3-15

DISCARD

BADGE
OF EVIL

BADGE OF EVIL

CRAIG HOROWITZ
& BILL STANTON

Regan Arts.
NEW YORK

Regan Arts.

65 Bleecker Street
New York, NY 10012

First Regan Arts hardcover edition, July 2015.

Library of Congress Control Number: 2015935083

ISBN 978-1-941393-59-8

Interior design by Nancy Singer
Jacket design by Ervin Serrano
Front jacket photographs: Police cars ©Joseph C. Justice Jr. / Getty Images; background lights © Jeff Spielman / Getty Images; water drops © Machmarsky / Shutterstock

Printed in the United States of America

10 9 8 7 6 5 4 3 2 1

For Rhonda,
my partner and best friend
Craig Horowitz

For Dr. Jane Fitzgerald
and her Bishop
Bill Stanton

. . . and ye shall know the truth, and the truth shall make you free.

The Gospel According to John
The New Testament

Truth is truth To the end of reckoning

Measure for Measure
William Shakespeare

PROLOGUE

KEVIN ANDERSON BLINKED a few times, hoping it would clear his eyes. It didn't work. He tried again, squeezing so hard now it made his ears ring. Still no luck. It was a Tuesday night near the end of March and Anderson was blitzed, totally wasted. Lying in bed at his beach house in the Hamptons, he felt like he was looking at his bedroom from behind wet glass. Everything was blurry and poorly defined. One object seemed to bleed into another. He couldn't tell where his antique dresser—the one he'd gotten with his wife on a romantic weekend in the Berkshires ten years ago—ended and the wall began. The longer he stared, the more it looked like everything was melting.

Anderson thought rubbing his eyes might help, but then he remembered he couldn't. His hands were cuffed to the bedposts. Same with his feet. A well-built thirty-seven-year-old black man, Anderson was lying there naked, limbs splayed so he looked like a big X. Maria, wearing only a baby-blue thong, was on the bed on all fours, leaning over him and snorting a line off his stomach. At least that's what he thought she was doing. Her long black hair hung down and partially obscured her face. Didn't matter. He was suddenly somewhere else, drifting out of his bed and floating inches above the ocean.

• • •

Maria moved lower on Anderson's body and went to work. Without looking up, she could tell he was awake now and could feel the wet warmth of the inside of her mouth as she took him in and his eyes rolled up in his head. He let out a little sigh. Maria turned toward him and smiled.

"Oh, baby," she said softly, stroking the side of his face as she reached for a loaded syringe on the nightstand.

Maria, a striking Latina in her midtwenties with black eyes and full natural breasts, had been in the house about an hour. She was, for all intents and purposes, a gift from one of Anderson's old friends. Anderson had called the guy a week earlier to ask for a favor, and the friend, whom he hadn't seen in quite a while, suggested they get together at Anderson's beach house and party like old times. He'd supply the entertainment.

The house—four thousand square feet, with four bedrooms and lots of undivided space on the main level—was set deep in the woods at the end of a long dirt road in Hampton Bays—the South Fork's "blue-collar beach town," where you could still buy a nice place with a pool for under $2 million. Maria had shown up at the house at eleven o'clock, right on schedule. She and Anderson started drinking tequila, took a little X, and made small talk for about half an hour. Then Anderson's friend called and said he'd been delayed, but he'd get there as soon as he could. They should start without him.

With that, Anderson and Maria headed for the master bedroom. On the way, she caught glimpses of what she assumed were vacation photos and pictures of Anderson's kids at various stages in their lives—little league, school concerts, holidays. *Nice-looking family*, she thought.

Now Maria took the syringe, which was loaded with a mixture of cocaine and heroin, and gently stuck it into the base of Anderson's erect penis. She squeezed the pump slowly to make sure she emptied all the liquid. Anderson was starting to look a little sad and she thought about untying him. She liked making people happy, and though he wasn't protesting, he no longer seemed like he was having fun. But her instructions were clear, not to untie him no matter what happened.

Just as she pulled the needle out, the doorbell rang. Maria glanced at the clock on the nightstand. Midnight, just like they'd arranged it. She liked punctuality when she was working. It was more efficient, made things simpler, and ultimately, since she lived by the clock, meant she'd make more money.

At the door was the swarthy middle-aged guy with the shaved head who'd hired her. She knew him only as Joe, which she was sure wasn't his real name. She knew he wasn't Anderson's friend, whom she'd never met, but his driver or bodyguard or assistant or something. She wasn't sure which, exactly, and she didn't care. All that really mattered was that when they made the deal, he paid her three times her normal rate. In advance.

"You told me to give him a party," she said brightly. "Mission accomplished."

"Go back upstairs," he said in the slightly odd accent Maria had noticed the first time they talked. "The boss'll be up in a minute."

As she padded up the stairs, still wearing only her little thong, he couldn't take his eyes off her. He watched her breasts bounce and her ass flutter ever so slightly and it was all he could do to maintain control and take care of business. He exhaled slowly. Hungering for her violated his religious beliefs. As an observant Muslim, he shouldn't even have been looking, and he was annoyed that he'd allowed himself to be distracted. He reached in his coat pocket for his walkie-talkie. He didn't bother taking it out, just clicked the point-to-point twice.

When Maria walked back into Anderson's bedroom, she paused by the door to primp a little. She smoothed her hair and, using both hands to pull the tiny triangle of cloth away from her body, straightened her thong. Suddenly, without warning, another man was standing in the doorway. He startled her.

"Ooh," she said, clutching her chest a little too dramatically, "I didn't hear you come up. You must be the friend who set this up." He just stared at her, expressionless. "You look a little tense. I'll bet I can help you relax."

Still no response as he intently looked over the scene. His eyes stopped briefly on Anderson, who, in his altered state, appeared to be sleeping. "C'mon, honey, no need to be shy with me," Maria said gamely. She walked over to him and stood so close her nipples were brushing the front of his shirt. She reached down and firmly rubbed his crotch. "Well, you may not be talking, but your body's speaking to me loud and clear."

For the first time his expression changed. The hint of a smile crossed his face. "Want to know what it's saying?" he asked in a low voice. With that, he sucked in his lower lip and backhanded her across the face with such power she stumbled backward for several steps before falling and hitting her head on the wall. He walked over to where she had collapsed and began to beat her with a slapper, a small cylinder of lead wrapped in leather.

Maria's soft, pretty face was quickly transformed into a bruised, swollen, nearly unidentifiable fleshy mess. Nose, cheekbones, and jaw all broken. Blood spattered everywhere. Like some crazed boxer, he got down in a low squat and worked her body, his stunning rage evident in the force of every blow. Then, just as abruptly as he had begun, he stopped.

Anderson, only partially lucid, couldn't believe what he was seeing. Was he actually watching his friend brutally beat a young hooker nearly to death? And for what? He began to sweat with fear. He tried to struggle against the cuffs securing him to the bed, but his limbs just wouldn't move. He tried to scream, but no sound came out of his mouth.

His friend was eyeing him now, boring in with a long, unblinking stare. He began to move toward the bed, slowly, deliberately, as if he were savoring every moment of the terror on Anderson's face. He raised his right hand like he was about to begin another savage beating, but then his hand came down slowly. Instead of attacking Anderson, he simply placed the slapper on his stomach. Then he looked at Anderson, whose face was covered in sweat and whose erection was long gone, and winked at him. Then he turned and walked out of the room. In the hallway, he passed Joe, giving him an almost imperceptible nod.

Downstairs, he stopped by an oak-framed mirror, carefully took off his bloody gloves, and admired his reflection. He lingered for a moment, turning his head a little to the right, then to the left. His breathing returned to normal. As he started to leave, a photograph on the fireplace mantel caught his eye. It was a picture of Anderson in his NYPD uniform, receiving his lieutenant's shield. In the photo, as was customary, were the newly promoted officer with his family and the police commissioner. He looked at the picture for several seconds. The corners of his mouth revealed the slightest hint of a smile before he walked out of the house and down the dark driveway to wait for Joe to finish up.

1

AT A LITTLE past one a.m. on a Thursday night, the streets of Bay Ridge were predictably desolate. Dark shadows mingled with the milky gray glow of the streetlights. Great puffs of steam rose from the manhole covers. There were no signs of life anywhere. The only movement, or at least what appeared to be movement, was actually an illusion—an erratically flickering neon sign in the window of a restaurant called Cleopatra's.

A light rain had been falling on and off for a couple of hours and the wet blacktop was as shiny as patent leather as New York City police commissioner Lawrence Brock's black Suburban rolled quietly—and without lights—along Third Avenue.

Brock put his window down, stuck his head out, and inhaled deeply. The cool, damp air made his face tingle. "Un-fuckin'-believable," he said as much to himself as to his driver. "Who gets to do shit like this besides us, right? They call this work? This must be how ballplayers feel. I swear I'd do this for free. This goes down as planned it's gonna be huge."

"Huge," his driver repeated.

Brock, a thick, muscular man of average height with a full head of silver hair and a face as round as a pie tin, had been twitchy with anticipation ever since he slipped into the midnight-blue jumpsuit back at police headquarters. From the moment Brock began to gear up for this operation, he was like a sprinter with his feet in the starting blocks, a coiled mass of energy waiting to explode.

For much of the ride out to Brooklyn, he had trouble sitting still. He fidgeted with his radio, tied and retied his twelve-inch boots, adjusted and readjusted his black Kevlar helmet, and repeatedly checked his side rig, a Glock nine-millimeter worn at midthigh, rather than in the traditional hip holster.

As they got closer to their target, he scanned the quiet streets and went over the details of the operation in his head. He was calm now, more focused. He could feel the weight of the Type III bulletproof vest pulling on his shoulders. With its hard ceramic plates, which were positioned to protect the vital organs, the vest pressed heavily against his chest muscles. Brock liked the discomfort. He found wearing a vest reassuring. Always had. Not because of the safety. He rarely thought about that. It was more visceral. The first time he strapped on body armor as a young soldier during basic training at Fort Benning was a revelation. It resolved life's great existential question—where do I belong, where's my place in the world? Dressing for battle that first time, putting on his vest and pulling the Velcro straps tight, Brock knew he was exactly where he was supposed to be. And it had been that way ever since.

Brock lived for action. Wearing a suit and tie, sitting in meetings, reviewing budgets, allocating resources, attending banquets, holding press conferences, planning, strategizing, and doing all of the things a police commissioner does was fine with Brock. Actually, it was better than fine. It was incredible. Every time he met with the mayor, addressed his troops, or discussed some critical issue with the city's business leaders, Brock had a flash of disbelief, literally a chill he felt run through his entire body. It was an instant when even he, with all his narcissistic bluster and general lack of self-awareness, was stunned by what he'd accomplished.

But as much ego gratification as Brock got from all this—and no one got off more on thinking of himself as a leader of men more than Lawrence Brock—there was nothing like the pure unrestrained physical joy of chasing a suspect, hitting an apartment, or getting in a shoot-out. This was why he had become a cop.

"Everything okay, boss?" his driver asked as they approached their destination.

"Never better," Brock said, his broad smile visible even in the dark cabin of the SUV.

They pulled over at Sixty-Third Street, behind the rest of their caravan. Almost immediately, several dozen Emergency Service Unit (ESU) cops piled out of the other vehicles and disappeared into the night, headed for their prearranged assignments. The target was a fourth-floor apartment in a modest five-story building a block away on Fourth Avenue. They parked around the corner on Third to keep their vehicles out of sight.

An ESU sniper team was on its way to the rooftop of a building directly across the street from the target, where they'd focus on the bedroom windows that faced the front. The snipers did not have a green light to shoot, no matter how good a shot they thought they had. Their orders were clear: zero in on the windows, sight the suspects, and wait for further instructions. They were a last resort. They knew they'd only get a shot if the raid went sideways.

The narrow alleys on both sides of the building were each covered by a pair of ESU cops. There were four more on the roof as well as in the small littered space in the back. Six men had the street in front. The intersections were sealed off by patrol cars and the bomb squad was on standby several blocks away.

At the tactics meeting in the war room at police headquarters, Brock had said (demanded, really) that he wanted to be a part of the acquisition team, the elite ten-man unit that would take apartment 4C. Inside were five suspected terrorists, four of them foreign nationals—two Saudis, one Pakistani, and a Palestinian—and one American, who had an Egyptian father and a mother from New Jersey.

After two months of blanket, round-the-clock surveillance, which included phone taps and highly sensitive listening devices actually placed in the apartment by TARU (the Technical Assistance Response Unit, the NYPD's high-tech gadget geeks), the cops decided it was time to move. Though it was unclear if the suspects had secured sufficient explosives to move forward, Brock believed the men were serious; waiting any longer would be too risky.

As best they could tell from the wiretaps and surveillance, the target was the Herald Square subway station on Thirty-Fourth Street. Each man would carry a backpack filled with explosives into the station during the morning rush hour. The plan was to spread the backpacks out to max-imize the death, destruction, and panic. But these men weren't suicide bombers. They'd use cell phones to detonate the explosives once they were safely outside.

It was highly unusual—unheard of, really—for a police commissioner to actually participate in a dangerous operation like this. But Brock was nothing if not unusual. He was an adrenaline junkie. High risk, high re-ward was the way he lived. As commissioner, he grabbed every possible opportunity to come down from his commanding wood-paneled perch on the top floor of One Police Plaza to do the things a regular cop does. He was both loved and hated for it. He was seen as a cop's cop by some and a grandstanding, ego-crazed cowboy by others.

Brock couldn't give a shit. He was having the time of his life. If people thought he was too tough or even a little crazy, that was fine with him. He'd happily wear those labels. He believed that every unconventional thing he did—even every mean-spirited, unpleasant rumor spread about him, for that matter—simply added to his growing legend.

But this night in Bay Ridge was extraordinary even for Brock. They were going to take down a heavily armed terror cell. There were seri-ous risks. ESU would have to work within the tight confines of a small two-bedroom apartment, and unexpected things, none of them good, often happen in small spaces.

The commanders had made the decision to grab the suspects in the middle of the night to minimize the size of the operation and the upset to the neighborhood. With businesses closed, the streets deserted, and everyone asleep, the cops hoped to get in and out quickly and cleanly. Though they were taking a chance by not evacuating the rest of the building, they felt it was worth it. The ESU commander, a muscular, six-foot-three-inch hard-ass named Anthony Z. Pennetta—everyone called him Zito—believed he had enough intelligence on the apartment's layout and what the suspects had going on inside to pull this off without endangering the neighbors or his men.

With everyone dispatched to their posts, Pennetta had ambled over to Brock to exchange greetings before the action started. "Evening, Commissioner," he said coldly.

"Zito," Brock said, acknowledging the commander with a nod. "Nice night to make the world a little safer for democracy?"

"Absolutely."

The two men stood on the street, in the shadows, facing each other in silence. A fine mist was in the air. Pennetta wasn't wearing his helmet and Brock noticed his hair was starting to thin. He almost smiled. Anything, no matter how small, that made Pennetta less perfect made Brock happy. He wasn't really in competition with Pennetta—he was the fucking police commissioner, after all, and Zito worked for him. But Pennetta made him uncomfortable. He was too tough, too confident, too tall, too smart, and too experienced. He didn't put up with any bullshit and he didn't give any either. He was straight up, almost too good to be believed, Brock felt.

Pennetta had been completely against Brock participating in the raid. So were his men. When Brock announced his intention in the tac meeting to be part of the team that would hit the apartment, Pennetta protested. Though he knew it was all about Brock grandstanding and getting post-raid face time on television, online, and in the papers, he tried to focus his argument on the safety issue.

If Brock wanted to risk his own ass, that was one thing. But Pennetta didn't want his men put at risk because the police commissioner was a reckless egomaniac. Hitting an apartment with five armed suspects inside required the kind of precision and coordinated teamwork that only comes from training together. "At crunch time," Pennetta would tell his guys, "it's all about instinct. You revert to what's most familiar. You're only as good as your training." ESU A-teams would practice this kind of exercise as a unit as often as a hundred times a year.

ESU was the police department's equivalent of the Special Forces. They handled the most dangerous, difficult assignments. They were the NYPD's elite—the fighter jocks, the fittest, best-trained cops on the force. They were mostly disdainful of other cops, whom they viewed as poorly trained slackers. They didn't like bosses either (Zito was the exception), who, in their view, did little except get in the way and suck up the credit. The last thing Zito's best guys, his number-one A-team, wanted to hear was that they had a new member, even if—especially if—he was the police commissioner.

They had no choice, of course. Brock was the final authority. In addition, he was the one who had received the original tip about the suspects. He'd passed the information to the head of the NYPD's counterterrorism bureau and they were off to the races. That's how this two-month investigation, which was about to reach its climax, got started. No one was sure how Brock had gotten the information, but it didn't seem to matter. Good intel was good intel.

With everyone in place, Brock and Pennetta walked briskly together to the scene. They were the entire command structure for the operation. In a typically ballsy maneuver, Brock had shut out the Feds. He'd never notified the Joint Terrorism Task Force—an uneasy alliance of cops and FBI agents—when they started surveillance of the suspected terror cell. And he'd kept a tight lid on while they were planning the operation as well. He had no interest in sharing any credit with another agency.

To prevent information about the raid from getting out now—and attracting half the cops in the city—nobody used the police radio. Everyone was communicating with point-to-point Nextel walkie-talkies. They were also intrinsically safe, which meant they gave off no spark that could, in a small space like the apartment they were about to hit, detonate explosives.

After walking almost an entire block in silence, Brock finally spoke. "I know what you're thinking and you're wrong," he said as they headed toward Fourth Avenue. "I'm ready."

"You have no idea what I'm thinking," Pennetta said as they turned onto Fourth Avenue, which looked like an armed camp. "Two things are lighting up the nerve endings in my head—getting the job done and getting my men out safely. I wasn't worried about you screwing up; you're not even on the radar screen. That said, with all due respect, *sir*, this is still the dumbest fuckin' thing I've ever seen anyone in this department do. With all the shit that's being thrown at us, the last thing this department needs, this city needs, is another incident for the left-wing cop bashers to grab on to."

Arrogant, self-righteous prick, Brock thought. *Fuck you. This is my department, not yours.* He was so angry now it was an actual physical sensation, as real as stomach cramps or a bad headache. He wanted to let it out, to explode, but he knew he couldn't, not now. Neither man said anything else, and in a few moments they were in front of the target.

It was a plain, unremarkable white-brick building, just like hundreds of others built in Brooklyn and Queens after World War II. There were double glass doors that led to a small alcove with mailboxes and doorbells on one wall. Through another set of glass doors were a long hallway, an elevator, and a staircase. The ground floor once had several apartments and a large restaurant with a separate entrance. All of that space was now occupied by al-Noor Mosque.

The mosque had been around for about ten years and had grown so steadily that it had expanded twice, each time taking over adjacent storefronts and knocking down the walls. But even with the additional space, accommodating the surging Muslim community in Bay Ridge was difficult. Al-Noor served as a community center and offered day care, a K–12 school, and adult classes on the Koran.

Politics at the mosque mostly revolved around local issues. There were passionate discussions, of course, about the problems facing Muslims in various parts of the world, but al-Noor was not known as a hothouse for radical Islam. On Friday afternoons, the focus was on handling the crowds, not, as it was at some of the city's other mosques, on the imam delivering a fiery postprayer diatribe.

Loudspeakers had to be placed out on the street so that the hundreds of Muslim men who couldn't get inside to pray—and who filled Fourth Avenue, kneeling and touching their foreheads to the ground—could participate in the service. This was the mosque where the five suspects worshipped. And one of them, the American, worked part-time at an Islamic bookstore just down the street.

Pennetta briefly huddled with an ESU captain. Everyone was in position and ready to go when Brock and Pennetta walked into the building. The A-team was on the stairs and lined up in its stack—the neat, single-file formation they'd use to enter the apartment. The first two cops in the stack carried the heavy ram to boom the door. Cops called it the key to the city. The next two cops, one carrying a bulletproof, Plexiglas shield and the other armed with an MP5 fully automatic, recoilless submachine gun, would be the first inside.

These two-man units were referred to as bunker teams, and there were three of them in the stack. If the suspects were armed and ready, the first bunker team would take the big hit for everyone else. Brock was the shooter in the second bunker team. The last guy in the stack, called the doorman, was responsible for covering the apartment with an M4, a long, penetrating rifle, to make sure no one got in or out. Pennetta would handle overall command from the hallway, out of the line of fire, where he'd be ready to deal with any contingency and call for backup, the bomb squad, or the EMTs.

Pennetta took a last hard look at Brock, who had moved into position in the stack. The commissioner, psyched and energized again, couldn't read his stare. He assumed it was expressing anger and left it at that. He didn't want any distractions. After a few moments, Pennetta motioned to everyone to turn off their walkie-talkies. All communication from this point forward would be hand signals until they were inside the apartment. Then he gave the sign that it was showtime.

The cops moved quietly up the stairs to the fourth floor. The stack formed on the hinge side of the doorway to apartment 4C. Brock licked his lips a few times and tried to keep his breathing slow and even. All of the training, the months of surveillance, the hours of planning and preparation, would now come down to a precious few minutes. Pennetta winked at the doorman, who then tapped the guy in front of him on the shoulder. Each cop in succession then tapped the next guy until it reached the first man in the stack. It was like lighting a human fuse.

THWACK. The night's silence was quickly, jarringly broken as the heavy apartment door was rammed and knocked to the floor. The bunker teams moved in rapidly.

"Police, get down. Police, get the fuck down," the first cop inside screamed. "Two perps right, doorway straight ahead. Two perps on the right, doorway straight ahead." The suspects were moving around, one behind an open sofa bed and the other across the living room by a big easy chair and a television. The apartment was dark and messy. There were clothes and papers on the floor; takeout containers were strewn all over a table in the living room.

"Stay the fuck down, you hear me? I said don't move. Not a fuckin' whisker," the cop barked as he and his partner moved deeper into the apartment. There was a kitchen on the left that was empty. As the cops inched their way past, they could see a small table with three chairs and a pile of dishes in the sink.

When Brock crossed the threshold and moved inside, the warm, stale air hit him immediately. He had his MP5 locked on the two men in the living room as he scanned the surroundings. The third bunker team was now also in the living room. Just as the cops reached one of the bedrooms in the back, where three more suspects were holed up, the words rang out like a piercing siren.

"Gun! Gun! I got a fuckin' gun!" Everything suddenly moved at hyperspeed, like a souped-up video game. The deafening bursts of MP5 gunfire filled the small space with as much noise as a jet engine. Flashes of flame-hot blue and red from the gun barrels lit up the dark space like strobe lights. As Brock pointed his weapon and squeezed his trigger, he saw one of the young Muslims reflexively lift up his empty right hand like he was trying to stop the bullets. Almost instantly his hand seemed to explode in midair—bits of bone and flesh and a quick spray of red in every direction.

The two bedroom doors in the back were kicked in and there was more gunfire. Then, suddenly, it all just stopped. The apartment was smoky now and Brock could taste the gunpowder. The blood was pounding in his ears and he was breathing too fast. He could feel the sweat under his Kevlar helmet. "Living room and kitchen secure," he yelled, catching his breath.

"Bedrooms and bathroom secure," came the response.

"Give me a count. Everybody up front's okay. I got two suspects down. Neither's breathing."

"Thumbs-up here too. Three perps down, one of the motherfuckers's still breathing. I need a bus. *Now*. Get 'em up here."

Pennetta came into the apartment, followed by the EMTs, who were directed straight to one of the back bedrooms. The commander scanned the carnage in the living room. It was a mess. "The hell happened?" he asked no one in particular.

"They were supposed to be sleeping, Captain," one of Pennetta's guys said to him. "But these bastards were up. I don't know, maybe they heard us coming."

Pennetta was skeptical but kept quiet. *No way they heard them coming,* he thought. He made a mental note to look into this later. "Start securing the rest of the building," he told his second in command. "I'm sure we managed to wake up the whole fuckin' neighborhood. Keep everybody in their apartments, got it? I don't want this turning into any more of a circus than it already is."

Then he turned toward the commissioner. "I'm fine," Brock said, fighting to suppress his excitement. "Thanks for asking. Rest of the guys are okay too."

"I don't want anything touched," Pennetta said tensely. "Not a goddamned dust ball. Everybody got that? I want this done absolutely straight up. No bullshit. Let Crime Scene and Internal Affairs do their job."

Looking at Brock, Pennetta said, "There's gonna be a major shitstorm and I don't want any of it coming back on my guys. You wanted some attention, Commissioner? Well, you're gonna get it."

Before Brock could respond, the EMTs came through with the lone survivor on a gurney. "What's his status?" Brock asked, noticing how young the suspect looked. He guessed he couldn't be more than twenty-one or twenty-two.

"Touch and go," said a short black woman with a stethoscope around her neck. "He's pretty torn up. We'll see if he makes it to the hospital."

Brock turned his attention back to Pennetta. He was too pumped to let the captain bring him down. "You're a terrific cop, Zito, but you got no fuckin' imagination. No creativity. No sense of the big picture."

Brock took a deep breath and started to smile as he felt the smoke in his nostrils and the back of his throat. He had the look of a man who'd just tasted a fantastic dish in a restaurant. "You're not gonna get anywhere with that narrow view of the world, Zito," he said to his commander. "You need to open up your mind, to develop a more global view of things, man. Shitstorm? Are you kidding? They're gonna throw me a freakin' ticker-tape parade. I'm gonna be a hero. These dead Muslims are *my* ticket to paradise."

2

"DAD. *DAAAAAD.* TELEPHONE!"

A. J. Ross was in the kitchen working on his third cup of coffee when he heard his fourteen-year-old daughter, Annie, yelling from her bedroom that he had a phone call. For a long moment, A. J. didn't move. He just sat there, staring blankly at the newspapers and listening to the radio. Actually, he wasn't really listening. A. J. had kind of zoned out until he was startled by his daughter's voice. "*Believe me,*" he now heard morning talk-show jock Don Imus ranting about some poor slob, "*that buck-toothed, beady-eyed, rodent-lookin' little weasel is gonna be sorry . . .*" It was seven forty-five a.m. *Fuck*, A. J. thought, feeling as cranky as Imus sounded, *no good ever comes from a phone call before breakfast.*

A. J. was having a more or less typical morning. He'd gotten up at six fifteen a.m., showered, shaved, and dressed. Then he'd checked his daughter's homework and read the news. It was one of those mornings when the big stories were breaking online and the printed editions of the newspapers were irrelevant before they even rolled off the presses. BROCK LEADS RAID ON SUSPECTED TERROR CELL was the headline stretched across the top of the *New York Times* website. CELL DAMAGE: COMMISH SHOOTS TERRORISTS, screamed the *Daily News* across its entire online front page. But it was the *Post*, as usual, that nailed it: BROCK KICKS ASS: COMMISH 4, TERRORISTS 0.

A. J. had more than a passing interest in the morning's stunning news story. In the media capital of the world, he was a franchise player, one of the best-known, best-connected journalists in the city. In ten years at *New York*, the thirty-eight-year-old had written seventy-five cover stories, won two National Magazine Awards, and always managed to score the big interview. Even with the decline in print sales in the digital era, his byline could still sell magazines, and it definitely generated page views. Though it was harder for any writer to have real impact, A. J. still produced work people talked about and people in power paid attention to.

"Daaaaaaaad. Daaaaa-aaaaaad!"

"Okay, okay," A. J. yelled to his daughter as he moved away from the table. "Hey," he said in a doleful tone of voice when he picked up the cordless.

"Morning, boss. Hope you didn't pull anything rushing to get the phone. Have you seen the headlines?" his assistant, Lucy, asked in her irresistibly throaty voice.

"I live in the suburbs, not Siberia. Of course I have. What'd you do, sleep in the office?"

"I was restless last night. I don't know, it was like I just couldn't get comfortable. So I got out early this morning, went to the gym, had a little breakfast, and got here around seven."

"I'm starting to worry about you, Luce. You need to have a little fun, relax a little, you know? There's not much more than headlines right now anyway. Everything happened too late. I haven't made any calls yet. Whaddaya hear from downtown?" A. J. asked as Annie came into the kitchen, dressed and dragging her school backpack across the floor. She pointed to her watch, indicating she needed to go. A. J. nodded, held up a couple of fingers, and silently mouthed the words "two minutes."

"So far nothing. There's a press conference at One Police Plaza at ten. Brock, the mayor, and Pennetta are supposed to be there," Lucy said.

"Zito? Man, they must've held a gun to his head. Well, they can make him show up but they can't make him talk. Actually, they'd never let him talk even if he suddenly wanted to. They're not sharing face time with anybody."

"Are you leaving now?" Lucy gently prodded.

"I'll get going right after I drive Annie to school. I'll meet you at One PP. I know it's early, but start making some phone calls on the suspects. Especially the one that's still breathing. And we need to find out where the hell the intelligence came from. Who tipped the cops about these guys?"

"I'll see what I can come up with. Listen, A. J., I don't want to overstep here, but can't Nikki drive Annie today?" Lucy asked, referring to his wife. "I mean, even if you leave now, with the traffic, you still probably won't make it."

Lucy Chapin had been A. J.'s assistant for about a year and a half. They'd met while she was a grad student at the Columbia School of Journalism. He delivered a guest lecture in one of her classes about how to develop sources. She was already an admirer, but once she heard him speak, she was determined to find a way to work for him. Not only was he enthusiastic, articulate, and smart, he seemed like a really decent guy. Lucy thought he was kind of cute, too, which didn't hurt.

She talked to him after his lecture, started e-mailing him at the magazine, and by the time she completed her master's, they'd developed enough of a relationship that it just seemed natural that she'd go to work for him. A. J. joked that Lucy was a good example of how unfair life can be. She was smart, funny, determined, and beautiful enough—five feet eight inches; thick, dark hair; light green eyes—to have paid her way through school by modeling.

Even her attitude was practically perfect. She was cynical and sarcastic—which A. J. loved—but never when it mattered, when there was something important at stake. She didn't take herself too seriously, but she was almost pathological about the work. You could argue, of course, that it's easy to be comfortable in your own skin when you've won the genetic equivalent of the Powerball lottery. But A. J. was often amazed by how many sore winners he ran into.

"Nikki is gonna drive Jack," A. J. said, referring to his nine-year-old son. "She also has an important meeting this morning and she can't be late. I, on the other hand, have no such critical obligation. The earth will not tip on its axis if I miss half an hour of Brock and the mayor blowing smoke up my ass. Besides—"

"A. J.," Lucy cut him off, "this is like the biggest—"

"Lucy, relax. You'll be fine and I won't be late."

It took A. J. about ten minutes to drive Annie to school. When he got back, he opened the garage, where he parked the minivan next to his three motorcycles. The black BMW R1200RT was the world's best all-around touring bike, equipped with GPS, stereo, ABS, and heated grips; A. J. only took it out on trips that lasted a week or more. Then there was the graphite-and-red MV Augusta F4, an exotic Italian racing bike he rode every once in a while at the track. Finally, there was the high-gloss midnight-blue Ducati Monster S4R S Testastretta, with a white racing stripe and a visible trellis frame that made A. J. smile every time he looked at it. The Monster was a bike he could ride anywhere, but it was especially ideal for scooting around the city and dealing with heavy traffic. It was light, easy to maneuver (flickable, gearheads called it), and blazingly fast. All of which made it ideal for lane-splitting—riding in between lanes to avoid sitting in stop-and-go traffic. A. J. wasn't sure if lane-splitting was legal in New York and New Jersey, but he didn't really care. It saved him too much time to give it up. And if he ever did get stopped, he had buddies in the police department who'd take care of the ticket.

He pulled his helmet on, secured the chin strap, lifted the face shield, and threw his right leg over the custom-made saddle. Sitting on the bike, he used his feet to push off and roll out of the garage. On the driveway, he turned the key and pressed the starter button, and the bike came to life with a roar. This unique, sweet rumble was Ducati's signature as much as the polo pony was Ralph Lauren's.

A. J. closed the Velcro on his gloves and checked his mirrors. He squeezed the clutch with his left hand, tapped the shifter into first gear with his left foot, and began to give the Monster some gas by twisting the throttle with his right hand. At the same time he let the clutch out slowly and he was off, the garage door closing automatically behind him.

Every time he rode, the first few minutes were always the same. Take it easy, get comfortable, and just enjoy the enormous fluid power under him. He leaned lightly into the first few turns, letting the tires warm up. This was critical. Cold tires on a bike have very little stick.

The satisfaction of riding a bike for A. J. really had two parts. First, of course, were the sensations: the thrill of pure speed, the exhilaration of hurtling through space on something so seemingly flimsy, and the tactile fulfillment of using both hands and both feet to operate the machine. There was also a physical pleasure, as there was in skiing, that came from linking turns together and developing a natural rhythm while riding. There is no steering wheel on a motorcycle. You don't actually turn it the way you do a car or a bicycle. To go left or right, you have to lean the bike in that direction rather than turn it. The sharper the turn, the more dramatic the lean, and the greater the rush.

The other key element that made riding so appealing for A. J. was the focus required. Writers spend a lot of time inside their own heads. They're always thinking, rethinking, examining, and analyzing their interactions, as well as replaying conversations. On the bike, however, A. J. had to turn all of that off. He had to clear his head. Riding demanded his full and complete attention. It was all about the machine and negotiating the environment around him. There was no margin for error. Sometimes he treated it like being inside a big video game. He rode like every car was out to kill him, which wasn't much of an exaggeration.

A. J. comfortably maneuvered the bike toward lower Manhattan, weaving in and out between cars, picking his line and leaning into the turns like a confident skier negotiating the gates on a slalom course. He glanced at the clock on the dash. It was 9:05. He'd make the press conference with ten or fifteen minutes to spare. In the distance he could see the brake lights where the backup began for the Holland Tunnel. With a small stretch of open road in front of him, A. J. gave the throttle a hard twist. The front tire lifted about six inches off the ground and he was gone in the blink of an eye.

• • •

The press conference lasted about forty-five minutes. It was the hottest ticket in town. Instead of the usual six or seven television cameras along the back wall of the police department's press room, there were more than twenty. The networks, the cable channels, and even Sky News and Al Jazeera sent crews. The room was meant to hold up to fifty reporters, plus the TV equipment, but there were at least twice that many crammed into the space. It was hot and stuffy, tempers were short, and several arguments erupted as reporters jostled for position. Those given temporary NYPD press passes were mostly relegated to the back of the room and whatever space they could find along the side walls.

The press room, on the second floor of police headquarters, had the standard run-down look of a city government facility: crappy linoleum floor, toxic fluorescent lighting, and walls that hadn't been painted in years. The only exception was the front wall, which served as the back-drop for any clips that TV viewers would see from the event. This wall had a ridged, dark oak paneling that could also be found in the lobby and on the top floor in the hallway outside the commissioner's office.

A. J. parked his bike on the side of the building, like he always did, where the cops kept their cars. Lucy looked relieved when she saw him walk in. She was in their usual spot, on the center aisle in the second row, and she was talking to Jerry Polone, the police reporter from the *New York Post*. Right in front of them was the guy from the *Times* who covered the cops, an annoying, imperious Ivy League nerd who acted like he was above all this.

The *Times* reporter had little interest in talking to the other report-ers, but when he did it was mostly to tell them that the police beat was a short-term assignment—he was only getting his ticket punched on his way to a job in the Washington bureau. A. J. thought his writing had the same clenched quality as his personality and his reporting rarely pene-trated the surface of a story because the cops couldn't stand him and he had no sources.

"Well, now I *know* this is a really big news day," Jerry said to Lucy with a smile as A. J. reached their seats. "Look who's come downtown. I'm honored, as always, to be in the presence of greatness."

"As I am to be so close to run-of-the-mill mediocrity," A. J. said good-naturedly. "What's up, Jerry? Harassing my coworker?"

"It's okay," Lucy said, "Jerry was just asking if he could come up to the office some afternoon and watch me lick stamps. I told him if I had no self-esteem or if we were living in, oh, 1950, I'd be flattered."

No one was sure exactly how long Jerry Polone had been covering the NYPD for the *Post* and he wasn't telling. A. J. figured out from their conversations that he had been around for at least eight police commissioners, which had to be twenty-five years or so. He knew everybody and he knew how everything worked. He'd always been incredibly gracious to A. J., including the first time A. J. showed up at police headquarters, essentially clueless, to work on a story. Though A. J. had never asked why, Polone told him who to talk to, how to get to them, and, in one or two cases, even what to ask.

"Whaddaya think?" Polone asked A. J.

"I hate to say it because he's such a self-absorbed ego-driven shitbag, but it looks like Brock's a . . . I don't know. I think the hero thing's a bit much, but it looks like this may be the real deal."

"Something's bothering me about it," Polone said. "There's something . . ."

"You mean, what the hell was the police commissioner of New York doing raiding an apartment?"

"There's that, for sure. But there's something else. I can't put my finger on it. But word's already going around questioning the assault. Where'd the intel come from, why didn't Brock tell any of the other agencies . . . ?"

"Maybe you're letting your personal feelings get in the way. I mean, we know Brock's a jerk, but he did get in a gun battle and—"

"No, it's not that. I just—"

At that moment the room fell silent and there was a sudden ripple of applause that seemed to move from front to back. It was 10:05 and Mayor Nicholas Domenico, Brock, and Pennetta walked into the room. A. J. and Jerry looked at each other in disbelief. Applause from the reporters? *This,* A. J. thought, *is going to be hard to sit through.*

The mayor, who was nearing the end of his second term, spoke to the reporters first. It was always his show, even now, when Brock was the reason for the huge media turnout. Domenico was only about five feet six inches and had a large head, a protruding brow, a huge expanse of forehead, and arms that seemed a little too short for his body. He looked like a mismatched set of parts, like he'd been drawn by a cartoonist. He also had an overpowering personality and an ego that was probably even bigger than Brock's. His need to fill every room he walked into was his great strength as well as his great weakness.

"Good morning," he said, getting things started. "As most of you know, public safety has been the cornerstone of my administration. From my very first day in office more than seven years ago, I have had no more important goal, no higher priority, and no greater purpose than keeping New Yorkers safe. I promised the people of this great city that I would do whatever it took to get this job done. And in the battles against crime and terrorism we have achieved historic results, results that continue to be the envy of cities all over the world. My partner in this noble cause—the tip of the spear, if you will—has been police commissioner Lawrence Brock. Though he has spent every single day of the last two years demonstrating his commitment to the people of New York—and, ironically, for security reasons you will never know the full extent of the success we've had foiling plots against our great city—last night he showed strength, courage, and a willingness to lay it all on the line that was extraordinary even for him."

When Brock stepped to the microphone, A. J. half expected the reporters to start rhythmically chanting his name: *Lar-ry, Lar-ry, Lar-ry.* He made a brief statement and then took some questions. He didn't put any meat on the bones of the story, and the questions were fairly straightforward and repetitive. A. J. never asked questions at these events. The daily reporters extracted the basic information, and he had no interest in asking anything that might reveal what he was thinking or how he was looking at a story.

Brock probably hadn't gotten any sleep after the shooting, and he looked wan and exhausted. His energy level, however, was still pretty high (adrenaline's amazing), and he said all the right things. No one ever wants to shoot someone, he said, while maintaining continuous eye contact with the reporter who asked the question. Yes, he was scared. No, he didn't regret his decision to go on the raid. Yes, he considered the danger to himself and the other cops. Yes, he discussed it beforehand with the mayor. And if he had it to do over again, he still wouldn't risk the success of the operation by telling the Joint Terrorism Task Force or the head of New York's FBI office. The wider the circle, the greater the chance of leaks.

Brock also said the department was putting together background information on the dead men, and there'd be an update on the lone surviving suspect as soon as one was available from the doctors. As expected, Pennetta stayed in the background and responded in the most cursory way when a question was specifically directed to him.

When it was over, A. J., Lucy, and Jerry walked out together.

"I want him," A. J. said outside on the street, with part of the Brooklyn Bridge visible over his shoulder. "I'd like to tell this story."

"You and a thousand other reporters," Jerry said, lighting a cigarette and taking a long, deep drag. "We're talking about *60 Minutes, Vanity Fair*. Shit, who knows, O'Reilly, an Oprah special . . ."

"Do me a favor, Jerry. Take another drag on the cigarette. Get some nicotine into your veins and get a little more blood flowing to your cerebral cortex and maybe your memory will start to come back. It's not like I haven't beaten all of them before."

"Whoa, down, boy," Jerry said with a little laugh. "That's true, but the mayor fucking hates you. He hasn't talked to you in—what—three years?"

"Four and a half, if you're actually counting."

"Fine, four and a half. And, by the way, what story do you wanna tell? The story of New York's fearless police commissioner? Lawrence Brock, superhero?"

"It's not compelling?"

"Of course it is," Jerry said, and then exhaled a long stream of smoke that prompted Lucy to cough with great exaggeration. "But it's bullshit. He's an ambitious opportunist. Maybe if you include the compromises, the bad behavior, the damage done to other people. Show his humanity. Or more accurately his inhumanity. And why would he let you do that? Especially now. You know, since even before Brock went all Jack Bauer on the terrorists, there've been whispers he might be up for Homeland Security. He's gonna want a wet kiss and he'll go with whoever he thinks will give it to him."

As the two men bantered back and forth, Lucy stood by quietly. She knew when not to talk. Yogi Berra once said, "You can observe a lot just by watching." You can also hear a lot just by listening.

"Don't forget," A. J. said, "Brock and I have a history. I wrote about him when he was still just a motorcycle cop, trying to start that foundation to get illegal guns off the street after his partner got shot, before anybody knew who the fuck he was. Or gave a shit."

"I guess it's possible he might feel some allegiance to you. And it's also possible that Lucy here is secretly madly in love with me. Possible, but highly unlikely. There's just no reason for him to take the risk."

"When it comes to the vanity of public officials, stranger things have happened."

Brock and Domenico took about twenty minutes after the press conference to do some quick one-on-one interviews for the cable news networks, the evening newscasts, and a few of the key papers. Then they took the five-minute walk to City Hall. Cars honked, drivers waved, people yelled encouragement out of their windows, and a few enthusiastic pedestrians came over to shake their hands and congratulate them.

Once they reached City Hall, the two men went to the mayor's office in the basement. The mayor had two offices at City Hall. There was one on the second floor, which was his official office. It was an elegant, formal setting where he signed bills, received dignitaries, gave important visitors a little face time, and staged photo ops. His real office, the place where he did his work, was in the basement. It was here, in this scruffy, windowless room, that Domenico lived up to his reputation as a mean-spirited, thin-skinned, vindictive politician. This was where he worked the phones, plotted strategy, made his deals, and badgered the weak. It was also the place where he kicked back with a cigar, a bottle of wine, and a little Puccini or Verdi booming on the stereo.

Domenico took off his jacket and loosened his tie as soon as he walked in. He hung his jacket carefully on the coatrack, then he sat down heavily in his leather chair, an indication—given his audible sigh—of annoyance rather than fatigue. "I thought that went pretty well," Brock said tentatively as he took a seat on the couch. "How about you?"

The mayor was silent for a while before responding. Finally he leaned across the desk, which made his oversize head look even bigger. "You think I give a shit about a bunch of annoying reporters?" Domenico said with controlled fury, keeping his voice barely above a whisper. "We go back a long way, Larry. You know how I feel about you. But you fucked up. I run things. I'm the mayor and you work for me. My name and my accomplishments and my fucking picture are what I wanna see in the papers. Not yours. *Not ever*, unless I say so."

Domenico stood up and leaned his hands on the desk. Brock could see a little white saliva bubbling at the corners of the mayor's mouth. He braced himself. "You hit the apartment without fucking telling me," Domenico said, his voice rising at the end of the sentence like it was a question.

"Are you nuts? What the fuck were you thinking? You forget who gave you this job? That I made you? Jesus fucking Christ. Every wonder why I chose you? Of all the people who wanted to work for me, to play a role, ever wonder why you? You were like this huge mound of shapeless clay. No real edges, no defining features. Except that you wanted it so bad. Make no mistake, there were plenty of others who wanted it. But none like you. You had this desperate, feral quality. I could smell it on you. I knew you'd do whatever had to be done, anything, and never look back or think twice," the mayor said, standing up straight now.

"When you stand at the edge of the abyss looking at nothing but darkness and fear, who's willing to step off the edge? Who's not only ready but eager to go forward into the black unknown? I never had any doubts about you. Till now. I call the shots here. If anybody's ass is gonna be kissed for his bravery, his tactical genius, and his devotion to the people of this city, it's gonna be mine, not yours. If anybody's gonna be anointed a goddamned American fuckin' hero, it's gonna be me. You get one mulligan. Fuck me again and you're gone. I don't care how far back we go."

Brock looked visibly shaken. All the color had drained from his face. The two men had been together for nearly eleven years, before Domenico had been elected mayor, and they had come to know each other in a way few friends ever do. They were demonstrative, even physical with one another, hugging and kissing with abandon. This was the first real breach between them.

"Look, boss—"

"Save it," Domenico said with a disgusted wave of his hand. "I'm not interested. You get another shot, which is one more than I would've given anyone else. So shut up and be grateful. You know how I feel, now let's move forward. What's with the suspect in the hospital?"

"The doctors are optimistic, but this weekend's critical. If he lasts till Monday, they believe he'll survive."

"I'm gonna assume there's nothing here I need to be concerned about. That you have everything under control. That the shoot was clean, and if it wasn't, whatever has to be taken care of will be. Discreetly."

"I'm on top of it," Brock said.

"You better be. Did you speak to the White House?"

"A secretary called earlier this morning to say the personnel director's gonna call today or tomorrow. They have my cell and all my other numbers."

"Good," Domenico said, beginning to look a little distracted, like he was ready to move on to other matters. "Don't make me sorry I set that in motion. I convinced them you're the guy for that spot. Anything else? No? Then we're done here. Keep me up to date."

"Absolutely, boss."

The two men shook hands and at the same time half hugged each other with their left arms.

Outside, on the top step of City Hall, Brock stood for a moment and looked out at the wide plaza that unfolded in front of the historic building. The cool air was bracing. He was exhausted, physically and emotionally. His shoulders and his legs ached. His head hurt. And his right hand felt like it was starting to cramp. But he was relieved. Brock knew how close he'd come to screwing everything up. He knew he'd just about pushed things too far. But he'd gotten away with it. He slowly began to smile. His plan was still on track.

He bounded down the steps to where his car was waiting.

"Let's swing by headquarters," he said to his driver, "and pick up Oz. Then we'll go get some lunch. I could eat a fuckin' elephant."

3

FRANK BISHOP WAS sitting on a black leather couch in a dimly lit room with red carpeting and a ceiling painted to look like a nighttime sky. In front of him there was a mirrored wall and a silver bucket with a $600 bottle of Beau Joie Champagne in it. Bishop, a thickly muscled, deeply tanned, thirty-six-year-old private investigator, couldn't imagine being much happier than he was at this moment. He could even see a little snippet of the broad smile on his face in the mirror.

Partially blocking his view were two large, perfectly shaped breasts that belonged to a "dancer" named Christina, hanging irresistibly in all their unencumbered naked beauty only a few inches from his face. Christina, who had been dancing for Bishop, was now on the couch straddling him and still moving rhythmically, but very slowly, to the background music.

"Sweetheart," Bishop said to her, "I could spend the rest of my life right here in this exact position looking at you. You're amazing."

Bishop was at V, the hottest strip club in New York, a place the city's tabloids still referred to (even though the line had long ago lost its clever ring) as "New York's mammary mecca." As strip clubs went, V was the high end of the genre, with shinier brass, softer leather, and thicker velvet than the competition. More important, it had the best-looking dancers, at

25

least by stripper standards, which were different from conventional standards. Stripper beautiful is to normal beautiful as a bodybuilder's physique
is to a gym-toned body—it's an aggressive exaggeration that screams its
intended message loud and clear. Huge gravity-defying sculpted breasts;
even bigger, usually blond, hair; collagen lips; cheek implants; big false
eyelashes; and makeup that often looked like it was applied with a paint-
brush and a putty knife. The club was huge, with a dining area where you
could actually eat dinner, two small stages next to the bar, a large main
stage, and a VIP deck. In addition to the businessmen who brought their
clients in, celebrities and athletes were a regular part of the late-night mix.

So was Frank Bishop. Some guys go to the golf club; he preferred the
strip club. It was his place, a hangout where he felt comfortable, enter-
tained, and, above all else, important. A couple of hours at V could easily
run several thousand dollars between money for the girls and drinks.
Bishop, however, never paid what he called the sucker's rate. Since he
often brought in wealthy clients, and occasionally a celebrity or two, his
visits were usually comped.

On this night, Bishop was in one of the club's private rooms with
Christina, another dancer named Chelsea, and one of his clients—a beautiful wannabe socialite named Elisabeth Merrill Bickers. Their little secret was that Bickers herself had once been a dancer at V. Fifteen years
ago, she'd met Quentin Merrill Bickers, an equity manager and partner at
Goldman Sachs, while dancing, and got to know him a little better in one
of these private rooms. Within a couple of months, she'd given up dancing.

Two kids, two dogs, and too many infidelities to count later, she had
reached the end of her rope with the marriage. She'd hired Bishop to get
dirt on her husband so she could get the maximum financial settlement.
At the moment, however, Bishop and Bickers were getting side-by-side
lap dances. On the floor, in between them, was a manila envelope with
Bishop's preliminary surveillance report and some photos. Christina
moved over to join her friend on Bickers's lap as the two women began
to make out with each other. Unoccupied for a moment, Bishop poured
himself a glass of Beau Joie.

Just as he took his first sip, his phone rang. He looked at the caller ID—Victoria Cannel. *Fuck*, he thought, *I'd better take this.* "Vic," he said with an enormous amount of false enthusiasm. "What's going on?"

"Let me guess, Frankie, you're at a titty bar, right? Don't bullshit me. I hear the awful music."

"C'mon, Vic, gimme a break. It's Friday night."

"I don't care if it's your fuckin' birthday. Lose the hard-on, put the little guy—and I do mean little—back in your pants, and meet me at Bell's, *now*. I got the kind of case you're gonna have to spend the rest of your cheesy life thanking me for. Are you leaving yet? I don't hear any movement. Tell Misty or Savannah or whichever Rhodes Scholar is rubbing her tits in your face to put the Champagne and her implants on ice. You gotta boogie."

"No wonder you're a defense attorney, Vic. All that compassion, all that obvious humanity and raging desire to help people. And don't worry, my hard-on looked like a frightened turtle retreating into its shell the moment I heard your voice. I'll be there in about fifteen minutes."

Bishop hung up and looked wistfully at the scene in front of him. Both strippers were kissing and fondling Bickers, whose dress was now half open, while she was putting the occasional hundred-dollar bill in their G-strings. He looked at the phone, he looked at them, and then he sighed heavily. He told them he had to leave for about an hour. Nobody paid attention.

He got up, went to the door, and said to Bickers loudly before opening it, "You okay with the bill?"

"No problem," she said, smiling. "I gave the waitress my black Amex."

"Aren't you worried your husband will see you were here?"

"Fuck him," Bickers said. "This is payback. And I'm only getting started. If you don't make it back tonight, let's have dinner next week so we can talk about my case," she said with a wink, turning her attention to the strippers.

"Trust me, sweetheart, I'm coming back."

Bishop had been drinking vodka at V (he never actually got a chance to have the Beau Joie), and when he walked into Bell's, it was on something less than rock-solid legs. The place was, as always, crowded and noisy. After thirty-plus years, and many premature pronouncements of its death, Bell's was still a solid, if somewhat tired, late-night hangout that continued to draw a reasonable number of the city's B- and C-list boldfaced names. It wasn't hip, it certainly wasn't hot—no chance anyone would confuse it with the rooftop at The Standard—and there was little to say that was positive about its look or the food. Still, it remained, for a certain class of privileged New Yorkers, a real saloon, in the best sense of the word—no blaring music, no annoying downtown wannabes or hipsters who thought they were too cool for the room, and no gawkers. It was a comfortable hangout for celebrities, journalists, attorneys, and cops.

Smiling and shaking hands, Bishop slowly tried to make his way past the high-visibility tables in the front along the wall opposite the bar. This was the gold coast, the best real estate in the joint, reserved for the regulars and the celebrated. "Frank, hey, Frank." Bishop heard his name being called through the din. It was Bell, sitting at a table with Sylvester Stallone and Alex Rodriguez. While making small talk with them, he spotted Victoria Cannel at a table farther back, with three people he didn't recognize and her assistant.

Bishop could see that she was telling a story and the people at the table were hanging on every word. Without missing a beat, she looked directly at Bishop and opened her big brown eyes a little wider in a why-aren't-you-on-your-way-over-here gesture. He gave her a slight nod of recognition and apologized to Bell, Stallone, and Rodriguez for not sitting down. "I'm actually working," he said, excusing himself a little sheepishly.

When he finally reached Cannel's table, she dismissed everyone except her assistant. "The usual, Mr. Bishop?" a waiter asked.

"Absolutely not," Cannel said before the PI could respond. "Bring him green tea. He's gotta get up early tomorrow."

"Well, you heard the lady. I guess I'll have green tea," Bishop said with a little wink. "So I guess we're on the clock starting now, right, Vic?" he said, looking at his watch.

"I need you awake and at your fucking best," Cannel said, ignoring his sarcasm. "You're meeting me at eight thirty sharp tomorrow morning at Bellevue. This is a real score, Frankie . . ."

"Vic, what the hell are you—"

"I got the kid, Ayad Jafaari—"

"The fucking terrorist? The guy Brock shot?"

"You mean the unfortunate kid who was caught in the wrong place at the wrong time?" Cannel said with a straight face. "You mean the dutiful son and brother, the honor student who worked part-time to put himself through school and help support his family? The kid who was wrongfully, horribly wounded by overzealous, trigger-happy cops? Yes, the kid Brock shot."

"Whoa, Victoria. Slow down. Slow way, way down. You're gonna defend some motherfuckin' Arab fanatic who wanted to blow shit up and kill people in my city? Our city? And you're gonna go up against Lawrence Brock, the red-blooded, all-American hero of the moment? And you want me to help? I'm not the smartest guy in the room, but I'm not that fuckin' stupid."

Bishop was quickly sobering up. He noticed a Page Six reporter from the *Post* sitting close by with a midlevel fashion designer. Both of them appeared to be trying to overhear what he and the lawyer were saying. Cannel, of course, had picked this up much earlier and was discreetly but purposefully playing to her audience. She *wanted* to see this in the paper, but now that she'd finished saying what she had to say for public consumption, she sent her assistant over to the reporter's table to buy her a drink and distract her.

She leaned in now to get close to Bishop, wrinkling her nose at the cheap stripper perfume that still clung to him. "Listen, Frank. This town is on fire. Brock's raid has the entire country focused on what's happening here. Talk about an opportunity. I want the terrorist scumbags eliminated as much as anyone. I'm just not willing to sacrifice the right to due process and the sacred concept that someone is innocent until proven guilty. And there's no fuckin' way I'm gonna cede those constitutional guarantees to that mouth-breathing Neanderthal Lawrence Brock.

I got a big problem with Brock turning the NYPD into his private army. Where was the Joint Terrorism Task Force? Where were the Feds? That cretinous fucker did this without telling anyone and led the goddamned assault himself."

"Who hired you?" Bishop asked, trying to process his thoughts and figure out what to do. He'd been involved in his share of big cases, but nothing like this. Not because of the publicity this would attract, but because it was so one-sided. No one was going to sympathize with the kid.

"His mother, who's American, by the way. Don't be a pussy, Frank. Show some guts. This is a once-in-a-lifetime kind of case, a case that'll make your career. The kid has no history of violence, no record, nothing. Help me find out what really happened last night. Help me—"

"Victoria, put away the talking-head bullshit for a moment and let's at least be honest. You're talking to me now. This case is about the front page of the *New York Times*, *60 Minutes*, and *People* fucking magazine. Don't wave the Constitution and the flag in my—"

"Of course it's about that. And it'll be about that for you too. But it's also about truth—"

"Justice, and the American way," Bishop said, finishing her sentence. "Yeah, yeah. I watched *Superman* on TV when I was a kid too. You wanna talk about injustice, less than an hour ago I had the world's most incredible pair of tits dangling in my face and three women making out in front of me . . ."

"Sometimes I really think you're hopeless. Like you're the same kid I met years ago with no direction, no skills, and no clue how the world worked. Back then at least you had ambition, you had balls, you were willing to take chances. This is the opportunity of a lifetime and all you wanna talk about's an easy pair of fake tits. I don't have the patience for this tonight. Are you in or not, tough guy?" Cannel asked.

"What do I need to know?"

"Meet me in the main lobby at Bellevue tomorrow at . . . let's make it eight fifteen. Wear one of your TV suits. We're having a press conference after we talk to the mother."

4

THE NEXT MORNING, when Bishop stepped into an elevator at Bellevue Hospital, he was not a happy boy. He'd only gotten about three hours' sleep, his head was killing him, and his stomach was fluttering wildly. He'd already had two cups of coffee, half a container of orange juice, and a bottle of water, and he still felt like he'd been licking talcum powder off the sidewalk. He must've had more to drink at V than he'd realized. And now he had to go interview some scumbag terrorist's mother. Great, just what he wanted to do. Victoria left a message on his cell that the hospital had offered the use of a conference room on the third floor and he should meet them there.

Bishop was wearing a navy-blue chalk-stripe suit, a light blue shirt, and a platinum tie. But even in the expensive, nicely tailored uniform of a successful executive, he still looked like a bouncer at a strip club. His skin was too brown from the tanning booth, his belt buckle was too big and too silver, and his shoes were too . . . well, his shoes were just wrong. But even if his skin tone had been normal, and the belt and shoes had been appropriate, his body would've given him away. No corporate clone or hedge-fund wizard was ever built like this.

In truth, Bishop looked only marginally more respectable in a conservative $2,000 suit than he did in his usual getup of Seven jeans, tight

Armani T-shirt, lizard cowboy boots, and a blazer—to cover the holster on his waist. His shoulders, chest, and upper arms were so beefy with muscle that even though the suit jacket fit him properly, the expensive worsted fabric looked like it was about to split open whenever he moved; like he was in the first stage of that explosive transformation the Incredible Hulk goes through when his muscles start to bulge and all his clothes start to tear.

Bishop had brought along two of his investigators. Paul was a just-retired lieutenant from the South Bronx with thirty-two years on the street. Like someone who can play a musical instrument by ear, Paul was a natural, a brilliant investigator with an acute intuitive sense. The younger investigator, Eddie, was the son and grandson of cops but had forsaken the NYPD for the allure of Hollywood. Along with acting, taking film school classes, and writing screenplays, he worked for Bishop to pay his rent—and maybe gather material for his writing. Bishop liked Eddie. He thought he had a lot of energy and the potential to be a good investigator. But mostly he kept him on because of his skill with a surveillance camera.

The conference room was at the end of a gauntlet of small, identical administrative offices occupied by people who stared at computer screens all day, keeping track of things like patient bills and insurance payments. Victoria, her assistant, and Mrs. Andrea Jafaari and her sixteen-year-old daughter were already there when Bishop and his crew walked in.

"I'm sorry," the private eye said as soon as he entered the room, "I hope we're not late."

"Actually, you're right on time," Victoria said. "We got here a little early to go over a few things. Frank Bishop, this is Andrea Jafaari and her daughter, Mary."

As the rest of the introductions were made, Bishop was a little confused. Andrea? Mary? What the hell was that about? He knew going in that the suspect's mother was American, but he never thought she'd be quite this American. He expected an older, dowdier woman in Middle Eastern dress, perhaps wearing the traditional Islamic head covering.

Instead, Jafaari, who appeared to be in her midforties, was completely unexceptional, an average, modestly dressed woman you'd never look at twice. Nothing about her was even remotely Arabic. And the daughter, meanwhile, was wearing Lululemon yoga pants and a necklace that said, PRINCESS.

Sensing his confusion, Victoria said, "We just got some terrific news from the doctors. Ayad was taken off the respirator this morning, he's breathing on his own, and they believe he's gonna pull through. He hasn't regained consciousness yet, but he's definitely turned the corner."

"That's great," Bishop said with considerably less enthusiasm than he wanted to muster.

"Why don't we get going since we have a lot of ground to cover?" Victoria said quickly, in the hope that no one else had noticed Bishop's lackluster response.

"I'm going to ask you a lot of questions, Mrs. Jafaari," Bishop said. "In order to help your son, I need to know what kind of kid he is, who he hangs out with, where he spends his time, what he's into. I need you to be completely honest with me. Even if there's bad stuff. I'm on your side here. The more I know about him and your family, the easier it'll be for us to conduct our investigation and hopefully help him."

The suspect's mother spoke softly, but she was articulate and direct. She was a fifth-grade teacher who lived in an apartment in Astoria, Queens, a neighborhood where there was a large Greek population and a growing Muslim community. When she was twenty-two she had met and married an Egyptian named Ibrahim Ayad Jafaari against the wishes of her parents. He was, she said, elegant and mysterious, and it was all very exciting. It became a lot less exciting, however, once they were married.

Ibrahim turned out to be moody, secretive, and intolerant. He was verbally abusive to her and their son, Ayad. He even smacked her once, hard, across the face. He had trouble adjusting to America, and when Ayad was not quite six years old, Ibrahim packed up and left. Just walked out one day with no warning, barely a good-bye and no forwarding address. He returned to Egypt and she never saw him or heard from him again. She was seven months pregnant when he abandoned her and Ayad, and she named her daughter Mary, the most American, Christian name she could think of, to spite him.

She raised Ayad and Mary on her own. To supplement her teaching salary, she occasionally worked weekends at a local travel agency that catered to Arabs. Most of the trips were visits home to the Middle East or pilgrimages to Mecca. The agency ran several annual hajj specials that kept them very busy in the months leading up to Ramadan.

"Sometimes I worked a lot of hours," she said, her voice starting to crack. "But Ayad was a good boy. He looked out for his sister and did whatever I asked him to do. He only got in trouble once. And it wasn't his fault. Six years ago—"

"Mom, *mom*, don't," her daughter suddenly said, trying to stop her from telling the story.

"It's okay," she said patiently to Mary, "they'll find out anyway. When Ayad was seventeen, a senior in high school, he was arrested for drugs. It was a big mistake. He was at a party and someone offered him a ride home. They got pulled over and there was a lot of marijuana in the car. Maybe some other things, too, I'm not really sure. It took a few days, but once the police realized he was telling the truth, that he knew nothing about the drugs, the charges were dropped and they let him go."

"That's it?" Bishop asked. "No other problems? Nothing else we should know about?"

"No," she said, suddenly weeping softly. "Nothing else. He was a good student and he worked part-time so he'd have spending money."

"Are you okay, Andrea?" Victoria asked, and handed her a tissue. "Do you want to take a break?"

Bishop snuck a glance at his watch. They'd been talking for nearly an hour.

"No," she responded. "I'm all right. I'd just like to finish and go be with Ayad."

"We're almost done," Bishop said. "You're doing great. How'd he meet the other suspects? The guys he was in the apartment with?"

"As I just mentioned, he worked part-time. In his second year at NYU, he took a class in Islamic studies. He'd always asked questions about his father; he was curious, as any child would be about a parent they never really knew. But he never expressed any interest in Islam or Arab culture. He was a typical teenager, focused on the usual things. But once he got to college and he began to pay a little more attention to what was going on in the world, he became interested in his heritage, his roots. So when he took that class, he also took a job at an Islamic bookstore in Bay Ridge. It's just down the street from the mosque and the apartment where he was . . . where he was shot. He met two of the men at the bookstore. And I think they introduced him to the other two."

"Did he ever talk about politics?" Bishop asked. "Was he angry or upset about the situation in the Middle East?"

"If you're asking me, Mr. Bishop, if he was a radical, or if he had extreme views, the answer is no. He was very passionate about politics, but what he wanted was peace and coexistence, not hate and war. At school he started an informal student group to promote campus coexistence. He has very close Christian, Jewish, and Muslim friends."

"But, Mrs. Jafaari, surely he must've—"

"Must've what, Mr. Bishop? Hated America? Wanted to commit jihad? Not Ayad. He loved rock and roll, football, and fast cars. He loved being able to think what he wanted and do what he wanted. Ayad loved being American. He was reading the Koran for the first time. He bought his first kufi. He was going to the mosque on Fridays. And you know what? He was beginning to understand and appreciate his heritage, but it actually sharpened his appreciation for this country. Helped him realize how lucky he was. He was curious, he was learning about who he was for the first time. But he was not a—"

"I'm sorry," Bishop interrupted. "It's just that it's a little hard to believe he was an innocent bystander in an apartment full of terrorists that got raided by the police."

"I don't know what Ayad was doing in that apartment. But the idea that he would do anything to hurt anyone, that he would do anything that involved bombs, or . . ." Her voice broke and she suddenly couldn't continue. She was weeping now. After nearly an hour and a half, she'd finally lost her composure.

"I think that's probably enough for now, Frank," Victoria said. "We need to get ready for the press conference anyway."

"Sure, I've got plenty to get started. When's the press conference, Vic?"

"In about fifteen minutes," she said.

"Good, then I'm gonna go powder my nose. See you in a few."

The two men embraced, exchanged pleasantries, and caught each other up on recent events. Then they got down to business. Something would have to be done about the kid, Ayad Jafaari.

"We can't risk leaving any loose ends," one said while sipping a cup of tea. "He's the only thing that can connect us to the apartment. We should move quickly."

"Perhaps it will take care of itself," the other one said optimistically. "If we let it be, if we just give it a little time, he may simply die from his injuries. We should know within a few days whether or not he'll survive. If he doesn't, then it's our good fortune, we don't have to do anything."

"I'm not willing to leave it to chance. There's too much at stake. It's simpler to just clean it up and then we can move forward."

The other man nodded and they sat in silence for a few moments.

Finally he said, "It will be very difficult, you know. Not impossible but certainly difficult. His hospital room is heavily guarded. There are police outside the door and police by the elevator to prevent access to the corridor. Lots of obstacles, very risky."

"I understand, but it's critical that we cover our tracks. I'm confident you'll think of something. You always do."

5

LUCY WAS ON the number 6 train, heading uptown along Manhattan's East Side. She'd gotten on the train in SoHo, about a block and a half from her small one-bedroom apartment. It was noon on a bright, cool Saturday, the kind of day she'd once imagined she'd spend jogging in Central Park, prowling exotic boutiques for fabulous clothes, lunching at some chic spot with her girlfriends, and maybe hitting the Met or the galleries downtown in the late afternoon. At least that's what she'd thought her Saturdays would be like before moving to New York.

The reality on this Saturday and many others, however, was a little different. She was working. After the Domenico-Brock press conference yesterday, she and A. J. had gone back to the office to map out their strategy. A. J. said he would work on getting access to Brock. He was confident that once he spoke to the police commissioner on the phone, he could at least convince him to have dinner—A. J. had his cell number and knew his favorite restaurant—to discuss the possibility of a profile.

"Okay," Lucy said, "then I'll work on this kid Jafaari and the backstory of the raid."

"That's exactly what I was going to tell you," A. J. said. "But there's something else I want you to do as well. Do you know the name Supreme? He's apparently some kind of music producer."

"Seriously?" Lucy said, tossing her hair back with a sexy little flick of her head. "You've never heard of Supreme? He's the founder of Black Ice Records. He's an entrepreneur like Russell Simmons or Jay Z, only he's not quite as well-known because he spends a lot less time hanging out with rich white people and mainstream celebrities. He's a lot more street."

"I'm impressed. Way to bring it . . ."

"You know I love you, A. J., but, really, don't do that. Even as a joke. You're like the preppiest guy I've ever seen outside of high school."

"Sorry. But you don't have to get all up in my grill about—"

"A. J. C'mon."

"Okay. I'm done now," he said, laughing. "Anyway, Supreme has left me several voice mails. Serious voice mails."

"He has? About what?"

"Did you see the story about ten days ago on that cop that was found dead in the Hamptons? The NYPD lieutenant? They found him in the bedroom of his house with a hooker who'd been beaten to death."

"Yeah, I remember. The *Times* buried it in the Metro section and the tabloids only played it for, like, one day. He was a decorated NYPD veteran who'd been suspended because of some kind of investigation by Internal Affairs. His name was Anderson, right?"

"That's the one." A. J. nodded. "Kevin Anderson."

"The papers said it looked like a murder-suicide. Like maybe he beat the hooker and then OD'd on drugs. Bizarre."

"It was beyond bizarre. And then the story just went away. Which was even more bizarre, given how much pop the tabloids could've gotten out of it. It was like the department shut it down or something. Anyway, Supreme claims to know something about it. Something big. Says it's all very sensitive and explosive. No idea if it's legit, but it's worth finding out. Call him and set up a meeting. If nothing else, it'll be a good exercise for you."

"Sure, okay."

"Anything else? No? Okay, then we're done here. Lemme know what happens."

• • •

Lucy had called Supreme as soon as they were finished. She said she was calling on behalf of A. J. Ross, almost like she was his secretary, which worked to get Supreme on the phone.

"Yo, when's he wanna sit down?" Supreme asked.

"Actually, he wants me to come and talk to you first so—"

"No deal," he snapped. "You tryin' to play me? I don't get to talk to the man himself, I ain't talkin'. Simple as that, know what I'm sayin'? You want the four-one-one, get me Ross. This shit's too important. Hey, I ain't frontin' here, people could end up dead over this. *I could end up dead.* And I ain't about to let that happen, know what I'm sayin'?"

Lucy remained calm, striking just the right balance of deference and resolve as she patiently explained to Supreme that this was standard operating procedure. "Please," she assured him, "there's no disrespect intended here. At any other time, given how important you are, I know A. J. would come see you himself. But surely you can understand that he can't always personally check out every tip that comes in—especially with everything going on in the city right now. Just as I'm sure you can't always personally go and listen to every new artist someone gives you a tip about. I'm sure there are times when you have no choice but to send a trusted associate to catch the performance first. Right?"

Lucy's gambit with Supreme worked perfectly. His attitude softened and he gave in. "I hope you as fine to look at as you are to listen to," he said. "C'mon up to my place tomorrow around lunchtime. You know, like one o'clock."

So, on a beautiful Saturday, Lucy was on her way to see Supreme. She got off the subway at Fifty-Ninth Street and Lexington Avenue. The street was crowded with shoppers, and Lucy had to maneuver to find a spot where she could pause for a moment and collect herself. She closed her eyes and took a few long, slow, deep breaths. She steadied her breathing, and her mind, which had been racing, gradually began to slow down.

As she started to walk uptown, she glanced in the windows of Bloomingdale's and stared at her own reflection. She paused, intending to smooth her clothes and maybe fix her hair a little. Instead, she just stood there, admiring the way she looked—the snug, but not too snug, fit of her dark low-rise pants and the irresistible silhouette her long legs created. Her short dark jacket with its little flared bottom and her man-tailored white shirt were perfect. She had a talent for creating a style that looked unstudied, like she'd grabbed the first things she saw in her closet and put them on. But the effect was irresistible, a casual look admired by both men and women. She got so completely absorbed in her reflection she didn't notice several harried people bump into her as they rushed by.

When the moment passed, Lucy was embarrassed and quickly looked around to see if anyone was watching. She felt a little silly, and a little mischievous, at having lost herself that way on a busy street. She took one more deep breath, shook her head side to side a couple of times as if literally trying to shake off the distractions, and started walking again.

Lucy realized she hadn't gone shopping in a long time. Though money was tight on her puny salary at the magazine, she tried to treat herself to something nice every once in a while—especially after completing a difficult assignment—and she made a mental note that it was time. She still had some money stashed away from her modeling days that she only touched occasionally, to reward herself with something she really wanted.

Supreme's elegant five-story town house was on East Sixty-Eighth Street between Madison and Park Avenues. Lucy had a pretty good sense of the Manhattan real estate market, mostly from the magazine's frequent coverage, and she was sure the town house was an eight-figure property. Given the location, the size, and the condition, it had to have cost Supreme at least $30 million. A small video camera was perched over the front door and another was focused on the garage. *Amazing,* Lucy thought. *How many people in Manhattan have their own garage?* At that moment, she noticed a huge, hulking figure about to get into a bright yellow, $300,000 Maybach.

"Afternoon," said the big man. "You Lucy?" She nodded. "The boss is expecting you. Ring the bell and someone will come right down."

Less than five minutes later, Lucy was sitting in a beyond-opulent living room with a ten-foot coffered ceiling. The furniture was classic, old-white-money stuffy and uncomfortable, with a few stunning antiques mixed in—the kind of pieces they sold at the auction houses. *Who was this guy?* she thought. She'd done some background work on him and knew he'd made some real money in the record business, but she didn't think it was this kind of money. And what was with the furnishings? The place looked like the Astors or the Vanderbilts were living in it. In fact, it probably had been owned by one of New York's old-line families at one time. You didn't have to watch BET to recognize this was not the way people who made hip-hop music decorated their houses. Where was all the contemporary stuff? The glass and stainless steel and leopard skin and the huge leather couches as big as minivans? Where were all the giant flat-screen TVs and the grown men wearing thick gold jewelry and brand-new, unlaced $300 sneakers, and sitting around playing Xbox?

Suddenly, two toddlers came running into the room, chased by a pretty nanny wearing a gray and white uniform. She apologized to Lucy in a German accent and said Mr. Clarence (Supreme's real name was Clarence Carter; his mother had named him after her favorite blues singer) was running a little late, but he'd be with her shortly. Just then, a trim white man in his forties walked in, wearing a trendy-looking black suit (Prada, Lucy guessed), and introduced himself as Ira Kleinberg. He was Supreme's business partner.

"How're you, Ms. Chapin?" Kleinberg asked with a smile.

"Please, call me Lucy. I'm—"

"Mmm, mmm, mmmmm." Supreme had come into the room and he was staring at Lucy. "Woman, you are a fine sight. Props to A. J. Ross."

Supreme was about five feet nine inches with a small but gym-produced muscular build. He had glistening skin that was so smooth it looked like it had just been buffed, and he was wearing a cream-colored velour tracksuit with a black stripe down the side of the pants. He had a small diamond stud in each ear and two big gold rings on each hand but no visible chains around his neck. He carried himself with the slouchy swagger of someone from the streets.

"How you doin', girl?" Supreme said to Lucy.

"Very well, thanks. And you?"

"Not bad for somebody with a motherfuckin' target on his head, know what I'm sayin'?"

"Actually, no, I—"

"Well, listen up. This is some serious shit I'm talkin' 'bout. I ain't playin'. I gotta cover my back on this 'cause I'm in it up to my mother-fuckin' neck, okay?"

"Okay," Lucy responded, though she wasn't at all sure she knew what he was talking about. "If you're referring to A. J. and me honoring what-ever kind of deal we make, you don't have to worry about that. I assume you called A. J. because you know his reputation."

"Girl, I got to worry 'bout everything. My stomach has more knots than the dreads on a Kingston reggae band. This goes bad, it's my black ass that's fucked," Supreme said, his mood suddenly darkening. "Maybe this is a bad idea, man. Shit, maybe I should just forget talkin'. I don't need to make this worse."

Lucy didn't really know what to say, so she didn't say anything. The wrong word, a misread facial expression, and Supreme could pull the plug on the whole thing. She looked at Kleinberg, who had been sitting quietly in a big, green velvet wingback chair. He stood up, walked around behind the chair, leaned forward against it on his forearms, and began talking.

"We've gone over this very carefully several times," Kleinberg said. "And we decided this was the best way to go, right? In fact, it's about the only way to go. Your life's on the line here, and unless we can get someone to pay some attention, the danger's only going to increase."

"No doubt," Supreme said softly, shaking his head back and forth. "No doubt. All right," he said with somewhat renewed spirit. "I ain't no fuckin' little girl, all scared and shit. Let's do this, let's rock somebody's world."

Relieved, Lucy reached into her bag without looking down and slowly, almost surreptitiously, removed her notebook and digital recorder.

"About four weeks ago, I got a call from Big K, telling me he wants to get together. You know, like old times. So I thought he was lookin' to get up on me, to shake me down for some money."

As Supreme talked, Lucy quietly turned on the recorder and placed it on the side table. "No way," Supreme said almost immediately, reaching for the recorder. "What the fuck? Take all the motherfuckin' notes you want, but ain't nobody gonna hear my voice except when I'm talkin' right now. No playback shit gonna be goin' on here, know what I'm sayin'?"

"Sorry," Lucy said without getting flustered. "We'll do this however you're comfortable. Could you start at the beginning? Like I don't know anything about this story, which I actually don't. Big K is Kevin Anderson? How do you know him?"

"I can't say no to those eyes again, baby," Supreme said with a smile. "Okay, you want it from the beginning, I'll give you the book of fuckin' Genesis. In the beginning, there was Church Jackson. Church was the baddest, smartest motherfucker in Harlem. He owned the drug business. I started runnin' for one of his crews when I was fourteen. You know, doing errands and shit. Gettin' them cigarettes, food, whatever they needed. It was what people downtown would call my internship. Slowly, I started doin' more serious shit. Drop-offs, pickups, and selling a little weed they'd throw me. I didn't actually meet Master Mind till I was like eighteen. He's layers removed from the street, insulated, for protection. Anyway, by the time I was twenty I was one of his go-to guys."

"So this all started around the mid-1990s?" Lucy asked.

"Yeah, I hooked up with them in '96. I met Big K like eight years later. February of 2004. I remember 'cause it was Valentine's Day and I was with my girl. It was a motherfuckin' cold night. I mean freeze-your-ass-right-off cold. Coldest night I can remember. I'd bought my girl some scorchin' Victoria's Secret shit, for a little holiday romance. But it was so cold that night she didn't even wanna take off her sweater.

"Anyway, Church Jackson called me around ten thirty, and I had to get all up outta bed, get dressed and shit, and meet him at an apartment on One Hundred Forty-Eighth Street and Frederick Douglass Boulevard. It was an unusual situation. Let's just say one of our sales managers seemed to be having a little problem with his bookkeeping, and we had a large shipment coming in that the motherfucker was supposed to be responsible for. So Church wanted us to pay him a little visit and make sure, you know, his spreadsheets were in order."

As Supreme talked, Lucy frantically took notes. She noticed that every once in a while the former drug dealer would lose the attitude and the edgy street argot and sound a lot smarter and more sophisticated than maybe he wanted to. Even though he lived in a Beaux Arts mansion, the whole gangsta thing was critical, she figured, to who he was and everything he was about.

Lucy didn't say anything while Supreme told his story, except to quietly utter an occasional "right," just to make sure he knew she was listening. A. J. had always told her to stay out of the way once someone gets rolling. "Let the momentum work. Allow your subject to unload whatever it is they need to unload. Do not interrupt," he'd tell her over and over. "Too many reporters want to hear themselves talk. They want their subject to like them or they want to show how smart they are. This is not about you. Save your questions until later. Even when a subject stops talking, don't say anything for a few minutes. Silence makes people uncomfortable, and their instinct is to keep talking to fill up the space. And sometimes that's when they let their guard down and give you the best stuff."

"So we're in this apartment, which we used for an 'office,'" Supreme said, actually making air quotes with his two hands around the word "office." He did it in such an exaggerated way that Lucy knew he was teasing her, making fun, she guessed, of what he considered an overused, twentysomething-white-girl gesture. He smiled at her in a surprisingly gentle way and she couldn't help but smile back.

"There was some serious fuckin' weight in that room and a substantial amount of cash too. We were explaining the importance of accurate accounting to this ignorant motherfucker who worked for us when the five-oh showed up. No knock, no shouted identification from the

hallway, no nothin', man. Two fuckin' uniforms, patrolmen of all goddamned things, came through the door with their guns drawn. I'm tellin'
you, it was no joke. There was enough rock and pure coke in that room
to send some niggas away for life, know what I'm sayin'? And the whole
thing was supposedly some stupid-ass screwup. A fuckin' mistake," Supreme said in disbelief, as if the incident had just happened.

"The cops said they were responding to a domestic-disturbance
call. Some drunk-ass fool was waving a piece at his old lady, scarin' her
and threatening to cap her ass or some shit. The cops were supposed to
hit apartment 504. But these two shining examples of New York's finest
musta been dyslexic or something, because the backward-ass motherfuckers came bustin' into 405, which was our place."

While Supreme's shock and indignation were sincere, it was all Lucy
could do to keep from exploding with laughter. The absurdity of the situation and Supreme's description of the cops were almost too much for her.

"So as I'm sure you can understand," he continued, "we were in a
severely compromised position. Totally fucked, actually. But somebody
musta been lookin' down on our asses. Hey, Ira," Supreme said, interrupting the story. "Ask Marta to bring us some iced tea or somethin',
okay? Iced tea okay?" he asked Lucy.

"Ah, sure. That'd be great."

"See, Kevin was one complicated nigga," Supreme continued. "He
was an opportunist, an aggressive, ambitious motherfucker. He wanted
to be a playa and he recognized immediately that night that his moment
had arrived. The fuck they say about luck? It's like when hard work and
preparation meet opportunity, or some shit like that, right? Well, that
night was Kevin's motherfuckin' shot at gettin' lucky. He wanted it, no
doubt. But did he have the balls to step up and take it?"

Supreme told Lucy that Kevin Anderson grew up in Mount Vernon, a
predominantly black suburb of New York, populated mostly by working-
and middle-class families. During his last semester at Tulane he was involved in an ugly scandal when campus security found a large quantity of
drugs and stolen final exams in his dorm. He blamed his roommate and the

guys next door. To avoid a scandal, the school agreed not to press charges and to sweep the whole thing under the rug if all of them agreed to leave.

Angry and bitter, Kevin returned to New York and finished his degree at City College. Then he entered the police academy. After graduation, he was assigned to uniform patrol in the Thirty-Third Precinct in Harlem. Supreme's territory. In those days it was Supreme's whole world. He knew every block of that precinct. And based on his experience getting stopped, hassled, chased, arrested, and slapped around a couple of times, Supreme believed there were basically three kinds of cops in the Three-Three, and probably everywhere else for that matter.

There was the cop who signed in every day, worked his straight eight, minded his own business, and went home. He was just trying to earn a living, put in his twenty, and retire. There was the really gung ho cop, the guy on a mission who wanted to protect and serve, the guy who believed he could make a difference, maybe even change the world. Lastly, there was the predator, the dangerous, aggressive, macho cop who just as easily could've gone the other way. This cop loved the action and lived to mix it up in the streets. He wanted to lock up the bad guys, but not for the right reasons. He was all about what was in it for him. This was Kevin Anderson.

"So Big K decided that night to step up and seize the motherfuckin' moment. Him and his partner cuffed us like we were gonna be arrested. But once they had us secured, that crazy nigga tells his partner to go for a walk. He tells him, 'No sweat, man, I'm huggin' this. I'm all over it. I'll meet you at the car in like fifteen minutes. I got somethin' I need to take care of here and you don't wanna be part of it.'"

Once the other cop was gone, Supreme said, Kevin announced that he was their new business partner. Unless they wanted to spend the next twenty-five years in prison, they were going to give him 15 percent of everything they did. "But here's the part that's really fuckin' wacked," Supreme said. "He wasn't just shakin' us down. He actually wanted to be *partners*. Big K was offering to earn his end. I thought he was trippin', man. The crazy-ass fucker told us he believed he could provide intelligence not only on police operations but on our competitors as well."

The plan was, in its way, genius. Kevin told Supreme that he was certain he could get his hands on CompStat data, the computer-generated statistical analysis of crime data the NYPD began using to clean up the city's streets in the midnineties.

For decades, cops had just muddled along, making an arrest when they saw a crime in progress or attempting to track down a perpetrator when someone reported being victimized. They were totally reactive. Prevention was not in the playbook. In truth, no one, not even the cops themselves, believed they could actually prevent crime.

Once a year, the FBI would publish crime figures for every city in America. *Once a year.* And this was the only accurate intel the cops got about what kinds of crime were being committed, how often, and in which locations. In essence, the NYPD's precincts functioned completely in the dark. How do you know where to put your resources if you don't even know where the crimes are being committed? It'd be like trying to run a company without having up-to-date sales figures.

CompStat changed all that. Every crime and police incident in every part of the city was tracked every single day by computer, which resulted in detailed street maps showing where the action occurred. So on any given day, a precinct commander knew exactly where the drug sales, the rapes, the purse snatchings, and the car thefts took place. And because he knew which corners, which alleys, which apartment buildings, and which subway stations had problems, he knew where to put his cops. It also meant that for the first time in the history of the New York City police department, precinct commanders could be held accountable for what took place on their watch.

Kevin's idea was to turn the CompStat process on its head. Used correctly, this information could be just as valuable to criminals as it was to the cops. For someone like Church Jackson, knowing where the cops were going to be, and knowing where his competitors were set up, was invaluable. Having this intelligence was like the street-crime equivalent of insider trading.

"So we make the deal with Kevin," Supreme continued. "I mean, what the fuck, yo, it's not like we had any choice. We set a meeting for later in the week to work out the rest of the details. He said he was gonna have a partner, some higher-up in the department who'd provide most of the info and additional protection. But this guy won't be at the meeting. He'll stay in the background, remain anonymous. Then he takes off the cuffs and tells us he needs fifty K. Now. He wants twenty-five as a motherfuckin' show of good faith, and twenty-five to make the cop who was with him look the other way. At that point I knew Big K wasn't just jammin'. This was no spontaneous fuckin' flash of lightnin', all right? Somehow the crazy motherfucker had planned it. Man," Supreme said, shaking his head and laughing, "that nigga was somethin'."

Lucy's mind was racing. She wanted to ask questions, to probe for details. But Supreme was clearly determined to continue telling the story and she didn't want to place any obstacles in front of him.

The partnership turned out to be an extraordinary arrangement for everyone. Church Jackson and Supreme made more money than ever— even with 15 percent coming off the top—and they didn't have to waste time and energy protecting their turf and fighting off the competition. Kevin and his anonymous partner, who were raking it in as well, pretty much took care of that. The deal even made Kevin look like a first-rate, kick-ass cop. With help from Church and Supreme—the intelligence exchange was a two-way street—his arrest numbers were very strong and he started getting regular promotions.

For five years, it was the perfect deal. And then Church Jackson turned up dead. Not just dead, but with his head and feet cut off. "The nigga was found in little pieces on a baseball field in Macombs Dam Park behind Yankee Stadium," Supreme said. "It was no joke. You gotta be one crazy-ass motherfucker to do that. I'm talkin' Jeffrey Dahmer, Hannibal Lecter, Osama bin motherfuckin' Laden crazy, know what I'm sayin'? They cut off his fingers and all ten digits were placed on the pitcher's mound. Tryin' to make it look like a ritualistic killing or some shit is one thing. But the psycho had to know if he dumped the body on that baseball field that a bunch of neighborhood kids would find it."

"Do you know—?" Lucy started to ask, but Supreme slowly held up his hand to stop her. He wasn't ready to take questions yet. He got up out of his chair and started pacing as he talked.

"This is where things really get fucked up. Church was into the whole secrecy thing. So even as tight as we were, there were still things he never told me. I don't know for sure how he ended up in motherfuckin' pieces spread out on the infield like human fertilizer, but I have a pretty good idea why. Big K's partner was done; he wanted out. Maybe he was tired of dealing with it, maybe he was climbin' the law enforcement ladder of success and he was worried about gettin' busted. Fuck if I know. But once he made his decision, guess what? The motherfucker didn't wanna worry about the shadows. He didn't wanna look in the rearview mirror and see anything but a long stretch of empty road. Nothing to connect him to our highly profitable little enterprise. At first I wasn't sure if it was Kevin or his partner who did Church. And for a while it didn't really matter," Supreme said, picking up his iced tea glass and taking a drink.

"Kevin came to me shortly after Church was eighty-sixed and said it was just us now. Me and him. His partner was retired, and I guess you could say, so was mine."

"Whoa," Lucy instinctively blurted, "weren't you concerned at that point about Kevin's partner? Why wouldn't he kill you too?"

Supreme allowed a half smile. "Patience, pretty girl, patience. I figured I was cool 'cause I had no idea who Kevin's other half was. He dealt only with Church. And if they were gonna do me, they woulda done it. Why dick around and waste time putting a new deal together between Big K and me? So Kevin and me continued to conduct business more or less like we had before. And then after two years or so of our new arrangement, I started to move into the music business and out of the drug business. Less stress, know what I'm sayin'?"

"So why the worry now?" Lucy asked.

"Kevin called me a few weeks ago. I hadn't heard from his ass in nearly two years. So I was surprised by the 'Hey, brutha, how you be' dial-up. The nigga says we need some face time, get together and talk about the old days, talk about business. Fuck, man, we ain't got no business no more, that street shit's behind me. In the rearview mirror. So I kinda played him, know what I'm sayin'? I said, 'Yeah, we should do that. Lemme get back to you.' Then the nigga turns up dead."

Supreme's demeanor was different now. He was less playful, less engaged by his own storytelling. Lucy thought that even his facial muscles seemed drawn a little tighter. "Once I heard that, I knew somethin' was goin' down. I knew he called with some real shit; he wasn't just trippin'. He didn't give anything up on the phone, but I knew that the chickens had come home to roost. Suicide?" Supreme said with a rueful laugh. "Yeah, right. Not a fuckin' chance."

"How can you be so sure?" Lucy asked. "Family man, decorated cop, under investigation by Internal Affairs according to the papers. Maybe it just got to be too much. Maybe IAB was closing in and the pressure was too much. Maybe—"

"Maybe he's in heaven now with Jesus and all the angels. Look," Supreme said, moving toward Lucy, "I'm not interested in fuckin' fairy tales and make-believe. Kevin was too tough, too smart, and too vain to kill himself. This motherfucker was raising a family and rising through the ranks of the NYPD while at the same time playin' a key role in runnin' a multimillion-dollar drug business. You wanna talk about stress? Pressure? My money's on his old partner. And guess what? I'm the last of the motherfuckin' Mohicans, the last critical loose end. If he's lookin' to clean the slate, I'm next up on the schedule."

"But you have no idea who he is," Lucy said.

"That's why I called A. J. He's got the best sources in the city. I've given you ninety percent of the puzzle. Go find the last piece. Quickly. Or this may be the last motherfuckin' afternoon you and I get to spend together. And that, shawty, would truly be a shame."

On the street, Lucy fumbled a little getting her iPhone out of her bag. She was so jacked up over Supreme's story that her hands were shaking. "Okay," she said to herself, "calm down. Take a few deep breaths and you'll be fine." The breathing helped a little, but what she felt like she really needed was a drink. That would have to wait. She wanted to get to A. J. while all of the details were still fresh. "YO," she typed quickly with her thumbs, "SUPREME STRY IS A MAJR SCORE. A GRND SLM . . ."

When her cell phone rang, she was already in a cab heading back to her apartment. "Hello," she said a little too loudly. She was still so energized her voice actually startled the cabdriver.

"So I guess it went pretty well," A. J. said.

"It was unbelievable," Lucy said, modulating her volume. "I don't even know what to say. I think I'm still in shock. Excuse me," she said to the cabdriver. "Can you pull over here? I'm sorry, I need to get out."

She felt guilty cutting the ride short, so she overtipped. She didn't want to discuss any details of the story within earshot of the cabbie. Now, standing in a doorway across from the public library on the corner of Forty-First Street and Fifth Avenue, she filled A. J. in on the details.

"He just gave it up," she gushed. "I mean all of it. The drug dealing, the complicit cops, how their system worked, using the CompStat intel, the murders, every amazing fucking piece of it."

"Good job, Luce. Make lots of additional notes now, okay?" A. J. said. "Where are you?"

"I'm right by the library."

"Perfect. Go grab a chair in Bryant Park, or go to a Starbucks or whatever. Put down your impressions of him, the town house, the atmosphere, his manner, all of it. Do it before you lose it. Same thing with the quotes. Go through your notes from the interview right now and add whatever you missed. Fill in the details. Put in his inflection, what he emphasized, where he paused, and what he was doing while he talked. Do it now and I'm telling you, you'll remember everything he said."

"Okay," Lucy said, "I'll start as soon as we're done. So whaddaya think?"

"It sounds promising. I think—"

"Promising? You're kidding, right?" Lucy blurted. "I mean, I know you always like to keep it low-key and all, but c'mon, A. J. This is fucking amazing!"

"Okay, okay. Yes, it's got amazing *possibilities* but we're not there yet. Right now all we have is him. We need more. And by the way, I'm not at all sure he's being completely straight."

"What? How much straighter could he be?"

"Well," A. J. said, "for starters, he knows who Kevin's partner was in the department. Or at least he has a very good idea. He may have a good reason for holding back, but I'm telling you he knows. Maybe he sees it as his ace in the hole, the one card he's got left to play. Or maybe he's not ready to completely trust us yet. But believe me, he knows."

"How can you be so sure?"

"I've done this a few times. And he sounds way too smart not to know who he was in bed with. The stakes were way too high. You did a really nice job here, Lucy. So let's do this: since I'm just getting started on the Brock thing, you can run with Supreme. Start talking to some other people about him, people from the old days and from the music business. Try to get some sense of what kind of guy he is, how other people see him."

"Oooooh, yeeesssss," Lucy squealed. "A. J., you're the best."

"Hey, no biggie, girl, you've earned it. Did you set up anything else with him?"

"He invited me to some, I don't know, I guess it's like a promo party for one of his new rappers. It's at a club in Brooklyn. I think it's actually like under the Brooklyn Bridge. It's later in the week."

"Of course he did. You don't have to go if you're not comfortable, or if—"

"A. J.," she cut him off. "I know that's coming from the right place but it's still patronizing. I'm a big girl. I'll be fine."

"Okay," he said with a heavy sigh. "Call me tomorrow and let me know how you're doing."

6

ON SUNDAY MORNING, Frank Bishop was his usual high-energy, hyper-active self. He'd had a really quiet Saturday night—no women, no booze, no carrying on—partly because he was tired but mostly because he simply couldn't deal. He'd once heard somebody say, "I hate everything and everybody and I hate everything about everybody," and that pretty much summed up how he was feeling by Saturday afternoon. It didn't happen often, but every once in a while, he just needed to totally retreat, to be by himself.

After he'd interviewed Andrea Jafaari at Bellevue, he'd gone to the press conference with her and Victoria Cannel. Essentially, he just stood there for almost forty-five minutes while Victoria strutted, preened, and served up witty, sometimes biting responses to the reporters' questions. Victoria was in fine form. She did righteous indignation with about as much over-the-top, almost campy, passion as Pacino in *Scarface*. *She looked great too,* Bishop thought, with her thick, lustrous hair swept back away from her face and her blue suit outlining the contours of her soft, fleshy curves. Though she was in her midforties and, as Bishop liked to say, way past warranty, she was clearly garage-kept. He passed the time imagining himself slowly undoing her skirt and watching it slide down to her ankles. Then he'd peel back her panties and bend her over one of the cheap brown folding chairs right there in that room with its toxic fluorescent lighting. He got so into it that at one point he started to close his eyes and breathe a little heavily, forgetting he was in front of a pha-lanx of reporters and cameras. By the time the press conference was over, he was drained instead of horny and he decided to simply head home.

Bishop lived in a stunning town house on East Seventy-Ninth Street off Madison, just a few blocks uptown from Supreme. Like much of the rest of his life, it was a cleverly negotiated arrangement. The house was owned by J.D. and Kiki Hiller of Power XXL, the largest independent oil company in America. Bishop had been their go-to guy for years, the "fixer" who, in return, got a two-bedroom apartment on the ground floor, accessible by the old servants' entrance, rent-free. The "real" front door opened into a black and white marble foyer with a small elevator and a grand winding staircase. The Hillers spent most of their time at their 55,000-acre Texas ranch, which meant that Bishop had the run of the place just about all the time.

When he walked into his apartment, his king shepherds, Gus and Woody, came running to greet him. Gus was named for Augustus McCrae and Woody for Woodrow F. Call, the two stalwart, irresistible cowboys at the heart of Larry McMurtry's *Lonesome Dove*. It was the best book Bishop had ever listened to. Bishop played with the dogs for a bit, went through the mail, checked his messages, and took a long, hot shower.

Then it was time to decompress. He ordered some pizza (sausage, extra cheese, as always), including enough for Teresa, the live-in house-keeper, turned off his cell phone and the house phone, and popped *The Good, the Bad,- and the Ugly* into the DVD player. The old spaghetti west-ern remained one of his favorite movies. He'd seen it dozens of times, but he still found it totally absorbing. It never failed to take his mind off whatever was bothering him.

Bishop loved Clint Eastwood's unflappable quiet cool. No matter how shitty his luck, no matter how bad things got, there wasn't even a hint of emotion in his facial expressions or his body language. He gave nothing away unless he wanted to.

In addition to the performances, the action, and the terrific scorched desert scenes, Bishop loved the movie because of its raw, cynical take on human nature. The most obvious piece of this, the fact that people will do anything for money, was a critical part of the story as the characters spent the movie desperately searching for a pile of stolen gold. But it went deeper than this. Bishop had once seen an interview with Sergio Leone, the legendary director, who said, when talking about the movie's story, that in the pursuit of profit there is no such thing as good and evil. Everything depends on chance—the circumstances you face, the choices you're forced to make. And in the end, he said, it's not the best man who wins but the luckiest. Bishop never forgot either of these things.

When he woke up, he was surprised to see that the TV and the DVD player were still on. He didn't remember nodding off. Unfortunately, he'd fallen asleep before the three-way shoot-out between Clint Eastwood, Lee Van Cleef, and Eli Wallach at the end of the movie. Bishop had gotten nearly ten hours of sleep, and physically, he was totally juiced, completely recharged.

Emotionally, however, it was another story. He'd had the Jafaari case for a little more than twenty-four hours and it was making him nuts. He'd gotten even more conflicted about it since interviewing the kid's mother. Bishop thought of himself as an extraordinary judge of character. He believed it was his strongest asset as an investigator. And his judgment told him that Andrea Jafaari was a decent, hardworking woman who did everything she could as a single parent to take care of her kids. When he talked to her in the conference room at Bellevue Hospital, she was distraught over her son, but she wasn't the least bit jittery. She maintained eye contact, she answered his questions directly, and she was, he was convinced, completely honest.

All of which just made things more complicated. Bishop was already plenty unhappy about working for a suspected terrorist. Now there was a possibility that he wasn't a terrorist, that maybe the cops had shot an innocent kid. Bishop felt like he was fucked either way. He couldn't decide which was worse: working for Jafaari if her son was a terrorist or working for Jafaari if he wasn't.

Bishop checked the time. It was nearly nine thirty. *Shit*, he thought, *I gotta get going*. As luck would have it, he was about to find out just how pissed some of his cop friends were that he had taken the Jafaari case. Once every eight weeks or so, Bishop and Chief Walter Fitzgerald would meet at the NYPD's outdoor firing range in the Bronx for a little shooting, a little training, and a little gossip. It was always on a Sunday morning, when the range was officially closed.

Known as Rodman's Neck, the range was tucked away on fifty-four acres in a corner of Pelham Bay Park, the largest park in the city. Used by the army and navy during World Wars I and II, the range had a dozen buildings, including a gun shop, classrooms, and full-scale mock-ups of various kinds of real buildings that ESU and other divisions of the NYPD used for training.

Thanks to some fairly uninhibited driving, Bishop managed to get to the range only ten minutes late. When he walked up to Fitzgerald and the two cops he'd brought along from his detail, he got exactly the kind of greeting he expected. "Holy shit," one of the cops, a detective named O'Brien, said, "get a load a this. It's Benedict fuckin' Bishop. What's up, man, ISIS take Sundays off? I thought Friday was their holy day of worship. Get yourself a fuckin' prayer mat yet, traitor? I actually bet everyone at Donohue's last night you didn't have the stones to show up this morning. Thanks a lot. You're still a shitbag traitor, and now I have to buy everyone drinks tonight."

"It's nice to know that no matter how fucked up the world gets," Bishop responded, "there'll always be a few things I can count on. Like you, O'Brien, being an idiot and a cheap prick."

"All right, guys," Fitzgerald said. "Dial it down a couple of notches, okay? You're about to have loaded weapons in your hands."

It was a command, not a request. The chief, in his midfifties, with nearly thirty years on the job, was old-school. He had a surprisingly smooth, unlined face for someone who'd led the kind of life he had, but it seemed capable of only one expression—a cross between a scowl and a sneer. He didn't talk a whole lot either, but when he did, people listened. He was a talented street cop and, as it turned out, a talented politician as well.

In the NYPD you can rise to the rank of captain simply by putting your time in and passing all the exams. It's very straightforward. Anything higher, however, only happens through an appointment by the police commissioner. It's personal and political. Fitzgerald had managed to thrive and advance from deputy inspector to inspector, then deputy chief to assistant chief, and finally chief, under three different commissioners. No small achievement, when you consider that the department's politics were so quirky and egocentric they'd have put a sorority house full of prom queens to shame.

The fifth member of the morning's shooting party was John Lee Russell, the range master, a small, wiry man in ninja pants and wraparound Oakleys. Russell was an internationally known combat instructor who looked—white hair, military demeanor, and all—like Senator John McCain's slightly demented younger brother. He was a former U.S. Marine who had trained the elite units that guarded Jordan's King Hussein and Egyptian president Hosni Mubarak. But on this morning, standing before a lifeless collection of targets and sand hills just across the water from City Island, he was about to put a few cops, and one private investigator, through their paces.

"Morning, ladies," Russell said, offering his standard greeting. "I trust you're all ready to go, right? Okay then, let's get to it. In a perfect world, when somebody's coming at you"—Bishop immediately thought, *Shit, in a perfect world nobody'd be coming at me*—"one shot between the nipples should cause the assailant a significant loss of morale. We know it never does. As often as not, after absorbing the impact of the first shot, the enemy will simply disregard any further ballistic insults. So let's work on the Mozambique."

With that, Russell turned around to face the targets, which were fifteen feet away. Without warning, he drew his weapon, shells flew, and the air reverberated with the sound of three quick shots. Bishop could taste the gunpowder. "That's the drill," Russell said with evident satisfaction. "Two to the chest and one to the center of the forehead. That'll drop anybody, even some crazy, drugged-up motherfucker."

The average cop with the standard amount of weapons training and practice should have been able to put two to the body and one to the head in about three seconds. A good shot could do it in two seconds, and an exceptional one in about a second and a half. On any given day, Bishop and the chief could be either good or exceptional.

"Feeling sharp today?" the chief asked Bishop. "Lunch says you're goin' down."

"You're on," Bishop said with a big smile.

As the other cops whooped it up taunting Bishop and making a couple of side bets, the two men prepared for their competition. Fitzgerald was carrying a Gold Cup Commander, a .45-caliber stainless-steel handgun with a seven-inch barrel. It was a beautiful weapon given to him by his men when he was promoted to chief. He carried it in a Fletch high-ride holster, which had a very narrow profile and sat at a slight angle on the hip.

Bishop had his Kimber Ultra Elite CQB, a lightweight .45-caliber aluminum pistol with a black finish, rosewood grip, and a satin slide. He wore it cocked and locked in a custom-made, non-thumb-break, high-ride leather holster designed for speed. He liked to say the Kimber was the Ferrari of handguns, and it seemed to shine even in the flat light of the dreary, sunless morning.

"Ready, ladies?" Russell asked.

Bishop and Fitzgerald looked at each other and then nodded to Russell.

"Okay, then. Make ready your weapons."

Both men felt for their holsters without taking their eyes off the targets. The tension was growing. "Don't think. React," Russell said.

"When you think, you get in trouble. Keep it simple. See the mother-fucker, shoot the motherfucker."

He waited another couple of seconds before shouting the command to fire. In a flash, both shooters sent two rounds to the body and one right between the eyebrows. They were dead even in movement, speed, and accuracy. They did two rounds like this and Russell decided to change the conditions. He added a tactical reload after the first two shots to the body. This meant releasing the magazine so it fell to the ground, insert-ing a new one, and getting off the last shot to the forehead. All, of course, while losing as little time as possible.

After several more rounds, it was still too close to call. "Last round," Russell announced before their seventh attempt at the Mozambique. "Ready?" When he shouted, "Fire," the chief was clearly a hair quicker to the draw. "That's too good," Bishop said, holding his hands up in mock surrender after both men hit their targets. "No way I can beat that."

While the chief talked to the range master, Bishop and the two cops picked up all their spent shells. This took a while since there were hundreds. Bishop was always surprised by how many rounds they fired in a short time. Then they all cleaned their weapons before Bishop and Fitzgerald took off for City Island to grab some lunch. Barely ten minutes from the range, City Island remained a great little hidden piece of New York, a tiny spit of land in Long Island Sound accessible only by a short bridge from the Bronx, with one main avenue that ran the mile-and-a-half length of the island and no street more than a couple of hundred yards from the water. It looked and felt like an old-time New England fishing village, with just over four thousand mostly middle- and working-class residents. It was the kind of place where property often stayed within families, which went a long way toward controlling the character of the place, keeping out both minorities and Manhattan yuppies looking for waterfront property.

Bishop and Fitzgerald, as always, went to Artie's, a local hangout right near the second of the three traffic lights on the island's main drag. Unlike most of the island's other restaurants, which had lots of glass and outdoor deck areas to take advantage of the water views, Artie's, with its brick interior, was as viewless as a vault. The food was the main attraction. Bishop and Fitzgerald took a table in the back along the wall.

After their time at the range, they were talking about guns and ammo. Specifically, they were engaged in the endless debate over the relative merits of a nine-millimeter versus a .45. Which inflicts more damage, the smaller, faster nine-millimeter round or the much larger, slower forty-five-millimeter bullet? It was the shooter's version of a couple of sports fans arguing over who's a better quarterback, Tom Brady or Peyton Manning.

They both ordered the lobster special, and when their drinks came, Fitzgerald changed the subject. "So when're you planning on tellin' me about your new case?" he asked. "You know, the one where you're trying to help get a terrorist off. The one where you're working for someone who wants to kill the same men, women, and children you once took an oath to protect and serve."

Bishop thought for a moment before responding. Though he had obviously known the subject would come up, he didn't expect the chief to come on so strong right out of the gate. It caught him off guard. "Oh, you heard about that, did you?" Bishop said, trying to be cute. The effort was pointless. The chief didn't crack even a hint of a smile, and Bishop suddenly couldn't think of anything clever to say.

"Shit," he mumbled finally, "what was I supposed to do, turn down the biggest fuckin' case I've ever been offered? Business is good, Chief, but it's not that good. I mean, think about the publicity and what this could do for my career. This could—"

"From where I sit, this looks like it could kill your career," the chief said, interrupting him. "But let's assume you're right, and maybe you are. Lawyers get rich and famous representing subhuman cocksuckers all the time. Is that all that matters? The money? The notoriety? You have no allegiances, no belief in right and wrong? You just sell yourself to the highest bidder?"

"Chief, with all due respect, I'm not a cop anymore. I'm a private fuckin' detective. And in case you hadn't noticed, it's usually not the good guys who hire me. This is not a calling, it's a job. And often it's a pretty shitty one. I spend half my time hiding in the bushes trying to get pictures of some selfish shithead cheating on his wife. Or I gotta chase some lonely, pissed-off wife who's tryin' to get even by sucking some other guy's dick. So if I'm not doing this for the money, Chief, what the hell'm I doin' it for? Maybe a little fame, I guess, which never hurts with the ladies. And, shit, I mean the adrenaline rush is great sometimes, but if I didn't need the money, I'd give this up in a fuckin' heartbeat."

"I understand all that, but I thought your reputation, at least within the department, meant something to you. First you leave the job under a cloud, and now this. You know, a lot of people have you in their sights right now."

"Is that coming from you, Chief? Or are you trying to give me a heads-up about what I can expect? 'Cause if it's a warning, I appreciate the thought, but I'm a big boy and I can handle whatever shit comes my way."

"It's nice to be confident, Frank, but when the commissioner gets wind of this he's gonna have a major hard-on for you."

"To tell you the truth, I never thought he was all that fond of me to begin with."

"He thinks you're completely full of shit. All style and no substance."

"I didn't realize he knew me that well," Bishop said with a smile. "Maybe the makin'-it-up-as-you-go-along thing cuts a little too close to home for him."

"Funny. But this is no laughing matter. We've been friends a long time, Frank, and I want you to listen to me. You fuck with the bull, you'll get the horns. Help nail this motherfuckin' terrorist and move on."

"But what if . . ." Bishop hesitated for a moment and then continued. "What if he's not a terrorist? What if he's—"

"See, that's the kind of subversive shit I'm talking about," the chief said, clearly angry now. "Nobody wants to hear that. Why would you even say that? *Jee-sus*, man. What the hell was he doin' in that apartment, then? Pickin' fuckin' wallpaper? Commissioner Brock was almost killed that night and your guy was right in the middle of the action. What more do you need?"

"Look, if this is as clear-cut as you and everybody else seem to think, then there's no problem. I'll do my investigation and the scumbag'll end up gettin' fried."

"Okay," the chief said finally, "let's get outta here."

Bishop paid the check and the two men headed for the parking lot. Walking toward his car, Fitzgerald looked back over his shoulder and asked, "Is Anthony Pennetta on your interview list?"

Bishop, about to open his car door, asked, "The ESU commander?"

"I guess that's a no. Just as well. Zito'd never talk to you anyway. He barely talks to anyone in the department unless he has to."

With that, the chief got into his unmarked police sedan with his detective driver. As the car started to pull out of the lot, he put the window down. "Watch your back on this, Frank," he said. "I'd hate to have to find a new sucker to hustle at the range."

The two men spoke by cell this time and it was a shorter conversation. No pleasantries and no effort to make small talk. It was strictly business.

"Have you made any progress on the project we talked about?" one of the men asked to begin the conversation.

"Indeed, I have," came the response. "I am quite gratified to say that I believe I have come up with the perfect solution. I think you'll be very pleased with the results. It will eliminate our problem and be untraceable."

"Security at the hospital won't be an issue?"

"None whatsoever."

"Timetable?"

"Resolution will be achieved within the next seventy-two hours. No need to give this any more thought. Consider it done."

"I knew my faith in you would be rewarded. Thank you, my friend. I'll talk to you soon."

7

AS BISHOP BEGAN the drive back to Manhattan he had a soft, relaxed smile on his face. It was a look of satisfaction. Just when he thought that maybe he'd gone too far and the chief was really pissed at him, the old guy tossed him a batting-practice fastball right down the center of the plate. ESU commander Anthony Pennetta. "Shit," Bishop said out loud in the car, "how the fuck could I have missed that?" He was relieved that the chief was still in his corner, but he was really annoyed with himself. He knew Pennetta should've been near the top of his interview list. The guy was in the goddamned hallway when the shooting started, and he was in the apartment only seconds after it stopped. And anyone with even a half-assed connection to the upper level of the police department and its factional, Iraqi-style politics knew Pennetta and Brock couldn't stand each other.

Nevertheless, Pennetta wasn't even on Bishop's list, and Bishop knew he'd fucked up. He'd gotten distracted by all the bullshit surrounding the case. Though Bishop seemed, to people who knew him only casually (which was most people), far more interested in getting drunk and getting laid than he was in getting the job done, he was in fact almost manic about his work.

He had no illusions. He was aware that people often thought of him as little more than a party boy, someone to hang out with. Even worse, however, he was sometimes seen as a kind of court jester, someone to provide a little diversionary entertainment and nothing more. For these people, laughing *at* Bishop was reason enough to hang out with him. By his own description, he was "the girl you wanted to fuck, not the one you wanted to take home." This image of him was mostly the result of his younger, significantly wilder days, and he was still struggling to overcome it.

But Bishop had no regrets. In the small, competitive world of celebrity private eyes, image and self-promotion are everything. "You've really got to bang the drum and make some noise to get them in the tent," Bishop told people. "But once they're inside, you've got to give them a good performance or they won't come back." He never forgot that without the wild-man, do-anything, take-your-pants-off-and-get-up-on-the-bar character he'd created early on, no one would've noticed him. It was the thing that separated him from everyone else.

That, and the Bishop charm, which for many people was an acquired taste. There was nothing subtle, sophisticated, or cool about Bishop. By contemporary standards, he was pure caveman—an honors graduate of the Frank Sinatra–Arnold Schwarzenegger finishing school. He was disarming and often shockingly blunt. At a chic Manhattan restaurant one night Bishop was chatting up several attractive, obviously successful women he'd just introduced himself to at the bar while everyone was waiting for a table. There was some mildly suggestive, playful teasing and everyone was all smiles. A little while later, when the women had been seated at a table next to Bishop's, one of them got up to go to the ladies' room.

She stopped and said something innocuous to Bishop about her after-dinner plans. He smiled; picked up the long, thick pepper mill from the table; and said, "How 'bout I get some batteries for this and we have a party?" Rather than smack him or walk away horrified, she smiled, leaned over, and began stroking his ridiculously ample chest.

One of Bishop's plugged-in friends had once told him you know you're totally wired in New York when you can get anything you need and anybody you want to reach with two phone calls, whether it was play-off tickets, restaurant reservations, or a favor from the mayor. It was all about who you knew, not how much you had. While Bishop hadn't quite reached the Zen plateau of two phone calls, he was getting close—it took five calls to find Anthony Pennetta.

Bishop's sources told him that outside of his family and his job, Pennetta's only real passion was flying. Early in his career, he had been in the Aviation Unit, where he got his pilot's license. When he was promoted to lieutenant, he went over to the Emergency Service Unit, but he never lost his love of flying. Pennetta had four kids and was completely devoted to his family, so money was always tight, but he'd worked out a deal for flying time in exchange for giving lessons at a flight school at Republic Airport in Farmingdale, Long Island, about a forty-five-minute drive from Manhattan on a relatively quiet, traffic-free Sunday afternoon like this.

Pennetta was making final preparations for the sky time he'd been looking forward to for days when Bishop unexpectedly rolled up. Though Pennetta had no idea who he was, he figured him for someone on the job with his cocky walk and badass attitude. When Bishop introduced himself, Pennetta just stared at him. He remained silent while the private detective told him he was representing the lone survivor of the terrorist raid.

The ESU commander was an imposing physical presence, a mass of tightly controlled energy. Bishop was rarely intimidated, but with Pennetta looming over him like a stack of boxes about to topple, he felt vaguely threatened. But since Pennetta didn't make a move toward him or turn his back and walk away, Bishop figured he'd better start talking. He had no idea how much time he might have before Pennetta decided to shut him down. He tried to make small talk about flying. The sense of freedom, the beauty, the adrenaline rush. But Pennetta was clearly not in the mood for charm and bullshit.

Fuck it, Bishop thought, *might as well be direct.*

"Look," he said, faltering, "I'm sorry I came out here and bothered you but I need some information. I'm not sure I can get it from anyone else. I'd never do anything to hurt an honest cop. I was on the job. I know cops make mistakes. Even the really good ones. Fuck, it happens. And if a good cop makes a mistake that's exactly what it is, a mistake."

Pennetta's face seemed like it was carved out of granite. It didn't move. Not an eyelash, nothing. He didn't even blink. He just maintained that hard stare.

"I don't need to make blood money by hanging a good cop for some scumbag wannabe terrorist," Bishop continued. "I'm just doin' my job here and trying to get the facts. So maybe you could cut me some slack and I'll owe you one."

Finally Pennetta moved. He shifted his weight from one leg to the other and scratched the top of his head a little with his right hand. "I don't have anything to say about what happened that night. You need somethin', you know how it works. Contact DCPI," he said, referring to the NYPD's deputy commissioner of public information. "And if that don't do it for you, talk to Commissioner Brock. I'm sure he'd be happy to give you every detail about his performance that night," he said without a hint of sarcasm.

"I'm done talking," Pennetta said. "I wish I could say it was nice to meet you. Now, if you get the fuck outta my face, I'll overlook the fact that you invaded my space on my day off. This time. But if you show up again, I promise I won't be so hospitable."

Bishop held his ground. Rather than attempt some kind of smart-ass remark, he was respectful. He told Pennetta he was absolutely right. "I never should've come out here without giving you a heads-up first. I'm really sorry about that. And I respect your feelings about that night. But if there's anything I can do to get you to change your mind, to talk to me, to tell me if anything unusual happened, please tell me," Bishop said as gently as he could.

Pennetta just stared at him. Bishop handed him his card. "Call me if you change your mind," he said.

• • •

Pennetta watched Bishop walk out of the hangar. When he was gone, Pennetta took out his cell phone and started dialing. "Chief Fitzgerald? Yeah, it's me. Bishop just left. No, I completely gave him the cold shoulder. Sure, anytime. Thanks for the heads-up."

Pennetta put the phone away. *At least the little fucker has balls*, he thought, and then he returned to his preflight safety check.

8

LAWRENCE BROCK WAS staring at his face in the bathroom mirror with the intensity of a plastic surgery patient who's just had his bandages taken off. He was so close to the glass his nose was almost touching it. Piece by piece, the commissioner examined his face. Slowly and gently, his right index finger traced the circles under his eyes, which seemed to have gotten noticeably darker since the last time he looked. *Fucking stress*, he thought. It had been an especially tough couple of weeks leading up to the Brooklyn raid, not to mention the fallout surrounding it. Disgustedly, he pinched a fold of skin under his chin. His neck was starting to get a little jowly and his cheeks were too fleshy. No one liked getting older, but Brock was pathological about it. It struck at the heart of how he thought of himself. This was a guy who believed he was invincible, bulletproof, literally and figuratively. "I get shot at, but I don't get hit," he'd often tell the guys in his detail. "I save other cops."

Just thinking about getting older completely changed Brock's mood. He'd gotten up feeling refreshed and vigorous following a night of great sex with Lynn Silvers, his girlfriend—helped, no doubt, by her willingness to keep telling him, as instructed, that he was the toughest, strongest, and most fearless son of a bitch in the city. "It's all you, baby," she'd panted as she pulled him into her mouth. "Eight million people in this city and every fucking one of 'em wishes they could be like you."

But now, the air had gone completely out of his balloon. Every time Brock stepped out of the shower in Silvers' $4 million Upper West Side apartment, he was unnerved by all the mirrored glass. *Jesus, what kind of self-absorbed head case puts floor-to-ceiling mirrors in the bathroom?* As vain as he was, the kaleidoscopic, funhouse-mirror view of his soggy, forty-seven-year-old body was even too much for him.

Brock backed away from the glass and he could see his whole body now. He flexed a little and smiled at his thick, tumescent biceps and his hard, taut forearms. But the rest of his body was starting to look a little like the before photo in a diet ad. The good life was taking its toll. Too many fancy lunches and dinners had left his once rock-hard chest and abs a little too soft and doughy. He vowed, as he often did in this bathroom, to start being more careful about what he ate and more disciplined about working out.

Brock dried himself off, shaved, and brushed his teeth. Then he took a small black leather pouch off the sink and opened the zipper. Carefully he took out a syringe and a tiny bottle of clear liquid. It was human growth hormone, known as HGH, a steroid commonly abused by athletes and weight lifters. He filled the syringe and then injected himself in the fleshy part of his ass. He put the syringe and the empty HGH bottle back into the pouch and finished getting ready.

It was Sunday morning, so he dressed casually in high-ranking-cop chic—black cashmere turtleneck, charcoal-gray pants, and a black Armani leather jacket. He looked at his watch. It was a little before eleven. He'd gotten up much earlier; checked in with his detail of two detectives, who were downstairs sitting in the car in front of the building; and found out nothing was happening. Since his cell phone and BlackBerry were also quiet, he and Lynn had rolled back into bed for one more round of Brock worship. She was a great find. Brock had met her at a black-tie benefit at the Metropolitan Museum of Art. A fiery redhead with nice legs and full lips, she came on to him as soon as she spotted him in the glass pyramid that housed the Temple of Dendur. She walked over and introduced herself, but Brock already knew who she was from the gossip columns.

Lynn Silvers was one of the best-known people in the media business. She had started her own newsy website, *The Silvers Report*, before the explosion of blogs and Web spin-offs by established media, and it was an immediate hit. Turning a profit for the site, which was part news aggregator, part original commentary—often from celebrities of one kind or another—took a little longer, but eventually she was able to sell it to a digital media conglomerate for several hundred million dollars.

Lynn was rich, powerful, and, according to what he'd read in the tabloids, crazy. They regularly portrayed her as mean, impossible to work for, even harder to have a relationship with. Brock found her to be none of these things. In truth, he preferred submissive women—especially in bed—because strong, powerful women scared him. But they also turned him on. And Lynn was as strong a woman as he'd ever met. He had to work hard to maintain the upper hand and often he used fear to exercise control.

Brock was completely taken with her—well, not with Lynn so much as what she could do for him. To be fair, Brock did like her and actually enjoyed spending time with her. She was interesting, funny, and hypercritical of just about everyone, which he loved. Unlike most women (and most men, for that matter), she was totally without pretense. She said exactly what she thought and didn't really give a shit how it sounded. And she was great in bed—she'd do whatever he wanted, no matter how outrageous.

But it was her juice, her influence, that Brock was really interested in. Though he had extraordinary access as police commissioner to powerful people—politicians and businessmen in particular—Lynn was plugged into a whole other world. They had dinner with some of the biggest names in the entertainment business—producers, directors, writers, and television personalities.

And then there was the film. They had begun preliminary work on a treatment for a documentary about Brock's life and career, and she was even more aggressive than he was about "massaging" the facts to intensify the drama and to make Brock a larger, more appealing figure. And since no one knew marketing, promotion, and media better than Lynn Silvers, once they started shopping it to producers, a big payday was almost guaranteed.

The film was one more piece of Brock's increasingly ambitious master plan. Over time, he'd developed a deeply held belief in his own destiny. In his heart he knew he was meant to do great things, and it was all starting to happen for him. He was also convinced that by carefully crafting his image, he could create his own reality. From his very first days as police commissioner, his strategy was to market himself, not just to the public, but to the cops on the force as well. It wasn't enough to be police commissioner; he wanted to be a cop's cop. He wanted the guys on the force to think he was just like them, not some tight-assed, out-of-touch bureaucrat. And in many respects, he was like them. He was a kid from the Bronx whose father was a junkie and a thief killed robbing a cabdriver when Brock was only six. His mother had cleaned houses and suffered from sometimes-debilitating depression. One day when he was ten, he came home from school and found her lying on the kitchen floor, dead. She had closed all the windows and turned on the gas in the oven.

Brock had come to love telling his personal story. And he was really good at it. He knew exactly when to pause, when to look sad, and when to appear triumphant to get the maximum impact. He could even produce tears. Over the years he'd refined his technique, added a few theatrics, and manipulated the facts to make an already moving tale even more dramatic. He never tired of watching people react, especially people like Lynn Silvers, upper-class white people, who, by being with the rough-edged Brock, seemed to get a little thrill from feeling like they were close, somehow, to the dangerous underbelly of the city. (New York's police commissioners had always found themselves condescended to by the city's elite. The prevailing attitude was "We'll invite you to our dinner parties as long as you have the job, but don't get too comfortable; we know you're still the help.")

In truth, Brock's life was an amazing, only-in-America tale of success. The story of a kid born with nothing—no money, no connections, and no real home life—who triumphed through hard work, cunning, and determination. How could people not be moved by the story of a lost, parentless kid, a troubled teen who eventually finds himself, straightens out, and somehow years later ends up running the NYPD, the largest, most sophisticated police force in the world, with nearly forty thousand cops and a yearly budget of more than $6 billion?

Brock's success was made still more remarkable by the fact that he'd only served on the force for thirteen years, and hadn't come anywhere close to the elite upper ranks of the NYPD before Domenico had named him police commissioner. This meant that unlike past commissioners, he didn't have to struggle to understand what the average street cop was thinking, because he'd just been a street cop himself.

He cleverly turned this into a management strategy only several weeks after he'd been sworn in. Brock was at home one night when he got a call at two in the morning that every big-city police commissioner dreads. A white cop on routine patrol had shot and killed a sixteen-year-old black kid on the roof of an apartment building in the projects. From the preliminary details it didn't look good. No weapon was recovered. The kid appeared to be unarmed. After going to the scene and listening to the reports from his command staff, Brock held a press conference barely twelve hours after the shooting. He didn't hesitate, he didn't equivocate, and he made no attempt to gloss over what happened. Looking directly into the TV cameras he said it was, based on the information he had, a bad shooting. Everyone was shocked. It was the last thing they'd expected to hear from him. The accepted wisdom, given his reputation, was that he'd back the cops no matter what. His straight talk defused a potentially explosive racial incident that easily could've rocked the entire city.

His only problem was the cops. There were rumblings that they felt betrayed, that their guy had sold them out. Again, striking just the right note, he did what he thought he would've wanted the police commissioner to do when he was a cop. Rather than try to patch things up by telling his troops he understood the difficulties they faced, he'd show them. The hapless cop who shot the kid had been on a routine vertical patrol. Cops hated doing these. Done at all the public housing projects around the city, vertical patrols required a cop to enter an apartment building and go floor by floor, using the stairs, to look for trouble. The patrol ended with a search of the roof. It was a high-risk, low-reward activity. The buildings had too many dark corners, too much low-level drug activity, and lots of potential for trouble. Many of the cops were actually scared, or at least jittery, when doing these. And while they weren't supposed to, most of them walked these patrols with their gun drawn and cocked at their side.

So Brock told one of his aides he wanted to do a vertical patrol. Unannounced. Find the most dangerous apartment building in the city, Brock said, and that's where we'll do it. Two weeks after the press conference about the Brooklyn shooting, cops around the city heard something over their radios one night that they'd never heard before: *Car one is in the three-oh for a 1075-V. Repeat, car one is in the three-oh for a 1075-V.* Car one was the commissioner's car and the three-oh was the Thirtieth Precinct in Harlem. Within minutes, word had spread to cops all over the city. *"Holy shit, the PC's doing a vertical."*

The commander of the Thirtieth Precinct, who'd been notified with barely enough time to get to the building just as the commissioner was about to hit the stairs, was having what one of Brock's aides called a major sphincter pucker. Somehow he figured if anything happened to the commissioner it'd be his career.

"Jesus, settle down," the aide told him. "Stop acting like a little girl. The PC's kicked more ass, been in more gunfights, and shot more bad guys than everyone else on those stairs combined. Nothin's gonna happen. I'm telling you, the guy's got eyes in the back of his fuckin' head or somethin'. Remember Magic Johnson, the basketball player? He could see shit on the court nobody else saw. Saw stuff behind him, on the sides. Made these unbelievable passes. That's what the PC's like."

Showered and dressed, Brock strode into Lynn's kitchen to grab a cup of coffee. She was sitting at the table looking at the Sunday papers. "Hey, baby," he said, and smiled at her.

"What's up for today?" she asked, cradling her coffee mug with both hands.

"Still seems pretty quiet, so I'm gonna pick up Oz and head over to Fat Jack's Steakhouse for lunch with my guys. You know, have a little celebration."

"He gives me the creeps," she said.

"Who, Oz?"

"Yeah. What the fuck is the deal with him, anyway?"

Brock laughed. "That's part of his appeal. Guy's a rock. More loyal and dependable than anyone I've ever met."

"He still makes my skin crawl. I hate the way he just looks at me with those empty eyes. Is he a cop or what?"

"He works directly for me, okay? That's all you need to know."

"Fine. By the way, don't you think it's a little premature to celebrate? Aren't you worried about jinxing things?"

"Not at all," Brock said, breaking off a piece of muffin from a plate on the table. "None of the guys except Oz even know the White House is supposed to call today. I mean, they've heard the rumors about the Homeland Security job, but I haven't said anything. They think we're celebrating the raid. You know, killing the terrorists."

"The papers say the surviving kid's mother's hired Victoria Cannel, and she's everywhere proclaiming his innocence. Says he's no terrorist and she intends to sue the city for fifty million dollars."

"Well, it's a free country. Even for the mother of a terrorist. Who was that guy you had dinner with on Friday night at Giovanelli's?"

"What? What guy?" she said, appearing startled.

"C'mon, Lynn. Don't fuck with me. The blond guy. You sat at a table by the end of the bar. You had the Dover sole and he had the lobster risotto."

"How do you—?"

Brock cut her off. "Hey, I asked you who he was!"

Lynn still looked startled, but she managed to compose herself. "He's an agent. He represents a writer I'm thinking about signing to write for my site. We were—"

Brock cut her off again. "I gotta go," he said. "I'm already late." He leaned in like he was going to kiss her good-bye and said quietly in her ear, "Whatever that is between you and him, it's over. Understand me? I don't wanna have to fuckin' tell you again. You need to see him, do it in the office. I'll call you later."

9

A. J. PARKED HIS Ducati on Sixty-Seventh Street near the corner of Columbus Avenue. He locked his helmet to the bike and ran his fingers through his hair over and over again as he started walking toward the Equinox health club just up the block. A. J. wore his hair, which was fairly thick, at a medium length, and it would get matted down by his helmet and look terrible. As long as it wasn't really hot and he wasn't sweating, though, A. J. was able to puff his hair up enough, using his hands, so it looked more or less okay.

It was nine forty-five on Monday morning and A. J. was on his way to try to find private investigator Frank Bishop. He'd never met Bishop, but he knew his reputation as a wild man and a world-class bullshit artist. Always doing his homework, A. J. had called a couple of people to see what else he could find out. "You wanna know what kind of PI he is?" asked one cop A. J. knew pretty well. "He couldn't find a fuckin' black guy in Harlem. Wait a second. Let me rephrase that in a more politically correct way. Bishop couldn't find Mickey fuckin' Mouse in Disneyland." A. J. also called one of the city's most successful investigators, a former detective he'd written about, who'd founded a security firm that grossed more than $30 million a year. Bishop had worked for the guy right after he left the police force. "Shit," the investigator said, laughing, "I sent that crazy fuck out on a routine surveillance nine years ago and I'm still waitin' for him to come back."

But A. J. was sure there had to be more to Bishop than what he'd been hearing. Otherwise, why would any of the city's top lawyers hire him, let alone a hypercompetitive, win-at-any-cost pit bull like Victoria Cannel? Victoria had called A. J. on Sunday afternoon to offer him an exclusive on her client, Ayad Jafaari. She promised complete access to the defense team, the kid's family, and possibly Ayad himself if and when he regained consciousness. Victoria was an egomaniac and a relentless self-promoter, but she'd always been straight with A. J. She never lied about the facts of a case or intentionally tried to mislead him. And she never blatantly, piggishly made it about her. She wanted her share of face time, of course— all the premier criminal defense attorneys were prima donnas with egos that would embarrass a rock star—but she never forgot that ultimately it was about the client.

A. J. had written a cover story not long ago about a cop who'd been convicted of brutalizing a suspect. There were four cops accused in the incident. One of them confessed and claimed he acted alone. The victim, however, swore that one cop grabbed him from behind and held him while the other guy beat him. He never saw the second cop's face. A. J.'s copiously reported 7,500-word piece laid out a convincing case that the wrong cop had been convicted of holding the victim during the beating. As a result, prosecutors reopened the case. When the piece initially came out, the wrongly convicted cop's lawyer called A. J.

"I just read your story," the lawyer said. "And you gotta be fuckin' kidding me."

"What?" A. J. blurted instinctively. He was caught completely off guard by the lawyer's reaction.

"After everything I did for you, all the time I gave you, that's the thanks I get? Where the fuck am I in the story? Where's my picture? There's like one quote from me in the whole goddamned thing."

"I'm sorry," A. J. said, his voice dripping in sarcasm. "I don't know what I was thinking. I had the mistaken impression that this was about your client, the guy who might spend the next fifteen years in jail for something he didn't do."

The lawyer just didn't get it. Victoria Cannel, on the other hand, was smart enough to know that if she was honest and helpful, her cases would get better coverage, and over the long haul, she'd get plenty of ink as well.

During their brief conversation, Victoria insisted that Jafaari was not a terrorist. She wasn't sure yet about the four dead guys, she said, but her client was an innocent kid in the wrong place at the wrong time. She suggested A. J. start by talking to Bishop, to get a feel for the case and what they had. Though she wasn't able to reach him, she told A. J. that most mornings Bishop was at the gym. "The one on the West Side," she said, "where all the celebrities go." A. J. didn't mention that he was just beginning to work on a piece about Police Commissioner Brock. No reason to. Both subjects were huge stories, and if the threads became intertwined, so be it. He'd go, as he always did, wherever the story took him.

A. J. spotted Frank Bishop almost as soon as he walked into the fully carpeted and mirrored gym. It was easy. Bishop was the tannest guy in the room, and in this room, that was saying something. The private eye was sitting at the edge of a flat bench, resting between sets. A. J. watched from a distance as he wiped his face, took a deep breath, and lay back down to do some more reps.

Bishop had 275 pounds on the bar, a considerable amount of weight to bench-press even for an accomplished lifter. It was the kind of weight that required complete focus. Bishop wanted to do another eight reps. He was on his third rep when, out of the corner of his eye, he noticed A. J. hovering off to the side. His concentration was totally broken. With a surge of adrenaline, Bishop threw the 275 pounds back onto the rack.

"Sorry," A. J. said as Bishop was getting up. "I guess I should've hung back farther until you were finished."

"Gee," Bishop said through his heavy breathing, "ya think?"

"My name is A. J. Ross, I'm—"

"I should've known," Bishop said, cutting him off. "You're the reporter.

Victoria left me like six messages last night and another bunch this morning. She says you're important. So far I'm not impressed."

"Fair enough," A. J. said, picking up a towel and handing it to Bishop.

"What is it I'm supposed to do for you anyway?" Bishop asked as he started walking toward the locker room. "Whaddaya want?"

"Information. I'm looking at doing a story about this kid Jafaari and the police raid on the apartment. I need material. I need to know what you know. I need to know what really happened."

"What makes you think anything happened other than what's been reported? If you're here to write some story that trashes the cops, I'm not gonna—"

"Whoa, slow down," A. J. said, putting up his hands. They were by Bishop's locker now, and as the private investigator peeled off his sweaty T-shirt, A. J. was astonished at the size of Bishop's chest and arms. "Look, that's not what I do. You obviously know nothing about me."

"I know you're a reporter, which in this case may be enough."

"Not much of an investigator, are you?"

"First you come in here and interrupt my workout, then you tell me you're gonna dump on the cops, and now you're insulting me. I can see why you're a big-deal reporter. Must be your winning personality."

"All right, look," A. J. said, clearly exasperated. "Why don't we start this whole thing over?"

"Okay by me," Bishop said, taking off his shorts. "But unless you want to wash my back, why don't we reconvene in the café after I shower?"

About twenty minutes later, a freshly scrubbed Bishop showed up dressed in his uniform: black Dan Post lizard-skin boots, snug Seven jeans, a skintight black Armani T-shirt, and a black custom-tailored blazer with a black pocket square. He grabbed a chair and sat down heavily at the small table where A. J. was drinking coffee and reading e-mail on his phone.

"How 'bout a cup of coffee?" A. J. asked him.

Bishop looked at his $5,700 Panerai GMT watch to check the time. "Sorry, we gotta go. Maybe we'll grab some coffee in Brooklyn."

"Brooklyn, who's going to Brooklyn?" A. J. asked.

"We are. I'll explain on the way."

Outside the gym, Bishop told A. J. they were going to Bay Ridge. "First, to the neighborhood where the raid went down, and from there to the local hooker bar." A. J. cracked up at this. "What?" Bishop asked. "What's so funny?"

"I think you mean hookah bar. H-o-o-k-a-h," A. J. said with a big grin. "Not 'hooker.'"

"What the fuck?" Bishop snapped. "Okay, egghead, I'll tell you what. Why don't we race to Brooklyn? If you win, you get full access, no bull-shit. If I win, you get to buy me dinner and the opportunity to convince me that I should help you. Where's your bike?"

"What bike?"

"That"—Bishop pointed at A. J.'s chest—"is a vintage Ducati jacket, and those"—he pointed down at A. J.'s feet—"are high-performance Sidi motorcycle boots. You're on a bike. Where is it?"

"And they told me you couldn't find Mickey Mouse in Disneyland. My bike's right over there," A. J. said, motioning across the street to his gleaming S4R S Monster, with its Testastretta V-twin engine. "But as far as the race goes, it's pointless. Victoria already promised me full access."

"If we're gonna work together, I want to get some idea of who I'm gonna be spending my time with. I want to see if you've got any balls. But I guess—"

"What's the address, caveman?" A. J. asked abruptly as he started putting on his helmet.

"6807 Fifth Avenue," Bishop said as he went to his Porsche Boxster S, parked two cars behind A. J. After he'd pulled out into the street and waited at the light at the corner of Sixty-Seventh and Columbus Avenue, A. J. rolled up alongside him, lifted his face shield, and asked, "Who says go?"

Bishop was looking at A. J. and listening to the low, fearsome rumble of the Ducati's engine. At the edge of his peripheral vision he could see the light they were sitting at turn yellow. Just as it was turning red, Bishop yelled, "I do. *Go!*" With that, the private detective slammed on the accelerator, screeched through the red light, and just missed getting walloped by oncoming traffic. A. J. was forced to sit and wait for the light to change.

Working the emergency brake, Bishop made a power turn onto Sixty-Fifth Street, heading east toward Central Park. At the entrance to the park he saw a cop directing traffic. Stopping momentarily, he flashed his ID and gave him fifteen seconds' worth of small talk before mentioning the commanding officer of the Twentieth Precinct (which handled the park) and asking for a small favor. He then banged fists with the cop, shot him a little salute, and, with a big grin, streaked across the park.

About sixty seconds later A. J. came across Sixty-Fifth Street on his bike and the cop waved at him to pull over. "Can I see your license and registration?" the cop said.

"Is there a problem?" A. J. asked, his mind racing, trying to figure out what he did wrong.

"I'll be right back," the cop said. A. J. watched in his side-view mirror as the officer walked away and then started talking into his walkie-talkie, apparently giving A. J.'s information over the radio.

Bishop was rocking down Fifth Avenue, past Tiffany, Saint Patrick's Cathedral, and Saks. The car's satellite radio was blasting the songs of the seventies, but he was laughing so hard thinking about that tight-ass A. J. Ross steaming while the cop checked his paperwork that he was having trouble singing along to "Brick House" by the Commodores. He turned left on Fortieth Street by the New York Public Library and then made a right onto Park Avenue.

Meanwhile, A. J. was still sitting and waiting. Finally, after nearly eight minutes, the cop returned and told A. J. everything seemed to be in order. He handed him his documents back and said, "Have a good day and please ride safely. Oh, and be sure to give my best to Frank Bishop next time you see him."

A. J. shook his head. "Fucking Bishop," he muttered. He was fuming, but he was also just a little impressed. For a guy who looked like he could have been Stallone's stunt double in the original *Rocky*—the one where he had the really thick, beefy body—Bishop was apparently pretty clever. A. J. slammed his face shield closed, fiercely twisted the throttle, and popped the clutch. The Ducati practically exploded forward, and A. J. was an instant blur, screaming across the park nearly fifteen minutes behind Bishop.

Bishop was all the way down in Chinatown, heading across Canal Street toward the Manhattan Bridge. When A. J. finally made his way across town, he decided to take the highway. He knew Bishop wouldn't take FDR Drive because he'd guess it would be too congested with traffic—congested for cars, that is. For A. J., though, it was like a live-action video game as he rolled down the highway, lane-splitting and threading the needle between the cars. He leaned the bike one way, then the other, working the controls with both hands and both feet, his timing exact and his rhythm, even when he slowed down, as perfect as if the whole thing were choreographed to music.

A. J. was quickly making up time and closing the gap with Bishop. By the time Bishop was getting on the bridge, A. J. could see it less than half a mile ahead. Knowing it would be a pain in the ass to access the Manhattan Bridge from the FDR, A. J. opted for the Brooklyn Bridge.

Bishop, doing nearly eighty, was already across the Manhattan Bridge and making a sharp turn onto Tillary Street, but he was driving so fast that even though he was listening to his GPS for directions, he made a wrong turn. Cursing, he punched the steering wheel several times while waiting for the GPS to reconfigure so he could find his way onto the Brooklyn–Queens Expressway.

A. J. was now on the Brooklyn Bridge. He had his face shield open so he could feel the cool air on his skin. He was wearing sunglasses but his eyes were still tearing from the wind. He was totally jazzed; he knew he was catching up.

• • •

When Bishop finally got onto the expressway, it was heavily pockmarked with potholes, making it very hard for the low-riding Boxster to maneuver. He was only a couple of miles from the destination. Ahead of him traffic was moderate to heavy. Bishop knew that if A. J. had any real skills on the bike he'd be closing in on him by now. Sure enough, at that moment, with the Gap Band's "Burn Rubber on Me" blasting from the speakers, Bishop spotted the Monster's single orb of a headlight weaving in and out of the traffic about a quarter of a mile back. He knew he was in trouble.

With A. J. gaining ground quickly, Bishop decided to use his secret weapon. He hesitated a moment, unsure if it was worth the risk. *Fuck it*, he thought. *Losing to this prick is not an option.* He reached under the passenger seat and pulled out the red light used on an unmarked detective's car. He plugged the cord into the cigarette lighter and put the big red cherry on the roof. He flicked the toggle switch, the light started flashing, and the siren sounded.

The light and siren worked like the parting of the Red Sea. Not only did it clear the way for Bishop, but the cars immediately closed in and filled the gap as soon as he passed, effectively blocking A. J. from advancing too quickly. As soon as Bishop got off the highway, he quickly put the light and siren away. The last thing he needed was to get pulled over for impersonating a cop and risk losing his gun license, his NYPD parking permit, his Taser, his pepper spray, and a host of other not-quite-legal gadgets and privileges.

As he made the turn onto Fifth Avenue, he spotted A. J. again, coming up fast. *Son of a bitch. Where the fuck did he come from?* Panicked, Bishop downshifted to first and floored the Boxster. But he let the clutch out too fast and stalled. He could hear the Ducati now, getting louder and louder. He fumbled to restart the car and managed this time to take off without stalling. He screeched up in front of 6807 Fifth Avenue less than ten seconds ahead of A. J. He was stepping out of his car with a huge grin on his face as A. J. rolled up.

A. J. parked the bike, took off his helmet and gloves, shook out his hair, and walked over to Bishop's car. As he approached, Bishop took a couple of steps toward him, stuck out his hand, and said, "Nice race." A. J. just gave him a long, hard stare. "Okay," he said finally, "now I know who I'm dealing with."

"What's that supposed to mean?" Bishop asked, almost sounding hurt. "I did what I needed to do to win."

"That's my point. No rules, no boundaries. The end justifies the means."

"Fuck you. Let's just say the better man won and leave it at that."

Both men were silent for a while, content, apparently, to collect themselves and let their heart rates return to normal after the adrenaline rush of the race. Bishop, of course, spoke first. "Guess you owe me dinner, biker boy."

"Yeah, whatever," a still-annoyed A. J. responded. "Why'd we come out here anyway? We're blocks from the apartment."

"I want to get a sense of the neighborhood, you know, get a feel for the place and the people. I'm sure you do the same thing when you're working on a story."

Fifth Avenue in Bay Ridge, between Sixty-Fifth and Ninety-Second Streets, is one of those colorful, messy, taken-for-granted New York commercial strips that go unnoticed but are a daily testament to the city's diversity. In the immediate vicinity of where Bishop and A. J. had parked, there was McCann's Pub, Jerusalem Hair Stylist, Cleopatra's, and China Pagoda, a restaurant whose sign also featured large Arabic script.

After about an hour and a half of canvassing the area, talking to local shop owners—at least the ones who spoke English and were willing to engage—Bishop decided it was time to hit the hookah bar.

The Magic Carpet, which had a red light over its front door, was at Fifth Avenue and Eighty-First Street, across from a pizza joint and right next to a cab company. Inside, it looked like a small Mediterranean restaurant with Moroccan-style chairs and about a dozen tables. There

was a counter at the back and the three tables closest to it were occupied by dark-haired, heavy-bearded men of various ages drinking tea
and smoking water pipes. Bishop and A. J. took a table near the back.
If Bishop went a couple of days without shaving, he could've fit right
in—dark skin, dark hair, dark eyes, heavy beard, and a generally swarthy
look. A. J., on the other hand, stuck out like a priest at a strip club.

An unsmiling waiter in his midtwenties asked them in a heavy Arabic accent what they wanted. "I'll have a Coors Light," Bishop said with great cheer.
A. J. just stared at him in disbelief. "We do not serve alcohol," the waiter said
curtly. A. J. ordered a pot of the house tea and Bishop, somewhat sheepishly,
asked for the same. When the waiter returned with the tea, Bishop whipped
out a photo of Ayad Jafaari and asked if he knew him. Without answering,
the waiter turned and walked over to a large, heavy man sitting at the corner
table in the back. He whispered in his ear and then disappeared into the
kitchen. All of the men were now staring at A. J. and Bishop.

"You know," A. J. said, leaning across the table, "I'm really starting
to feel like I'm in the presence of a master. Subtle, graceful, amazingly
skilled at making people feel comfortable and coaxing information from
them. No wonder the best lawyers hire you. *Are you nuts?*" A. J. hissed.
"You ask for a beer? Have you done any homework? Do you have any
clue about what you're doing?"

"Sit back and learn," Bishop said as he got up and walked over to sit
down at the big fat guy's table. "I'm not sure if you speak English," Bishop
said, breaking the ice, "but you're obviously the man to talk to around
here. My name is—"

The fat guy, whom Bishop decided looked like Chris Christie's darker,
fatter, sweatier brother, held up his right hand, motioning for Bishop to
stop. He was in the middle of a long, deep draw on his water pipe. Bishop
complied. He smiled to try to conceal his disgust at the man's cheap white
shirt and dark suit, his long dirty fingernails, and the thick stubble on his
greasy-looking face. Finally, he exhaled a huge plume of smoke, most of
which was blown right in Bishop's face.

"I know who you are, Mr. Bishop, and I have no interest in talking to you."

Bishop turned and gave A. J. an everything's-under-control wink. Turning back to the fat guy, Bishop said, "If you know who I am, then you know I'm trying to help someone from your community and you should cooperate."

"Cooperate? I don't think so. I'm a businessman. I have enough headaches without you."

"I'm trying to help one of your—"

The guy cut him off. "Do not treat me like a fool, Mr. Bishop. You used to be a police officer. Why would you help Ayad? This would only make trouble for the police who shot him. Now, if you will excuse me."

"Wait a minute," Bishop said in a suddenly aggressive tone. "Every time I talk to you people I get the same shit."

"What do you mean, 'you people'?"

"All you motherfucking Muslims say the same shit, whether it's on the news, picking me up in a cab, or selling me a fucking shish kebab on some street corner at one in the morning. 'Oh, we love America. Muslims are a gentle, peace-loving people. The terrorists should be punished.' Well, you're just proving yet again that it's all bullshit. You have a chance here to either help one of your own prove his innocence or, if he's guilty, to help lock up a terrorist. Yet you won't even answer a few questions. I'll tell you what. Give me ten minutes and I'll buy the next bong. Whaddaya say, Muhammad?"

"My name is not Muhammad. This conversation is over, Mr. Bishop," the shop owner said, nodding almost imperceptibly to the waiter, who scurried into the back again.

Three big, bulky men came in the front door led by the waiter. Bishop, still sitting at the table with "Muhammad," had his back to them but sensed their presence even before he saw their reflection in a silver platter mounted on the wall. As the biggest of the trio, who looked to be about six feet four, two hundred fifty pounds, moved forward, Bishop got up, pushing the table with his hips directly into "Muhammad" in a single fluid movement. He kicked the chair out behind him with his right leg, startling the big Muslim coming at him, and then grabbed a cup of scalding tea, spun around, and threw it in the guy's face. As his attacker clutched his face in pain, Bishop punched him in the throat with everything he had. One down.

With the biggest dog out of the fight, Bishop was feeling pretty good as the two other guys approached. One veered off toward A. J., his hand already raised. A. J. said something to him in what Bishop figured was Arabic, and the guy turned back toward Bishop. His partner charged Bishop, who delivered a front snap kick directly to the guy's groin, but he kept coming and he grabbed Bishop's midsection, driving him backward. Bishop was able to spin around and use the guy's own momentum to throw him directly into the table where he'd been sitting and right on top of "Muhammad," who hadn't gotten up from the table yet.

Looking around for A. J., who was apparently gone, Bishop saw the remaining thug coming at him with a chair. Expecting Bishop to back up, he was quickly moving forward with the chair held directly over his head. Bishop closed the distance between them and landed a right hook directly on the guy's jaw. He went down almost comically with the heavy Moroccan-style chair falling right on top of him. Bishop's amusement, however, was short-lived.

An angry crowd of twenty-five or thirty people had gathered outside the tea shop to watch the ugly melee. Now some of the crowd was coming inside and Bishop began to backpedal. *Now what?* he thought, running through a mental checklist. In high-stress situations like this, Bishop would get strangely calm. He remembered that when he was a cop, whenever he got in a jam, he'd begin to see things like there was a strobe effect—as the action sped up, he actually saw everything moving slower. He was running through his checklist now: *Any sign of a gun or a knife? Who looks like he's going to make a move first? What's my exit strategy? Do I pull my weapon?*

Bishop knew that once he broke leather and the .45 came out, everything would go to a different level. There were now at least half a dozen of the angry onlookers inside, shouting at him in Arabic. Bishop decided to move first. He held up the index finger of his left hand, leaned forward in a boxer's stance, threw back his jacket, and pulled up his T-shirt to reveal the gun. His right hand was on the grip now and his thumb was already disengaging the safety. From this position, he could draw the weapon and get off several shots in mere seconds. The gambit didn't work. Several of the men began to move toward him.

Without hesitation, Bishop pulled out the .45 and grabbed "Muhammad," who was just now stumbling to his feet, around the throat with his free arm. With the gun pressed against the man's temple, Bishop started moving forward and screaming, "Out, cocksuckers. You hear me? Get the fuck out. *Now!*" He didn't know how many of them spoke English, but apparently they all got the idea. When the last guy was on the street, Bishop locked the front door. He then dragged "Muhammad" into the kitchen area.

Bishop began to hear sirens. He didn't have much time. "Okay, fatso, let's see how tough you are now. It's time for us to have a conversation." With the sirens getting louder, he pulled "Muhammad" over to the stove and pushed his face down close to one of the open flames—so close that some of his hair began to singe. "Start talking," Bishop commanded. "Why the strong-arm? Why try and play it so tough?"

Sweat was literally pouring off the guy now and Bishop thought he might be having a little trouble breathing. Through clenched teeth he said, "It was your people who told me not to talk."

"My people?" Bishop said incredulously. "The fuck you talkin' about, 'my people'?"

"The cops. They threatened me—"

Just then Bishop heard the sound of breaking glass and the front door being smashed in. "Shit," he said out loud, "I guess your friends are back." He also heard the sirens out front now and the sound of screeching brakes. Keeping the gun against the head of his hostage, Bishop moved back into the front room, where nearly thirty people were screaming and yelling and on the verge of starting a riot with Bishop at the center. Then there was a sea of blue pushing through the mob. Bishop shoved "Muhammad" toward the enraged Muslims and quickly holstered his weapon.

Raising his hands high above his head, he started yelling, "I'm retired off the job. I'm retired off the job."

The sergeant came over to Bishop. "Ever think of becoming a diplomat?" he asked him. "What the hell happened here? Never mind, I don't wanna know. Did you call in the ten-thirteen?"

"A ten-thirteen?" Bishop said, repeating the urgent radio code used when an officer needs assistance. "I didn't call any ten-thirteen in. But I'm pretty sure I know who did."

About forty-five minutes later, the crowd had been uneventfully dispersed, police were taking statements, and Bishop was sitting in the back of a patrol car two blocks away, hands cuffed behind his back. He was tired and dirty and his side ached where one of the Muslim goons had rammed his shoulder into him. But more than anything else, Bishop was worried about damage control. He'd have to call Victoria, a call he dreaded, because he knew she'd go nuts on him. And what could he say? How would he explain what happened? *Fuck*, he thought, *this is a disaster.* Bishop was angry with himself for letting it happen—no, for *making* it happen. He had too much at stake now to eagerly get into these kinds of brawls. But he kept pushing anyway. It was like he couldn't stop himself. It was time to grow up. He rubbed his side where it was sore. He wished he had some Motrin.

He also wished he could bitch-slap that arrogant little prick A. J. Ross for bolting on him when things heated up. Not that he was expecting any help, but still . . . On the other hand, he did call in a 10-13 to bring out the cavalry. Whatever. He needed to focus. Maybe he should call Chief Fitzgerald. Why would the cops threaten "Muhammad" and tell him not to talk? Just then, the car door opened and a big man with broad shoulders that spanned a good portion of the front seat got in.

"You really fucked up, Bishop," the man said in a deep voice without looking in the rearview mirror to make eye contact with Bishop. "Big-

shot PI. Always on the cable shows shootin' your mouth off, gettin' mentioned in the papers. This time you went too far, jerk-off. You're sticking
your fuckin' nose in shit that doesn't concern you."

"Are you reading that off your sleeve or did you memorize it?" Bishop
asked.

"That's funny, dickhead. But we'll see who's laughing at the end of
the day."

"Who the hell are you and why are we sitting in the car?" Bishop
asked, thinking maybe the guy looked and sounded familiar. He was
huge, about six feet six, and black.

"Shut up and do as I say or you'll end up at Central Booking, which
is where you belong. Here's how it's gonna work. We're going for a little
ride. There's someone who wants to talk to you," he said, starting the car.

"Hey, Frankenstein. Can I call you Frankenstein even though you're
black? I mean, I'm not violating some politically correct race thing if I do
that, am I? I can't think of any black monsters. Does Blacula count? Sorry,
I meant Count Blacula," Bishop said, laughing at his own lame joke. "I
don't think there were any actual black monsters, were there? Whatever.
Anyway, we're going for a little ride? Are you kidding me with this bull—"

"*Shut the FUCK up!*" the guy screamed, cutting him off. "That's your
last warning. You either shut up and listen or you can kiss your pistol
license and your PI license good-bye. Am I clear?"

Bishop didn't say anything, just sat back and tried to place the guy.
Who in the NYPD would be able to take a precinct sector car off-line and
use it at will, like his personal vehicle? No detective he knew could do
that. And the guy's suit was way too nice for a detective. Maybe he was a
chief? But Bishop was pretty sure he knew all the chiefs. One thing was
clear as they got on the expressway—they were headed to Manhattan.

Traffic was very light and in no time they were in midtown. Bishop
still had no idea what was going on. They pulled over on Fifty-Third
Street and Broadway, to a side entrance of the Sheraton. The guy helped
Bishop out of the car and—*finally!*—took the cuffs off. "Remember," he
said as they headed into the hotel, "behave." Once they were inside the

Sheraton's blue and beige lobby, it was clear that some event was about to start, as hundreds of expensively dressed people were funneling into the main ballroom. Security personnel were everywhere. People in and out of uniform acknowledged the big guy and Bishop. Some of them were talking into their wrist, and Bishop wondered if they were Secret Service or part of the NYPD's Intelligence Division. Almost everyone, guests and security alike, was in black tie.

"Hey, Frankenstein," Bishop said quietly as they got into a side elevator, "if you'd given me a heads-up I would've had my tux ready. I own three, in case you were wondering. One's a Hugo Boss, six-button double-breasted model with peaked lapels. Another is a shawl collar—"

"Shut up," the big guy said, cutting Bishop off, and Bishop could see by the look on his face he was serious.

The elevator stopped on the fifteenth floor, where there was a security guy waiting, and the three of them headed to the corner suite. The double doors swung open and revealed a huge living area done in subtle beige tones, with lots of marble, an oak dining table, a plush leather couch, and a flat-screen TV. Standing by the floor-to-ceiling windows that looked south on Times Square was A. J. Ross. A bored-looking female security agent stood by the dining table.

Bishop looked at A. J. and with a shrug of his shoulders said, "What the fuck? What is this, the NYPD's rendition program?"

"Cute," A. J. said, obviously annoyed. "Guys," he said, looking at his watch and turning to the security agents, "I've been here a long time. I know he's doing me a favor, but I gotta tell you, if he doesn't show in the next five or ten minutes, I'm outta here. My time is valuable as well."

Almost on cue, the female agent, with her head cocked and her index finger pressed to her IFB wireless earpiece, said into her wrist: "Affirmative, both subjects are here awaiting the Eagle, ten-four." Looking at A. J., she said, "He's in the elevator and on the way up."

"Hey," Bishop said, "is anybody gonna tell me what the fuck is going on?"

"No," A. J. responded. "Just shut up."

Before Bishop could fire back, the doors swung open, there was a flurry of activity, and moving like a fighter surrounded by his entourage on his way to the ring, Lawrence Brock made his entrance. Wearing a tuxedo and holding an unlit cigar the size of an electric toothbrush in his left hand, Brock was all smiles. While the people around him all seemed to be talking on their cell phones, the commissioner shook hands with A. J. and Bishop.

"Let's step in the other room so we can have some privacy," he told them. "I apologize that I'm a little pressed for time, but I've got to get downstairs shortly and introduce the mayor. It's a fund-raising dinner."

"Commissioner," one of his aides said, "please remember we need to go over your speech again."

"I know, I know," he said, raising his cigar-laden hand. "Give me five minutes with no interruptions." The aide looked at her watch, smiled curtly, took out her cell, and began dialing.

The commissioner ushered A. J. and Bishop into the other room of the suite and closed the door behind them. Lighting his cigar, Brock said behind a big puff of smoke, "Guys, before I ask how the two of you know each other, I've got a more important question. What the fuck are you doing?"

Both men were dumbfounded. They stared at him not knowing what to say. "Really, boys," Brock began again, as if he were talking to two mischievous children. "What are you doing? The entire city is kissing my ass. They want me canonized, and you morons are out in Brooklyn turning over rocks to try and find some fuckin' Muslim to piss on me and the department. I don't get it. Bishop, if it wasn't for A. J. here calling me, you'd be down at Central Booking right now getting your picture taken. A. J., I thought you keep better company than this. You can kiss your exclusive good-bye if this is who you're gonna run around with."

Brock paused for a moment, checked his watch, and took a long drag on his cigar. Exhaling, he said, "We can all get what we want here. A. J., call my office tomorrow and let's schedule dinner. Bishop, if you stop chasing ambulances and trying to make me look like an asshole, I could probably even throw you a bone."

"Hey, Commish," Bishop said, "I was just wonderin'. Who's the Frankenstein-looking assbag who drove me here?"

Brock smiled. "You're a piece of fuckin' work. That's Chester, he's part of my detail. Think you could take him? I'd like to see that."

Bishop didn't say anything. "All right, guys," Brock said finally, "I gotta get going. I assume we're clear on this. I'd invite you to the dinner downstairs, but you both look like you're in desperate need of a shower. Not to mention a tailor."

With that, Brock walked past Bishop without acknowledging him and enthusiastically shook A. J.'s hand. "Call my office to set up the dinner." Then, from the other room: "And don't forget you owe me now, A. J."

As Brock went out the door, everyone else followed. In an instant, the suite was empty except for A. J. and Bishop. For a moment they just stood there staring at each other.

"Shit," Bishop said suddenly through a half-cracked smile. "My fucking car is still in Brooklyn."

10

LUCY WAS AT her desk at the *New York* offices, which was right outside A. J.'s office. Her cubicle was small but comfortable and had the cluttered look of someone who was not just busy, but busy working on a variety of different projects simultaneously. There were stacks of press releases and invitations on her desk, a growing tower of newspapers on the floor, and dozens of Post-it notes with instructions from A. J. stuck all over the place like random yellow decorations. There were no personal items except for one small photo of Lucy and her father taken at his sixtieth-birthday party.

She was on the phone with a news producer at a local TV station, hoping to track down footage of the Kevin Anderson murder-suicide scene in the Hamptons. As she was wrapping up the call, she saw Frank Bishop approaching her cubicle. She recognized him from his TV appearances. "Hi," she said, "can I help you?"

"Ah, I'm sure you could," he responded lecherously, with a big snow-white, bleached-teeth grin. "But right now I'm looking for A. J. Ross."

Lucy ignored the lame attempt at . . . what, charm? Flattery? Wit? She wasn't sure what it was. She felt like it was just one of those days when every guy she dealt with seemed more immature than the last.

"He's not in the office," she said with just a hint of edge in her voice. "I'm his assistant."

"My name is Frank Bishop. I'm a private investigator," he said completely straight, having noted Lucy's icy reaction to his opening line.

"Yes, A. J. told me about you."

"Okay, given how this is going so far, I can guess what he said. Anyway, I need to talk to him."

"Don't you have his cell—"

"It's Lucy, right?" Bishop asked, cutting her off. "I do," he lied, "but I really need a face-to-face. It's important."

"Well, he won't be back this afternoon. He coaches his daughter's softball team and they have practice today."

"I don't suppose there's any chance I can get you to—"

"What? Tell you where they practice? I'll make you a deal, Mr. Bishop. I have to drop off some papers for him. If you promise you'll tell him you forced me at gunpoint, I'll let you drive me out there."

Twenty minutes later, Bishop and Lucy were on the West Side Highway heading toward the George Washington Bridge. The decision to take the bridge and not the Lincoln Tunnel was made only after a brief argument. Lucy pushed for the tunnel because it was more direct. But it was a beautiful afternoon and Bishop, predictably, wanted to put the top down on his Porsche and enjoy the ride. Once the small talk began, it made Lucy wish they were still arguing about the route.

"So," Bishop asked with a smirk on his face, "what's a nice girl like you doing working for an elitist, liberal douchebag like Ross?"

Normally, Lucy would've gone nuts over a remark like that, but she was certain Bishop was intentionally baiting her, crudely probing to get some idea of who she was. "Does this technique work with all the women you try to fuck? Or fuck with?" Lucy asked, deciding to dive straight in.

"Ooooooh, I love it when you talk dirty. But I don't know what you mean."

"Whatever," Lucy replied, rolling her eyes and shrugging her shoulders.

After a few minutes of quiet, they filled the rest of the forty-five-minute ride into New Jersey with meaningless chatter about politics. They agreed on practically nothing but managed to keep the conversation pleasant. Bishop was amazed that someone so hot could be so smart—and not be jaded. Lucy was optimistic in a way he hadn't seen in a long time.

At Lucy's direction, they pulled off the highway at a very expensive, upscale suburban town and drove to a large, meticulously kept municipal park. In the front area where you drove in, there was a gleaming public pool, basketball courts, a roller-hockey rink, and eight tennis courts. "Keep going past the last tennis court," Lucy told Bishop. "The fields are in the back." There were three baseball diamonds and two softball fields, all of them buzzing with activity. Bishop drove out to the farthest field, where A. J. was standing at home plate and hitting grounders to the infielders. As he and Lucy got out of the car and walked toward the field, they could hear him giving instructions to the girls. He was direct but encouraging, demanding but with a deft touch. It was easy to see he cared about the girls and they hung on his every word.

"Ash," he said to a girl playing third base, "make sure you stay down on the ball and look it all the way into your glove. And remember, on a hard-hit ball like that you've got plenty of time to make the throw."

A. J. saw Lucy and Bishop walking toward the field, but he didn't acknowledge them for more than fifteen minutes. His focus was on the girls. Finally, he told the team to take a couple of laps and then get some water. Only after the girls started running did he walk over and say hello. He looked at his watch and then at Lucy.

"Weren't you supposed to call me?" he asked her. Lucy began to stammer. "And what time were you supposed to meet me?"

"You said six fifteen at your house," Lucy responded haltingly.

"And where are we now and what time is it?"

Bishop tried to interject. Without even looking at him, A. J. held up his hand and said, "Am I cross-eyed? I didn't think so. I'm talking to Lucy, not you."

Bishop laughed it off, but Lucy, who usually had all the self-assurance and poise of someone with twice her experience, suddenly looked like one of the teenage girls on the field trying to please the coach.

"I'm sorry, A. J., it's my fault," she said.

"Okay," he said. "I just wanted to make sure there was no confusion about my instructions. Let's move forward."

A. J. was wearing warm-up pants and a Brooklyn Half Finisher T-shirt from the previous year's race. He looked warm, dusty, and sweaty. He went over to the dugout and picked up a water bottle.

"We need to talk," Bishop said.

"Okay. Lucy, do me a favor and hang here till the girls are done running. When they finish, tell them to get a drink, take a little breather, and then do the over-under drill. They'll understand. I'll be back before they're done. Bishop, let's take a walk."

A. J. and Bishop headed toward the other field. Bishop was amazed by how many girls were out practicing on a Tuesday afternoon. And they all looked like ballplayers. They threw hard, they hit screaming line drives, they dove for grounders, and the pitching was downright frightening. He couldn't believe how fast they threw. He knew girls played, but not like this.

"They're pretty good, aren't they?" A. J. said. "People who've never seen athletic teenage girls play softball are always amazed. You play ball in school?"

"Me?" Bishop said. "No. I was awful. I had to play ball in shoes when I was younger. My father said I was so bad it was a waste of money to buy me sneakers. My brother was the athlete and he got all the equipment. It's one of the reasons I started working out."

"Listen," A. J. said after an awkward pause. "You didn't have to come all the way out here to apologize. A phone call would've been sufficient."

"That's funny," Bishop said without a smile. "This is a nice life you've got here. I never would've taken you for a girls' softball coach."

"Why would you assume anything about me? You're an investigator, but you have no clue who I am. You don't know anything about me."

"You lived in the Bronx until you were five," Bishop countered. "Then you moved to a modest two-family house in Queens, which your parents could only afford to buy by renting half of it. Your father had a nondescript office job with the city and making ends meet was always a struggle. Your intellectual gifts were recognized early and you skipped fourth grade. You also skipped eighth grade. You went to Stuyvesant High School, which meant you commuted by subway for an hour and fifteen minutes each way. You were basically a lazy student, bored probably, who got by on natural ability. You went to City College, lived at home, and mostly skipped classes and hung out with your friends. You dropped out after your sophomore year and worked at odd jobs for a while before talking your way into a bottom-rung job at the *Daily News*. That lasted about four years—"

"Okay, okay, I get the point," A. J. said, cutting him off. Now it was his turn to be surprised. "You know how to use Google and did some homework. I stand corrected."

"Not exactly the preppy, Ivy League, top-tier background people probably assume the buttoned-up, accomplished journalist A. J. Ross would have, right?"

"Are you gonna continue with this?" A. J. said, starting to get a little annoyed. "Besides, people who live in half–Puerto Rican, half-Polish houses shouldn't throw stones."

Bishop laughed. "Good comeback," he said. "Let's call it a draw. Besides, I didn't come out here to talk about you. Or me, believe it or not. I came to talk about the case. I appreciate what you did in Brooklyn, calling in the cops. You didn't have to help me. Especially after the way I treated you. I gave you no intel at all and I'm sure you figured I was just winging it. But my guys did some legwork in the neighborhood—they ran Jafaari's phone bill and his credit cards—so the places I went and the people I talked to weren't random. I had a plan. Not a very good one, I'll admit, but it was a plan. I went out there intending to shake things up a little. I just left the blender on too long."

"Way too long," A. J. said.

"I shouldn't have gotten you in the middle of it. Anyway, I'm here to tell you that even though I'm under orders to work with you, I want to voluntarily cooperate on this."

A. J. was watching the action on the field while he listened. He didn't say anything for a few minutes after Bishop finished. Bishop thought maybe he was still pissed. Then he stood up and stepped off the bleachers. "You see that girl at shortstop?" A. J. asked, stretching his legs. "Watch how she gets ready on every pitch. Her knees are bent, she's on the balls of her feet, and both of her hands are low to the ground and a little out in front of her. She's balanced, focused, and ready to move. When a ball's hit to her, there's no excess motion, no showy maneuvers. On a hard grounder she doesn't have to waste time getting her hands down to where the ball is and then bringing them back up to throw. They're already in position and the only direction they go is up, when she brings the ball into her body after she catches it. She hasn't missed a ball since we've been here. It's all about fundamentals. Doing the little things right. You want to be a real player, that's how you build your game."

"So, is that an 'Okay, Frank, good, I want to cooperate on this too'?" Bishop asked, aware of what A. J. was saying.

"I guess," A. J. responded without much enthusiasm as he started walking back to the other field. "But no more bullshit."

"Okay," Bishop agreed.

"Something's not right about this case. I'm not even talking about the fact that Brock participated in the raid. I mean, the police commissioner has us both brought to the Sheraton, where he's introducing Mayor Domenico at a major fund-raiser, just so he can tell us to back off? What the hell was that?"

"There's more," Bishop said. "When I held that fat guy's head to the fire in the hookah bar—"

"The expression," A. J. interrupted, "is to hold someone's *feet* to the fire."

"I know the expression," Bishop said, "but I literally held his fucking head to the fire. After you bailed on me when the fighting started, I took care of the thugs from next door. Then, in the little time I had before the mob overran the place and the cops showed up, I wanted to persuade that fat fuck that it was in his best interest to talk to me. So we had a brief chat over the kitchen stove."

"And?"

"Well . . . ," Bishop said, watching a vicious line drive rocket over the left-center-field fence. "Shit, did you see that shot? One of your girls hit that?"

"It was my daughter. Remember, focus. So what'd he say?"

"I can't believe a girl hit that. I mean, no offense. Anyway, when I asked him why he'd immediately taken such a hard line, he said it was 'my people' who told him he better not talk."

"Hold on," A. J. said, waving one of his players over and telling her to bring the team off the field. Practice was over. "What the hell's that mean, your people?"

"The cops."

"He said the cops told him to keep his mouth shut?"

"Yup."

"Okay," A. J. said. "That takes this to a whole new level of strange. Did he say anything else?"

"No, that's when all hell broke loose."

A. J. told the girls to get all the gear together and then take a seat in the usual place. They dutifully rounded up three buckets of softballs, the bases, two mesh hitting screens, batting helmets, bats, orange cones, and some other miscellaneous items. Without being told, they picked up the empty water and Gatorade bottles and tossed them, and when they finished, they sat in a little circle on the grass in right field. A. J. went over what they needed to work on, told them what they had done well, and answered a few questions. Then he said he'd see them Friday.

With that, he turned to Bishop and Lucy and said, "Let's go, we're gonna be late for dinner. I'll meet you at the house. Lucy knows the way. Annie," he yelled to his daughter, who'd already rounded up several teammates she was bringing back to the house for dinner. "You ready? Good, let's rock."

None of them noticed the dark blue sedan with New York plates and tinted windows parked on the street just beyond the left-field fence. Someone inside was watching them.

11

"COMMISH, YOU SURE you don't want me to drive? No? Okay. Lemme know if you change your mind."

Lawrence Brock was on the New Jersey Turnpike heading toward Washington, DC. His moment had finally arrived. He was going to the White House to meet with the president, who was set to ask him to become the nation's chief of Homeland Security. "A fucking cabinet post," Brock kept repeating to himself. He still couldn't believe it. There he was, with his GED and his murdered, drug-addict father, about to become a member of the president's cabinet. God bless America. Even though he felt like he'd spent thirty years training for this moment—and it was part of his *plan*—he was still shocked and amazed that it was actually happening. Most of the candidates for these jobs were groomed to go this route from very early on. They went to the right schools, clerked for the right judges, worked at the right law firms and investment banks, and schmoozed the right political people. Brock's resume included none of the classic qualifications. He was like someone from a parallel universe: the tatted-up bad boy the debutante takes home to meet her parents.

Of course, to see the president, he actually had to get to Washington, which, as he sat in turnpike traffic that was barely moving, was starting to look like no small task. A steady, heavy rain had been falling for several hours and the roads were a mess. Brock had already been in the car for nearly three hours and he was still only in some unidentifiably ugly part of South Jersey. Though he was in his personal car, a Lincoln Navigator, rather than his official city car, he had two detectives with him. Sam Cho, Brock's number one and his main bodyguard, was, as usual, in the front passenger seat, while Chester Mickens sat in back. He'd brought them along more for companionship than anything else, and he hadn't yet decided if the city was picking up the tab.

Brock had been the subject of Homeland Security rumors for weeks, at least a month or more before he'd initially heard from the White House. The first contact was an e-mail, which directed him to call someone on the president's staff the next day. This message was very clear that no commitment was being made and he should tell absolutely no one, not even the mayor (who had virtually engineered the whole thing, collecting on the favors he was owed for tirelessly campaigning on behalf of the president in last year's election). The exchanges between the White House and Brock rapidly progressed from an e-mail and a short phone call to a résumé, completion of a tedious sixty-four-page application, ten years' worth of financial data, and excruciating details about every hangnail, hiccup, and untraditional event in his very untraditional life. Given Brock's motley, unlovely background, this was a significant undertaking. The phone calls and paperwork were endless. He had spent nearly two hours on Sunday afternoon sitting in the back room at Fat Jack's Steakhouse, talking on his cell phone to the Attorney General.

Considering how sensitive presidents had become to the embarrassment of having a nominee forced to withdraw as a result of some unexpected revelation, it was hard to believe that Brock could even make it through the background check. But there were two huge factors clearing his path. The White House staff naturally assumed that as New York City's police commissioner, Brock had already been heavily scrutinized and picked apart by the toughest, most rapacious media in the country. More important, the president really liked Brock, specifically because of his up-from-the-streets, take-no-prisoners, regular-guy personality.

Sitting in the car, though, Brock wasn't thinking about any of the messy details or the risk of exposure. He wanted to enjoy the moment. He was completely taken by what he'd achieved and exuberant almost to the point of being silly. He called his wife. Twice. "Hey, know where I'm going?" he asked her playfully each time. "That's right, sweetheart, the fucking White House." The he hung up and made the same call to Lynn.

"Commish," the detective in the backseat said, almost like a child talking to his father, "tell us about that Washington Heights bust you made as an undercover where you scored ten million dollars' worth of coke."

When he finally arrived in the capital, after another five hours on the road, Brock was wiped out and happy just to follow the instructions the White House had given him. One of the absurdities of the appointment process was the obsession with secrecy. It was a strange little game. Names always leaked, official sources issued perfunctory denials, reporters continued the chase, and the White House struggled to thoroughly vet their candidates while trying to keep everything under wraps. He checked into the Marriott and went straight to his room. He had been told to stay there—no going out and taking the risk of being seen—so he made a few phone calls, ordered dinner, and watched TV. It felt good just to stretch out on the bed and relax.

A presidential staffer called around nine p.m. and told Brock to come to the White House the next morning at ten thirty. He was instructed to drive past the main gate, where there'd be a black Ford Taurus he was to follow. After a good night's sleep, he showered, shaved, and dressed. He put on a simple but elegant dark blue suit, a white shirt, a pair of gold Statue of Liberty cuff links (he'd had a dozen pairs specially made for himself and the mayor), and a dark, muted tie. He had breakfast in his room, and at ten o'clock sharp, he went out to get the car.

When he reached the White House, he dutifully followed the Taurus onto the grounds through a side entrance. Someone was waiting at the door and ushered him straight to an elevator so no one would see him. Brock thought all the secrecy was amusing and totally unnecessary. The elevator opened onto the area just outside the Oval Office, where several secretaries sat. Brock had barely taken half a dozen steps out of the elevator when the president appeared, shook his hand, and told him to come on in. The two men had met once before when the president visited New York. Now, as then, Brock was physically demonstrative with the president, grabbing his right hand in a bearish grip and using his left to squeeze the president's shoulder. It was part of his working-class charm. His enthusiastic display of affection was the kind of thing real men—cops, mob guys, athletes, and soldiers—did with one another to show their camaraderie. The president loved it. It made him feel like he belonged, like he was one of the guys. Never mind that he was the most powerful man on the face of the earth. What the president craved was the kind of hairy, anti-intellectual, muscular, physical camaraderie shared by men like Brock.

When they walked into the Oval Office, it was not the size or the look of the room that overwhelmed him but the symbolism. Brock felt like he had penetrated the inner sanctum. After a few minutes of small talk, the president got down to business. He told Brock he was looking for someone to take over the Department of Homeland Security and asked if he was interested. "Yes, sir, I am," he said. "It would be an honor to serve."

There was no discussion of policy, no questions for Brock about where he stood on critical issues. This was not an interview about the finer points of protecting the First Amendment while engaged in crucial domestic surveillance, any more than it was about the nuances of border control and the question of amnesty for illegals already here. The president told Brock he had chosen him because the antiterrorism work he had done in New York gave him an understanding of the threats America faced in a way most people would never appreciate. "You've been on the front lines," the president said, "and I believe that you can effectively communicate those threats to Congress and the American people."

The president then paused and leaned forward. "Larry," he said—Brock loved it when the president called him Larry—"I'm not looking for someone who's going to maintain the status quo. We're facing more serious threats and challenges than ever. I need someone to shake things up, to really give 'em hell. We've gotta step it up and take this thing to the next level."

And that was it. That was the sum total of the conversation about policy. The remaining fifteen minutes or so were spent talking about how the White House worked and the chain of command. Then, right on cue, the president's chief of staff walked in. Immediately, the president said, "I'd like to introduce you to the new Homeland Security designee." Then he asked when they should make the announcement. "Let's do it tomorrow, right after lunch," the chief of staff said, "before it leaks out."

"Tomorrow it is," the president said cheerily. "Larry, get your wife and daughter down here, and I'll see you tomorrow."

Brock walked out of the Oval Office stunned. He was thrilled, but he was also a little nervous. He had just agreed to take on one of the most important jobs in government. He'd be responsible for 22 separate agencies with a total of more than 189,000 employees. And his job was to somehow use that lumbering, discordant bureaucracy to keep America safe. The chief of staff led him to a small West Wing office where he could sit down and make some calls. "There's a list on the desk of the various congressional committee chairmen and their phone numbers," he said. "You need to call and start romancing them. They're a bunch of raving egomaniacs and if you don't make them feel important they'll make your life miserable. To be honest, they'll probably make your life miserable anyway, but it's always nice to begin on a positive note. Start with them and then you can move on to individual House and Senate members who can help you. Do as much of that today as you feel like and I'll get you the details for tomorrow's press conference. Let us know when your wife's gonna get in, and we'll get her picked up at the airport. Congratulations, Larry. Just remember, this is the high point. The nasty, partisan, ego-driven, mean-spirited Washington bullshit hasn't started yet. But, believe me, it will. The confirmation process is grueling. Pace yourself."

• • •

While Brock was at the White House meeting with the president, Andrea Jafaari was at the John F. Kennedy Elementary School in Queens. The fifth-grade classroom on the second floor, with its metal desks, Apple computers, and walls decorated with self-portraits the kids had drawn, had become her refuge. Here, surrounded by the energy and enthusiasm of her students, and the moment-to-moment demands of keeping them focused, she was able to forget—however briefly—that her son, Ayad, was lying in a hospital bed in a coma.

Andrea was a dedicated teacher who really cared about her students. She was strict but widely loved. If someone needed help, she stayed after school for as long as it took. If a student wasn't doing his work, she called the parents. She took a meaningful interest in every one of the kids in her class. The students were mostly too young to understand what she was going through, but their parents and her colleagues were horrified. Unlike the rest of the city, which had branded her the mother of a terrorist, at school she received almost unanimous love and support. They refused to believe that their favorite fifth-grade teacher had raised a Muslim terrorist. When she told them it was all a horrible mistake, they took her at her word.

Andrea had an unusually light day. She had no after-school appointments scheduled and no meetings. She did have some tests to grade, but she'd do that at home. So when the final bell rang at three, her day was over. She taught in Woodside, and the drive to her Astoria neighborhood usually took about twenty minutes. But it had been pouring all day so traffic was slow. She was too exhausted, emotionally and physically, to care. She tapped her fingers on the steering wheel and thought about buying a pack of cigarettes. She'd quit years ago, but all week, ever since her son had been shot, she'd had this intense, unshakable craving. It calmed her just to think about taking a long drag, feeling the smoke go down into her lungs, and then slowly, soothingly exhaling a long funnel of smoke. One of Ayad's doctors had offered her something to calm her nerves, to help her relax, but she wasn't interested. She didn't want to dull her senses. There were so many decisions to make about Ayad's medical care and his defense; she needed to be as sharp as possible. It was all-consuming, the horror, the shock, the confusion. Andrea bounced back and forth uncontrollably between anger and overwhelming sadness. As awful as she felt, however, she tried very hard not to forget about her daughter, Mary, and the impact all of this was having on her. The kids at her high school were not nearly as understanding as Andrea's coworkers.

As Andrea got close to home, she passed a bodega and then a super-market and debated pulling over. The refrigerator was starting to look a little bare. *Tomorrow*, she thought. *I'll deal with it tomorrow.* She circled her block for about ten minutes and finally found a parking spot right by the prewar apartment building where she lived. As she labored up the stairs to the fifth floor, she remembered hassling with the landlord over the rent when she signed her first lease fifteen years ago. It seemed like a lifetime. "I have an infant and a toddler," she argued, "and there's no elevator. How am I going to get a stroller up and down? Take fifty dollars a month off." He refused, but she signed the lease anyway.

While she fumbled for her keys, she could hear Mary's music blasting from inside the apartment. She'd asked her over and over again not to play it so loud. As annoying as this was, there was also something comforting in the fact that no matter how crazy her life had become, some things never changed. She opened the door and stepped into the small entry hall of the two-bedroom apartment. Andrea put her pocketbook and brief-case on a chair in the modestly furnished living room—which was where she slept on a pullout sofa, so the kids could have their own bedrooms.

Mary's book bag and her jacket were, as usual, strewn on the floor where she'd dropped them. Andrea called to Mary to lower the music. Not surprisingly, there was no response. She yelled her name three more times. Nothing. Now she was getting angry. *Just once*, Andrea thought, *can't she be a little considerate?* She stormed down the hall to Mary's room, where she expected to see her on the phone and the computer simultaneously.

Instead, she was stunned when she opened the door to find her daughter duct-taped to her desk chair, a sock stuffed in her mouth. A bald, swarthy man with square shoulders and thick lips was holding a knife to her throat. Andrea stood frozen in the doorway. Mary's usually perfect hair was disheveled, her forehead glistened with sweat, and her pretty green eyes were screaming with fear.

Andrea's stomach was suddenly all twisted up and she was having trouble breathing. She gagged a little and then gasped for air a couple of times like an asthma sufferer in need of an inhaler. The intruder, who Andrea thought had a frighteningly empty look on his face, almost like someone who was medicated, used his free hand to hit the remote and turn off the stereo. "Please don't scream or make any sudden moves," he said in a quiet, uninflected voice. "If you remain calm and do exactly as I say everything will be fine. Now, sit on the bed."

Andrea stood there, still unable to move. She was desperately trying to process what was happening. The stranger, the knife, Mary bound and gagged. "Sit down," he said much more harshly, this time in Arabic.

Though Andrea was American, she knew some Arabic from her ex-husband. Slowly, she sat on the edge of the bed. "What do you want?" she managed to ask, beginning to steady her breathing. She couldn't stop staring at Mary's wide, frightened eyes.

"What I want is very simple. I want time," he said, keeping the knife pressed against Mary's throat. "I need several days to help certain people return to their homeland."

"I don't understand," Andrea said. "What's that got to do with us?"

"To ensure their safe departure, I need to know your son will not interfere. I need to be certain he will remain unconscious for at least another three or four days." As he talked, Andrea looked first into his dark eyes and then she tried desperately to take stock of the situation. Was there something, *anything*, she could do to make him go away? Her mind raced, but nothing made any sense.

"On the bed where you are sitting is a leather pouch," he continued. "In it is a syringe filled with a low dose of fentanyl, a narcotic that will keep him unconscious for several days. It will have no effect whatsoever on his overall condition. Here is what you will do: Go to the hospital for your regular visit. When you pass the reporters and then go through security, just behave as you normally do. Then, when you are alone with Ayad, empty the contents of the syringe into his IV bag. Stay as long as you like and then come directly home. It's quite simple really. It only gets messy if you don't follow my instructions. Do not call anyone and do not go to the police. You will leave your cell phone with me. I have people at the hospital. You'll be watched. And just to make sure you do exactly as you have been told, I'll be here waiting with your beautiful daughter," he said, brushing the back of his pale, spindly fingers against her cheek.

"But what if—"

"There are no what-ifs," he said, cutting her off. "I have given you your instructions. Please do not try my patience."

"I got it," Brock practically screamed into the phone when he called Mayor Domenico.

"Congratulations," Domenico said. "This is what we've worked for. I used some juice on this so my credibility's on the line. Keep your fucking head down and do what you're supposed to. No showboating. I mean it. I wanna make the most of this—for both of us."

"No worries, boss. I know what's at stake. And thanks again for everything."

"Just be careful. Washington's not like New York. We're not in control there. Keep me updated."

Brock spent the rest of the afternoon on the phone unleashing his charm offensive. He shamelessly stroked key legislators and various Washington power brokers, telling them exactly what they wanted to hear. It was a roaring success. Whatever else he was, Brock was a world-class salesman when it came to selling himself. By five o'clock, though, he could no longer listen to the sound of his own bullshit—a rare development. He was spent. He called his two detectives, who'd been hanging around the hotel pretty much all day, and told them to grab a cab to the White House. He had the car and he was ready to leave.

About half an hour later, the three of them were in the Navigator. Brock sat in the backseat working his BlackBerry. In addition to the BlackBerry, which he used for e-mails and texts, he had two other phones. One was principally for personal use, family and close friends, and the other, which Sam handled most of the time, was the "Bat Phone," the number used only by a handful of critical people, like Mayor Domenico, his three deputy police commissioners, and now the White House. These were all "official" city government phones. But Brock had a fourth "unofficial" phone, an untraceable, disposable $50 cell. It was ironic in this age of high-tech surveillance, obsessive security, and relentless intelligence gathering how anonymous someone could be with a prepaid cell phone. A throwaway phone effectively thwarted eavesdropping and electronic tracking.

While Brock sat hunched over his BlackBerry, the two detectives talked quietly about who was going to do the late shift with the commissioner. As soon as Brock lifted his head, they were silent. "Okay, guys," Brock said, looking at his watch, "I've been cooped up inside all day. I need to clear my head. Let's hit Rock Creek Park, I wanna take a walk."

It might've seemed like an odd request, but the detectives were used to the unexpected with Brock. One time he was on his way to give a speech, and he jumped out of his car in downtown Brooklyn to chase a suspect he saw run out of a store. Brock caught up to the guy, tackled him, and held him down until Sam and Chester showed up to put the cuffs on. He then went on to his appearance with torn pants, a fresh scrape on his face, and a dirty suit jacket. It made for a great opening anecdote and the crowd loved it. "Hey, I'm still a cop, right?" he told them. "What was I supposed to do, watch the lowlife run away? Ain't gonna happen." He got a ten-minute standing ovation.

Brock was nothing if not unpredictable. Sam and Chester often picked him up or dropped him off at odd hours in strange places. So when the commissioner said he wanted to take a walk in the park, they didn't question him. They didn't even put up much of a protest when he said he was doing it alone. "Commish," Sam said, going through the motions, "let us walk with you. Please. We'll hang back a ways if you want."

"I got it covered, guys," Brock said. "If I need you, I'll call. Sit tight. I'll be back in about twenty."

As Brock walked into the park, the sun had already gone down. It was dark. Sam and Chester were not happy. "What the fuck?" Chester said. "If somethin' happens to the boss, it's on us."

"Not really," Sam said. "You're just following orders. I'm head of the detail, so I'm the one that's fucked. But hey, we've been down this road before. There's nothing we can do but ride it out."

"So if the boss gets this Homeland Security gig, are we history? Or do we get to be like 007 guys?"

"Right now," Sam said, "all I give a shit about is getting the big guy back in this car, taking him to the hotel, and keeping his ass whole until tomorrow's press conference. And, of course, fillin' out my fuckin' overtime voucher."

"I was just wonderin'," Chester said. "Think we'll get to eat tonight?"

Andrea Jafaari did exactly as she was told. What choice did she have? She had no doubt that the terrifying man in her apartment would kill Mary if she deviated from his instructions. She knew from his weirdly calm, almost disconnected attitude that he was serious. Clearly he'd done this kind of thing before. So how could she risk going to the police? It wasn't an option. Her only hope was that he was telling the truth. When she arrived at Bellevue, she barely noticed the small crowd of reporters clamoring for a comment from her. It was like she was underwater and their voices were muffled and distant. She breezed through the entrance checkpoint where, fortunately, they didn't ask to open her bag. Ayad's room was on the fourth floor. The cops had wanted him isolated, for security reasons, so there were no other patients in his corridor. When she reached his room at the end of a long hall, there were two cops standing like sentries on either side of the door. They nodded to her as she approached. Andrea didn't acknowledge them. She simply went inside and closed the door behind her.

When she was finally at Ayad's bedside, she realized she'd been so preoccupied since she left her apartment that she had no recollection whatsoever of her trip from Astoria to the hospital. She had traveled by some kind of autopilot. Andrea took off her coat, put her bag down on a chair, and moved in close enough to Ayad that her hip was pressed against the bedside. He seemed so peaceful. Even with all the tubes, the mass of monitors, and the bad fluorescent lighting, he looked, to Andrea, almost exactly as he did when he was a little boy and she would go into his bedroom to kiss him good night before she went to sleep. His skin was still so smooth and his features had barely changed.

"What did you do, my beautiful boy?" she said softly as she stroked his forehead. "Whatever it was, please don't leave me. I miss you, baby, please come back." She sat on the bed for a long time. Tears were streaming down her cheeks. She cried quietly. Andrea didn't want the cops to hear her suffering. After a while, she wiped her face with the back of her hand and then she leaned in and kissed Ayad. She kept her face pressed against his and whispered, "We're waiting for you, baby. Everything's gonna be okay. Just please don't leave me. Please, baby, we're waiting for you to come home." She sat up slowly, wiped her face once more, and got off the bed.

She straightened the front of her dress, patted her hair, and took several long, deep breaths. It was only six thirty but the hospital seemed very quiet. Moving deliberately, Andrea opened her pocketbook and took out the syringe. "Forgive me, baby," she said as she inserted the needle into his IV bag and squeezed the plunger. The clear liquid emptied quickly. Then she just stood there, syringe at her side, staring at the heart monitor. When it didn't flatline, which was what she was convinced would happen, she was relieved, for a moment, anyway. At least she hadn't killed her son, she thought. Maybe there was hope.

Andrea began to move more quickly now, with a pronounced sense

of purpose. She wanted to get home and see Mary. She put on her coat, threw her bag over her shoulder, and took one long last look at Ayad before leaving. In the elevator, she put her hands in her pockets and felt a cell phone. It was Mary's. She was always yelling at her about being more careful with it. Andrea's fingers nervously played with the keypad and spun the phone around and around in her pocket. She desperately wanted to call home to make sure Mary was all right. Once outside the hospital, she lost her resolve. She pulled the phone from her pocket and frantically dialed her apartment. When the answering machine clicked on, she quickly hung up. She tried three more times and still no answer. Panicked now, she raced to her car. She opened the door, threw her bag across the seat, and got in. She was trying not to get hysterical. She leaned forward, resting her forehead on the top of the steering wheel, struggling to hold herself together. In a moment, she sat back up. Feeling a little calmer, she went to put the key in the ignition.

"Hello, Mrs. Jafaari." The intruder from the apartment popped up in the backseat. Andrea was so startled she threw her keys in the air and her heart raced so fast it felt like it was going to explode in her throat.

"I . . . I . . . I did everything," she somehow managed to say.

"I know," he said with a blank expression. Then he calmly slid his left arm around her throat. He leaned over the front seat a little, and with his right hand he simultaneously grabbed her hand, pushed a .38 into it, and lifted it up to her head. The gun was pointing at her temple. She began to struggle, but he was simply too strong. Quickly, with her hand under his, he pulled the trigger. The shot inside the car was deafening, but he was wearing earplugs. If anyone in the parking lot had been watching, they would've seen a quick flash of light and heard something that sounded like a balloon popping. But no one was there, and the parking lot's security cameras had been disconnected hours earlier. Leaving the gun in Andrea's hand, the killer got out of the car and disappeared.

Brock walked into the park at a brisk pace, and he was quickly beyond the sight of his detectives. He turned his suit collar up against the chill

of the damp night air and shoved his hands deep in his pockets. As he walked, he was recapping events in his head. In his mind's eye he went through the images quickly. It was like cataloging snapshots. He didn't dwell on any one thing for very long. He reveled in the mythic image he had of himself. He saw himself as a man like Odysseus, a fearless warrior who had spent years overcoming great odds and conquering insurmountable obstacles to reach his destination. For Odysseus, the journey ended where it began, at home. But Brock had no interest in going back. He felt like a man standing on a precipice, the promised land stretched out in front of him. All he had to do was keep moving forward.

Brock was not completely lost in his fantasy, however. As he walked, he remained the ultimate predator. He scanned his surroundings, eyeing the park benches, the bushes, the trees. He saw an approaching jogger, about fifty yards away, and he calculated his pace at eight minutes a mile. *Not bad*, he thought. When he spotted a man with a dog he immediately wondered if he was legit. Maybe he was doing surveillance.

He had been walking for nearly seven minutes when he came to an artery where a road cut through the park to the other side of town. A taxi rolled to a stop just as Brock approached the intersection. He opened the door and got in. "Twice around the park," he said to the driver, who was a Middle Eastern man with dark features and a thick black beard. Almost a full minute passed before another word was spoken. The cabbie looked directly at Brock in his rearview mirror. Their eyes met. The cabbie broke the silence by saying something in Arabic.

"Yes, Abdullah," Brock responded, "it's done. Tomorrow the president will make the official announcement."

Abdullah nodded and Brock thought he saw something he hadn't seen in the twenty years the two men had known each other—the hint of a smile. "Praise be to Allah."

Brock had first met Abdullah al-Rasheed when he was stationed in Saudi Arabia and had been assigned to a military detail that occasionally provided additional security for the Saudi royal family. Brock stayed in

the country for two years after his discharge, taking a job with an American contractor, and that's when the relationship between the two men really developed, though it had been several years since their last meeting. The last time was when he was about to be named New York City's police commissioner. Abdullah moved in and out of Brock's life, appearing at critical moments. Brock's wife was Abdullah's cousin, though he didn't find out until after they were married. There were nights when Brock couldn't sleep and he'd lie awake next to her, wondering if she was a plant, some kind of operative whose assignment was to seduce him and then keep an eye on him.

It was not something he allowed himself to think about very often. Mostly because it raised other, even more troubling questions. If she'd married him by design, if it was her *assignment*, then who was really in control? Brock or his Muslim benefactors? Who was the puppet and who was the puppeteer? Was he pulling the strings and simply using them— over the years, they'd been helpful when he needed money and other kinds of assistance—to achieve his ambitions? Or was he their tool, a potential weapon about to be placed deep inside the president's cabinet? They'd never asked him for anything; they knew he wasn't interested in religion and couldn't have cared less about the subtleties and nuances of Middle East politics. Brock's only agenda was ambition, ego, and personal gratification—there was little else that motivated him.

As Abdullah drove through the beautiful park, Brock was momentarily amused by the idea of his real story, the whole story, somehow getting out. *No one would believe it*, he thought. The version of his life that the public had been given was already unbelievable enough. But when he thought about the planning, the scheming, and the sheer dumb luck that had brought him to where he was now—his complete life story—it was almost enough to make him think there actually was a God.

In his insatiable quest for power he was never bothered by conscience and only rarely by self-doubt. Through cunning and guile and an uninhibited willingness to do whatever was necessary, he had always engineered his own fate, created his own outcomes. Or at least he thought he had. But now, on the eve of his cabinet appointment, his greatest achievement, for one brief moment he considered the ramifications. Had the man in the seat in front of him played him all these years? If that was true, Brock realized, he had no real idea why. Was Abdullah expecting to call in his favors once Brock was in the cabinet? *Doesn't matter*, he thought. *I'll be the one holding all the cards. Fuck him.*

Despite their long association, Brock didn't really know Abdullah very well at all. There had been times when Brock tried to uncover his history, to learn something about his background. But he always came up empty. Every road was a dead end. Even when he'd question his wife about her cousin, she'd feed him some crap about how Muslim women were always kept in the dark, or how while they were cousins in name, it was not like being cousins in America, where you spend the holidays with your extended family. They were never close, she explained, and why would they be? Her cousins numbered in the triple digits, and while she knew many of them by name, that was really all she knew.

Abdullah finally broke the silence. "What are you thinking, my friend?"

"I always knew I'd get here," Brock said. "But it's amazing now that I actually have."

"You have done well. This is only the beginning," Abdullah said, "the beginning of what Allah has planned for us." Abdullah had already begun to circle back to where he picked Brock up. "This is quite possibly our last meeting," Abdullah said. "You will be too visible. Any information we need to deliver will pass through Oz."

As the cab pulled over to the spot where Brock had gotten in, the two men said good-bye. "Take care," Brock said as he moved toward the door.

"You too, my friend."

Brock nodded and got out. He shivered for a moment as a strange chill ran down his body from his head to his feet. Then he started walking back to meet Sam and Chester. When he was about halfway there, he felt his phone vibrating in his pocket. It was the disposable. There was a text from Oz. "PROBLEM PUT TO REST. 3 DWN. C U SOON." Brock stared at the message for a few moments as he walked and then put the phone away.

When he emerged from the park, Sam and Chester looked relieved. "That got the blood flowing," Brock said, rubbing his hands together. "Anybody hungry? I'm fuckin' starving, let's go get some dinner."

12

"IT'S DEPRESSING TO say it, but I'm getting too old for this." Lucy was talking to Bishop at the bar in a club called Roxx. It was just past eleven thirty and they were having a drink while they waited for Supreme, who was supposed to arrive at midnight. Roxx was in Brooklyn, in a former warehouse on Dock Street, literally under the Brooklyn Bridge. The out-of-the-way location was part of the club's exotic aura, amplified by the décor; Supreme was a silent partner in the club and had it designed to look like a forest, filled with rocks and trees and a couple of man-made waterfalls. It was an ideal setting for the live animals Supreme had brought in to create a little additional excitement. There were several tigers, two bears, and a leopard.

The dance floor in the main room could probably hold a couple of thousand people; there were nearly that many out there already, and Supreme and his crew hadn't even arrived yet. There were also several smaller private-party and VIP areas. The back wall of the main room was almost all glass, providing a stunning view of lower Manhattan and the dark underbelly of the bridge. Several well-known young rappers were in the house as well; word had gone out that Supreme was throwing a party for his latest protégé and everyone wanted to be there.

"I wouldn't worry about feeling old," Bishop told Lucy with a smile. "It happens to the best of us. Especially when this kind of shit's going on.

I mean, what the fuck is this? Live animals? The hookers, strippers, and rappers aren't enough? Shit, I'm an Olympic gold medalist in partying with marathon-runner stamina, and this crazy shit makes *me* feel tired."

"Thanks," Lucy said. "But that doesn't make me feel any better. You actually *are* a lot older. I still can't believe this place. You know Supreme prepaid sixty thousand dollars for alcohol for his crew tonight? In cash."

"See, I don't understand black people. No, wait," he said as Lucy rolled her eyes at him. "Hear me out on this. Supreme is obviously a smart guy, but c'mon, you gotta admit this is fucked up. I mean, as soon as black people get some money, they get stupid. Look, I'm half Puerto Rican, so I kinda understand. But you don't see Bill Gates and Warren Buffett throwin' parties like this. Fuckin' tigers and leopards? No way. You ever see that movie *Soul Plane*, where the plane's painted purple and it's got chrome rims and big fish tanks and huge flat-screen TVs? I'm telling you, that's how black people think."

"Thanks for the sophisticated analysis of race and consumer spending in America. Nicely done."

"C'mon," Bishop said, laughing, "you know I'm right. You're just too politically correct to say so."

"Actually, I'm too politically correct to tell you how ridiculous and racist your remarks were. I'm afraid I'd offend all the half Puerto Ricans— not to mention all the other half-wits."

Bishop laughed a little too hard and a little too long at this. Truth was, he had no comeback. Again, Lucy had left him speechless. She was just too quick. Wherever he went, she was already there, blocking any potential opening. But he was not about to give up.

"Bishop," Lucy said, smiling, "if you're gonna sit there with your jaw hanging down like that, don't embarrass yourself. At least have one of these." She handed him one of the shots of vodka she'd ordered for the two of them and threw down her own glass. Bishop did his best not to wince as he downed his shot, but he did. She smiled.

"Hey," he protested, "the first one always goes down hard. But it's the last man standing that wins the prize."

Feeling ballsy again, Bishop decided to take another whack at it. "I know that in this new spirit of cooperation between my team and A. J.'s, we're sharing information and helping each other out, but I'm still wondering why you invited me tonight. I have to believe it goes beyond professional courtesy."

"I like you, Bishop," Lucy said in a tone he couldn't read at all. "But you gotta stop trying so hard. And give it up with the canned banter . . ."

Bishop hesitated for a moment, trying, despite the thumping music, the crowd, the flashing lights, and the vodka, to think about Lucy's remark before responding. "What do you mean 'canned banter'?"

"C'mon, do you really want to talk about this? I don't want to insult you."

"I've always been able to take constructive criticism. But just understand that in the days of the caveman, when Fred Flintstone would see a woman he liked, he'd walk up to her, hit her with his club, and pull her by her hair back to his cave. Then he'd hit her with his other club." He winked when he finished.

"See what I mean?" Lucy said with a straight face. "That's just so lame. Don't you have any cultural references from, oh, I don't know, *now*? It's like you're stuck in some kind of weird time warp. Every TV show or movie you mention is several decades old. Have you just totally tuned out the last twenty years?"

"That's the stuff I like. And as far as the banter thing goes," Bishop said, undeterred, "a guy's got two things, either a black Amex card, which I don't have, or good verbal skills and a sense of humor, which I do have. I like the give-and-take, the mental fencing, you might call it. It's like a love dance."

"So, you consider yourself a romantic?"

Bishop caught the bartender's eye and signaled for another round. "Yes," he said, "I consider myself a twenty-first-century Renaissance man."

"Really. Then explain to me how four of my girlfriends in this town all claim to have dated you within the last year. And I use the term 'dated' loosely. Whenever your name comes up, the story's always the same. After the introductory conversation—let's call it your entertaining little sales pitch—it leads to nowhere except the same old tired MO. You take them to Bell's to try and impress them by having the boldfaced names come by your table to chat. Then, around eleven thirty—by the way, feel free to interrupt at any time if I'm getting any of this wrong—you leave Bell's and take them to Marquis. Yeah, yeah, I know, it's the hottest club in Manhattan at the moment. With the line of people dying to get in stretched around the block, you walking right to the front, finding one of your good friends, Jason or Noah, never neglecting to tell the girl that they're the owners."

Bishop interrupted to hand her the next drink. "Well, they are the owners."

She waved off the drink but motioned for him to feel free. He did this shot without a wince and, putting the glass down on the bar, said, "Continue."

"Anyway, after you get into Marquis, you sit at a table with a celebrity. Brianna was quite impressed and told everyone at the dinner party how she got to sit at the same private banquette as Chelsea Clinton. By the way, how do you know Chelsea Clinton?"

"If I answered that, it'd just look like a lame attempt to impress you. Continue."

"Fine," Lucy replied with a genuine smile. "Now, that puts you at Marquis around two a.m. As if setting your watch by it, you then head to your 'unofficial office,' V, where you finish the night on a high note by getting them lap dances and massages from all the highly evolved, postfeminist Ivy League grads who work there. Then, more often than not, you attempt a little heavy petting in your convertible, like Fonzie at make-out point."

"Hey," Bishop interrupted, "that's one of my favorite seventies cultural references."

"I'm sure," Lucy said. "Finally, you drop them off between six and seven a.m. So, how'd I do?"

"Well, if you wanna reduce my finely honed, carefully choreographed seduction dance to a simple schedule of events, you did very nicely. But that ignores the charm, the humor, the romance."

"I'm sure there's plenty of all that," Lucy said, laughing a little. "But here's my question. Why don't you take them home?"

"I'm saving that for you," Bishop responded. "Only a really special girl gets to go back to the cave with yours truly. That's a pretty good job profiling me. Four girlfriends, you say? That's not that bad."

"Actually it is," she said, "considering I only have five girlfriends in this town and the only one you haven't dated is the one who's not a model."

"Let's be fair. I obviously want to take you out. You're not a model."

"That's right, but I was. That's how I paid for school."

"Well, I still think it shows I've gotten past my really bad-boy stage. That I've matured. My turn-ons are not what you'd probably think—at least not anymore. It's not about big tits or a great face or money or celebrity or any of that stuff. I mean, it is sometimes, but mostly now it's about content for me. It's about what kind of game you bring. The other shit gets boring real fast."

With that, she did her shot.

"What about you?" Bishop asked.

"What about me?"

"Let me profile you, Clarice, darling."

Whether it was the music, the alcohol, or maybe the fact that she was actually curious about Bishop, she begrudgingly decided to indulge him. "Okay, Dr. Lecter, ask away!"

"Are your parents still married?"

"Yes," she replied. "Very happily devoted to each other for thirty-nine years."

"Well, that explains a lot. Especially the confidence you have in who you are."

"Uh-oh, you're not trying to analyze me with a bunch of psychobabble bullshit, are you?"

"No, no," Bishop said quickly, hoping he hadn't screwed up again. "I just think it's interesting that people whose parents stay together seem to have a certain comfort level that . . . Uh, okay, never mind. So where'd you grow up?"

"My formative years were in Orange County, California. The infamous OC. I was pretty athletic and competed in all the OC glamour sports: tennis, swimming, softball, volleyball. Oh, and I surfed a little, though not well."

"What about boys?"

"I had to beat them off with a stick. Is that what you want to hear? Look, I had my share of fun, but I kept everything in perspective. My parents taught me what was important. I wasn't turning my life upside down for some pimply-faced, horny primate. School and sports were the dominant things in my life through most of college."

"Maybe sometime I'll get you to give me some of the details of the fun you've had with boys."

"C'mon, Bishop, even you can do better than that." Lucy suddenly seemed a little distracted. She looked at her watch. "Listen, I'd love to continue this fascinating dialogue, and especially to talk more about me, but it's time to go to work. It's almost midnight and Supreme wanted me to meet him out front. And remember, I fly solo when Supreme gets here. You can be my wingman and watch me from the bar or wherever."

Bishop tried to protest, but she cut him off. "Listen, this is my call, my lead, A. J.'s story. I'm sure you want to give me all that macho bullshit about how you've got my back. Save it. That's a given. Otherwise I never would've asked you to come with me. You can pout while I party with Supreme. But don't feel too bad. If this goes well, maybe I'll consider letting you take me where I've never been before."

Bishop suddenly had the bright, expectant look of a kid on Christmas Eve. "You'll come back to my place?"

"Are you nuts? Of course not. You think I wanna get hit with your club, Mr. Flintstone? I'm talking about V. But it'd have to be our secret."

• • •

The scene out on the street in front of Roxx was a kind of controlled chaos. The lines of people hoping to get in now flanked both sides of the main doors. The people were six deep behind the barricades and the lines stretched well beyond where Lucy could see. Limos and SUVs were double and triple parked, a small but active swarm of paparazzi and reporters bumped and elbowed one another in a penned-off area near the entrance, and security seemed to be hovering everywhere.

Lucy and Bishop didn't have to wait outside for long. At a couple of minutes past midnight, two black tour buses rolled up carrying Supreme and about a hundred members of his crew. Showing up together this way made a big, splashy statement, emphasized how tight they were, and enabled them to party together on the way to the party. Most of the guys getting off the buses were wearing black T-shirts promoting Supreme's company, Black Ice Records. Black Ice medallions emblazoned with the company slogan—THE ICE AGE IS HERE—were everywhere as well.

As a model, Lucy had been to her share of high-profile events in LA, New York, Paris, and Milan. She'd walked the red carpet at movie premieres, charity events, and, of course, major fashion happenings. She'd even gone to the Grammys one year on the arm of the president of a major recording company. But she'd never seen a spectacle like Supreme's entrance.

When Supreme saw Lucy, his eyes lit up. "Girl, you are a fine sight," he said, kissing her on each cheek. "We gonna party tonight. I got a secluded spot inside. You'll come sit with me. Who's the beef?" he asked, looking at Bishop and then back at Lucy. "You think you need protection?"

"Actually, he's just a—"

"Frank Bishop," he said, cutting her off. "I was just keeping her company until you got here. I'll entertain myself while you guys talk." With that, he left them and headed back into the club.

Once inside, Bishop made his way to a spot at the bar where he had a clear view of Supreme's private banquette in the VIP section. Lucy smiled at him as she turned and headed for Supreme's table.

• • •

"C'mon now, girls, make a little room here, know what I'm sayin'? Back it up and let this fine lady come sit down with me." Supreme had come into the club with three bodyguards and five sparingly dressed young women—three black and two white—who looked like they'd just stepped out of one of his rap videos. He patted the banquette next to him and motioned to Lucy to come sit down. "What can I get you?" he asked her when she finally made her way past the other women in the booth. They were clearly pissed.

"Uh, K One, straight up, chilled," she said. "This place is amazing."

"That's for real," Supreme said. "It's been open for just about a year now and it's killin'. Practically every night we open it's like this. Already covered all the up-front costs. Construction, supplies. I own the building, so everything from here out's pretty much just icing."

"Wow," Lucy said, surprised.

"But no business tonight, okay, pretty girl? No trippin' on Big K gettin' capped, crooked cops, or any of that unpleasant shit. Let's just chill and enjoy the night. Things are gonna get pretty crazy, so just sit back and let it flow."

Bishop was watching Lucy and Supreme closely but discreetly, and given his surveillance training, it was unlikely anyone would've noticed what he was doing. He saw immediately that Supreme was taken with Lucy. No serious detective work needed there. Supreme dismissively shoved the *mamacitas* he'd come in with out of the way for her and then took control of the entire VIP section, coordinating who sat where and what kind of alcohol he wanted. Once that was done, all of his attention was focused on Lucy.

Bishop assessed Supreme's security. There were two NFL-lineman-sized bodyguards flanking his table as well as two more positioned in the front of the VIP section. Bishop also spotted a fifth man by the entrance to the club. They were all big, well dressed, and, as best he could tell, armed—though probably unlicensed. He pegged them for amateurs, all show and no go. It's one thing to carry a gun; knowing how to use it is a whole other ball game.

Bishop continued to scan the club, scoping out the exits and noting the easiest, quickest way to bolt, just in case something bad went down. He wasn't expecting trouble. But he'd learned the hard way over the years that having an escape route was always a good idea. Bishop was also running through a checklist in his head. He had his investigators tapping every source they had in the police department, especially in ESU, to try to get some useful information on the raid. So far it had been slow going, but he was still hopeful something would break.

He was also wondering why he was so attracted to Lucy. The strippers were a lot easier to play mental chess with—actually, most of them only played checkers. And not very well either. Lucy was certainly beautiful, but in a much more classic, understated way than the exaggerated Barbie look Bishop usually went for. But what Bishop found particularly appealing about Lucy was her personality. She was quick, funny, smart, and didn't give a moment's thought to impressing him. Coming with her to Roxx was not part of his deal with A. J., but he couldn't resist when she'd asked him. Truth be told, he was flattered.

The bar was busy, but not as busy as it should've been given how crowded the club was. When Bishop was a cop, the bars he went to were usually three people deep and it was all you could do to get a cocktail. Nowadays it was a lot easier to get a drink at these clubs, given the number of people on designer drugs, most often Ecstasy. And designer water was often the preferred beverage of the evening.

"Goddamn it," Bishop muttered as his cell phone started to vibrate. He knew who it was before he even looked. It was Victoria calling for maybe the fifteenth time in the last two hours. The club was too loud to hear or be heard in, and he didn't feel like talking to her now anyway. She'd have to wait. He'd give her a full rundown tomorrow. He shut off his phone, put it in his pocket, and turned his attention back to Lucy.

At the end of the bar, a man was watching not just Bishop, but Lucy and Supreme as well. It was Oz, disguised to blend in. He was wearing sunglasses and a blazer over a prewashed tie-dyed T-shirt with a pair of jeans. With a full head of black hair, he looked like an older rocker cruising for a piece of ass. He appeared to be drinking a martini while intensely observing the exchange between Lucy and Supreme. The wig, the sunglasses, and the whole getup worked perfectly. Bishop had glanced in his direction several times already, and each time he'd looked right through Oz as if he weren't there.

Oz may have been Brock's closest aide and confidant, but he was a mystery within the police department. Everyone at police headquarters knew the commissioner had this strange, virtually anonymous guy who worked for him, who never said anything and had complete access to Brock all the time. He even rode the commissioner's private elevator. But he had no rank and no official title. It was unclear even to Brock's deputy commissioners if he was on the payroll. And no one was about to ask. People who ran into Oz at One Police Plaza didn't even want to make sustained eye contact with him. His eyes were black as coal and the rumor was—there's no better incubator for rumors than police headquarters—if you stared too long you'd fall under his control. As absurd as this notion seemed, no one in the building appeared willing to put it to the test.

Oz, whose full name was Kareem Ozmehet Said, was born and raised in Brixton, a poor, mostly black and Muslim suburb of London. His plan was to go to college and study engineering, but when he was sixteen, he began hanging around a group called al-Muhajiroun, an extremist organization dedicated to creating a worldwide Islamic society governed by sharia, Muslim law. The group was eventually outlawed in England. Instead of college, al-Muhajiroun sent Oz to Pakistan to study Islam in a madrasa and train in a terrorist camp in the mountains. The teen who once wanted to be an engineer became a jihadist, a highly trained guerrilla fighter. He learned hand-to-hand combat and tracking and reconnaissance techniques, and he was schooled in the use of a variety of weapons, including handguns, knives, AK-47s, RPGs, small explosives, and sniper rifles. He was introduced to Brock in Saudi Arabia by Abdullah al-Rasheed, and they became close very quickly.

Only hours earlier, Oz had pulled off what he believed was a perfect crime, tying up three loose ends with one knot—Ayad, Andrea, and Mary. Now it was time to take care of his last piece of business. Oz had done his homework. He was familiar with Supreme's club antics and he had come prepared. He'd slipped the doorman a $100 bill to get into Roxx, he'd dressed the part, and he had a pretty good idea about when he wanted to take care of business.

Oz had come to Roxx not long after shooting Andrea Jafaari, taking just enough time to go home, change clothes, and put on his wig. He could have hired someone else for this job, but that always had the potential to get messy, no matter how meticulous the preparation, and then he'd have another loose end to eliminate. Too bad, because in this case it would've been particularly easy, and cheap, to hire someone. There was no shortage of jealous guys from the neighborhood who would've been willing to smoke Supreme just for the fun of it. And the cops would've happily classified it as another rap music feud. In the end, however, Oz had decided, as he always did, to handle the matter himself.

Bishop couldn't believe what he was watching. About half an hour after Supreme had settled in with Lucy in the VIP area, the rapper everyone had been waiting to see, TnT—"Tuff 'n' Tuffer," he growled—took the stage. After one song, Supreme decided to crank things up. "Watch this," he said to Lucy as he got up and motioned to two of his assistants. They brought over two Hermes bags, stuffed with thousands of dollars in fives, tens, and twenties. "Okay, yo," Supreme said to his guys, "it's time to make it rain." Smiling now, Supreme and the two men all reached into the bags, grabbed handfuls of cash, and began throwing them out over the crowd on the dance floor. They repeated this several times and it quickly looked like it was raining money.

"What're you doing?" Lucy asked, stunned.

"Just makin' the people happy, girl, just givin' 'em what they want. You think all these people rolled up tonight just to hear TnT? And all those people outside huggin' the block, waitin' for hours and hopin' to get in? Shit, they came 'cause they knew this would get crazy. They knew I'd make it rain, and who knows what other shit might go down?"

"But how much money can anybody actually get?" she asked.

"Girl, you missin' the point. It's not about the money. It's about the show, it's about the craziness. It's about bein' part of some shit nobody else is part of. That's why they come."

"And why do you do it?" Lucy shouted into Supreme's ear so she'd be heard over TnT, who'd started performing again.

"That's easy. 'Cause it brings 'em out. Wherever I go now, they expect all this. It creates major attention for my artists. Believe me, pretty girl, I more than get my money's worth. It's cheap but effective promotion."

"Are you finished, or do you do it again?"

"It's definitely gonna rain again."

"Can I help?" Lucy asked, excited now.

Supreme laughed. Lucy liked when he laughed; he had a nice smile and it made him look like an innocent young boy. "Pretty girl, get ready to rock the house. But when we done here, tell A. J. the clock is ticking. I need to see him."

"Absolutely. First thing tomorrow."

With that, Supreme motioned to his people again to bring back the money.

Oz had just come out of the men's room wearing latex gloves, and he began to work his way across the dance floor. Even though he was aware that he couldn't be identified by his prints—they'd been altered years ago, along with several of his features—he felt he could never be too careful. The dance floor was packed with nearly two thousand hot, sweaty people jumping up and down and screaming. Oz just kept moving forward, pushing and shoving whenever he needed to. As he got closer to the VIP area, he reached into his waistband and pulled out the Glock. He held it low at his side, along his thigh. Getting spotted was a nonissue. In this crowd, he felt like he could've been carrying a rocket-propelled-grenade launcher on his shoulder and no one would've given him a look. And Supreme, dressed in all white, was the perfect target.

His bling didn't just make him more visible; the "piece" around his neck was like a big bull's-eye. A piece in the hip-hop world was that singular emblem that represented who you were. It was the symbol of your success and your empire. Jay Z had a "Roc" piece, after his company Roc-A-Fella; 50 Cent had a "G-Unit" piece. Supreme's piece, a sparkling medallion of white gold and colored diamonds that said, "Black Ice," was so blindingly bright it looked like it had its own light source. He'd had it custom-made for $500,000. Pieces were also phallic; they were a visible representation, in precious stones and metal, of the wearer's manhood. They were usually worn on a thick chain and hung in the center of the body. The greatest affront in the rap world was to steal somebody's piece. But to take it, you had to be man enough—or crazy enough—to rip it off someone's neck. Oz couldn't have cared less about hip-hop rituals, but he thought he'd give Supreme's piece to Brock.

Supreme turned to Lucy and asked, "Ready?"

"You bet."

"Then let's do it. But not till I give you the signal." At this point, all he had to do was stand up and the crowd surged toward him. Just for fun, he did this twice without making it rain. Finally, he dug into the Hermes bag and pulled out a huge wad of bills. As he raised his arms to let the money go, Oz lifted the hand holding the Glock nine-millimeter, loosening his grip slowly as he squeezed the trigger.

Supreme let the money fly and it floated down on the crowd like a torrent of leaves on a windy fall day. Just as the hammer hit the primer of the nine-millimeter round, Oz was bumped from behind in the wild orgy of hands and elbows and limbs. The bullet hit Supreme's body-guard in the mouth showering blood, shattered teeth, and tissue all over Supreme's immaculate white suit. At first, no one seemed to notice what had happened. Or maybe they didn't care. But the next three shots got everyone's attention. Now there was a different kind of hysteria.

At first Bishop wasn't sure what he'd seen. He barely realized that shots had been fired—they sounded like muffled firecrackers in the din of the blaring music and the screams over the money. But as soon as he saw the blood splatter, he knew. To his credit, Bishop thought, Supreme reacted quickly, grabbing Lucy by the wrist and pulling her along with him as he ran.

After the fourth round Oz knew he had to go. All four shots had missed their mark. He dropped the gun and pulled off his wig and glasses while walking calmly in the opposite direction of the crowd. He was sure no one would remember his profile. He was headed to a rear door.

Bishop spotted Lucy and was fighting through the crowd, which was rushing en masse toward the exits, to try to reach her. Supreme held on to the back of his bodyguard's jacket and followed him through the turbulent sea of people, all the while maintaining his hold on Lucy's wrist. The bodyguard had little trouble using his bulk to clear a path. It almost looked like some weird football play, with Lucy following her blockers.

Once they were out on the street, the bodyguard opened the door of the Rolls, and Supreme and Lucy spilled into the back. Lucy was panting and trying to catch her breath. "Get the fuck out of here! *Now.* Go, go, go," Supreme screamed at his driver as Lucy struggled to catch her breath. Without hesitation, the driver floored the gas pedal and clipped a cop as the car peeled away from the front of the club. The officer was sent reeling to the ground. The driver didn't stop.

At the corner, Supreme yelled, "Run the light, run the light!" In the middle of the intersection, the Rolls smashed into the side of a patrol car. Still determined to get away, Supreme was shouting "Back out, motherfucker, back out and go! Get us the hell out of here!" But before the driver could get the car in reverse, four cops with their guns drawn had surrounded the vehicle.

"Get the fuck out of the car!" the cop in charge bellowed several times. Finally, but very slowly, the doors opened and the driver, the bodyguard, Supreme, and Lucy sheepishly got out of the Rolls. Moving deliberately, the cops got all four up against the car, patted them down, and then put the cuffs on.

Bishop made it to the street just in time to see Lucy being put into a squad car, which pulled away with its lights and siren blaring.

"Shit," he said, looking around at the mess. "A. J.'s gonna be pissed."

13

SIX HOURS AFTER all hell had broken loose at Roxx, Bishop was sitting at a table in an otherwise empty Bell's chugging coffee. He had a splitting headache centered right between his temples and he was so physically tired that the mug actually felt heavy when he picked it up. But more than anything else, he was pissed—punch-a-hole-in-the-wall, scream-at-the-help, kick-the-dog pissed. Bishop knew he'd been useless. When the shooting started, he was little more than a spectator. He didn't even get a decent look at the gunman. And his impotence, metaphorically speaking, was not likely to improve his standing with Lucy. The only way the night could've been worse was if Lucy had gotten shot or if he'd gotten arrested.

"So I go to the fuckin' precinct, figuring, you know, maybe I can at least get some information. Maybe they'd even let me talk to Lucy," a frustrated Bishop was telling Bell, who sat across the table from him. "I thought they'd extend me some professional courtesy. So what happens? I walk into the Seven-Seven and introduce myself to the desk sergeant. I ask him if he could help me out, you know, do me a favor since I used to be on the job. He looks at my ID and the first thing he does is lean back in his chair and start stroking his chin like he's the CEO of some big corporation and he's trying to figure out how to deal with the fuckin'

135

shareholders. It was unbelievable. I wanted to tell him, 'Hey, shithead, it's been a long night and you better start smiling, 'cause I'm one wrong look away from losing it. Just gimme what I need so I can get outta here. It's not that big a thing.' But I figured I better keep my mouth shut. So he's pondering the situation like he's got some critical decision to make. I mean he's totally caught up in this little power game. That's what I love about cops. That petty bullshit. Their world can be so small sometimes."

Bishop paused for a moment to refill his coffee cup and pour himself a glass of water. He loved being at Bell's when it was closed and no one was there. It made him feel like the ultimate insider. "By the way," he continued, "I ever tell you about the fuckin' cops who work the midnight tour? Shit, what a bunch of freaks. The cops of the night, my first partner used to call them. They're like a totally separate breed from the rest of the force. Really weird. Believe me, it's no accident that every time some black guy gets beaten, sodomized, or shot forty times, or some other crazy shit takes place, it happens on the midnight tour. You know most cops look pretty sharp now. But these guys on the midnight tour got food stains on their shirts, their shoes are scuffed, even their holsters look worn. I mean, who they dressing up for, right?"

"Get to the point, Frankie," Bell interrupted, in a tobacco-soaked voice as scratchy and abrasive as a nail file. "I'm tired, I worked all night, and I gotta go home and get some sleep."

"Sorry, Bell," Bishop said, reaching out and affectionately touching her arm. "So the desk sergeant is leaning back and saying to himself, 'Bishop, Bishop, why does that name ring a bell?' Then, all of a sudden it clicks. 'Bishop,' he says, 'you're that scumbag working for the terrorist, right?' Then he yells to a couple of the other cops, 'Hey, look who we got here askin' for favors. It's Frank fuckin' Bishop, the Page Six PI.' I was lucky at that point to even find out what Lucy was charged with: section 265.001 of the penal code, criminal possession of a firearm, 'cause she was in the car with all the guns."

Bishop had left the precinct before things got really ugly, called his guys, and told them to meet him at the "Fat Lady's." Whenever the shit

hit the fan and his team needed to go to the mattresses, they always went to Bell's.

Victoria had called A. J. around three thirty a.m., practically psychotic. Ayad Jafaari had gone into cardiac arrest around midnight and died shortly thereafter. Then she couldn't get ahold of Bishop for several hours. When she finally heard from him, he told her Lucy and Supreme had been arrested. A. J. did the best he could, particularly considering it was the middle of the night, to settle her down so he could get some information.

Driving into the city in his BMW Z4, A. J. was feverishly working the cell phone, trying to reach his contacts at police headquarters and talking to his editor about getting Lucy out of jail. Since the magazine's lawyers only handled contracts and libel issues, A. J. suggested they hire either Victoria or one of the city's other top criminal defense attorneys.

His next call was to Jerry Polone at the *Post*, to try to get a little more information about what happened to Ayad Jafaari, and that's when he found out about the mother and sister. "The cops are calling it a double murder–suicide," Jerry told him. "The official line is the mother killed the daughter, then they think she went to the hospital and probably injected something into the son's IV that killed him, then blew her brains out in the parking garage. Off the record, I hear there was a suicide note left on her laptop in the apartment. Said the pressure, the humiliation, and the certainty that her son was either going to die or get the death penalty as a terrorist were just too much too bear."

"You hearing anything different on the inside?" A. J. asked.

"Yeah, there's a decent amount of skepticism about that scenario. I don't know why, but a couple of detectives I talked to this morning aren't buying it. At least not yet. They don't have anything definitive, it's just their instincts. They're waiting on the autopsy and the toxicology report to find out exactly what killed Jafaari and they're waiting for ballistics on the gun. Just doesn't feel right as a murder-suicide, they said. But it would be aw- fully neat and convenient for the department, and especially your buddy

Brock, to write it off that way. Hey, what was Lucy doing hanging out with a drug-dealing shithead like Supreme?"

"She was working a story."

"That's what I figured. Speaking of which, how's that piece going on Brock and the 'Great Raid'?"

"Well, it gets more complicated all the time. And now that the Jafaari kid's dead, there are no more eyewitnesses to the raid other than the cops. I haven't really turned the screws on the reporting yet, but I will over the next several days. Something doesn't feel right about the raid either, but that's just my gut."

"Any idea how Lucy's doing?"

"I'm sure she's fine," A. J. said, doing his best to mask his concern. "She's a lot tougher than she looks. Listen, I gotta run. Let's try and catch up later. Thanks for the update. You're the best."

Bishop, his two investigators, Bell, and one of Victoria's drivers were all sitting at the big table up front when A. J. walked in. Victoria was on the phone, pacing, lionlike, back and forth in a short, tight line. In the back, the Mexican porters were doing what they always do in the early morning—putting the chairs on top of the tables, sweeping and mopping the floors, and getting ready for the next night's dinner crowd. John, the headwaiter, had his tie off and his sleeves rolled up, and he was trying to tally the night's receipts. He was also doing triple duty as waiter, bartender, and cook to Bishop and his crew.

"Everyone just ordered breakfast," he said to A. J. in greeting. "What can I make you?"

"Are you cooking? 'Cause I don't want you to go to any trouble just for me," A. J. said. "I can just have some coffee."

"It's no trouble, I'm cooking anyway."

"All right, I'll have some eggs, well-done bacon, whole wheat toast, and coffee."

"Got it. How d'you like your eggs?"

"Whatever you do best."

John disappeared into the kitchen and A. J. looked directly at Bishop. "Long night, huh?" A. J. said. "Whaddaya got for me?"

"How do you wanna be updated?" Bishop asked, looking at A. J. through half-closed eyes. "Listen, before we get started, I want you to know there was nothing I could've done. Lucy didn't want me breathing down her neck, and when the shit came down, it happened too fast and the crowd was too thick for me to get to her."

"I have no problem with you on this," A. J. said. "She's a big girl and I'm sure you did whatever you could. Just give me everything from the beginning."

Before Bishop had a chance to respond, the room was filled with the sound of Victoria screaming into the phone. "I don't give a fuck what has to be done," she practically shrieked. "I want it done now. Got it? Don't fuck with me on this unless you'd like to see a story in the paper about some late-night trips the judge makes to a certain West Village apartment, with you named as the source. I'll be downtown before the judge gets there. Don't worry about that. You just get Lucy Chapin out of there." She ended the call, fully aware that everyone in the room was watching her. She now turned her attention, and her wrath, toward them.

"Maybe someone can explain to me why every time I have to call in a favor it's to bail one of your dumb asses out of the fire?" As she railed at them, they sat stone-faced. No one made a sound. There was, they all knew, little if any real anger behind the rant. It was all about the performance, which was, as these kinds of things went, first-rate.

"How is it, A. J., that I'm here at eight thirty in the morning, *eight thirty in the morning*," she continued, "to pull some strings and browbeat a few people so I can bail your assistant out of jail? Someone, *anyone*, please explain that to me. I just lost my client and his entire fuckin' family. I've got every newspaper and TV station on my back. Do you have any idea how many phone calls and e-mails I've gotten in the last five or six hours? Believe me, you don't. And on top of that, I've gotta go practically all night without being able to get ahold of my crack private investigator because he's babysitting your assistant," she said, glaring at A. J. "And why is he doing that? Is it to benefit my case somehow? No. It's on the pathetic hope that he can get in her pants. It's unbelievable. I'm surrounded by incompetence. I have to do everything myself."

With a nice dramatic flourish, she spun around, scooped up her coat, and started toward the exit. Without missing a beat, her driver was in position, standing like a sentry, ready to hold the door open so she could depart. On her way out, she paused one final time and turned to face the table. "While I'm downtown making sure A. J's pretty little assistant doesn't have to spend the weekend in jail, perhaps the rest of you can do something useful for a change. Like figuring out what the fuck is going on, for starters. And, A. J., you smug son of a bitch, you owe me. Big time. I'll be back in two hours." With that, she was gone.

"You gotta love the set of balls on that woman," Bell said, laughing.

"She gets the job done," A. J. said. "If Lucy had just about any other lawyer handling this she'd be cooling her jets in a cell until Monday morning. And my money says she comes back from downtown with Supreme as her new client."

"She's calculating and aggressive," Bishop said, "but you think she's *that* calculating and aggressive? It's only been a few hours since the whole goddamned Jafaari family went belly-up. Somewhere under all those expensive clothes, even Victoria has some feelings, right?"

A. J. just looked at him.

"Okay, you're right. Supreme's a lock," Bishop conceded. "You think she sleeps in her makeup? Who the hell looks that perfect at eight thirty in the morning? How long you think it takes her to get ready?"

Bell shook her head. "On that note, I'm going home to bed. You guys should do the same. Send John home after he feeds you. And the porters'll lock up after you leave."

When Bell gathered her things, Bishop directed his two guys to take her home. Then it was just A. J. and Bishop, sitting alone at the front table. For a moment, neither man said anything and the only sounds in the restaurant were the muffled voices of the porters and the occasional splat of a wet mop hitting the floor.

"The way it went down was surreal," Bishop said, breaking the silence. "You couldn't even hear the shots because of the music and the people going nuts over the money Supreme was throwing into the crowd. When you think about it," he continued, taking his phone off his belt and putting it on the table, "it's the perfect place and time to commit a crime. It's like a riot, so nobody hears or notices anything. And they don't give a shit even if they do. I heard no shots and all of a sudden the body-guard's head just explodes. Hardly anybody even saw it; they were too busy scrambling for the cash. I only saw it 'cause he was standing right by Lucy and I was watching her. I really tried, but by the time I was able to fight through the crowd and get anywhere close to her, she was being pulled into Supreme's car."

"Hey," John the waiter said, coming out of the kitchen, straining a little because he had both arms loaded with plates of hot food. "Where'd everybody go?"

"No worries," Bishop said. "Everything smells great. Just put the plates down and we'll have a buffet. Just make sure you give me my chicken."

Bishop saw A. J. staring at him. "What?" he said as John laid the plates down on the table. "I told you I did the best I could but there was no way to get to her."

"Chicken," A. J. said incredulously. "You're eating roast chicken and mashed potatoes for breakfast? What're we, in college? You want a beer with that?"

The table was crowded with plates of eggs, pancakes, bacon, and toast. The only exception was right in front of Bishop. He was about to dig into the previous night's dinner special.

"What time you have?" Bishop asked.

"Eight forty-five," A. J. said.

"That's funny," Bishop said smiling. "I've got nine o'clock."

"Okay, what's your point?"

"You have your time, I have my time. My stomach doesn't wear a watch," Bishop told him. "It wants chicken, I give it chicken. Get off my fucking back!"

Before John left, he brought in all the morning papers, which A. J. and Bishop read intently and mostly in silence. They were desperate to get as much information as they could about what happened to Lucy and Supreme as well as to the Jafaari family. While he was reading the half dozen newspapers, A. J. watched in amazement as Bishop methodically worked his way through about three-quarters of the food on the table. Not only did he devour the roast chicken, mashed potatoes, and string beans, he also ate an order of pancakes, three eggs over easy, bacon, and at least one piece of toast. When he started on a plate of sausage, A. J. could no longer restrain himself.

"You always eat like this?" he asked.

"Whaddaya mean?"

"What do I mean?" A. J. said. "What I mean is, like a pig, like someone who hasn't had any food in a week, like someone who's not going to have any food for another week, like a condemned man. I swear, you've got the biggest fucking appetite I've ever seen."

"I'm hungry," Bishop responded while putting a sausage in his mouth. "I didn't have dinner last night. What the fuck, anyway? What're you, my mother?"

"Whatever," A. J. said, rolling his eyes.

The two men sat with their plates in front of them, facing the TV, which hung above the front door of the restaurant near the bar. All morning, the cable networks had been running teasers for a live announcement by the president introducing New York City police commissioner—and "hero in the war on terror"—Lawrence Brock as his choice to be secretary of Homeland Security.

"Unbelievable," A. J. said right after one of the promos for the Brock announcement. "Well, at least I get another chapter for my book."

"What's unbelievable?" Bishop asked. "Brock's nomination? What book?"

"Yeah," A. J. said. "Brock's nomination. I mean, who would believe that could happen? A cabinet post for a knock-around guy like him? A guy with his background? Man, it gets harder all the time not to be completely cynical and disillusioned. It's a book I joke about writing called *Why Good Things Happen to Bad People.*"

Bishop smiled. "I like that. Listen," he said during a break in the news, "about last night—"

"I already told you," A. J. said, interrupting him, "I don't hold you—"

"I got that," Bishop said, cutting him off and pushing his plate away like he was finally done eating. "But the truth is, I don't even know what the fuck I was doing there. I mean, Lucy asked me to go, okay. But there's obviously something going on here I don't know about. I'm still waiting for someone to tell me what this has to do with anything."

"Well, last night notwithstanding, Supreme's got nothing to do with you," A. J. said. "Remember a couple of weeks ago, that detective was found dead with a hooker in his house in the Hamptons? It was classified a murder-suicide."

"Sure, I remember thinking it was a strange story. There were all kinds of things about it that didn't seem to make sense. What was the cop's name again?"

"Kevin Anderson," A. J. said.

"Right, Kevin Anderson. When that story broke, one of my investigators mentioned he was briefly assigned to the same precinct as Anderson, who was like some kind of one-man wrecking crew trying to wipe out the drug business single-handedly."

"As it turns out, he was a one-man wrecking crew trying to wipe out the competition. He was *in* the drug business."

A. J. recounted Supreme's story in detail. The mysterious voice mails he'd left for A. J. at the magazine, his meeting with Lucy at his town house when he told her all about Anderson and the drug business, and his pronounced fear that someone was going to kill him—the same way they killed Kevin Anderson. "I was a little skeptical about the threat, but I'd say last night pretty much confirms his claim," A. J. said.

"I'm guessing you think there's something else going on," Bishop said.

"Well, you were a cop. You tell me. Don'tcha think it's been a pretty unusual couple of weeks? I mean, first there's a high-profile murder-suicide in the Hamptons. How often's that happen? Then Supreme starts calling and leaving me panicky messages about the urgent need for a sit-down. Next there's the commissioner's one-man war on terror, his 'Great Raid,' that leaves four Muslims, and actually now a fifth, dead. And the commissioner—the fucking New York City police commissioner—shot at least one or maybe even two of them himself. Now we have yesterday's murder-suicide of the Jafaaris and last night's attempt to kill Supreme."

"It could just be coincidence," Bishop said. "This is New York, shit does happen."

"You don't believe that any more than I do."

"Okay, Sherlock, what's the connection?"

"I don't know," A. J. said with a heavy sigh, clearly frustrated. "That's the problem. But there's something going on here. It's right in front of us. You're the fuckin' detective; help me out."

"It is compelling, I'll give you that," Bishop conceded. "But there's no common thread. And even if there was, what the fuck do we care? It's not gonna put any shekels in my pocket, is it? No, it's not. My case is over."

"We care because people were killed—your client, for chrissakes—and the way things look now, the killing's probably not finished. And in case you hadn't noticed, we're kind of in the middle of it."

"Maybe you're in the middle of it, 'cause you've got a couple of sto-ries going here on the commissioner and Supreme. But like you said, my client's dead. I'm done."

A. J. ran his hands through his hair a couple of times and then folded his arms across his chest. "All right," he said after a few moments, "let me try this another way. Even if you don't care about police corruption and a couple of dead people you don't really know, what about the bigger picture?"

"What bigger picture?" Bishop said with a little smile, clearly enjoy-ing A. J.'s frustration with him.

"Doesn't it bother you at all that the president's about to announce that he's picked Lawrence Brock to become director of Homeland Security? Aren't you just a little concerned about that? You know his reputation probably better than I do. He's a bully and a taker who's not exactly known for his ethical standards. Is that who you want in charge of the country's security? Don't you give a shit about anything other than yourself?"

"That's exactly the kind of red, white, and blue bullshit that got me into this in the first place," Bishop said, no longer amused. "Victoria ran that same game on me about patriotism and the flag and all the rest of that crap. That's how I ended up working for a terrorist. Well, know what? I'm taking the kid's murder as an unexpected but welcomed out for me. I see it as a lucky break to get off a case I shouldn't have been on in the first place."

Before A. J. could respond, the front door flew open and Victoria swept in with a subdued Lucy not far behind her. Victoria looked almost radiant. Her cheeks were a little flushed, no doubt from the running around she'd been doing. Nothing made her eyes brighter than a good fight, and now she had a fresh one. While she'd gotten Lucy arraigned and out of jail, she was less successful with her other new client: Supreme. But partial success only made her more energized.

Lucy, on the other hand, looked terrible—as terrible as someone could look with near-perfect cheekbones, flawless skin, snow-white teeth, and a nose that every sixteen-year-old getting rhinoplasty would kill for, anyway. She was still in the same clothes she had been wearing at the club, including the blouse stained with the blood of Supreme's bodyguard.

As soon as Lucy saw A. J., she wanted to run to him. But she controlled herself, knowing everyone was watching. She certainly didn't want Bishop to see her vulnerable, to see her acting, as he would probably put it, like a girl. Lucy walked over to A. J. and he put his arms around her and held her the way he would have held his daughter. Though he knew men his age who were having affairs with women younger than Lucy, that wasn't A. J.'s style. He had too much character for that. Though he would never have admitted it, lest he get branded a chauvinist, or at the very least an anachronism, he felt responsible for her in a kind of old-fashioned way. Though she was incredibly beautiful, his affection for her was paternal, not sexual.

Lucy had managed to maintain her composure through the shooting, the crazy scramble to get out of the club in the middle of a near riot, the arrest, and the arraignment. But now, with her head buried in A. J.'s chest, she lost it. She burst into tears and sobbed quietly.

"You want something to drink?" A. J. asked her after a few minutes when she stopped crying and regained control.

"I guess a cup of coffee would be nice," she said softly. "But what I'd really like is to get out of these clothes, take a shower, and sleep for about a week. I feel so dirty."

"Of course," A. J. said, glancing at his watch. "I just need you to hold on for a little longer. I need you to tell me what happened. I'm sure you've already gone over everything ad nauseam with Victoria and the cops, but I need to hear it. It's important. If you want, you can wash up a little first in the back."

Lucy shook her head no and began to go through the evening for A. J.: the silly small talk with Bishop, the mistake of having several vodkas, Supreme's entrance, the insanity when he "made it rain," and the shooting. A. J., following his own advice, didn't interrupt her. He let Lucy get out whatever she needed to expel. He took a few notes while she talked.

"I was standing next to Supreme and throwing the money for maybe fifteen seconds when I felt a splash on my face. I had no idea what it was. The only way I can describe it is it felt like someone had thrown half-set, warm Jell-O on me. Then, almost in the same instant, the bodyguard fell backward, pushing me into Supreme. I tried wiping my face, and when I took my hand away I saw it was blood. I thought I was gonna lose it. Just for like a split second, just before I felt the splash on my face, I saw a strange long-haired white guy wearing sunglasses out in the crowd raise and point what looked like a gun. But I turned when the bodyguard fell on me, and when I looked back out over the dance floor, the long-haired guy had vanished into the crowd."

"My guess is that guy was the shooter," A. J. said. "Listen, I'm really proud of the way you've handled yourself."

A. J. told her he'd get her home shortly. What he wanted to do was bring her home with him and have her spend a little time with Nikki, just to make sure she was okay. Lucy didn't protest.

"Hey," Victoria yelled, "get a load of this." On the television, the president was walking confidently toward a lectern with Lawrence Brock alongside him. The lectern was set up in front of a portrait of Teddy Roosevelt on horseback, dressed in his uniform as commander of the Rough Riders. The big, beautiful, wild-looking horse had reared up on its hind legs and Roosevelt, sitting majestically on its back, exuded strength, courage, and leadership. *Son of a bitch,* A. J. said to himself, *they're making the announcement in the Roosevelt Room.* Primarily used as a conference room, it was not the usual choice for this kind of event, but A. J. had to admit it was a perfect symbolic choice—in addition to being one of America's best-known presidents, Roosevelt happened to be New York City's most famous police commissioner.

Everyone in Bell's went silent as the president stepped to the microphone and Brock, in a nicely tailored gray suit, white shirt, and red tie, stood about a step behind him on his left side. With his chest out, his shoulders back, and his gaze fixed on the commander in chief, Brock looked very confident. "Good morning," the president began. "I'm proud to announce my nomination of Commissioner Lawrence Brock as the secretary of Homeland Security." Right on cue, Victoria let loose a huge raspberry. "Very mature," A. J. said, laughing.

"Lawrence Brock is one of the most accomplished and effective leaders of law enforcement in America," the president continued. "Throughout his career, he has demonstrated a deep commitment to justice, a heart for the innocent, and a record of great success."

"All right," Victoria said loudly, "that's it. I don't know about the rest of you, but I can't take any more of this. It's bad enough that fat skirt chaser, who by the way hits on me every fucking time I see him, has become some kind of national hero and he's keeping me off the front page, but Homeland Security? Jesus Christ."

As Victoria ranted, A. J. continued to catch pieces of the president's introduction of Brock. ". . . he understands the duties that came to America on September 11. Commissioner Brock takes that responsibility so seriously, so personally, that last week he put his own life at risk in the active pursuit of those who seek to destroy us. In the name of freedom, he rushed into a dark, danger-filled apartment—"

"A. J., A. J." The sound from the TV cut out, and A. J. realized Victoria was calling his name, waving the remote in her hand.

"Uh, sorry," he said a little sheepishly, "I was listening to the president."

"Well, now it's time to listen to me," Victoria bellowed. "We need to figure out what the fuck is going on here. First off, I'm now representing Supreme. Bishop, that means your lazy ass is still on the payroll."

Bishop looked at A. J. and shrugged his shoulders in a gesture of resignation. "Okay," Bishop said, principally to A. J., "now I have a reason to stay in the game."

"But there'll be no more episodes like last night," Victoria continued, "or we're done. When I call, I need to be able to reach you. Understood? The next time you turn your phone off when I want you will be the last time I want you. And the first thing I want you to do is find out who got to the judge. I want to know why I wasn't able to get Supreme released on bail."

A. J. stole a look at the screen. As the president finished his announcement, Brock stepped forward. As was his custom, he threw his right arm around the president's shoulder and gave him a good squeeze. The president smiled and then stepped back, allowing Brock to have center stage for his brief statement. A. J. turned to the group and began to explain his feeling about the extraordinary events of the past two weeks to Victoria and Lucy.

"I don't know exactly what's going on here," Bishop said, jumping in, "but something's fucked up. No way two murder-suicides are a random coincidence. No way the Jafaari deaths are murder-suicide at all. I only met the mother once, but there's no chance she killed both her kids and then offed herself. When I talked to her, she was relaxed, focused, and strong. And it was clear she loved her kids. Nothing in her profile would suggest suicide, let alone murder. My investigators'll be all over Bellevue to find out what went down."

Lucy, her eyes puffy and red, looked at Bishop, then Victoria, and turned finally to A. J. "You need to talk to Supreme."

"Absolutely," A. J. said. "And I need to get my meeting scheduled with Brock as well."

A. J. picked up his coffee cup and took a drink. "Ugh," he said. "It's ice-cold. All right," he said, getting up from the table. "We really need to start rockin'. If there's any chance something's really amiss with Brock, besides his being a power-hungry, self-absorbed prick, we better find out before he's confirmed by the Senate."

"We need a plan of attack," Lucy said.

"That's exactly what I'm about to give you," A. J. said with a smile. "Once the two of you get a little rest and you're able to recharge, here's what I want you to do. Bishop, your guys have been all over Brock's raid, right? Good. Then it's time for you to see what they have. We need to find out where the tip came from, how Brock got involved, and whether the whole thing was clean. And we need to find out why the cops are threatening people to keep them quiet. Lucy, you should make contact with Anderson's wife. Go see her in person, if she'll let you, and get whatever you can from her. She had to have some sense of what he was up to."

A. J. then looked at Victoria and glanced quickly at the television. Brock and the president were turning and walking out of the Roosevelt

Room. The press conference was over and Brock's nomination was official. "Vic," A. J. said, "you need to get Supreme out of jail. And while you're doing that, you think you can get me into Rikers for a visit?"

"Even if I have to blow the warden," she said.

"Hey, Vic," Bishop said, "I thought you did that for your last case."

14

ON MOST DAYS, Walter Fitzgerald was okay with his place in the world. He had reached the upper ranks of the NYPD and achieved more success than he could've imagined as a working-class Irish kid growing up on Belmont Avenue in the Bronx. This was not one of those days. This was a day when he felt shortchanged and overlooked. A day when all of his resentments about having to take orders from people with less experience who were not nearly as smart as he was bubbled to the surface. It had been some time since Fitzgerald recognized he'd never get the top job, that despite his wealth of experience, political savvy, and street smarts, he'd never be police commissioner. And, for the most part, he'd made his peace with it. After more than thirty years in the department, he still loved his job, and even if he wasn't going all the way to the top, he'd come pretty damn close. The fact that he'd outlasted five mayors and half a dozen police commissioners was a badge of honor he wore proudly. "In order to thrive, you must survive," he often said, and that was the goal: survive and thrive.

He'd actually started the day feeling pretty good. It was a Saturday, so he slept in till seven forty-five. Then he made himself a nice big breakfast of ham and eggs, some fresh fruit he'd picked up the day before at a farmer's market in Union Square, and plenty of fresh ground coffee.

He was meeting Commissioner Brock at eleven o'clock at police headquarters and he couldn't wait. Fitzgerald was almost as excited about the
get-together as he was the first time he was ever called to the commissioner's office nearly twenty years earlier. Back then, the invitation was to
recognize and reward him for his outstanding leadership. Two priests in
lower Manhattan had been tortured and murdered, and within ten days,
the detectives in his command made an arrest.

Since then, he'd had hundreds, maybe even thousands of meetings
with all the various police commissioners, and he couldn't remember
the last time he was this eager. He was thrilled for Brock, his onetime
protégé, who was just back from Washington and his star turn with the
president, and he knew that as manic as the commissioner was, he would
be sky-high over the nomination. Fitzgerald couldn't wait to hear the
gossip and dirty details from Washington.

But now, as he sat in the back of his Crown Victoria at the foot of
the Brooklyn Bridge, he was more pissed than pumped. He'd shown up
at Brock's office right on time, only to be directed by the commissioner's
secretary to the Manhattan side of the Brooklyn Bridge. She didn't know
why Brock wanted to meet him there and neither did Fitzgerald—at least
not at first. On his way over, he figured Brock must be planning some
kind of press event, otherwise why would they be meeting outside?

Some guys just never get enough, he thought. He knew the commissioner as well as anyone and he'd seen outrageous displays of his ego many
times. But this was off the charts, even for Brock. How needy and fucked
up could one person be that he'd still be craving attention after a week
like the one Brock had had? Any public display at this point, Fitzgerald
believed, was an unnecessary distraction with no upside. Brock had already won the big prize. There was serious business to take care of, like
the complicated minefield of the confirmation process. Not to mention
the little problem of A. J. Ross and Frank Bishop snooping around and
looking into the Kevin Anderson situation. They needed to be stopped
before they caused real trouble, and Brock's continuing to scream, "Look
at me, look at me," was definitely not the way to do it. *If ever there was a*

time to just keep your head down and enjoy the spoils, the chief thought, *it was now.*

So as Fitzgerald sat in his car waiting for Brock, his mood had darkened considerably. He no longer even cared much about what happened in Washington. His primary concern now was taking care of business in New York, *his* business. After three decades of extraordinary police work and even more skillful, meticulously planned political maneuvering, Fitzgerald was not about to let someone else's carelessness—even if it was the commissioner's—destroy everything he'd worked so hard to achieve.

While he waited, he took a picture of his daughter out of his wallet. Bright blue eyes, luminous smile. He remembered how excited he was when the doctor announced, "It's a girl!"

His reverie was abruptly broken when the Emergency Service Unit vehicle pulled up. Brock and his entourage arrived a few minutes later. When the commissioner got out, he was grinning like a six-year-old at recess. He walked over and wrapped Fitzgerald in a big, tight bear hug. He squeezed hard for several seconds before letting go. "We did it, man, we actually fucking did it," Brock said, laughing.

"Congratulations," Fitzgerald responded soberly.

"'Congratulations,'" Brock repeated incredulously. "That's it? That's all you got? What the hell's the matter with you, man? How 'bout some excitement? How 'bout some noise? How 'bout some 'Holy fuckin' shit, Commish, you're unbelievable'? C'mon, Fitz, it doesn't get any bigger than this."

"Sorry, Commissioner, I got a lot on my mind. I really am thrilled for you."

"Well, you're doing a great job of hiding it."

"Listen, couldn't we do this at Nello's or Fat Jack's or some other restaurant? I'll buy."

"Fuck you," Brock said, smiling. "This is gonna be great. I already made us a reservation and it's only two hundred seventy-six feet away."

"You're kidding, right?" an anxious Fitzgerald asked.

"The fuck I am, brother." But even before Brock answered, Fitzgerald saw two ESU officers approaching with harnesses, one for each of them. As the chief slipped into the canvas and leather contraption, which was not unlike the kind used by window washers, he knew what Brock was doing. The two of them were going to climb to the top of one of the towers on the Brooklyn Bridge. He felt like he wanted to strangle Brock. *This compulsion to engage in risky behavior must be some kind of sickness*, Fitzgerald thought. There was no other way to explain it. Brock was at the absolute pinnacle of his career; why would he stupidly dance along the edge and risk losing everything? Fitzgerald had about as much patience for pop psychology as he did for the ACLU, but in this case he was seriously starting to wonder if Brock's compulsion to tempt fate was really a subconscious effort to sabotage himself.

Fitzgerald didn't dwell on his simplified attempt at analysis. At that moment he had more pressing concerns—like how the fuck he was supposed to get to the top of the tower? The main suspension cables came up out of the ground at the foot of the bridge. There was one on the right side and one on the left. They gradually rose to the top of the first tower at about a thirty-degree incline, and then they stretched straight across to the next tower. From there, they began their descent down to the ground on the other side of the East River. Each of these cables was about the width of a diving board, but of course they weren't flat. They were cylinders. Walking on one was like walking on one of those balance beams that gymnasts use. You had to work to maintain your equilibrium and watch every step. Each main cable, about the thickness of a good-size log, was flanked on both sides by two narrower ones that ran parallel all the way up and across the span. These secondary cables were about at waist height, so, like a couple of window washers clamping onto the side of a building, Brock and Fitzgerald locked onto these cables with straps attached to each hip. They could also use them to hold on to during their ascent. As they began their climb, there were two beefy ESU officers in front of them and two behind as a safety precaution.

It was a beautiful day with the kind of cloudless blue sky that sometimes causes outfielders to lose track of simple fly balls. Fitzgerald was breathing heavily as he climbed and he could feel the sweat underneath his shirt and dripping down his face. He focused intently on every step, carefully and slowly placing one foot in front of the other. Though he was afraid he'd lose his balance if he turned his head and really looked around, he could still see how spectacular the 360-degree view was. Unfortunately, he could also sense what was below him—on one side was the roadway and on the other was the blackness of the East River.

The climb, which probably could've been done in twenty minutes, took nearly twice that time because of the chief's cautious pace. When they reached the top of the tower, there was a flat surface about twenty feet by twenty feet where they could sit, relax, talk, and have lunch. Brock took a long, deep breath and exhaled slowly with a big smile on his face. "How great is this, huh, Fitz? Really makes you feel alive."

"Fuck you, cocksucker," Fitzgerald responded. "I'm gonna get even with you for this."

"Hey, hey, watch your mouth," Brock said. "Let's have a little respect. What's the matter with you, anyway? You afraid of heights?"

"Who the fuck isn't?"

Brock had made sure one of the ESU guys brought along a camera; he'd taken a few pictures during the climb and he was taking some now with the skyline in the background. One of the other officers was unloading his pack, which contained drinks and sandwiches from Brock's favorite restaurant. "Hey, guys," the commissioner said. "Do me a favor. Go down to the truck and take out a bottle of champagne. I forgot to put it in the pack. I need all four of you to go." The sergeant hesitated, not wanting to abandon his responsibility, but one quick look from the commissioner was all it took. He knew Brock wanted to be alone with the chief and he was not to be argued with.

Once the ESU guys started their descent, Brock looked at Fitzgerald, who still seemed to be scowling. "You know this is not just about me," the commissioner said. "This is for all of us, everybody in the crew. When one of us succeeds, we all succeed. That's what we always said. So you're coming with me." Before Fitzgerald could protest, he said, "I don't want to hear anything, Chief, you're coming to Washington. But first you need to clean up the mess with Bishop and A. J. There's nothing they can do to hurt us. They'll never connect the dots. All the same, make it go away. That motherfucker Bishop has always been a pain in the ass, even when he was a cop. Maybe someday you'll explain to me why you protect him. As far as Supreme goes, leave him to me. We can't have any loose ends. The FBI's gonna be all over the vetting process and I need to look clean. And so, by the way, do you."

Fitzgerald knew better than to argue when Brock was like this. The commissioner was pacing back and forth on the tower, each time coming and closer to the edge. Fitzgerald just sat and watched, careful not to send any signals with his body language or his facial expressions to antagonize the commissioner. He was just trying to ride out the storm. But he knew that ultimately something did need to be done about Bishop and A. J.

"Everything's under control, Commish," Fitzgerald said finally. "I pulled a few strings, so Supreme's not getting outta Rikers any time soon, even though he's got that bitch Victoria Cannel representing him now. His bail was denied. I got him being watched, and I got Bishop and A. J. Ross and his assistant under surveillance as well. Whenever any one of 'em takes a piss, I'll know what shade of yellow it is."

The commissioner, certain he'd gotten his message across, had relaxed and became upbeat again. He walked to one corner of the tower and motioned for Fitzgerald to join him. When the chief reluctantly complied, Brock put his arm around him and fully extended his other arm, pointing north. Fitzgerald was wondering what the hell the commissioner was doing. It was a strange, almost statuelike pose. Then it clicked. The chief looked down and saw a throng of reporters and cameras gathered at the foot of the bridge, tipped off to the photo op, no doubt, by Brock's people.

The wind picked up a little, swirling around the two men as they stood together stiffly for another few moments. Fitzgerald looked at the pleasure-boat traffic on the water. For just an instant, he had a wistful, envious sensation. How nice it would be, he thought, to spend a Saturday on the river, or in a park, or lying on the couch like a normal person. Maybe he'd reached the time in his life when he wanted to be able to go home on Friday and shut down, to leave it all at the office until after the weekend.

"Chief, Chief." He suddenly realized Brock was trying to get his attention. "Are you with me? All right, it's time to go down."

The moment of doubt for Fitzgerald passed. "What's the mayor gonna say when he sees photos of this little escapade?" he asked.

"Well, I guess I'll find out shortly. I'm going to see him as soon as we're done."

"Aren't you concerned?" Fitzgerald asked.

"Fuck him," Brock said with a full measure of arrogance. "This is our time."

Mayor Domenico was uncharacteristically subdued when Brock met with him. There was no yelling, no grand theatrical gestures, and no playing to the cheap seats. He sat behind his desk and was pretty much all business. He had his glasses on, his sleeves rolled up, and an unlit cigar stuck in his left hand. Brock was a little disappointed, but he knew this was a session they had to have. Domenico was in operational mode. He'd been a high-ranking attorney in the Justice Department, so he knew the system and he knew exactly how the process would go. He had his secretary bring in a pad for Brock so he could take notes. The mayor then spent about thirty minutes briefing the police commissioner on who he needed to call, which lawyers had to be involved, what paperwork had to be pristinely presented, and which of his cronies he'd have to jettison.

The mayor asked Brock several times if he anticipated any hot spots, anything the investigators might find that could potentially be a problem. Each time he asked, Brock responded in the same way: No, sir, there was nothing he was aware of that should cause any problems. And each time it came up, the mayor reminded Brock in a severe but muted tone that this was not just about him. The mayor told Brock, as if it needed repeating, that his long-term plan was a run for the White

House, otherwise he might've taken the Homeland Security job himself. Therefore, any embarrassment, any humiliating surprise during the approval process, was absolutely unacceptable, since it would potentially damage much more than just Brock's nomination.

It was a painfully difficult position for the mayor to be in. Though he wasn't his usual demonstrative self, he was seething. Despite the intense closeness of Domenico's relationship with Brock, and the fact that Brock had always unquestioningly deferred to his authority, Domenico was, for the first time, concerned that the police commissioner might ultimately be impossible to control. It was a bitter pill for him to swallow. Domenico had built his entire public life on the themes of discipline, personal accountability, and control. Every fire, every shooting, every water-main break, Domenico was there in his windbreaker letting everyone know he was in charge. It was always *his* cops and *his* crime-control strategies that made the city safe. If a reporter asked him why the schools were failing, he'd say it was because he didn't control them. But it turned out that the arrogant tough guy now might not be able to control his police commissioner—a monster that he, in true Dr. Frankenstein fashion, had created. He'd fired one of Brock's predecessors, one of the most effective police commissioners in decades, just because he thought the guy was getting too much press. Now, with Brock, he'd begun to have real moments of doubt.

"What about the raid?" Domenico asked, getting up from behind his desk for the first time. "What's the status of the various investigations?"

"We'll be fine," Brock said without any attitude. He sensed the mayor's quiet agitation. "Now that the last Arab's dead, there are no witnesses other than cops. The investigations at this point are simply routine and should be wrapped up shortly."

"What about the deaths of Jafaari and his family?"

"I have no reason at this point to think it was anything other than what's been reported, a distraught mother who killed her son and took her own life," Brock said.

The mayor, who'd been walking around the office for the last five minutes or so, now leaned against his desk, right in front of Brock. "Get moving right away on those instructions I gave you earlier," he said. "The sooner you get started, the less friction there'll be in the process."

They shook hands and Brock stood up to leave. When he was by the door, the mayor said, "Oh, I almost forgot. One more stunt like this morning's little show on the bridge, and I'll pull the fucking plug on your nomination myself. Close the door on your way out."

15

THE LATE SATURDAY-morning sun hit Lucy right in the face, momentarily blinding her as she drove east out of Manhattan in her rental car. She fumbled with her right hand to get her sunglasses out of the bag resting on the seat next to her. Once she got them on, the road reappeared and she was able to relax. Lucy loved to drive and it was something she'd rarely gotten to do since moving to the city. She was still a little tired from the all-night ordeal that began at Roxx and ended with her getting booked downtown, but she was feeling really good. She'd slept through most of the afternoon and then gotten another solid ten hours that night. More important, she was very happy with the way she'd handled herself when things got ugly. She'd never really been tested that way before, and she was thrilled that she'd been tough enough to maintain her composure and deal with it like a professional.

When they left Bell's yesterday, A. J. had tried to get her to go home with him so his wife, Nikki, could pamper her and she'd be guaranteed some rest. But Lucy just wanted to lie down in her own bed and sleep. Surprisingly, A. J. relented, dropping her off at her apartment once she'd promised to call when she got up. On the way there, she convinced A. J. that she was fine, just a little tired, and he should let her go to the Hamptons to interview Kevin Anderson's wife. He was resistant, but she got him to cave on this, too, making it clear to him that he couldn't be in two places at once and his priority, given everything that had happened, should be a face-to-face with Supreme at Rikers Island.

Lucy had made this trip to the Hamptons countless times over many summers. It was almost a ritual. For a while, it was all partying all the time. She'd stay at some rich player's house with her model girlfriends; they'd hang out poolside during the day, and at night they'd go from one A-list event to another. She was on every publicist's guest list. Eventually she graduated to more sophisticated outings where the conversation was a little more interesting and the people had a lot more money, but the bottom line was more or less the same—too many annoying men hitting on her, a memorable hangover, and a really empty feeling the next day.

This trip would be very different. She thought about how far she'd come in such a short period of time. It was strange. In some ways, it seemed like only yesterday that she'd been a model, and in other ways it seemed like another lifetime. Lucy never thought of modeling as a long-term thing, but the money had been great, the perks even better, and for a while the whole thing just became irresistible. It was also fairly easy. Mindless, but easy. She remembered the moment she knew she was done. She was at a studio shoot in SoHo for the spring lines from the hot new Italian designers of the season, and for the first time in her career she decided to make a creative suggestion. She wasn't being annoying or temperamental or acting like a diva. She simply thought the setup for the shot could be more interesting. Lucy was standing under the lights and a stylist was primping and fussing with her clothes when she offered her suggestion. There was no response. No one even looked at her. The music in the studio was pretty loud so at first she thought maybe no one heard her. She said it again, a little more assertively, and there was still no response. This time it was clear they were ignoring her. Finally, when she'd repeated it a third time the photographer said, "Sweetheart, please don't worry about anything other than looking beautiful. It'll give you wrinkles." That afternoon she went online and began the application process for grad school. She continued to model quite a bit that spring, but she knew the end was in sight. She took the summer off, and in September, she started classes at Columbia to get her master's in journalism.

As she passed Exit 60 on the Long Island Expressway, Lucy turned off the radio and plugged in her iPod to play her favorite recording of Vivaldi's *The Four Seasons*, featuring Isaac Stern, Pinchas Zukerman, Itzhak Perlman, and Shlomo Mintz. She needed to focus on the task at hand and classical music always helped her concentrate. Almost over-night, she'd gone from handling mostly banal, run-of-the-mill research tasks and the occasionally interesting background interview for A. J. to serious reporting. Every interview she did now was crucial and had the potential to break a big story. More important, lives were possibly on the line. Lucy knew she needed to get this right, but she just wasn't sure about the best way to handle a woman whose husband had been found dead in the bedroom of their house with a naked hooker who'd been beaten to death.

While Lucy was on her way out to Long Island to see Yvette Anderson, A. J. trekked uptown to Harlem for a little background work and some waffles and fried chicken at Willie's Uptown, a restaurant that served what was often called the "best Southern food north of the Mason-Dixon Line." A few minutes after A. J. walked in and sat down at a table, the owner, a very large man named Willie Lynch, came out of the kitchen to say hello. "It's been too long, brother," Willie said warmly. "We gotta get you uptown more often."

"You know I love coming here," A. J. said with a smile, "but every time you feed me, I've gotta spend a week at the gym doing double time."

"Hey, no talk about waistlines today. I'm gonna make sure you and the reverend leave my place happy."

"You always do, but don't go to any trouble for me," A. J. said.

"It's no trouble. It's what I love to do, especially for good people like you and the Rev."

With that, the front door opened and the Reverend Kellen "Muddy"

Watters walked in. There were few bigger head-turners in New York than Watters. Whatever else he was, and he was many things, he was a transcendent celebrity, the kind of personality that made people of every color and from every walk of life stop and take notice when they saw him. Even people who couldn't stand him had to acknowledge his extraordinary television presence and his skill at manipulating the conventions and symbols of the black struggle for civil rights. Every aggravating Day of Outrage he conducted, every mindless cry of "No justice, no peace!" and every appearance with a black family grieving over the murder of one of its members had left an image of Watters burned into the public psyche.

"A. J. Ross," Watters boomed, "I know if you've come up to Harlem for breakfast you must need somethin' from me. What's up? That magazine you write for need a little newsstand rejuvenation? You come up here to put me on the cover again so you can actually sell some copies?" he said with great laughter. "How are you? It's been a while."

"It has indeed," A. J. said. "You look good, man. Nice to see you."

A. J. had known Watters for more than a decade, and in that time he'd written two cover stories about him. He'd followed the reverend's transformation from a grotesquely overweight buffoon to a legitimate political power broker with his own cable news show, a progression that surprised just about everyone except the reverend himself. Nevertheless, he remained for many white people the worst kind of opportunist—someone who drove them nuts, a small but significant annoyance like a pebble stuck in their shoe. And he remained for many blacks—precisely because he drove white people nuts—a crusader.

As A. J. looked at the reverend now, slimmed down from a scale-busting 325 pounds to a ridiculously svelte, almost sickly 165, looking very sharp in his dark three-piece suit, white shirt, and silver tie, he thought pretty much what he always thought about him: *So much wasted potential.* Watters would no doubt argue he'd accomplished a huge amount as an activist (an agitator, really) working outside the system.

But the reality, whether he wanted to admit it or not, was that for most white people, and some blacks as well, he'd never be more than a fraud, a disgrace to the cloth, and the ringmaster of the racial circus that had played on and off in New York for almost two decades.

But, man, could he preach: arm-waving, bellowing, Bible-quoting, foot-stomping, hellfire-threatening, old-fashioned shaking-the-pulpit-and-moving-people-to-tears Baptist preaching. It was something to see.

A. J. had come to Willie's to talk to Watters about Supreme, to draw on his street connections to hopefully get some useful background. They made some small talk about politics, starting with Mayor Domenico, who had done the worst possible thing someone could do to Watters: he'd ignored him. He'd seriously diminished the reverend's clout by simply acting as if he didn't exist. Domenico had made a strategic decision when he became mayor that he wouldn't take the reverend's bait. He didn't respond to anything he said, he never sat down with him, and he never bowed to any community or activist pressure on the issue of race. Not surprisingly, being shut out infuriated the reverend.

"How 'bout Brock?" A. J. asked.

"Good for me, good for my community," the reverend said in between bites of his waffles and fried chicken. "Despite Domenico's outrageous refusal to recognize me, Brock knows if he wants to get any cooperation from me and the other community leaders in this city, he has to spend some time courting us."

"What'd Brock do to reach out?"

"Well, he'd do things both over and under the table, like having all of the black community leaders in the city come down to police headquarters, where his people would explain his crime-fighting initiatives. Especially any time he introduced anything new. He also made sure the precinct commanders reached out to people in the neighborhoods. A little goes a long way, know what I'm saying? But you're not here to talk about Brock, are you?"

"No, I'm not," A. J. said. "I'm here to talk about Supreme. How well do you know him?"

The corners of the reverend's mouth curled into a hint of a smile. "We on or off the record?" he asked.

"We're whatever you want us to be," A. J. said, playing his role in their little dance. "We've known each other long enough, so you know you can trust me. I need real, honest information. If you can only do it on background, that's fine. I'd rather you be candid and tell me what you know."

"What're you looking for?" Watters asked, motioning for the waiter. He asked for more water and another glass of lemonade. "Is this about the incident with the gun the other night? He's in Rikers now, right?"

"Yes and no," A. J. said. "Yes, he's being held at Rikers without bail, but no, this isn't about the thing with the gun. I'm not looking to hurt him. Just between us, he's reached out to me for some help and I'm trying to find out what I'm getting myself into. I'm trying to get some details on his background. Real stuff, not the record company's bullshit. Anything you can give me here would really be appreciated."

The reverend looked around for a moment and wiped his mouth with his napkin before saying anything. "Supreme was always different in this neighborhood. He did what he had to do, but he did it responsibly."

"You'll forgive me, Reverend, but I didn't know drug dealers could be responsible."

"Anybody can be responsible, even journalists. That's why I'm sitting here talking to you, A. J. Let me explain. Church Jackson, his predecessor, was a mean, violent man. He was ruthless and he didn't care who he hurt. But when Supreme took over, the neighborhood got smooth. He was chill and everybody was able to just mind their own business."

"I don't understand what you're saying," A. J. said.

"When Church Jackson was running the streets, it was all about war, constant violence. Innocent bystanders sometimes got hurt, and it was really bad for the neighborhood. All that violence kept people indoors, so it was bad for business. It also created a negative atmosphere. That meant no new investment, no people moving here, no new housing built. But once Supreme took over, there was peace in the streets. It was like a combination of the bad guys doing what they had to do and the cops filling in the gaps."

"What do you mean?"

"Well, you had Supreme controlling most of the trade with the other major guys apparently okay with a smaller piece of the pie. And whenever somebody got stupid trying to make a name for himself, the NYPD upped their game. They'd step in and make arrests. If I didn't know better, I would've said they were working together."

"Maybe it was all just a coincidence," A. J. said. "When Church Jackson was running things, crime was out of control everywhere. The city was a mess until the police department started implementing Comp-Stat and things began to settle down. Then Supreme takes over. So maybe it was all just timing."

"No question the city was like the Wild West and it was every man for himself," the reverend conceded. "It was very hard to get anything going by way of real organization. So Church Jackson's strategy, if you can call it a strategy, was basically kill them all and let God sort it out. At some point, it all changed and order was brought to the neighborhood. I always figured it was Supreme. Look, don't get me wrong," Watters said, sitting back and putting his hands on his vest-covered belly as the waiter cleared the dishes from the table. "We're talking about a drug dealer. No question. But given that Supreme was a significant drug dealer, he was also, in that context, a decent guy. I've never heard that he himself committed any acts of violence or that he had his guys doing it. And his rep on the street was he was always available if someone needed help—money or whatever. People knew they could go to him."

"I think I'll let someone else nominate him for man of the year," A. J. said sarcastically. "But as far as the business goes, you're saying Supreme was able to build up his empire because of the lack of competition, right?"

A. J. was fascinated by the way the whole enterprise worked and how it had all gelled because of Kevin Anderson and the NYPD. Everything Watters was telling him fit perfectly into the story Lucy had gotten from

Supreme. It was mind-blowing. And Watters essentially had it figured out; he just didn't realize it.

A. J. took the check when it came, and he thanked the reverend for his help as they walked out together. "As always, it's been enlightening. And a pleasure."

"I'm always happy to eat Willie's cooking, but we hardly talked about me," Watters said with a big smile. "What about my story?"

"Reverend," A. J. said as they shook hands out on the sidewalk, "I'll get back to you on that."

Bishop had spent most of last night poring over all of the intel his investigators had gathered. He put it all into separate piles: one for the information related to Brock's raid and the Emergency Service Unit, another for the medical examiner's report on the dead terrorists and witness statements, a third for background info on the terrorists, and one more for everything they came up with on the Jafaari family. It was a lot to process.

Just before turning in, he highlighted a statement in one of the follow-up reports on the raid. One of the ESU officers on the entry team, the first guy in the stack, said he thought he heard a cell phone go off inside the apartment just moments before they hit the door. He realized only afterward that it had to be a cell, because the apartment didn't have a landline. The detail nagged at Bishop as he lay in bed and drifted off to sleep, and was still lodged in his brain when he woke up, sandwiched between his two king shepherds.

Wouldn't the ESU command cut off all cell phone use in the area before making their entry? Standard procedure dictated they shut down all communication and eliminate the possibility of anyone using a wireless signal to detonate an explosive. He got out of bed feeling strong and reenergized. This was going to be his kind of day. He had every intention of pissing someone off. And at the top of his list was ESU commander Anthony Pennetta.

He'd showered and gotten dressed quickly and was walking to his car when a black Crown Victoria pulled up to the curb next to him and the back door opened. "We need to talk," Chief Fitzgerald said, raising his hand to cut Bishop off before he could respond.

Bishop quickly looked up and down the street through his rimless Revo sunglasses. No one was around, and running was probably a bad idea. He had no doubt he could get away—Manhattan was a really easy place to quickly get lost in—but the last thing he wanted to do was look scared. He reluctantly got into the backseat.

The driver continued down the block and turned when they hit Lexington Avenue, heading downtown. "We've been friends a long time," Fitzgerald said. "I've helped you whenever you came to me and I've saved your ass more than a couple of times. Now listen to me closely, because I'm only gonna say this once. I'm asking you as a friend, and I'm telling you as a chief, back off of this case. Officially and unofficially."

"What case, Chief? My client's dead."

"Don't fuck with me, Bishop. I'm talking about the whole god-damned mess. The Muslim scumbag and his whore of a mother who killed him and his sister and then herself. And I'm talking about that drug-dealin' nigger Supreme, who, as far as I'm concerned, is a domestic terrorist."

When the chief used the word "nigger," Bishop looked at his driver, who was black. Whatever he was thinking, his face gave nothing away. The ugly language was nothing new—that was just the lazy, dismissive way cops often talked to one another when no one else was around. They rarely meant anything by it. They mocked everybody. But this was different. In all the years he'd known Fitzgerald, Bishop had never seen this kind of rage from him. This wasn't just cop talk. The chief's remarks were loaded with real hate.

"Chief, forgive me here for a moment, but why the fuck do you care if I'm handling Supreme's case?"

"You don't need to know why, Bishop, you just need to fucking do what I tell you," he said, the veins in his neck bulging.

"And if I don't?" Bishop asked with a little more edge than he'd meant.

"If you don't, you're on your own and it's gonna get really ugly. Where elephants tread, ants get trampled." With that, the driver pulled over to let Bishop out.

Bishop stood motionless on the street as the car sped away and realized that something had changed forever. He'd just been threatened by the NYPD's chief of detectives but also, more to the point, by his long-time friend.

16

LUCY WAS SMOOTHING her skirt and adjusting the clips in her hair while she sat in the living room of Kevin Anderson's house in the Hamptons. She'd been there for about ten minutes and was waiting for Yvette Anderson to return with coffee. The house was bigger than she'd expected, and the main floor had lots of open space and a striking glass wall that overlooked the pool and the backyard. *Not exactly the kind of place a cop could afford,* Lucy thought. The furniture was tasteful contemporary— sleek leather couches with very clean lines in muted earth tones—and there was a huge floor-to-ceiling fireplace with a glass mantel. There were also large cartons, the kind used for moving, scattered around the room in various stages of being filled.

Yvette had wanted to be packed and out of the house by now, but she couldn't start the process until she had clearance from the cops. And they were in no hurry. First the whole place was sealed off as a crime scene and cops from the Hampton Bays Police Department went over every inch of the house. Yvette had no idea what they were looking for or why they cared about any area other than the master bedroom, where her husband's body was found. Then came the NYPD investigators, along with several cops from the Internal Affairs Division. It was only after all of them were finished that Mrs. Anderson was allowed to go back into her home and start packing.

Lucy tried to look beyond the furniture for some clues about who these people were. She walked over to the fireplace, which was beautifully done, to take a look at the several dozen photographs on the mantel and the wall. It was a mix of family shots at life-cycle events like weddings and christenings, vacation photos of the Andersons skiing and on the beach with their two kids, and a smattering of the kids at school functions and participating in sports. *What a shame for the kids*, Lucy thought. It was bad enough to lose a parent, but she couldn't even imagine the difficulties involved when it happened under horrible circumstances like these.

There were also several photos of Kevin Anderson in uniform with what appeared to be his partners and a few ceremonial photos of Kevin getting promoted and receiving awards. She even saw one with Kevin surrounded by family, shaking hands with police commissioner Brock on the day he was promoted to lieutenant. The photograph was obviously taken by a family member or a friend, not a professional, so it wasn't framed that well. There were five people in the background; four of them appeared to be chiefs, judging by the scrambled eggs on their hats. But there was another guy dressed in a dark suit Lucy thought looked familiar, though she couldn't quite place him.

"That was a wonderful day," Yvette said when she walked into the living room carrying a tray with coffee and cups. "Everyone was so proud of Kevin when he became a lieutenant." She stopped for a moment, staring at Lucy. "I know what you're thinking," she continued, now with a sharp edge to her voice. "You and all the other outsiders who come here assuming you know something about my husband because of what happened. Well, you don't know anything."

Lucy relied on her training and remained quiet and impassive. She could hear A. J.'s voice in her head: "If she didn't want to talk to you, she wouldn't have let you into her house in the first place. Let her vent. Let her say what she has to say. It's not about you. It's about getting the story, so shut up and listen."

Yvette was a good-looking woman, with high cheekbones, lovely mocha skin, and almond-shaped eyes; Lucy guessed she was in her mid-to late thirties. She was well dressed, and her hair and nails had been done in a salon. Lucy thought she looked like the kind of woman who'd have a house like this—and nothing like the average cop wife.

Most cops come from a working-class background, and their average career path keeps them firmly rooted in that socioeconomic milieu. New York City requires at least two years of college to join the NYPD, and it's a given that most of the candidates go to community college to get the minimum number of credits they need to get into the academy. The starting salary is about $25,000, which gets bumped to $35,000 after the first year. It's a tough economic road given the cost of living in New York. Cops often live with their parents until well into their thirties or until they marry their neighborhood sweetheart, who has to work to help make ends meet. Lucy had seen some statistics somewhere that said if a New York City cop were to get married, have two kids, and have his wife stay at home, that family would have to go on some kind of government assistance just to get by.

The Andersons didn't fit the profile. Yvette had met Kevin when they were juniors at Tulane, where they were both prelaw. When he was quietly asked to leave in his senior year, she stayed on at school to graduate. She went to NYU law school and worked part-time while Kevin began his career as a cop.

"Look, I didn't mean to snap," Yvette said after a pause. "It's just been a very difficult time."

"I'm sure," Lucy said quietly.

"Anyway," she continued, seeming to regain some of her buoyancy, "the weather was perfect that day and Kevin was so happy. I thought he'd lost his passion for being a cop and it'd become just a job, something he had to do. You know, just work. But that day I realized I was wrong. No matter what he did, or what people think he did, he really loved being a cop. I've never told anybody this. When I got up that morning to get ready—the ceremony was downtown at eleven—Kevin wasn't in the house. I thought maybe he'd gone for a run. He got back by the time I'd showered and dressed. I was in the kitchen having a cup of coffee when he walked in. When I asked him where he'd been, he told me he'd gone to the cemetery. He went to his father's grave. Now," Yvette said, pouring coffee for herself and Lucy, "he hadn't been to the cemetery since his father's funeral seven years earlier. I didn't ask him why he went. I knew. He wanted to tell his father in person that he was becoming a lieutenant. That's how much it meant to him."

Yvette sat down on the couch and Lucy sat across from her. They quietly sipped their coffee for a few moments. Lucy desperately wanted to take out her notebook, but she was concerned it would disrupt the flow. So she began to take mental notes, hoping she'd be able to remember everything later.

"Look," Yvette said, breaking the silence, "I don't know what kind of story you came here to do, but God knows there's enough salacious misinformation and bullshit out there to fill a book. You know, crooked cop found with dead hooker. I've heard it all. I mean, my husband gets murdered and I don't even get the opportunity to grieve because I have to put up with all these intrusions, all this other crap. It's like he was such an awful person, who cares what happened to him. Well, let me tell you, *I care* and *my kids care.*"

"Why do you believe your husband was murdered?" Lucy asked.

"Are you gonna give me that nonsense that my husband was so despondent that he was being investigated by Internal Affairs that he beat a hooker to death and then killed himself with drugs?" Yvette snapped. "That's bullshit. And if you're here just to tell the same story that's been in the papers over and over again, you can leave now. I have no interest in talking to you."

"No, no," Lucy protested gently, trying to reassure her. "The last thing I want to do is to tell the same story again. I want to tell *your* story. That's why I came to see you."

"Excuse me a moment, please." Yvette walked out of the room. While she was gone, Lucy quickly took out her notebook and furiously began writing things down. When she heard footsteps, she closed the notebook but left it sitting on her lap. Yvette walked back into the room, wearing a light sweater now.

"Sorry, I felt a little chill. I went and raised the heat. Are you okay? You sure? You know, it's ironic, I never wanted this house," Yvette said, shaking her head and looking around. "I don't really like the people out here; it's all too flashy and way too busy during the season. I prefer western Connecticut, where it's a lot quieter and more laid-back. That's why I'm packing up and selling the house. Of course, I can't go into the bedroom anymore, either. I haven't been in that room since Kevin's body was found."

"Mrs. Anderson—" Lucy began.

Yvette interrupted her. "Listen, girl, if we're going to talk about very personal matters, you've got to stop calling me Mrs. Anderson."

"Sorry," Lucy said with a sheepish look on her face. "Yvette, for me to do this story, *your* story, I need to be able to ask you anything. I need to know I can bring up any subject, no matter how sensitive."

"What?" Yvette replied. "The house, the money, the hooker, the rumors about Kevin? We can talk about all of it, as long as you give me your word you'll keep an open mind. No preconceived notions about who Kevin was or what he did. If you're good with that, then let's do it. But not here. Let's go for a walk."

There was now a light mist falling. Yvette gave Lucy a nylon windbreaker and had an umbrella for the two of them as well. They walked down the gravel driveway and then on the long dirt road that led out to the main drag. They made a left to walk along the side of the road.

"I want to tell you up front that I loved my husband," she said as they walked. "He had lots of flaws, and I know he did some bad things, but I still loved him. It's certainly not my intent to run down his name. But I can't say anything at this point that could be worse than what's already been said. I want to set the record straight. Well, as much as I can anyway, and I want to nail those hypocritical bastards to the wall who did much worse things than he ever did and are now trying to make him the fall guy. So, tell me what you've heard."

Lucy gave Yvette a short version of the story Supreme had told her about Kevin Anderson forcing his way into Church Jackson's drug trade, and how he'd used information from Church and Supreme to build an amazing arrest record while eliminating the competition. Yvette didn't say much, but when Lucy finished, a broad smile finally crossed her face. "I'll bet you're expecting me to dispute all of this," she said, "and protest that my husband would never do something like that, the same way I did for Internal Affairs and all of the self-righteous investigators who questioned me. But not today. Today's your lucky day, Lucy. I don't have anything that'll help you prove Supreme's claims, but I can tell you that I buy it, that it makes sense based on what I know."

Lucy stopped walking and turned to face Yvette. "What are you saying?" she asked.

"I'm saying that I believe it. I never knew the specifics, but the way you laid it out just now sounds about right. You ever watch *The Sopranos*?" Yvette asked.

Lucy nodded.

"Well, I'm not Carmela Soprano. I didn't stay with him for the lifestyle, for the material things he provided. I have a career of my own. I didn't need Kevin's money. I stayed with him because I loved him, and because despite it all, he was a good father. You ever love someone who wasn't perfect? We're all human and we're all flawed."

"So you knew," Lucy said.

"Look, there's knowing and there's *knowing*. I obviously knew we weren't living this way on a cop's salary. But whenever I did ask, he assured me he wasn't doing anything to hurt anyone. I got the rationalization that people have their vices—drugs, gambling, prostitution, or whatever—and they're gonna find a way to indulge no matter what the cops do. So if he could play some role in somehow making things safer, and make a few dollars at the same time, why not? That's about as detailed as the discussion ever got. And whenever I expressed concerns about him, his safety, and the risk of getting in real trouble, he always assured me he was protected. He laughed it off. Look, he couldn't have done this by himself, without cooperation from someone higher up. And he always said he had an insurance policy. He knew too much for anything to happen."

Yvette stopped walking. She turned and looked at Lucy. Beads of water were dripping off the edge of the umbrella. "He was my husband and I loved him for who he was and despite who he was. Part of me viewed him as a real man—tough and strong and resolute, with the guts to go out and do what he believed he had to do to take care of his family regardless of the risk and the danger. I don't know what that makes me, but that's the truth. And now that I've given you what you came for, I'd really like you to do something for me."

"If I can," Lucy said. "What is it?"

"My husband did not kill himself and he certainly didn't beat that poor girl to death. He'd never lay a finger on a woman. Not a chance."

Lucy thought about what she said for a moment. "Well, what about the pressure from Internal Affairs?"

Yvette laughed. "Shit, Kevin knew from day one the kind of scrutiny he'd get. So now, after all this time, he suddenly gets jumpy about IAB? No way. It doesn't make sense. The only thing I can figure is somebody else is involved in this—probably a higher-up in the department, I don't know—but I'm guessing somebody suddenly decided he wanted one less partner. Or whatever. But I'm telling you the whole murder-suicide thing is bullshit. The autopsy found Viagra in his system. And there's not a chance he would've taken that."

Lucy started to say something, but Yvette cut her off. "Let me finish. There's no doubt Kevin liked to take a hard-on drug every once in a while for recreation, you know, to really have some fun and last a little longer. But he wouldn't have taken Viagra because it gave him severe migraines. Girl, you're not blushing, are you? You can't be that innocent. Anyway, he had a prescription and a full bottle of Cialis in his nightstand. He'd never take Viagra. So please tell me you'll look into this."

"I assure you A. J. and I will look at every possibility," Lucy said.

As they walked back to the house, Lucy knew she needed to ask about the prostitute. "Don'tcha think that in this context that's the least of it?" Yvette said, laughing. "Sorry. But if I don't laugh I'm afraid I'll cry. We've already established that Kevin was no saint. And he was a man with large appetites. But I know I had his heart."

As they were turning the corner to head down the dirt road back to the house, Yvette said, "Oh, there's one more thing. Look down the street. You see the Chrysler with the tinted windows? They're here all the time. My guess is they'll follow you now, too, or somebody just like them. Sorry, but you asked for it."

17

A. J. HATED GOING to Rikers Island. It was a dreadful, depressing place, and every time he went, he felt like it sucked the life out of him. No matter who he had to see or why he needed to see them, it always seemed to take all day. And by the time he finished, he'd be practically gasping for air. He wasn't claustrophobic, but the inside of a prison always made him feel like he couldn't get enough oxygen, like his breathing passages were closing up.

At least he'd been able to eliminate most of the bureaucratic hassles involved in getting access, thanks to connections he'd made among the wardens and senior corrections officers. One phone call usually got him whatever he needed.

The inmates simply referred to it as "the Rock," but to most New Yorkers, Rikers Island was some unspeakably wretched place they preferred not to think about. Ever. If you asked someone in the city where Rikers Island was located, the response was usually a quick, "Oh, it's in . . . it's near the . . . um . . . you can see it from the Triborough Bridge, right? Well," they'd invariably say after a few moments, "I know it's in the river somewhere."

It's actually a 415-acre island in the East River, just off the shoreline of Astoria, Queens, and only about a hundred feet from the end of Runway 22 at LaGuardia Airport. Though the swirling currents of the East River once guaranteed that no inmate could make it off the island alive, airport expansion and its proximity to the island had resulted in a few prisoner sightings at the end of the runway. (All, however, had been quickly apprehended.) Most people were surprised that Rikers had not one but ten separate jails and was the largest penal colony in the world, a motley collection of old-style penitentiaries, modern prefab jails, modular units where prisoners lived in dormitory-style housing, and trailers. Every day, in addition to about sixteen thousand inmates, there were seven thousand guards, three thousand nonuniformed staff, and as many as thirteen thousand vehicles on the island, which was accessible only by a two-lane bridge. It was big enough to qualify as a medium-size town, with its own power plant, a firehouse, a bakery capable of making enough bread every day for more than twenty-five thousand people, a marine unit, and even a makeshift courthouse where prisoners could file the more than two hundred writs a week they brought against the system.

A. J. stopped at the guard shack on the Queens side of the bridge, got his visiting press pass, and proceeded onto the island. Supreme was being held in the James A. Thomas Center, a maximum-security jail. Though A. J. figured Supreme could buy whatever he needed while inside— everything was for sale, including drugs, sex, and protection from the other inmates—he knew he'd still be out of his mind about being locked up. Justifiably so. He should've gotten bail, but somebody with juice obviously wanted him inside. Ironically, through all his years in the drug business, Supreme had never done a single day of jail time.

It was a little past noon when A. J. parked. He'd come straight from his breakfast with Reverend Watters, and he was still full. As always, he'd eaten one too many waffles and he felt a little sluggish now. The bright blue sky coupled with the warmth of the sun made him think for an instant about getting back in the car and bolting. He could go home and play some tennis, take one of the bikes out for a ride, throw a softball around with his daughter. *Anything* except this. Rikers was just about the last place he wanted to be, especially on a Saturday.

Only moments later, however, having decided to do the responsible thing, A. J. heard the large steel door slam shut behind him. He was immediately overwhelmed by the smell of disinfectant, an unfortunate fact of institutional life. The noise level was unbearable, with the inmates yelling; the guards screaming; electronic jail doors relentlessly beeping, squealing, and clanging; planes roaring overhead; and music blaring.

It took A. J. about ten minutes to clear security, which included a full-body pat-down, a walk through the metal detector, and the surrender of various personal items like his cell phone and press ID. Then he was told to sit and wait. He tried reading the newspaper, but he was too distracted. He watched small groups of desultory inmates grudgingly being herded along the dreary hallways. The guards were constantly at them to stay within the lines painted on the floor. They all seemed to have bad skin, bad teeth, tattooed arms and necks, and a simmering disdain for everybody and everything.

Before A. J. even realized it, he'd been sitting for half an hour. He got up and asked the guard at the entry station what was happening. "I'm not really sure" was his response. "Can you please try to find out?" A. J. asked. He tried to be as polite as possible, knowing that any attitude would only slow things down even further. It was another twenty minutes before he heard anything. "Hey," the guard called out to him, "I just got word that there's been some kind of emergency. That's the holdup. The inmate you're supposed to visit was taken to the emergency room."

A. J. jumped up out of the hard plastic chair he was sitting on. "What?" he said. "What happened?"

"I don't have any other information. They said you should sit tight, and somebody'll be out here shortly."

A. J. had already surrendered his phone, so he couldn't call anybody. He began to pace and run through various possibilities in his head, none of them good. What could've happened to Supreme that would require taking him to the emergency room? Maybe he got sick from the food. Maybe he . . . A. J. stopped himself. The speculation was useless. He continued pacing and getting more agitated by the minute. He was also starting to feel crummy. The stale air was making him nauseous.

Finally, after more than an hour and a half, Captain Reggie Stack-house, a normally affable corrections officer A. J. had met several times before, came out with a dour look on his face. "Hey, A. J.," Stackhouse said.

"What the hell's going on, Reggie?" A. J. asked.

"Supreme got shanked sometime during the night and they rushed him to the emergency room."

"And . . . ?" A. J. said.

"He didn't make it. He died about half an hour ago."

"Oh, fuck. Are you kidding me? Tell me you're joking, Reggie."

"Nothin' funny about it. The details aren't real clear. The official line is it was some kind of rap war revenge thing."

"That's complete bullshit," A. J. said, running his right hand through his hair. "How could that happen? A high-profile inmate like that and nobody's watching? Where the hell were the guards?"

"Look, I came in this morning and got the news. That's all I know. I don't know what else to tell you."

"This is just . . . *fuck*. I can't believe it. Did anybody see what happened? I'm sure the guards aren't talking, but what about the inmates? Who controls the cell block where he was taken out?"

"Supreme got knifed out in 6A. Guy from the Latin Kings they call Chooch runs that house."

"Look, Reg, I've been sitting here for nearly two hours with my thumb up my ass. You gotta do something to help me out here. How 'bout letting me talk to Chooch? Can you take me to see him?"

"I don't know, A. J. The official clampdown on this is really tight. The brass don't want nobody talking."

"C'mon, Reggie, for me man, I'll owe you one."

"You owe me more than one already, brother. Listen, I'll take you over, but it's between us, right? Nothin' in print, A. J. It could be my job."

"No worries, man. I got you covered."

"Where's Chooch at? *Heeeey*, listen up," the captain yelled. "I'm lookin' for Chooch. Yo, brother, *bru-tha*. Yeah, you. Where he at, I said? In the back? Go tell 'im to get his bony ass out here. Tell 'im someone's here to make him famous."

A. J. and Stackhouse were in cell block 6A. There were three tiers of cells stacked on top of one another with a narrow catwalk at each level. The place had been built in the late thirties and it looked like the big house from an old James Cagney movie. Few of the inmates bothered to even look up. Blank-faced, empty-eyed, they wandered aimlessly around the cramped space outside the cells, moving so slowly they looked like they were underwater.

"Hey, Captain, what's happening? You wanna see me?" A shirtless Hispanic inmate with a gold stud through his left nostril, a dark sculpted beard that traced the outline of his jaw, and CHRISTINA IS MINE tattooed on his left bicep ambled over.

"Chooch," the captain said happily, flashing a luminous, toothy smile. "How you be living, dude?"

"You know, Captain, jail is jail."

"C'mon, Chooch, tell my friend A. J. here how you really living." The captain was in Chooch's face now, still smiling but leaning in to make his point.

"Hey, man, this is the danger zone, for real, know what I'm sayin'? We killin' each other up in here for the phone, the TV . . . anything. You feel me? You got to stay to yourself. You show you're scared, you got real problems. Only the strong survive, bro, only the strong."

"Stop frontin', Chooch. You jailin' too long for that. I asked you how *you're* living, okay? There ain't gonna be no payback. Just keep it real, that's all. Maybe we should go in the back and take a look inside your cell. Take a look at that fuckin' WalMart you got runnin' back up in there. Right? You the Sam fuckin' Walton of Riker's Island, a budding entrepreneur."

"C'mon, Captain. What you be talkin' all that shit for? I ain't got no—"

"Last time I'm gonna ask, Chooch. I told you, keep it real. Okay? Now, tell my friend A. J. here how you living."

"Okay man, I hear you. Truth is, yo, I be livin' lovely. You feel me?"

Though Chooch was practically running a full-service convenience store out of his cell—inmates and guards could buy anything from junk food, cigarettes, and batteries to sex and drugs—his commitment to commerce didn't extend to Supreme's killing. He either had nothing to trade or he had no interest in giving anything up. After about fifteen minutes of conversation, all they got was that a Jamaican inmate had been grabbed for the murder.

"Let's put it this way," Chooch said as they continued to prod him. "You might as well cut my fuckin' tongue out, 'cause I ain't sayin' shit about no stabbing."

"What's it take to be in charge here?" A. J. asked.

"It doesn't matter *where* you come from," Chooch replied. "It only matters *how* you come. Real niggas recognize real niggas. Simple as that." Then he curled his right hand into a fist and pounded his chest. "You need it right here. You feel me? You need heart."

"With all that heart, you're still afraid to tell me what happened last night," A. J. said, challenging him.

"You chickenshit yuppie cocksucker," Chooch snarled, rage washing over his angular face. "Don't come talk shit to me in my house unless you wanna bleed motherfucker. What happened last night had nothin' to do with anything in here, got it? Now get out my face, yo, before I lose it."

On the way out, Stackhouse told A. J. he thought he'd taken a stupid risk talking to Chooch like that. "You know what Chooch meant by 'heart'?" he asked A. J.

"When he says you got to have heart, he means you have to be able to stick a shank in somebody's eye and go on about your business. He means you got to be able to take a razor and slash somebody's face from his ear down to his mouth, giving him a scar he'll have for the rest of his life, a scar he'll see every fuckin' time he looks in the mirror . . . and never give it a minute's thought. When he says you need heart, that's what he means. Whatever it takes, whatever's necessary, no matter the consequences."

A. J. desperately wanted to talk to the Jamaican before leaving. When they reached the main area by the entrance to the building, the security station where A. J. had to leave his cell phone, his car keys, and his ID, he looked at Stackhouse. Before he said anything, Stackhouse knew what he wanted. "You gonna get me a nice cushy job at your magazine so I can still support my family when I get fired from corrections? You know, you used to be my favorite reporter. Actually, you're the only reporter I know."

"You just made my day. I was feeling awful about having to spend time here in Dante's seventh circle of hell, Reg, but you've made it all worthwhile. So how 'bout it? Can I talk to the Jamaican?"

"*Shee-it*, man. All right, let me get a name, and then I'll give you five minutes. No more. We gotta go in and out fast."

"You're the best, Reggie."

The Jamaican was being held in another part of the building, an area called the Central Punitive Segregation Unit, or, as it was known in the jails, the Bing. On an island filled with thousands of murderers, rapists, child molesters, armed robbers, drug dealers, muggers, and arsonists, the city's toughest, meanest, least reconstructible miscreants are held in several maximum-maximum-security cell blocks. This was supposed to be real hard time—prisoners here were locked in for more than twenty-three hours a day and were not allowed to smoke, watch TV, have radios, or put pictures on the walls of their cells. And though it was designed as a thirty-to-ninety-day punishment unit, the reality was there were guys who racked up more than a thousand days of this kind of confinement. This was where the Jamaican prisoner, Worrell Brown, was being held.

When A. J. and Captain Stackhouse got to the Bing, there was, as usual, some kind of incident in progress. Anguished cries echoed off the mustard-colored tile walls, and they were, at first, bone-chilling. "*There are dead bodies in the yard . . . there are dead bodies in the yard*," a hollow-sounding voice screamed over and over. No one paid any attention because four cells over, guards were just finishing putting out a fire.

An inmate had taken some toilet paper and held it to the naked lightbulb in his cell until it caught. Then he burned his mattress, the sheets, and the pillowcases.

"Hey, Captain, welcome to paradise," one of the guards said to Stackhouse.

"What's up with the fire?"

"The guy's pissed 'cause he's got a court date tomorrow and he says he didn't get a haircut. Fuck his ass, man. Like a new do's gonna change his miserable life. What brings you up in here?"

"You got the Jamaican brought in last night for shanking another inmate?"

"The guy who cut the big celebrity, right? He's in number fourteen, but he hasn't said a word since he got here. Strong, silent type."

"Thanks."

"There are dead bodies in the yard. There are dead bodies in the yard."

A. J. watched as an officer finally made his way down the cell block toward the crazy screamer. As he passed one cell, a food tray came flying out through the slot in the door. It didn't miss him by much, and when it crashed against the wall, milk and juice and unidentifiable globs of food splattered everywhere. "Go ahead and write the ticket, man," the disoriented-looking inmate screamed when a guard tried talking to him. "I don't give a fuck about no infraction. You disrespected me."

While he continued to rant, another inmate was yelling, "Yo, I say yo, can I get some attention in here?" A third inmate, who had his arms hanging out his cell door so he could follow A. J. and Stackhouse in the reflection on the glass face of his watch, was screaming, "I wanna see that reporter. Make sure you bring that reporter down here, know what I'm sayin'? I got some stories to tell his ass, yo. Bring that motherfucker here *now*."

A. J. gave the captain a disgusted look. "Guess he's spotted your notebook. Hey, we came up here for you, remember?" Stackhouse said. "So don't gimme any grief. Let's just see your guy and get the fuck out of here."

"Good idea," A. J. said.

The Jamaican kid was a skinny twenty-three-year-old with a big sixties-style Afro and a scar that started at the corner of his mouth and ran halfway across his face. He'd already done over a hundred days of Bing time and had just been put back in the general population when the incident with Supreme took place. "Hey, Worrell," Stackhouse said to the Jamaican, who was lying down. "Get your ass up and come over here, someone wants to talk to you."

"I don't feel like entertaining guests right now, fuck face."

"Then you're gonna be one unhappy camper over the next several weeks, I promise you that."

Worrell didn't say anything and didn't move. Then, after a few minutes, he slowly began to lift himself off the bunk and shuffled over to the cell door. A. J. identified himself and then began asking questions about Supreme and the previous night. But he was coming up empty. The Jamaican claimed he didn't know anything.

"How 'bout you cut the crap and tell the man what he wants to know and then we'll be out your face," Stackhouse said.

"Look," he said with his eyes fixed on Stackhouse. "You work in here, so I know you can't be too bright. For your dumb-ass benefit, I'll say it again. I don't know anything, okay? Now," he said, turning to A. J., "white meat here is a different—" Worrell suddenly lunged at A. J. through the bars. A. J. was caught completely off guard. He jumped backward, stumbling a little, but managed not to trip over his own feet and go down. He dropped his notebook and pen. His heart was racing.

"Surprised you, didn't I?" Worrell chuckled.

"Yes you did," A. J. said, a little embarrassed.

"I'm telling you the truth," the inmate said, more seriously now. "I was asleep last night when two guards came and dragged me out of bed and up here. I didn't cut nobody. I have no reason to lie. Look at my record. I'm never getting the fuck out. And the guy was some kind of fuckin' big shot, right mon? A celebrity. You don't think I'd want props for that? C'mon. But I'm telling you it wasn't me."

Back out front, near the entrance to the building, A. J. collected his belongings that had been left with the guards. "I think the guy was telling the truth," he said. "And Chooch claimed the attack had nothing to do with anything in here. Something's clearly not right about this."

"I agree," Stackhouse said. "Any of it make sense to you?"

"Part of it. Maybe. I don't know. Listen, thanks for all the help today."

"I'd say 'anytime,' but I'm afraid you'll take me up on it," the captain said with a smile.

"Hey, no worries, Reg. Try and make me come back here. I'm done with this place for a while."

"Yeah, till the next time."

A. J. knew he had to call Victoria, Bishop, and Lucy. But when he got outside, he just stood there for a while, breathing deeply and looking at the sky.

18

BISHOP WAS PISSED, but he was also a little disoriented. He'd been threatened—seriously, angrily, menacingly threatened—by someone he'd trusted and relied on for years. Fitzgerald had been Bishop's mentor when he was a young cop, and when he got in serious trouble on the job, the chief saved his disability pension and enabled him to resign from the force with dignity. But the most hurtful thing of all for Bishop was that one of his best friends had chosen Brock over him. "Commissioners come and go," Fitzgerald had always said, "but friendship is forever." Apparently not anymore.

He walked for a couple of blocks to clear his head and make a few phone calls. Then he grabbed a cab back to his apartment to get his car. Saturday traffic was light, so it only took him about twenty-five minutes to get to the Rodman's Neck firing range in the Bronx, where he'd learned Anthony Pennetta would be training with one of his ESU teams. He was told they'd be doing search-and-rescue drills at the Tactics House, a mock three-story apartment building with windows, fire escapes, and a full complement of realistic details. The inside of the building could be con-figured in a variety of ways, enabling ESU to train for different scenarios.

When Bishop pulled into the parking lot, it looked as if they were taking a break. Pennetta and his team were seated at a table outside of the Tactics House loading the magazines of their MP5s and tactical shot-guns. Bishop saw Pennetta spot him, say something to his men, and then head in Bishop's direction. Pennetta was a big man, but he moved with the ease and grace of an athlete. *Motherfucker, here we go again*, Bishop thought.

As Pennetta made his way over, Bishop checked out the equipment the ESU team was using, from the commando-style holsters to the high-tech Kevlar vests. Two of the men were carrying MP5s, another had a nine-millimeter, and one had a long gun, a Colt .223 M4, essentially a short M16. His inventory was interrupted when Pennetta got right in his face. He didn't seem particularly angry, but Bishop figured that was just his style—controlled fury; never let 'em see your emotions; focus on the challenge, not your opponent; all that Zen crap.

"What the fuck did I tell you the last time you just popped in on me?" Pennetta said. "Didn't I tell you I had no interest in talking to you? Are you stupid? No wonder you're a fucking rent-a-cop. I have no inten-tion of discussing department business or anything else with you, got it?" he sneered. "Go catch some cheating husband and stay out of shit that's way over your head."

"C'mon, gimme a break, will ya," Bishop said in a voice that almost sounded like he was pleading. He wasn't above playing the loser private investigator if it got him what he needed. "I'm just trying to make a liv-ing here. All I need are a few answers, man. That's all and then I'm outta here."

Bishop and Pennetta were only about thirty yards from the ESU cops, who were tending to their weapons and trying not to look like they were watching the exchange. But it wasn't working. Instead they were like players on a football team watching their captain argue with some guy from a rival high school. But when Pennetta glanced over his shoulder he noticed one of his guys making no attempt to fake it—he was staring at them intently while talking on a cell phone.

When Pennetta turned back to Bishop, the private investiga-tor thought for a moment that he saw a change in the commander's expression. He thought Pennetta suddenly looked angrier. But he didn't waste time dwelling on it. He knew the clock was ticking and Pennetta might blow up at any moment, so he just forged ahead. "Did you read all of the incident reports after the raid in Brooklyn?"

"Who the fuck do you think wrote them up?" Pennetta asked. "What's your point, Bishop? I don't have time to play here."

"The point is why would someone on your entry team hear a fucking telephone go off just before they're about to hit an apartment full of ter- rorists?" Bishop knew as soon as he got the question out that he'd struck a nerve. "Didn't you kill all cell phone activity in the area before going in, to prevent anyone from tipping off the targets?"

"I don't know what the fuck you're talking about, but you're finished here," Pennetta barked, no longer trying to sound measured.

Never satisfied, of course, until he poked the bear hard enough to make him charge, Bishop pointed his stick at Pennetta one more time. "What are you covering up?"

Pennetta pivoted his hips slightly. Bishop read the body language and he knew a left hook was coming. But Pennetta moved surprisingly fast for a man his size, especially with the amount of tactical gear he had on, and he was still able to land a glancing blow to the right side of Bishop's face. Bishop's hands were already up to cover his head when Pennetta fol- lowed up with a right cross, but the force of the blow knocked him down on one knee. Bishop knew he was in trouble. He was in the right position to deliver a quick body shot to Pennetta's midsection, but that was useless since he had his heavy vest on. He'd probably just break his hand. While Bishop was capable of benching over three hundred pounds, Pennetta was his equal and then some. He was also seven inches taller and forty pounds heavier. And when two alpha dogs are in the pit fighting, the bigger dog almost always beats the smaller dog.

As Bishop started to get up, Pennetta landed another right, this time flush on the chin and with all his weight behind it. Bishop was out cold by the time he hit the ground. The entire altercation had taken less than forty-five seconds.

When Bishop started to come to, he slowly opened his eyes and blinked half a dozen times to try to get rid of the blurriness. His face felt like it had been stepped on by a horse. He did a quick audit of the damage. Happily, he seemed to have all his teeth, his jaw didn't feel broken, and there were no visible signs of blood. He shook his head side to side a couple of times. He was still a little dizzy, but he was starting to get his bearings. Almost fully lucid again, he realized he was sitting in the passenger seat of his car in a parking lot. But it wasn't the parking lot at Rodman's Neck. This lot was at least ten times the size of the one at the range. Then it clicked. He was in the middle of the parking lot at Orchard Beach, about a five-minute drive from the range. Someone had obviously dropped him off there. He was just about to slide over to the driver's side when his cell phone rang.

He didn't recognize the number but answered anyway.

"It's Zito" he heard the voice say.

"You really didn't have to call," Bishop said, trying to act like he wasn't hurting. "Flowers would've been sufficient."

"Unbelievable. Always the smart mouth. Meet me at my plane on Long Island. The hangar where you first came out to see me. We'll discuss everything then."

"Now you wanna talk to me?" Bishop said.

"Look, just be there in three hours." The telephone went dead.

Bishop stared at the phone for a couple of minutes and rubbed his aching chin. "Musta been my charming personality that won him over," he said to himself. "Wait till he really gets to know me."

19

LUCY HAD TRIED not to seem concerned in front of Yvette Anderson. A. J. always told her not to reveal anything when she was doing an interview. It was more effective to be stoic, he'd say, not to show much emotion to the person she was interviewing. It was okay to appear friendly, sympathetic, and understanding; that was all part of the seduction, part of making someone comfortable and eager to talk. But let the emotions come from them.

As Lucy said good-bye to Yvette and drove down the driveway and out the dirt road, though, she was a little rattled, and her anxiety went up another couple of notches once she got out on the main road and thought she saw the sedan Yvette had pointed out at the house following her several car lengths behind. She called A. J., hoping for advice but also just wanting to hear the reassuring sound of his voice. Unfortunately, the call went straight to voice mail.

Then she called Bishop . . . no luck there either. She tapped her fingers nervously on the steering wheel and looked in the rearview mirror. She was sure the car was still there. *Why would anyone follow me?* she wondered. Was it her connection to Supreme? The shooting at Roxx? Her trip to the Anderson house? As she ticked off the list in her head, she almost started to laugh. She realized it could be any of them, or all of them. She knew at that moment, in a way she hadn't before, not even when she was arrested, that this was real. When she used to fantasize about being a reporter in New York City, this was what she pictured—drama, intrigue, dealing in sensitive information, upsetting people in power, and, yes, even a little danger. It made Lucy think of her father, who often used the old cliché "Be careful what you wish for."

She looked at the speedometer—she was doing eighty. Lucy quickly slowed down and checked the mirror again. The car that had been tailing her was gone. *That's weird*, she thought. Maybe she'd been mistaken; maybe there was never a car there in the first place. Could she have imagined it? *Relax*, Lucy told herself. *Breathe slowly and evenly, slowly and evenly.*

It was late in the day and she was tired and hungry. A wave of exhaustion washed over her. Her limbs felt heavy and weak. Maybe the past few days had taken more of a toll than she'd realized. The last thing she wanted to do was deal with the long drive back to the city. She opened her window to get some air, hoping that would help her snap out of it. She decided to stop, get a bite to eat, and call one of her friends, who was dating a big-shot divorce lawyer with a house on Shelter Island. She'd stayed there once before, and since it was the off-season, she figured the house was probably empty and she could stay there overnight, then head back into the city in the morning.

"Hey, Sue," Lucy said when her friend answered. "What's up, girl?"

"Lucy, I'm good. How're you? Everything okay?"

"Good, good. Listen, I need a favor. I'm out in the Hamptons working on a story. It's getting kinda late, I'm tired, and rather than drive back to town, I was hoping maybe I could crash at your friend's house on Shelter Island."

"Absolutely. You sure everything's okay? You sound a little, I don't know, stressed or something."

"No, no, I'm fine, just tired and focused on this story I'm working on. We'll catch up in the next couple of days when things settle down a little."

"Okay. Lemme give you the security code. It's the same for the gate and the front door. Type 'Atticus Finch' on the keypad, all lowercase."

"Seriously?"

"Don't even ask. There's a key under the flowerpot next to the front door. Fridge is probably empty, but the liquor cabinet'll be stocked."

"You're the best. Speak to you in a couple of days. Love you."

"Hey, love you too."

Lucy pulled into a diner in Westhampton, parked the car, and dragged her weary body inside. She ordered a cup of coffee, grilled chicken, and a Greek salad.

After dinner and two more cups of coffee, she was happy to get back in the car, especially when she looked around and didn't see anyone following her. As she was driving to Sag Harbor to catch the ferry to Shelter Island, Lucy kept the window down a little for air, clicked Gary Clark Jr. on her iPod to up the energy level, cranked the volume, and bounced in her seat to the stunning guitar riffs.

She almost didn't hear the phone ring. It was Bishop. He apologized for not being reachable earlier, explaining that he was on the phone with his investigators, who'd found out some very interesting stuff that he would fill her in on later. Lucy was surprised at how happy she was to hear from Bishop. She gave him the highlights from her time with Yvette Anderson and then mentioned that she was on her way to the Shelter Island ferry. "My friend's dating this lawyer who's got a house there," she said. "The lawyer's kind of a dick, an arrogant gasbag, but he won't be there and the house is amazing."

Bishop started getting a little pumped. He thought this was leading to an invitation. He didn't know Lucy that well, but he did know it was out of character for her to get excited about material things—especially a house that was probably an ostentatious, overdone monument to the lawyer's money and ego. He could also tell, from the sound of her voice when she told him her suspicions about being followed, that she was worried. Sure enough, she made him an offer.

"Wanna come out and keep me company?" she asked in an irresistibly girlish voice. "I could use somebody with a big club to protect me."

"Well, when you put it that way . . ." Bishop was already headed in that direction to meet Pennetta at the airport, but even if he hadn't been, there was no way he'd have turned down an offer like this. "I'm not sure what time I'll get there," he said, "I gotta make a stop first. But, yeah, I'll come out and keep you company. Text me the address so I can put it in the GPS."

"Just remember," Lucy said, "the ferry stops running at midnight. And I promise I'll make up a room for you all nice and cozy. See you later."

Bishop took that as shorthand for "Sorry, you're not getting laid tonight." He hung up the phone and laughed.

As Lucy said good-bye, she was already on the ferry sitting in her car. The boat was fairly small and held, at most, fifteen cars. It was early evening, and given that it was the off-season, the ferry was only about half full. She did a quick scan, looking for the dark-colored sedan she thought had been following her earlier. No sign of it.

If she'd had a more experienced, trained eye, like that of Bishop or A. J., she would have profiled all seven cars on the ferry. She would have seen the old sea salt in the pickup full of lobster pots; the mom in the Subaru station wagon with her three children; what appeared to be a young college student in a beat-up Toyota. And she would've seen two guys wearing jeans and heavy winter coats in a late-model Jeep Cherokee. They were the second surveillance team.

Bishop got to the Long Island airport early and circled the hangar where Pennetta kept his plane to make sure the meeting wasn't some kind of setup, then parked his car facing the gate so he could see everyone going in and out. Bishop's jaw still hurt and he had a dull headache. But there was work to do. He pulled out a legal pad to make some notes. He put down "Andrea Jafaari" and then drew a box around her name. From there, he drew a line that ended at a question mark and another box. In the box he wrote, *Why kill son, daughter, and self? Honest. Strong willed. Hardworking. Good mother.* He drew another line leading to another box, this one with Ayad's name. *Motivation to become a radical? How did he die? What drug was used?* Bishop flipped the page over and put Kevin Anderson's name in a box. In the connecting box with the question mark he put, *Corrupt cop. Accomplices? Murder-suicide? Get tox report, compare to tox report from Jafaaris.* He flipped the page again and wrote down, *Raid in Brooklyn. Have Victoria subpoena Internal Affairs incident report as well as additional reports or files on any of the team members involved in the raid.*

Bishop knew he was all over the place. His jaw was throbbing, and trying to make sense of the information made his headache worse. Any one of these investigations presented a mountain of questions and obstacles, some of which seemed almost insurmountable. But he was determined to figure it out, to find the connective tissue he knew in his gut was there. A. J. was right; these events were not random.

He was staring blankly at his boxes and question marks when Pennetta pulled up in his red Silverado. He flashed his high beams at Bishop and then pointed toward the hangar. Bishop followed him in and they parked.

Pennetta was out of uniform. He was wearing jeans, an L.L.Bean-style twill shirt, and work boots. He was staring at Bishop's slightly swollen, discolored jaw when he walked over. "You look disappointed you didn't do more damage," Bishop said with a bit of attitude.

"I don't blame you for being pissed," Pennetta told him. "I'm sorry I had to do that, but there's a leak in my unit. I had to put on a little show to make it clear that I want no part of you. I'm not sure who the information's going to, but I have my suspicions. This goes way beyond bullshit gossip and interdepartmental politics. Cops are being put in danger. *My cops.*"

"Any idea why?" Bishop asked.

"Not yet. But before I share anything else with you," Pennetta said, folding his arms across his chest and leaning against his truck, "I need some disclosure. Why're you doing this, Bishop? From what I hear, you're just a fucking mercenary. The only thing you care about's yourself. And even though you were on the job, you could give a fuck about your fellow officers."

"I'm not gonna lie to you," Bishop said, trying to look sincere, "you're right. You pretty much got me pegged. My sympathetic, feel-bad-for-the-other-guy, help-the-underdog days are long fucking gone. And so are my days of bleeding NYPD blue. If it weren't for Chief Fitzgerald, the department would've kicked me to the curb without a pension. And now even he's turned on me. It's a cold and ugly world out there, and we're in it all alone." Bishop rubbed his sore jaw with his right hand.

"When I was a rookie," he continued, "my first partner used to tell me, 'You want a loyal friend, get a fuckin' puppy, 'cause you ain't gonna be able to count on anyone else.' He always upset me when he said that. But I just thought, *Okay, he's a disillusioned, cynical old crank.* Turns out he was right. So to answer your question, yeah, I'm in it for the buck. And if you're gonna tell me you believe in all the bullshit about how the NYPD is a family, how the department really cares, then maybe you're not as sharp as I thought you were. It's all about ambition and politics and collars for dollars. The mayor wants to get reelected, the police commissioner wants to keep his job, the brass wanna get promoted. And the bad guys get locked up because it serves those ends. But the normal balance, fucked up as it is, has been thrown off. I don't know exactly what's going on, but something's up." He thought he saw Pennetta's face soften just a little.

"Bad shit happens, I get it," Bishop said, warming to his task. "Decent people screw up. Bad people hurt decent people and the good guys rarely win. There is no reward for doing the right thing. Not in this life. God or some fucking cosmic force wreaks havoc indiscriminately and everyone suffers. It's all as random as lottery numbers. I accept that. So I've adapted. I've minimized my expectations. I expect nothing from people so I'm rarely disappointed. It's all about small victories and learning to pick your spots. I ignore the endless open pit of human suffering. I find happiness where I can. A great pair of tits, solving a difficult case.

"But," he said, holding up one finger as if asking Pennetta to wait another moment before drawing any conclusions, "all of this enables me to maintain a certain balance in my world. A kind of homegrown equilibrium. But every once in a while, some prick shows up and does something that throws everything out of balance. A prick like Brock, who marches around doing whatever the fuck he wants, breaking all the rules, pissing on everybody beneath him, just because he can. When that kind of thing happens, I will put my beliefs aside, go off the clock, and do what I have to do."

Pennetta wasn't quite sure what to think, but he felt Bishop was trying to be honest. And he really didn't have much choice. He couldn't even trust anyone in his own department, so he decided to risk talking to Bishop.

He began with the Brooklyn raid. He explained how the whole thing was wrong, how the operation was micromanaged by Brock from the beginning, and none of the standard regulations or procedures were followed. ESU was only notified the actual day of the raid that they'd be hitting an apartment full of suspected terrorists that night. Brock kept the whole thing under wraps, not telling anyone anything. They had strict orders not to inform the Joint Terrorism Task Force, the NYPD's Intelligence Division, or the deputy commissioner in charge of terrorism operations. No one knew the source of the tip or how long the suspects had been under surveillance. Every order, every piece of the planning, and every decision, no matter how minor, had gone through Brock. Worst of all, perhaps, was the commissioner's demand to be part of the entry team. Pennetta said that when he made the mistake of venting to his men, he heard from Brock less than half an hour later. The commissioner pulled him to the side to address his specific concerns, solidifying the fact that one of his own men was whispering in Brock's ear. There had been additional evidence of the leak since the raid.

He told Bishop that he too had noticed when reviewing the reports that one of his men on the stairs heard a telephone ring possibly as much as two minutes before they hit the door. He went to the commanding officer in charge of logistics. "Weren't all cell repeaters in that area shut off?" he demanded. "Shouldn't everyone within a four-block radius, not just the terrorists, have been effectively shut down?" Pennetta said the CO got very nervous and said, "Yes, everything was shut down and no telephone should have been working."

When Pennetta went to the property clerk's office to go through Ayad Jafaari's belongings, there was no cell phone with his things, nor was there one listed in the inventory of his possessions. But one of his guys told him the kid definitely had a phone in the apartment. It was in his pocket when they checked him after the shooting stopped to see if he was still breathing. Pennetta did a little digging, pulled the phone records, and discovered that Jafaari did receive a call just about five minutes before ESU boomed the apartment door. "Someone tipped those motherfuckers off," Pennetta told Bishop angrily, "right before we breached. Someone put my guys in danger."

Bishop's adrenaline had begun to pump while he listened to Pennetta. This was the commander of the NYPD's Emergency Service Unit, the man in charge of the department's most elite cops, spilling about serious violations of procedure, leaks, screwups putting cops at risk, and possible corruption, all related to the biggest, most celebrated bust in years.

"Commander," Bishop told him, clearly unable to contain his excitement, "we need to get a cup of coffee and talk."

20

THE RIDE TO Shelter Island on the South Ferry was only about five minutes. Once there, Lucy quickly found her way to Route 114 and she was at the house in about fifteen minutes. At the front gate, she punched in the security code and drove down what seemed like several hundred yards of gravel driveway that ended at the huge house. It was fairly secluded by the significant setback from the road, tall hedgerows on two sides, and a backyard that literally spilled into the ocean. Lucy found the key under the flowerpot and let herself in, entering the alarm code as she shut the door behind her.

She stepped out of the foyer and into the soaring two-story living room, where the cold-looking furniture and the antiseptic modern art made the already gymnasium-like room seem even more cavernous. Lucy was no authority, but she knew a little about painting, and this stuff was mostly dreadful—expensive, but dreadful. The living room had a bunch of black, European-looking leather sofas, chairs, and ottomans, and an enormous flat-screen TV. She was ready to settle in on one of the black leather sofas, open a bottle of wine, and maybe watch a movie while she waited for Bishop to show. But first she wanted to shower. It had been a long day. She figured she'd borrow a pair of sweats—her friend said to take whatever she needed from the closet—to get comfortable. She also really wanted to talk to A. J.

• • •

Fitzgerald felt his phone start to vibrate.

"Whaddaya got?" he asked, recognizing the number immediately.

"We followed her to some giant fucking house on Shelter Island," one of Fitzgerald's detectives said. "You should see this place, Chief. Unbelievable. Must belong to some guy who's hosing her. Anyway, I'm guessing she's in for the night at this point. We've been sitting on the house for, like, an hour. We're about twenty-five yards or so from the main gate, and Sherlock here is bitching he's hungry and tired," he said, jabbing a finger at his partner, who was sitting next to him in the Jeep Cherokee.

"Jeez, act like a professional," Fitzgerald said. "Okay, call it night. I'll talk to you in the morning. Good work."

Fitzgerald called Commissioner Brock. "That's a coincidence," the commissioner said. "I was just about to call you. Listen, Chief, bring in your men. At least for tonight. I don't wanna risk having them spotted. That would be a bad thing."

The chief didn't tell Brock that his guys were already on their way home. And Brock didn't tell the chief the real reason he wanted Fitzgerald's men gone. He picked up the phone and called Oz. "You have the location, right? Good, let's get this taken care of tonight."

After having a cup of coffee with Pennetta at a diner near the airport, Bishop knew he was at least headed down the right road. He wasn't quite sure where it was taking him, but he figured that would come in time. There were still too many unanswered questions. But even with the questions, it was possible to begin putting some of the pieces of the puzzle together. At least it would've been if Bishop had been able to put aside his personal feelings and his long-standing loyalties. He essentially refused to recognize what was taking shape right in front of his eyes. Despite all of his tough talk about the NYPD and its failings, he was still connected to the police department in a deep and meaningful way. In his heart he was still a cop and probably always would be. So he simply couldn't admit the link between Kevin Anderson, Supreme, the Brooklyn raid, and the deaths of the Jafaari family. At least not yet. Because it looked like all roads were leading to the police department—and specifically to Brock and Fitzgerald.

Bishop jumped back on the LIE and took it to the last exit heading toward Greenport. It was starting to get late. He knew he was getting old since he was looking forward to a good night's sleep rather than taking a shot at coaxing Lucy into the sack. When would he ever have a better opportunity? A Saturday night, just the two of them all alone in a huge house on Shelter Island? She was feeling a little vulnerable . . . *Okay*, he thought, *I better get a second wind here*. He called Teresa, the live-in maid at his house in the city, and asked her to make sure she fed and walked Gus and Woody. It was, as always, a negotiation. He had to promise to take her to Target and Walmart on Long Island over the next weekend.

As A. J. walked back to his car from the jail at Rikers, he felt like he wanted to grab somebody by the throat. He was furious about Supreme's murder. He didn't believe it was the result of a screwup. The only way a high-profile inmate like Supreme could've been shanked was if somebody in a position of authority wanted it to happen.

A. J. got in the car and turned on his phone. Though it had only been a matter of hours since he'd had brunch with Reverend Watters in Harlem, it felt like a different day. He had fifteen voice mails and too many texts and e-mails to bother counting. They'd all have to wait. He called Nikki to make sure everything was okay. He told her not to wait up and to kiss the kids good night for him since he'd probably be late. Then he tried Lucy and Bishop. He didn't reach either one of them. He wanted to tell Lucy about Supreme before she heard it on the news, and he wanted to find out how she did with Anderson's wife.

A. J. knew what he had to do. He needed a face-to-face with Brock. Maybe he could push a few buttons and get the commissioner to inadvertently give something up. Experience had taught him over the years that the more arrogant the subject, the easier they were to manipulate. He decided to head into the city. A call to the commissioner's office gave him nothing. Brock wasn't in. Why would he be on a Saturday night?

And the cop who answered the phone didn't give anything up. But A. J. was pretty sure he could find the commissioner.

First, though, he drove to his office in midtown. He felt really dirty after Rikers and wanted to wash up and put on a fresh shirt. No one was in, of course, and he left his editor a handwritten note. It seemed a little more personal than sending her another e-mail. He hadn't seen her in more than a week, which was not all that unusual. He rarely spent much time in the office, particularly when he was in the thick of a story. She knew he was working on Brock, but she had no idea the direction the reporting had taken. He'd fill her in when he could do it in person.

He called a couple of the photo agencies that assigned photographers to stake out celebrities at restaurants, clubs, hotels, theaters, or anywhere else they might turn up. Normally, New York's police commissioner wouldn't be on the paparazzi's "it" list of hot targets, but since the Brooklyn raid, Brock, America's hero, was as marketable as Brad and Angelina. Sure enough, they all had Brock at the Broken Wing, a hole-in-the-wall restaurant on West Twenty-Second Street. A. J. knew the place. The commissioner usually favored high-visibility spots like Nello's, Cipriani, and Da Silvano, but he liked occasionally trading war stories with the Broken Wing's owner, a former Green Beret, and it was a place where he could relax, have a leisurely dinner, and spend several hours drinking wine without being hassled.

A. J. returned a few calls and answered some e-mail, killing time until he was sufficiently calmed down from the whole Supreme-Rikers episode that he'd be able to control himself with Brock. He wanted to maintain the upper hand, which meant, as he'd always told Lucy, never let them know what you're thinking. The last thing he wanted to do with the police commissioner was get angry and lose his head.

A. J. drove past the restaurant and immediately spotted Brock's security detail outside. There were also a couple of photographers hanging around, smoking, bitching, talking on the phone, and hoping to get the money shot when Brock came out after dinner. A. J. parked the car down the block; smoothed his dark blue cashmere blazer; adjusted the collar and cuffs on his button-down, Bengal-stripe oxford shirt; and walked back to the Broken Wing and went right past the security guys. They knew who he was, but they'd reacted too slowly to stop him.

Oozing determination, A. J. headed directly to the big round table in the back by the brick wall. Brock was sitting with his girlfriend, Lynn Silvers, and one of his flunkies, a civilian named Johnnie Dell. A. J. had never met Dell, but his name had come up over and over again in his reporting. Though A. J. hadn't yet been able to find any proof, the rumor was that he served as a kind of bagman for Brock, arranging under-the-table deals and payoffs for access and preferential treatment.

A. J. got all the way to the table before two of Brock's security guys caught up to him. They each took one of his arms. Brock looked up and smiled. Then he quickly waved them off. A. J. was not happy about being manhandled. "You might want to reevaluate your security detail, Commissioner," A. J. said, smirking, "if a physically unimposing writer can come right up on you in the middle of dinner."

"You may be right," Brock replied calmly. "How are you, A. J.? What brings you here unannounced?"

Dell and Silvers were both staring at A. J. with unmasked expressions of disdain. Brock didn't invite A. J. to sit down, though there was plenty of room at the table.

"Standing here talking to you like a delinquent schoolkid facing the principal doesn't work for me. We need a few minutes to talk," A. J. said, looking directly at Dell and Silvers. "Just you and me. No girlfriend, and no . . . friend."

Without showing the least bit of anger, Brock signaled his companions to give him a moment. Once they'd left, A. J. sat down. The waiter came over and refilled the commissioner's wineglass. It was an expensive bottle to be sure, but A. J. was certain Brock was not paying the check. He'd eaten enough meals with the commissioner to know he never put his hand in his pocket. Dinner was on either Dell, Silvers, or the restaurant. When the waiter then put a fresh glass down in front of A. J., Brock held up his hand. "He won't be drinking," he said. The waited nodded and left the table.

"What's up, A. J.? I told you the story is yours, even though they're all still calling. *60 Minutes, Vanity Fair*, everybody. But I'm going with you. You've earned it."

"Don't patronize me. I don't give a shit about *60 Minutes* or *Vanity Fair*. You want to give your story to one of them, be my guest. I've got enough now to kill you with a thousand cuts."

Brock sat up straight and slowly took a sip of wine before responding. "You've obviously got something on your mind, A. J. So let's talk, as long as you're not wired."

A. J. opened his blazer. Brock looked at him and then he pushed out his chair to frisk A. J. while he was sitting down. He did it so inconspicuously that no one would've noticed, even if they'd been looking at them from one of the other tables.

"Why the paranoia, Commissioner? You worried about something?"

"Worried?" Brock laughed. "You burst in here with no warning and then you tell me you're gonna cut me up. Don'tcha think I should be a little concerned?"

"What happened to Supreme?" A. J. asked flatly, ignoring Brock's remarks.

Brock's face was impassive. "Is that what this is about? A fucking drug dealer? It's my understanding that someone took a shot at him, and his bodyguard took the hit. So what, that's news? And then the pussy tries making a getaway and clips one of my officers, and he was carrying without a permit. So he gets to cool off at Rikers. What's the problem?"

"He's just been murdered."

"Forgive me if I don't rush to Rikers and offer my condolences. Look, make your point, A. J., because you're starting to annoy me."

"My point is Supreme. My point is Kevin Anderson. My point is Andrea Jafaari, Mary Jafaari, and Ayad Jafaari. All dead, all on your watch, all somehow connected. Something's going down and you're in the middle of it. I don't know if you're behind it or just caught up in it, but I'm gonna find out."

A. J. watched as Brock squeezed his napkin until his knuckles turned white. He had wanted to rile the commissioner, but now he was worried he might've gone too far.

"Are you nuts?" Brock said quietly, though his jaw was tightening. "You wanna play hardball? Let me tell you something, you little fuckin' pip-squeak, don't ever make the mistake of trying to intimidate me. You fuck with me and I promise you'll be sorry. Maybe you should be more concerned about your family and the predators that sometimes lurk in parks and watch young girls at play. Or your lovely assistant. What's her name again? Lucy? Perhaps you should be a little more concerned about her."

A. J. stared at Brock and tried to maintain his composure.

"So here's my advice," Brock continued. "Do your profile of me, tell a good story the way you always do, and enjoy the recognition. Your editor'll be happy, you'll get plenty of face time on TV talking about me, and you'll get lots of credit for the big exclusive with America's hero Lawrence Brock. Then you can take care of those close to you and move on to the next story. Have I made my point?"

"Here's my advice to you, Commissioner Brock," A. J. said, surprising himself with the force of his voice. "Don't start packing for Washington. This isn't over. Not even close."

Without waiting for a response, A. J. got up and started to walk out of the restaurant. His heart was racing and he didn't dare even take a breath, afraid that he'd start hyperventilating. He kept his eyes fixed straight ahead. He tried not to walk too fast so it didn't look like he was rushing to get away.

When he got in the car, he locked the doors and fumbled to put the key in the ignition. His hands were trembling and he tried to get his breathing under control. He was scared, but he was also proud of himself for not folding. He knew, now more than ever, that there was no way Lawrence Brock could be allowed to take over Homeland Security.

21

BISHOP FELT LIKE it took forever to get to Greenport and the ferry to Shelter Island. He wasn't sure if the drive seemed so long because he was tired or because he was starting to get excited about seeing Lucy. He couldn't remember ever feeling this way about a woman before. His relationships all followed a fairly predictable pattern. He'd spot somebody he was attracted to, he'd romance her a little—take her to dinner, out to the clubs—and the goal was always the same: to get into her pants.

But his feelings for Lucy were completely different. Yes, he had the hots for her, and, yes, he absolutely wanted to get into her pants. But it went way beyond that. He actually found himself thinking that she was the perfect woman: sexy, funny, interesting, not too girlie, and smart. Not name–the–five–Great Lakes kind of smart, but smart in her ability to read people. She was as intuitive as a skilled investigator. Talking to her was as much fun as Bishop could imagine having that didn't involve guns, cars, or getting naked.

Greenport was half an hour from the last exit on the Long Island Expressway. Bishop finally rolled up to the ferry dock at a few minutes after eleven p.m. The ferry was scheduled to leave at eleven fifteen and from Greenport, unlike the shorter Sag Harbor ferry, it was a fifteen-minute ride. He figured that would get him to Lucy around eleven forty-five. The gate was open and Bishop eased his Boxster up on the boat. Then he hopped out and popped open the trunk.

Bishop liked to be spontaneous but found it always worked better when he did a little preparation. Nestled in the back of his trunk and covered with a small blanket, he kept spare "get-lucky bottles" for nights just like this, when the possibility of scoring came up unexpectedly. Confirming that he had wine and Beau Joie in hand, he smiled, closed the trunk, and got back into the car to wait for the ferry to take off.

Lucy was busy getting herself comfortable in the big house. She'd showered, put on sweats, and turned on the fireplace, and now she was curled up on the huge living room couch. The weather was getting nasty. A storm was coming in, which was a surprise given how beautiful it had been only a few hours earlier. The wind was already whipping around the house and beating against the glass doors that faced the ocean. She was multitasking: watching *Cinema Paradiso*, one of her favorite movies, on the big flat-screen, while typing up the information she'd gathered from her conversation with Yvette on her laptop. She had opened a bottle of wine and was almost two glasses in when she found her eyes were getting heavy. She looked at her watch. It was just after eleven p.m. Bishop had texted her to say he'd be at the house around quarter to twelve. She was determined to stay awake, but it was a losing battle. A few minutes after finishing her second glass of wine, she was out cold.

Oz watched Lucy put the glass of wine down on the coffee table and drift off to sleep in the glow of her laptop. He was actually feeling a little tired himself. It had been an exhausting and not altogether successful week. He was still stewing about his failure to take out Supreme at Roxx. Sloppy work upset him. It was not the way he did things. There were still too many loose ends, too many possibilities for their plans to be disrupted. Ever the loyal soldier, Oz didn't complain to Brock, but the truth was he was unhappy about having to work this way. Even he occasionally needed rest to be as sharp as possible, and he needed time to properly prepare for these assignments. Failure was not an option, but Brock had continued to put both of them in a difficult, precarious position.

After Chief Fitzgerald had called Brock earlier in the evening, the commissioner decided it was time to regain control of the situation with Frank Bishop and A. J. Ross. So right after directing Fitzgerald to bring his men in, he dispatched Oz to go send a message to "the three fucking stooges." They had become a serious nuisance, and what better way to intimidate them than to hit the weakest link: A. J.'s assistant, Lucy Chapin.

His directive was simple and to the point. "Scare the fucking daylights out of her. I want her so terrorized that the other two morons get too scared to do anything. Leave no marks, leave no sign you were there, and do not get identified." Brock had one additional request. He wanted Oz to tape his encounter with Lucy. He wanted to hear her cries for help, the desperate screams, the pleading for her life. He had begun to get excited just giving this last instruction to Oz.

Oz had been with Brock for years, but there were still many things about his boss he didn't understand. He would never challenge him, but requests like this last one—and it wasn't the first time he'd asked for something like this—left him puzzled. There was no pleasure or excitement in hurting people for Oz. He did it because he had to do it, because it served the cause. There were no pangs of remorse, no guilt, and he never felt empathy for his victims. He'd decided long ago that it was God's way, that God had given him the tools to do what he needed to do. Killing, for Oz, was simply the means to achieve his objectives for Allah. Oz wasn't sure what Brock believed. He had moments when he doubted Brock believed in anything.

While Bishop waited for the ferry to leave Greenport, he called his guys and left messages detailing what he needed them to accomplish the next day. He wanted to get phone dumps on all the Jafaari family members, as well as the bank statements and the credit card bills of Kevin and Yvette Anderson.

He also tried to reach Lucy, but her phone went straight to voice mail. Just as well, he thought; he didn't want her to get the idea he was too eager. But the more he thought about her, the more he wondered if he actually had a shot with her. Not at just a couple of meaningless dates, but at a real relationship. It was the kind of thing he'd never thought about before. With Lucy, he found himself wondering not so much about what she'd be like in bed, although that had crossed his mind over and over since they'd met, but more about what it would be like if they went away together. How would they spend a summer weekend on Shelter Island? What kinds of things would they do?

Bishop was snapped out of his reverie as a wave smacked the side of the ferry and water splashed onto the hood of his car. The winds were picking up and the sea was getting choppy as the storm moved in. He could see the Shelter Island dock about two hundred yards ahead; he figured another twenty minutes or so and he'd see Lucy's irresistible smile.

Lucy's eyes fluttered as she slowly began to wake up. She was totally disoriented. It felt like her blood was rushing to her head. It took a couple of moments before she realized she was hanging upside down. She tried to move but felt constricted. It took another moment until she was lucid enough to fully recognize her predicament: she had been duct-taped, naked, to an inversion table. Her feet were in gravity boots and the tape was across her throat, her shoulders, and her thighs. Her hands and wrists had been taped down as well.

When Lucy had turned the alarm off, she never turned it back on. Oz had easily slipped into the house through a window. Lucy was already asleep, so his job was simple. He didn't have to subdue her to inject one hundred milligrams of fentanyl into her carotid artery, which guaranteed that she'd be out for at least ten to fifteen minutes. After a quick search of the house to make sure no one else was there, he found the inversion table in the master bedroom. Oz was essentially winging it—he hadn't had time to formulate a real plan—so the table was, in its way, the answer to his prayers. It was the perfect torture device.

Working quickly, he undressed Lucy, placed her on the inversion table, and put her feet in the gravity boots. To make sure she was completely restrained, he used the duct tape to bind her tightly to the table. Then he turned her naked body upside down. Oz was an observant Muslim. He stripped Lucy to maximize her vulnerability and feelings of helplessness, not for any sexual reasons—though it was impossible not to notice how beautiful she was.

He'd also found a pivoting full-length mirror that he placed directly in front of Lucy. Oz put Lucy and the mirror in the middle of the pitch-black room. Then he placed a flashlight on the floor. It provided just enough illumination for Lucy to see herself taped, naked, and hanging upside down in the dark. This alone was enough to fill the house with her screams. The closest neighbor was about two thousand yards away, and with the storm winds howling off the ocean, Oz was not at all concerned that someone would hear her.

Bishop had rolled off the ferry and onto the island and was trying to put the address into his GPS, but it wasn't working. He relied on the device for getting around and it rarely let him down. But now he was only getting Route 114, the island's main road, and virtually nothing else. Shelter Island was indeed sheltered. He'd have to do what any good PI would do . . . look for the nearest gas station and hope the Pakistani working there knew the neighborhood.

Lucy was sobbing softly. She could feel whoever did this to her in the room. She tried to stifle her sobs so she could listen, but it was like trying to stop a fit of hiccups. She was breathing hard and the blood pumping in her head was making her ears throb. She was cold and trembling.

Suddenly, from a dark corner of the room she heard a very soft "Sssssh," almost as if a parent were hushing a baby. Then a breathy male voice, nearly a whisper, said, "Listen."

Bishop was driving down Route 114 looking for 76 Winter Street. "How fucking big can this island be?" he muttered. "I gotta find someone to help me out here." He was barely half a mile down the road when he saw a bar and decided to go in and ask for directions. Since it was the off-season and almost midnight, with a hard rain already starting to come down, it looked like the bartender was getting ready to close, but when Bishop decided to have a shot of Ketel One to take the edge off, the guy served him happily, then wrote down directions to the house where Lucy was staying.

With Lucy's chest heaving, she heard the voice from the dark again, this time much closer to her. "Listen very carefully," he said, close enough now that she could almost taste his scent. She couldn't see him, but she could feel his index finger touching her now, gently tracing a line from the top of her pubic hair to her belly button, across her stomach, and down and around her breasts. He circled each nipple twice. It was a very light stroke and when he finally reached her neck, his full hand closed around her throat momentarily. Not tight, but just enough to apply a little pressure.

"This is not a game," he whispered in her ear. "You and your two friends are in the middle of something that's none of your concern. This all goes away when the three of you go away. If you ignore my suggestion and continue to pursue these matters, the three of you will die. You will also place your families at risk. I assure you I am serious. Do not make me prove it." He had barely started to walk away when Lucy let out a piercing scream.

When she stopped, the room was silent. A few moments later, she heard something from outside the room. She tried to focus and listen carefully, but the blood was still pounding in her ears and she continued to sob. It sounded like her attacker was in the kitchen going through the silverware drawer. Then she heard what she thought was a knife being sharpened. Lucy became hysterical. She was sure she was going to die. Her mind raced. She closed her eyes, which alleviated some of the dizziness from being upside down, and images flashed in her head like a high-speed slide show. Her parents. A. J. Her first dog, Ellroy. Main Street in Telluride. Grace Bay in Turks and Caicos. Summer nights on the beach after high school graduation. She opened her eyes again. The images were far too painful. She'd rather be dizzy. Then she began to do something she hadn't done since she was a little girl—she started to pray.

The rain was getting heavier. Bishop tried one last time to call Lucy, but he still wasn't getting a signal. Then he saw the mailbox and the front gate and realized he was there. Lucy had given him the code, but the gate was open. *Strange*, he thought as he pulled up to the front of the house. He pulled in behind Lucy's car, opened his trunk, and quickly grabbed the bottle of Beau Joie.

With the shot of vodka running through him, he felt energized. He walked to the front door and peered through the glass pane of the decorative side panel. He saw the living room with the huge TV screen. There was a movie playing, but he couldn't tell what it was. Directly across from the living room, he saw the only light on in the house. It looked like the kitchen and he thought he saw Lucy. He decided to go around back and surprise her. He figured he'd better do it quickly, since he was already getting soaked.

As Bishop moved to the side of the house he heard the roar of the waves hitting the seawall of what looked, even on a stormy night, like a beautiful place. He had to remember to check it out come morning. On second thought, he hoped he'd be preoccupied in the morning. He walked up on the deck and approached the glass doors.

He was caught completely off guard by what he saw. He was so stunned that for a moment he wasn't even sure what the hell he was looking at. As he stood in plain sight facing the kitchen of the lawyer's multimillion-dollar beach house, he saw the lean figure of a man, approximately five feet eleven inches, dressed all in black, including gloves, and wearing what appeared to be a Casper the Friendly Ghost Halloween mask. He was standing at the counter sharpening a knife.

Oz had almost finished with Lucy. There wasn't much more he could do, short of starting to cut her or torture her in a way that would leave marks, and Brock had specifically told him not to do this. She seemed about as terrified as anyone he'd ever worked on. Just to make sure, he decided he'd toy with her a little longer, until she either urinated on herself or screamed so hard she burned out her vocal cords. He was certain sharpening the knife within earshot would get her to do one or the other.

Oz was about to go back into the darkened room when he sensed something behind him. He stopped sharpening the knife, placed it on the counter, and in one fluid movement pulled a SIG Sauer .223 semi-automatic from his waist holster. He spun and was almost as shocked to see Frank Bishop, standing outside with a Champagne bottle in his hand, as Bishop had been to see him. He pointed the SIG and fired three times in rapid succession. The first round shattered the sliding glass door. The second shot shattered the champagne bottle in Bishop's hand, wiping the last vestige of a grin off his rain-soaked face, while the third shot whizzed by his left ear—all in less than two seconds.

By the time the third shot narrowly missed him, Bishop was already in a combat stance and firing back, but his target was now on the move. He burst through the shattered glass door into the house, broken shards of glass crunching under his wet shoes. As soon as he got out of the storm, he could hear Lucy's screams echo throughout the house. Bishop felt like every nerve was on fire as he carefully moved toward the sound.

Whoever was in the house was good and Bishop knew the guy had the advantage. He'd had time to get a sense of the layout and a feel for where things were. Plus he probably had a plan just in case someone showed up. Bishop's only plan for the evening was seducing Lucy.

It was hard to hear anything over Lucy's screams. Bishop finally yelled out, "Lucy, its Bishop. Are you okay?" To which Lucy's crying reply was, "Please, *please* help me." He worked his way down the corridor to the master bedroom in a low crouch.

Oz watched Bishop from a darkened corner of the dining room, his back against the wall. As always, he was completely calm. He felt confident he could take Bishop out if he had to, though he was impressed with the PI's reaction time. Oz was, however, disappointed with himself. He despised inefficiency and shoddy performance. This was the second time in less than a week that he had fired his weapon to kill someone and missed. He had shot at Bishop from an odd angle, and the heavy glass of the sliding doors further deflected his aim, but there was still no excuse for his failure.

The question was, should he kill Bishop now, if he got the opportunity? Would that put an end to their problems or would it just create new ones? Oz decided not to kill Bishop unless he had to. He'd left no evidence, no proof that he'd been there, and they had no way to identify him. If he got out now, he would have accomplished his mission. He'd made his point: they were all vulnerable. He could get to any one of them at any time. He'd put the fear of God in the woman, and if they were smart, they would get the message.

Bishop had reached the doorway of the master bedroom. When he saw Lucy naked, bound with duct tape, and hanging upside down, it sent a chill through his body. He was enraged, but there was a touch of fear as well. What kind of sick fuck would do something like this? He fought the urge to run to her. He knew the motherfucker was still in the house. Crouching down, he asked her in a low voice, "Are you hurt?"

Lucy, sobbing softly again, managed to choke out a soft no.

Keeping his gun hand extended in the direction of the doorway, Bishop slowly backed into the bedroom. He reached into his left pocket and pulled out a CRKT pocket blade, which was about the size of a money clip and razor sharp. Without taking his eyes off the door, he pushed the mirror out of the way and brought the inversion table parallel to the floor. "Are you all right?" he asked.

"Yes," she replied through choked sobs.

Working quickly, Bishop cut the duct tape around her neck and shoulders and the tape binding her arms and wrists. He reached over to the bed, pulled off the blanket, and covered her. His mind was going at warp speed. Was the intruder still in the house? He gently put the knife in Lucy's hand and whispered in her ear, "Can you cut yourself out the rest of the way?" She nodded. "Good," he said, softly stroking her cheek. "Once you're free, dial 911, and wait in the closet. Hang in there, sweetheart, I'll be back shortly."

Not much more than sixty seconds had elapsed from the time Bishop entered the room, cut Lucy's hands free, gave her instructions, and got himself back to the doorway. Oz started toward the front door. He saw Bishop poke his head out of the bedroom doorway, and he fired to keep him pinned down. Bishop quickly ducked back in. Bishop waited and listened. When he heard the front door opening, he bolted in pursuit. He saw the intruder run down the gravel driveway and disappear into the darkness. He had about a thirty-yard head start.

When Bishop ran after him he was greeted by pelting rain and powerful winds. He realized whoever this guy was, he must've parked close by, probably down a side road, and was now racing back to get his car. Bishop decided to cut him off. He fired up the Boxster, threw it into first, and hit the accelerator so hard he kicked rocks up everywhere. The car's rear end fishtailed violently before he regained control and headed down the driveway. Even with his high beams and fog lights, he saw nothing but blackness surrounding him and sheets of rain blasting against his windshield.

At the mouth of the driveway, he paused to look for a sign, any sign, of whether to go left or right. He looked to his left and suddenly out of the darkness came a pair of high beams racing directly toward him. He was momentarily blinded as Casper the Friendly Ghost blew past him going at least eighty miles an hour. Taking a long blink to clear his eyes, Bishop slammed down on the accelerator and went after him.

He drove over a slight rise and around a curve and saw Casper's taillights about a hundred yards ahead. Spotting Bishop behind him and closing ground, he turned off his lights. No headlights, no taillights. Now he was driving in total darkness. Bishop completely lost sight of him and was only able to spot him sporadically, when his brake lights came on briefly. The roads were awful, slippery, narrow, and made nearly invisible by the storm. Bishop had started talking to himself. "Let's go, mother-fucker," he said loudly. "I own you now."

By the way the guy was driving, Bishop was pretty sure he had no idea where he was going. He made a series of lefts and rights, then rights and lefts. Bishop wondered what he was thinking. They were back on the main road, Route 114, when the car suddenly spun out. Sensing the opportunity, Bishop accelerated. But just as he picked up speed, five or six deer appeared out of nowhere in his headlights. Bishop cut the wheel hard to the left and spun out himself. He missed the deer but went off the road into a soft muddy quagmire.

He saw the brake lights of the other car, now only about twenty-five yards in front of him, pull back onto the road and head down the hill. Bishop tried to follow, but he was stuck in the mud, which reached nearly halfway up his wheel wells. The faster his wheels spun, the deeper he sunk. He started to get angry, but then it struck him that Casper the friendly motherfucker wasn't going anywhere either. The last ferry of the night had come and gone.

Through the sheets of rain, Bishop could see the ferry station and the lights of the parking lot at the bottom of the hill, several hundreds of yards in the distance. Bishop got out and kept one hand on the car to keep from sinking in the mud as he made his way to the trunk. He fig-ured he had time for a tactical reload. He grabbed and opened a box of .45 rounds. They were custom MagSafes; he put some in his pocket, and he put a fresh magazine into his Kimber and reholstered. Then he high-stepped his way out of the mud and started a slow jog toward the lights.

He was jogging right down the middle of the road on the north side of the island through Shelter Island Heights, beautiful landmark homes to his left and right. As he loped past the tennis courts at the top of the hill facing the ferry, he saw Casper darting away from the ferry house. He laughed to himself. "Gotcha, motherfucker! Stupid bastard should've read the ferry schedule."

Instead of reconstructing the action movies he'd seen a gazillion times, Bishop was trying to talk himself into a state of calm. If he was going to kill this asshole, he needed to be in complete control; he had to achieve an almost Zenlike state. He looked down the hill and there was a moment when Casper looked back up at him; even across several hundred yards on a stormy night, they locked on to each other. The connection was just as real and just as potent as if their eyes had met across a well-lit room. Now that he'd been spotted, Bishop got in a low crouch and started running in a zigzag pattern.

The rain was very cold and it was coming down hard, pelting his face. His soaking-wet shoes and clothes weighed him down, but his adrenaline was pumping. He'd closed the gap between him and Casper to about two hundred yards when the guy suddenly turned back. There were two bright flashes, quickly followed by what sounded like muffled firecracker pops. Bishop saw the grass in front of him kick up. He tucked and rolled and came up ready to fire back.

While it was too far to fire a shot, he was able to see the guy was headed toward a short bridge. Bishop saw the bridge led to a tiny hamlet, which looked like maybe it had some kind of small shop, a bait store perhaps, a tavern, and—*HOLY SHIT*—a boatyard. This cocksucker was looking to get off the island by stealing a boat. Bishop pulled off his waterlogged jacket, holstered his gun, and sprinted to the bridge.

Bishop saw Casper stop to catch his breath in the middle of the bridge. While he couldn't make out the guy's features, the bridge was lit brightly enough for him to see the mask was gone. The man was white, middle-aged, and had a shaved head. He started to head toward the boatyard again. Bishop, fortified by about fifteen seconds' rest, took off after him.

By the time Bishop got to the foot of the boatyard, he had his gun out. He stood very still, hoping to hear the assailant, but the wind, the rain, and the waves drowned out anything else. He decided to take a risk. He was desperate now and intentionally moved into the light, knowing that made him an open target. He was hoping the guy would take a shot and give away his position. He waited. Suddenly, through all of Mother Nature's background noise, he heard the grumble of heavy engines throttling up. He ran down the dock and saw a twenty-six-foot Boston whaler backing out of its slip like a drunk pulling out of a packed parking lot. It crashed into the dock and knocked Bishop down hard. When he hit the boards, his gun slid out of his hand. Groping around in the dark, he finally got his hand on it, but the whaler was already pulling out.

Bishop got back on his feet and ran ahead. When he got to the end of the dock, he went down on one knee, aimed at the fast-fading whaler, and emptied his mag. Then all he saw was darkness.

22

IT WASN'T ONE of Bishop's better nights. He'd lost the chase, his car was stuck in the mud, and he wasn't sure what the story was with Lucy. He didn't know how long she'd been terrorized, what exactly had been done to her, or how she'd be handling it now. He was pretty sure whoever broke into the house only wanted to scare her. Otherwise, why go to all that trouble? If he'd wanted to kill her he would've just done it. As Bishop began the two-mile walk back to the house, the rain was still coming down heavily. He was exhausted, chilled, soaked to his bones, and about half covered in mud. If he hadn't been so pissed about losing Casper the fucking assailant, he might've laughed at how ridiculous he probably looked. There he was, trudging along on the side of the road in the dark, his feet squishing in his cowboy boots, the rain dripping into his ears.

Since he had nothing but time—the walk would probably take thirty or forty minutes—he kept going over what happened in his head. He didn't think there was much he could've done differently. Maybe the only significant thing, the one move that might've made a difference, would've been to anticipate the guy would go for a boat. If he'd realized that was his likely move, Bishop might have been able to stop him, but he couldn't be sure.

When he finally got back to the house, Lucy was obviously freaked but remarkably under control given what she'd been through. Oz had cut the phone lines and Lucy couldn't get a signal on her cell, so she'd never called the cops. *Just as well,* Bishop thought. *How big a force could they have on a small island like this anyway,* he speculated, *two guys tops during the off-season?* If they'd come, he would've been obligated to either lie or give a full report about what happened, and the cops would've seized his weapons, which would've been a serious problem.

By the time Bishop finally managed to get a signal on his cell, he'd decided to leave the cops out of it. The first thing he did was call his guys, Eddie and Paul, and tell them to beeline it to Shelter Island on the first morning ferry. He put Paul on surveillance at the parking lot, hoping the prick would be dumb enough to come back to retrieve the car he'd ditched. Bishop knew this was unlikely, since the guy seemed like a pro, but it was worth a shot. He dispatched Eddie to get his car out of the mud.

His next call was to A. J. Though they could've talked for hours, given how much information they had to exchange, they kept it brief. Bishop gave A. J. the key points of his meeting with Pennetta and told him what had happened to Lucy. A. J. told Bishop about Supreme's murder and his confrontation in the restaurant with Brock. Their first decision was easy. Lucy and A. J.'s family needed to be moved somewhere to guarantee their safety. Bishop said he had the perfect place and they could meet there tomorrow.

He had a billionaire client named Lee Morgan who lived on a sprawling 250-acre estate in the most exclusive part of Greenwich, Connecticut. The main house was twenty thousand square feet, and there were several guest cottages and servant's quarters, a landscaping shack, and a security house. Over the years, Bishop had handled various cases for Morgan, some of them very sensitive and requiring what Bishop referred to as "off-the grid" work. Their relationship developed into one of mutual respect and friendship. It was rare that Bishop asked Morgan for a favor, but he needed one now. His estate was the perfect haven for Lucy and A. J.'s family to spend the next couple of days.

It was very late, but it was Saturday night, and Bishop knew if Morgan were sleeping his cell wouldn't be on. Sure enough, he was still up. The only question he asked Bishop was if he'd be harboring fugitives. Bishop replied negative, and when he started to explain, Morgan stopped him. "No need," he said. "I'll make sure your friends are well taken care of."

With his phone calls done, he needed to find something to cover the shattered sliding glass door, since the wind and rain were blowing into the house. Once that was done, it was time to turn his attention back to Lucy. She was in a fragile state and certainly didn't want to go anywhere near the bedroom. "Can we sit on the couch and maybe you could just hold me for a while?" she asked so sweetly it almost made Bishop cry. Within minutes, she fell asleep in his arms. Bishop stroked her hair and tried to stay alert. He wasn't sure if someone was coming back. He thought it was unlikely, but just in case, he barely dozed the rest of the night.

In the early afternoon on Sunday, Lucy and A. J.'s family were dropped off in Connecticut, but not without significant protest. They all thought it was ridiculous—even Lucy, who was still shaky from the previous night. A. J. let them vent, and when he thought they'd made their points, he ended the discussion. They were staying and that was final, he told them, reminding them to shut off their cell phones as well. Once they were settled in, A. J. and Bishop took Lucy's rental car and started back to the city. Since A. J. had gotten a couple of hours' sleep, he drove and Bishop dozed. They stopped in the Bronx to get gas, grab a bite, and call Pennetta from a pay phone. They were now convinced their cell phones were being monitored. They gave Pennetta an account of what had transpired over the last eighteen hours or so and set up a meeting for later in the day in Flushing, Queens, in the shadow of Citi Field.

After making certain they weren't being tailed, they headed to Al's Custom Motors, a detailing and custom car shop owned by one of A. J.'s childhood friends. A. J. and Al Tessa, the owner, had been friends since grade school. What better place to have a meeting and ensure there was no eavesdropping?

Pulling into the garage around six p.m., they saw that Pennetta was already there and was talking car engines with Al Tessa. Al was waving his arms and extolling the virtues of the legendary '66 Pontiac GTO, with its 396-cubic-inch V8 and its three two-barrel carburetors, while Pennetta was arguing on behalf of the 2013 Shelby Mustang GT500, the ultimate modern muscle car. After a quick hug with A. J. and an introduction to Bishop, Al showed them where the coffeepot was and then excused himself, heading to his loft office so they could have some privacy.

Forty-five minutes later, Pennetta, with the veins bulging in his neck, said, "You expect me to believe a sitting New York City police commissioner is complicit in not one murder but more than half a dozen, including an NYPD lieutenant?"

"I know it sounds preposterous," A. J. said. "I'm just asking you to keep an open mind and look at the information. Think about it for a second. If the three of us hadn't come together and we only had the facts we have individually, I agree it wouldn't add up. But when you put all the pieces together, what other possibility is there? First Anderson and the hooker, then the suspects in the apartment, the Jafaari family, and then Supreme. Brock's connected to every one of them."

"To my knowledge," Pennetta said, picking up a ratchet and playing with it nervously while he talked, "Brock was never in the Three-Three's command. And that's where you place Anderson when he made this supposed deal with Supreme. And while I know Brock and Fitzgerald are tight, you should be ashamed of yourself, Bishop. There's no doubt Brock's a scumbag and a grandstander and a media whore, but I thought Fitzgerald was the guy who saved your ass."

"Now who's a fucking hypocrite?" Bishop said to Pennetta. "You only go after the guys you don't like?"

A. J. stepped in before things got too heated. "Hey, guys, we're not the enemy. Focus, okay? How do we figure this out? How do we find the connection between Brock and Anderson?"

"Roll call," Bishop said immediately.

A. J. looked at him quizzically.

"That's right," Pennetta said eagerly. "There's a roll call for everyone who's in the precinct, not just the guys who work a particular tour. It's the CO's roll call, and it's a complete list of everyone, including civilians, who's assigned to that particular precinct on a given day."

Pennetta got up and moved over to the red Snap-on toolbox that stood almost six feet high. He opened one of the drawers, put the ratchet away, and turned to A. J. "What he's saying is we need to look at that roll call and see if we can link Brock and Anderson."

"You know anyone in the Thirty-Third Precinct?" A. J. asked Bishop.

Bishop frowned and shook his head slowly from side to side.

Pennetta, looking just as dour, raised his hand and surprisingly said, "I do. I'm tight with the administrative lieutenant. I'll take the day myself and go up there tomorrow."

"Fine by me," Bishop said. "I'm completely fuckin' exhausted."

"Now," Pennetta said, "what about you being followed?"

"They've absolutely got our houses staked out, and they're tracking our cell phones. We need to pick up prepaid phones and communicate that way."

It seemed, for the moment at least, that they were done. A. J. gently ran his hand along the fender of a bright red, fully restored '69 Firebird. "That's a beauty, isn't it?" Pennetta asked.

"I had a '72," A. J. said. "It was totally stock, but it was a great car."

"Listen," Bishop said to A. J. as they were leaving. "No one's getting into my place unless I want them to. Why don't you stay with me? I'm sure you wanna see Nikki and the kids, but it'll save you the ride in from Greenwich."

A. J. thought about it for a moment. "Okay," he said. "Thanks. Tomorrow Brock and I need to have a serious sit-down."

23

A. J. WOKE UP on Monday morning around eight and found himself nose to nose with what he thought was a large wolf. There were several seconds of terror until he remembered where he was. He rolled over and it was like he was seeing double. Two massive king shepherds had climbed up on the pullout couch where A. J. was sleeping at Bishop's place and surrounded him. With their tails wagging, they started happily licking him. He pulled the covers over his head for a few moments, but when he peeked out the dogs were right there waiting. At 135 pounds each, they weren't easy to push off the bed.

Teresa, the live-in, came down and started chasing the dogs away in Spanish. She greeted A. J. with a perky "*buenos dias*" and a big mug of coffee.

"*Gracias*," A. J. said appreciatively, "that's great. Just what I need."

Bishop, who was already dressed and ready to roll, came into the room humming. "Jeez, still in bed?" he said. "I always heard reporters were lazy."

"Nice," A. J. said, sitting up now on the bed. "Good morning to you too, asshole. Zito coming to pick you up?"

"No," Bishop said, laughing. "I'm meeting him up at the Three-Three. The last thing we need is for whoever's watching the house to connect Zito to us."

"Mr. Bishop," Teresa said, "you no walk dogs again? Babies playtime. *Ay dios mío*, these dogs pull me down the street every time they see a squirrel."

"*Muchas gracias*," Bishop said. "I promise I'll take you shopping next weekend. Target, Walmart, Costco, anyplace you want. I'm just really swamped right now. I'll make it up to you. Hey, I'll buy you the Clapper, clap on, clap off, my treat."

"Wow," A. J. said, "now that's gratitude. Big spender!"

As Bishop pulled on his jacket and drank the last of a protein shake, he told A. J. that Teresa would cook anything he wanted, and Eddie, who had successfully managed to extricate his Porsche from the Shelter Island mud yesterday, would give him a lift anywhere he needed to go. Concerned about being followed, Bishop would make his way to the Three-Three via some combination of subway and taxi.

Pennetta and Bishop shared coffee and doughnuts and an hour of war stories with the administrative lieutenant at the Thirty-Third Precinct. Pennetta told the lieutenant he was planning a reunion for everybody he'd worked with at the precinct more than a decade ago—hence the need to go through the roll call. With no reason to doubt Pennetta's story, the lieutenant took them to the basement records room and let them loose on the files.

"Fuck," Bishop said, taking a look around at the stacks of boxes everywhere. It was a daunting sight. The shelves ran from the floor almost to the seven-foot ceiling and they were packed with decrepit-looking boxes. The low ceiling made an already cramped, uncomfortable space even more unpleasant. Since the period they were interested in was before the department's records were fully computerized, they'd have to fight through the cobwebs, dust, and mold to examine the contents of at least two dozen musty cartons of paperwork. Making matters worse, organization of old files was not exactly a priority for the NYPD.

"You know how much I normally get an hour?" Bishop asked. "This is way below my pay grade."

"You hide in the bushes with a camera to try and catch cheating husbands to earn a living," Pennetta said. "Lose the fucking prima donna attitude and get started on the left side there. I'll take the right."

After Teresa whipped up a sumptuous Mexican breakfast of frittatas and huevos rancheros for A. J., Eddie showed up a little after nine, obviously tired from working pretty much around the clock but happy to tell A. J. all about himself. He was in his early twenties and for a brief moment had considered going into the family business—the NYPD. So far, however, things hadn't quite gone as planned. His PI work left little time for anything else.

While A. J. and Eddie were talking about movies, A. J.'s cell phone rang. It was Brock's office calling him back. One of the commissioner's aides told him he should come to Brock's office at One Police Plaza at two o'clock.

A. J. hung up and looked at his watch. He really wanted to see Nikki and the kids and Lucy. He wished he had one of his bikes in the city. But he had a plan B. He thought if Eddie were willing to have a little fun and drive a little faster than he probably should, they could still shoot up to Greenwich for an hour or so to see everybody and get back in time for his meeting with Brock. A. J. put the cell phone in his pocket and told Eddie what he had in mind. He also told him it was a little more complicated than just getting there and back. There was a surveillance team watching him, so they'd have to shake the tail before they could head to Connecticut. He asked Eddie if he was up for it. Eddie was quiet for a moment and then smiled. "You kidding me? he said. "It'll make a great scene in one of my movies."

"Tell you what, kid," A. J. said. "Get this done and I'll write an Oscar-worthy story for you to direct. But if it turns out the way I think it's going to, no one'll believe it."

Bishop and Pennetta had been at it for several hours. Their shirts were dirty and stained with sweat. Their throats were scratchy and their

mouths were dry. They still hadn't found the specific box labeled "Roll Call" for the years 2004 through 2009. "Why the fuck couldn't we just grab this guy's ten card?" Bishop complained. He knew the answer; he just needed to vent. In the NYPD, the ten card essentially documents your history in the police department from the day you're sworn in to the day you retire. It covers all essential information—what commands you've been on, what firearms you own, and so on. If it had been virtually anyone else but the police commissioner, this process could have been cut short. But there was no ten card for the PC. Bishop was moaning about this when Pennetta yelled, "*Bingo! Got it!*"

Going through the roll calls, he'd finally found Kevin Anderson's name. On some roll call sheets he'd be on a foot post, on others he'd be in "Sector Boy" or "Sector David," which meant he was in a patrol car responsible for covering an area in the precinct designated as Sector B or Sector D. But so far, there was no connection to Brock. They continued to tear through the boxes until Bishop suddenly stopped. With a file in his hand, he slowly looked up at the ceiling for a moment, then turned around and walked out from between the shelves. In an open area near the door, he fell to his knees like he was in church, stared hard at the floor, and dropped the roll call sheet. Then he rubbed his eyes with his palms, as if pushing back tears. Pennetta stopped what he was doing, looked up, and watched.

Bishop got up, went toward the door, and, never turning around, walked out. Over his shoulder he said, "I've gotta get some air." Pennetta picked up the roll call sheet and scanned the lists of names. It said, *Assigned to Sector Boy, Kevin Anderson.* The name next to Anderson's was John Keno. Still no Brock. He continued looking down the sheet and then he saw it: *Integrity Control Officer, Lt. Thomas Fitzgerald.*

Eddie was having a blast. He was doing nearly ninety on the Connecticut Turnpike heading back to the city with A. J. They'd just come from Greenwich, where, after going through what felt like presidential-level security, A. J. had been able to spend a little time with his family and

Lucy. Eddie kind of watched the visit but wasn't close enough to hear anything. After A. J. said his good-byes, hugging everyone and saving an especially long embrace for his wife, Nikki, all he said to Eddie was a short "Let's go."

A. J. barely said a word to Eddie in the car. When they got to One Police Plaza it was five minutes to two. Perfect. A. J. thanked Eddie for his help and told him to call if he ever needed anything, writing advice or whatever. Eddie wanted to wait, but A. J. said he'd find his own way back. He knew Bishop had given Eddie a pile of stuff to do.

A. J. stood in front of police headquarters and gazed up at the fourteen-story brick building sometimes called Puzzle Palace, for the Byzantine bureaucracy and the political intrigue that bubbled inside. A. J. took a deep breath and started walking across the wide, redbrick plaza. About a hundred yards from the entrance to One Police Plaza, he showed his press credentials at the security checkpoint and the cop on duty called the commissioner's office to check his appointment. Then, with his visitor's pass in hand, he headed for the building. When he was just about at the entrance, a bald man in a suit with a shaved head approached him. "Mr. Ross?" he said. "I'm a special assistant to Commissioner Brock."

"Haven't we met?" A. J. asked. "I'm sure we have. I'm sorry, but I don't remember your name."

"It's Kareem Ozmehet Said," the man said, smiling.

"Ah," A. J. said. "How could I forget? What's up with the commissioner?"

"He has been unexpectedly called to Washington, and as a result he's on his way to catch a flight out of Newark. But he knows your meeting is important, so he respectfully asked if you could meet him at the airport. There will be time to talk before his flight leaves."

A. J. considered protesting but then thought better of it. He needed to have it out with Brock, and if it happened in a public space like the airport, that could be even better.

Oz led A. J. around to the back of One Police Plaza and directed him to a slightly beat-up Jeep Cherokee with blacked-out windows. He opened the front door, and when A. J. looked inside, he saw the broad smile of Chief Walter Fitzgerald, dressed casually in jeans and a red plaid shirt. Oz got into the backseat and directed A. J. to the front. He slid in, and the chief pulled the SUV out slowly and headed toward the Holland Tunnel.

Lee Morgan's estate was spectacular. No detail, no matter how small, had been overlooked. The main house had been built at the turn of the last century, and the facade featured elaborate stonework and filigree that could never be duplicated today. Along with the pool, there was a red clay tennis court, and the gently rolling, sculpted grounds led down to the water.

Lucy was walking in the lush gardens alone. She was having a hard time. Though part of her felt great relief to be able to relax in this beautiful protective cocoon, she was conflicted. She felt guilty that she'd been ostensibly taken out of the game, benched at the most critical time. She even felt a little like a coward, though in her heart she knew she had absolutely nothing to be ashamed of. As awful as her experience at the house on Shelter Island had been, she was still angry and a little embarrassed that the psycho had been able to make her scream.

She wasn't normally prone to feeling sorry for herself, and she knew this was a bad time to start. She was desperately trying to think of something she could do to help A. J. and Bishop nail Brock and whoever else was involved. She'd been going over everything that happened in her head, first forward and then backward. She knew she was missing something. Lucy remembered the day of the press conference after Brock's raid, the day when all of this started. It seemed so long ago even though it was only a little more than a week. She recalled meeting Supreme, whom she'd actually begun to grow fond of, and now he was gone, murdered in jail. She thought about the night at Roxx with Bishop and how much fun she was having before she ended up with blood on her clothes. She replayed her visit to Yvette Anderson and momentarily felt a little surge of pride that she was able to get information from her that no one else had gotten. She pictured the house and the huge living room fireplace with its photo wall. Then she froze.

A. J.'s wife Nikki was relaxing out on the lawn with the kids. Nikki was sitting in an Adirondack chair reading the paper, and the kids were throwing a ball around and chasing each other. Nikki looked across the broad expanse of property at Lucy. She was just standing there, staring down at the grass. She wondered what Lucy was doing. Nikki was very fond of Lucy and looked at her almost like she was Annie's older sister. She felt terrible about what had happened on Shelter Island and hoped it wouldn't have any lasting effects. Nikki was just about to call out Lucy's name to see if she was okay when all of a sudden Lucy started running in her direction. She wasn't jogging; this was a flat-out sprint, and she had a wild look on her face.

Nikki stood up as Lucy approached and she reached out to grab her. "Please, please, Nikki," Lucy blurted, barely able to catch her breath. "I have to get to A. J. I have to talk to him *now!*"

Racing into the guesthouse, she went straight to the phone. She desperately needed to tell A. J. what she'd just realized. The morning Brock spoke at the press conference after the raid; the photo by the fireplace of Anderson receiving his lieutenant's shield from police commissioner Brock; the night of the murder attempt on Supreme at Roxx. All of these had one thing in common—Lucy didn't know the man's name, but she remembered his swarthy, slightly fleshy face. She remembered him standing in the background behind Brock at the press conference. She could picture his face in the corner of Kevin Anderson's promotion photo. And now she could see the night at Roxx in her mind's eye. In that split second after the third shot rang out, after Supreme's bodyguard had been hit, she looked into the crowd and saw a white guy, pulling off a wig, revealing his shaved head. He stood out because he was the only middle-aged white guy besides Bishop in the club. As she struggled to dial A. J.'s cell number with her trembling hand, she guessed that he was probably also the sick fuck who'd terrorized her on Shelter Island. She had to let A. J. know.

24

BISHOP RUSHED OUT of the Thirty-Third Precinct and started walking down Amsterdam Avenue. It was about two in the afternoon and the streets were crowded. This far uptown, Manhattan looked and felt more like one of the outer boroughs. The buildings were much smaller, traffic was lighter, the streets seemed wider, everything felt more open. There were also very few white people. About two blocks from the precinct, Bishop saw a bar and went in. He needed a drink.

As Bishop took a seat at the far end of the bar, the door opened. Pennetta walked in and took the empty seat next to him.

They both ordered two shots of vodka, then sat for a while in silence. A small TV over the bar was playing one of the daytime courtroom shows with no sound. Finally, after about ten minutes, Bishop spoke first. "Why?" was all he said. Pennetta let the question hang in the air. "Why?" Bishop asked again. "It makes no sense. Everything good about the job, everything right about being a cop, I got from Chief Fitzgerald. Whenever I felt like it was all a bunch of crap and none of it meant anything, he was the guy who showed me I was wrong. He could always make me feel like being a cop made a difference," he said, downing his second shot, then swiveling in his seat to look at Pennetta.

"I know the chief's not about money," he continued. "He never gave a shit about anything other than the fucking job. I had a gig once and I really hit a home run for the client, and he gave me a Rolex. I already had one so I decided to give it to the chief, you know, as a thank-you for all the shit he put up with from me. And he wouldn't take it. 'What the fuck am I gonna do with something like that?' he said to me. 'Where am I gonna wear it?' He wouldn't take a fuckin' watch as a gift. So this, this just makes no sense."

"Stop feeling sorry for yourself for a moment 'cause you lost your mentor," Pennetta said. "Fitzgerald didn't do it for the money, at least not in the way you're looking at it. Stop for a minute and think about this. What happened to him like twelve or thirteen years ago when he started drinking again?"

Bishop looked down at his glass. At first he didn't remember. But then it came back to him.

Pennetta saw the look of recognition on Bishop's face. "That's right," he said, "Fitzgerald's daughter!"

"Shit," Bishop said, shaking his head. "We never really talked much about it. He never wanted to and I never pushed him. I remember she was born with all kinds of medical problems—like she had cystic fibrosis and some kind of rare blood disease. I remember at one point when I was still practically a rookie there were fliers posted around the precincts advertising fund-raisers for a Lieutenant Walter Fitzgerald. I didn't know him then. We met like four or five years after she was born, and he almost never mentioned her."

Bishop stared at himself in the mirror behind the bar, then turned away when Pennetta started talking. "All the special treatments, the drugs, the home care, must have cost huge amounts of money. I think she was even in some kind of facility for the last two years before she passed. It would be very easy to justify doing anything when you're trying to save your daughter's life."

Bishop was disgusted. *Nothing*, he thought, *is ever what it seems.* The bartender passed and he ordered another round.

• • •

Traffic in the Holland Tunnel was light, and Chief Fitzgerald appeared relaxed as he drove. He looked at A. J., who was sitting next to him, and noticed how active his eyes were, taking in everything. Oz, sitting in the back, hadn't said anything since they left police headquarters. "So what's the deal, Chief?" A. J. said. "You're looking a little informal today. The department have casual Mondays now?"

Fitzgerald laughed. "Casual Mondays, that's funny. Today's just my regular day off. But apparently the PC has something to tell us, and he insisted we all be there."

"Any idea what it is?" A. J. asked.

"Not a fucking clue," the chief said. "Maybe you're gonna get that big scoop you've been looking for."

Before A. J. had a chance to respond, his cell phone started vibrating. He had a policy of not taking calls when he was working, so he let it go to voice mail.

Lucy looked at the phone and cursed as soon as she heard A. J.'s voice mail. She knew his rule about not taking calls when he was reporting a story, but this was different. She had promised him she wouldn't use her cell phone, but she had to get a message to him somehow.

"If the commissioner's taking the shuttle to DC, why didn't he just go Delta out of LaGuardia?" A. J. asked as the Cherokee came out of the tunnel and into New Jersey. The chief smiled uneasily at him.

A. J.'s phone buzzed again. Annoyed, he took it out of his pocket to see who was trying to reach him. It was a text from Lucy. "CALL ME ASAP —U R N DANGER—BROCK'S RT HAND MAN WAS SHOOTER AT ROXX."

A. J. looked at the text and realized how stupid he'd been. He'd let hubris completely cloud his judgment. He was angry about everything that had happened and so intent on having it out with Brock, he'd missed all the obvious signs—Oz intercepting him in front of police headquarters, traveling in a Jeep Cherokee instead of an official car, and Fitzgerald out of uniform on supposed official business. Of course they weren't going to Newark.

Oz said it first. "*He knows.*"

"I know he does," Fitzgerald responded calmly as he plucked the cell phone out of A. J.'s hand. "But A. J.'s not stupid. He's aware that you have a silenced automatic pointed at the small of his back and that doing something heroic would not be in his best interest. He should realize if he behaves and does what he's told, he'll be able to walk away from this without a scratch."

The conversation reminded A. J. of the way Nikki and his kids would sometimes talk about him at the dinner table as if he weren't there. He shook his head. Now was not a good time to think about his family. He needed to focus; he needed to figure out what the hell he was going to do. He looked at the signs as they passed the exit for the Newark airport and headed south on the New Jersey Turnpike. The three of them rode in silence.

Bishop rarely did any serious drinking with the guys. For him, alcohol, and vodka in particular, was simply a means to an end. The end being the beginning of a great time between the sheets. Nevertheless, Bishop and Pennetta were half in the bag when Bishop's cell began buzzing. It was Lucy. With a wry, half-drunk smile, Bishop showed the phone to Pennetta so he could see it was Lucy calling. Prepared to be playful and sexy when he answered, Bishop quickly lost his buzz when he heard her voice. She was frantic, talking so fast Bishop at first had trouble understanding.

"*It's him, it's him,*" she screamed over and over.

"Lucy," Bishop implored her. "Lucy, slow down, I can't—"

"Listen to me," she said, controlling her breathing now—inhaling and exhaling slowly, one breath at a time—the way A. J. often told her to. "There's no time to explain. The shooter at Roxx was the guy who works for Brock, that weird, creepy guy. You know who I mean? The bald, Middle Eastern guy. And I'm guessing he's the freak from Shelter Island too."

"How do you know? What is—"

Lucy cut him off. "The only thing that matters is A. J.! We need to find him."

"Okay, okay," Bishop said. "I hear you. Listen to me, don't say anything to Nikki yet. No need to panic anyone. I'm here with Zito and we got it—"

Before Bishop could say covered, Lucy, fully composed now, was on him.

"Just please get it done," she barked at him. "Now!" And she hung up.

Bishop looked at Pennetta, who had overheard most of the short conversation.

"Oz," he said. "That's the name of Brock's guy." The lieutenant said he was a mysterious figure around police headquarters whom he'd met a couple of times when dealing with the commissioner.

Since there was little they could do, except stop drinking, they decided to wait at Pennetta's house in Wantagh, out on Long Island. They figured that was the safest place, given that no one had any idea Pennetta was involved. The house was a fairly typical split-level, the kind found in middle-class suburbs by the thousands. What was atypical was the number of women living there. Pennetta, who was in his early fifties, lived with his mother-in-law, his wife, and his four daughters—a thirty-year-old from his first marriage, a twenty-two-year-old from his second marriage, and a six- and nine-year-old from his current wife. The place was like a life-size dollhouse, with loads of pink and frills and stuffed animals everywhere. Bishop thought it was a riot. *Serves the testosterone-loaded fucker right*, he thought. *It's great how nature works to balance the universe.*

The basement was Pennetta's sanctuary. All of the girls, including his wife and mother-in-law, knew not to go downstairs for any reason. It was his place. In contrast to the rest of the house, it was a man's space, with a big-screen TV for sports, dark wood paneling, and two beat-up old couches. Against one wall was a bar and on the opposite one was his wall of fame. There were photos of him as a young marine in uniform, photos of him in the Aviation Unit, and a big eleven-by-fourteen of Zito in full assault gear with his ESU team.

Several hours had passed since the call from Lucy, and there still hadn't been any word from A. J. Bishop had called Eddie and verified that he'd dropped A. J. off at One Police Plaza and left after A. J. told him not to wait. He'd also gone through the motions of calling Brock's and Fitzgerald's offices. As expected, he was told on each call, "I'm sorry, he's out of the office. Would you like to leave a message?" The hours went by. At a little after midnight, both Pennetta and Bishop were passed out on separate couches in the basement.

Around one thirty a.m., Chief Fitzgerald, in complete darkness save for his headlights, pulled off the main road in Morganton, North Carolina, and onto a dirt track. The dirt road continued for about a quarter mile, where it came to a stream and a small wooden bridge just wide enough on each side for the Jeep to cross. Just beyond the stream an open field stretched for several hundred yards in every direction. The road continued up a gentle rise to the base of a mountain, where, on a piece of land cut out in the forest, there was a nearly ninety-two-year-old two-story house, built right into the side of the hill so that the main floor was level with the ground and the second floor was up on the grade of the hill.

The place, the chief had mentioned a few miles back, had been in his wife's family for years. There was a big utility barn that housed a tractor, a lawn mower, a snowplow, and assorted farm equipment. There was an old chicken coop that hadn't been used in years and an old dilapidated, unused outhouse as well. The place was so off the beaten path that there was a hunting lodge about two miles west of the house, and in season, lost hunters would often knock on the door to ask for directions.

Fitzgerald found the house by memory. When he shut off the car lights, he couldn't see his hand in front of his face. He'd driven the entire way, nearly twelve hours, and he was tired. The drive had been more tedious than usual because the car was so quiet. No one said a word practically the entire trip. A. J. had spent the twelve-hour ride trying to figure out what they were up to. He wasn't particularly scared; he was really more concerned than frightened. He thought if they wanted to kill him, they probably would've done it already and just dumped him somewhere in South Jersey. They obviously needed or wanted something, but he had no idea what it was.

Fitzgerald's head was in a completely different place. *How,* he wondered, *could this have happened?* How did almost forty years of devoted service to the NYPD come to this—first a kidnapping, and now he was on the threshold of possibly getting involved in murder? He was a good man, a devoted husband, and a responsible father. He'd overcome many obstacles in his life. Ironically, were it not for his devotion to his family, he wouldn't have been here in the dark in the middle of the night with A. J. and Oz. *Sometimes life really sucks,* he thought. When Brock had offered him the opportunity to make some money all those years ago, he wanted to say no. More than anything, he wanted to tell him to go to hell. He despised crooked cops, and he despised Brock for even thinking he could come to him with such a proposition. But he was desperate. The drugs were going to be on the street anyway, he started rationalizing; wouldn't it be better if he helped control the violence? In the end, what difference did it make if he made a few bucks on it to help his daughter? But he never really believed that. He never managed to convince himself it was okay, and his life was never the same once he started taking the money. And now, it was only about to get worse.

Oz, on the other hand, was, as usual, completely indifferent. It was all about the goal; the means were unimportant. He looked at things like an accountant, and he needed to balance and close out the books for this quarter. In his mind, the business was about to start showing landmark results, and the only things standing in the way were what he looked at as several accounting anomalies—A. J., Lucy, and Bishop.

Bishop felt somebody watching him. It was Pennetta's six-year-old daughter. Her mother yelled from upstairs for her. "You'd better get up here and into this kitchen yesterday! If your father catches you, you're going to get it."

Bishop, with his eyes still mostly closed, flashed a big smile at her.

Without saying a word she ran up the stairs, only to be met by her father, who scooped her up and playfully whacked her on her bottom. He put her down and said, "You know better than to go down to the basement. Get ready for school and come kiss me good-bye before you go."

Bishop sat up on the couch, grabbing his back. "Sorry," Pennetta said, already up and moving. "We're not really set up here for overnight guests." Bishop stood up, shook his head, and stretched a little. He had more pressing concerns. Where the hell was his newfound partner? He picked up the house phone and started dialing. "You have an idea that'll help us find A. J.?" Pennetta asked.

Bishop held up his hand to quiet him, pressed the telephone against his chest, and said, "No. I mean yes. But I'm calling about my dogs. I'll tell you my idea right after this call."

A. J. opened his eyes and saw a bed with a patchwork quilt, an old rocking chair, and some pictures hanging on the wall that looked like Norman Rockwell prints. It would've made a cozy room at a rural bed-and-breakfast. Too bad A. J. had spent the night on the floor, handcuffed to an old radiator.

When Fitzgerald came into the room, he was dressed pretty much the same way he had been the day before, in jeans, a plaid shirt, and hiking boots. He would've looked like a country gentleman if it weren't for the Glock nine-millimeter holstered on his side. "Look," Fitzgerald said with what A. J. thought was resignation in his voice, "I'm going to uncuff you to go to the bathroom. Don't be stupid, okay? You're in the middle of nowhere, and if you act up, Oz will make things uncomfortable for you."

A. J. simply nodded. Fitzgerald took the cuffs off and A. J. got up slowly. He was stiff and sore from sleeping on the floor and his wrists hurt from the cuffs. Fitzgerald led him into the bathroom across the hall. He told him to leave the door open. A. J. knew better than to protest.

After calling Teresa and arranging for the dogs to be fed and walked, Bishop called Fitzgerald at home. There was nothing unusual about this.

From time to time, Bishop would stop by the chief's house for dinner or call about setting up a shooting trip. So Fitzgerald's wife wasn't surprised to hear from him, except for the fact that Bishop was calling at such an early hour. When Bishop asked for the chief, she told him he was away for a few days on some kind of training trip. Bishop thanked her and hung up. If there'd been any doubt that Fitzgerald was involved, any possibility that he was innocent, all of that disappeared when Bishop hung up the phone.

A. J. was led into the living room as the morning sun was pouring in through the bay window. He could see that there were several laptops set up on the kitchen table. Oz, who was looking at the screens, turned and watched as Fitzgerald guided A. J. down the stairs to the root cellar, then sat him down in a big old chair and began to bind his forearms and ankles to it with plastic flex cuffs.

A. J. was trying to decide if he should resist. Even though Fitzgerald was at least fifteen years older than he was, A. J. was still pretty sure the chief could kick his ass. And then there was Oz. It quickly became a moot point. Once he was entirely bound to the chair, fighting back was no longer an option. A. J. was left with only one weapon—his intellect—and he was becoming convinced that if he wanted to stay alive, he'd better start using it.

25

"THIS NEEDS TO be contained," Fitzgerald yelled at Oz. "The more people brought in, the greater the chance of exposure."

"The plan was discussed with the commissioner," Oz said calmly. "He felt this was the best way to ensure an end to our problems once and for all."

"Well, fuck that," Fitzgerald responded, his face turning red with anger. "Nobody consulted me and I don't like it. We should've just finished this, you and me, and gotten the fuck outta here."

A. J. could hear the two men arguing from the cellar. He'd been sitting in the dark for what he thought was hours, amid a bunch of old rusty tools, a few tires, assorted boxes, and preserve jars that had probably been there for years. A. J. had started to feel like he was trapped in a Quentin Tarantino movie, except this was real. He was working very hard not to panic, to try to stay focused on figuring out some way to improve his chances.

The two men were in the living room. Oz, displaying his usual detachment, had matter-of-factly informed the chief that two additional men were coming to help, and they were due to arrive at any moment. The chief got really agitated when he learned they weren't from the department.

Not long after, an old Honda Civic came up the dirt road to the house, and two men in their twenties with tobacco-colored skin and dark hair got out. As they came into the house, Fitzgerald looked like he was about to have a stroke. "The commissioner has used these assets in the past for deep undercover work, even to penetrate possible terror cells," Oz said, anticipating his complaints.

"I can see why," Fitzgerald said, practically spitting the words out, he was so angry. "They look just like the guys we lit up in last week's raid. Same shit, different names, is my guess."

The two men completely ignored Fitzgerald and started talking to Oz in what sounded like Arabic. The chief just stood there listening and shaking his head. "You gotta be fucking be kidding me," he muttered. Then they sat down in the living room and discussed the plan.

Bishop was sitting and having a cup of coffee with Pennetta when his cell phone rang just before ten a.m. The number came up "Restricted," but he knew who it was. The voice was cold and direct. "Mr. Bishop, get a pen and take down these instructions. I'm only going to give them once." Bishop signaled for Pennetta to get a pen and paper. Then Bishop said, "Go ahead."

"By now you know the situation. We have your friend. I'm not going to waste time on the obvious. I'll assume you know what'll happen if you don't follow my instructions exactly."

"Listen to me, cocksucker. I know who you are, *Oz*, and I'm gonna nail your fucking head to the hood of my car and drive down—"

Oz abruptly cut him off. "Save the tough-guy talk for the slutty women you're always trying to impress, Mr. Bishop. You and I know you're not really up to the task. You *didn't get it done* at Roxx, did you? And be happy I didn't kill you on Shelter Island—"

"You dirty fucking—"

"Enough," Oz said, cutting him off again. "I suggest you shut up and listen to what I have to say. The clock is ticking and you're wasting time. *Your time.* You and your lovely friend Lucy Chapin are going to take a little trip. Your journey will begin precisely at eleven thirty. You'll be told when and where to stop and we'll be watching you. No one is to come other than the two of you. You'll be given additional directions at each of your stops."

Bishop's mind was going a thousand miles a minute. "What the fuck do you want, you murdering piece of shit?" he said, knowing how ridiculous he sounded even as it was coming out of his mouth. But he couldn't help himself.

Oz ignored the outburst. "We know where you are and we know where Lucy is, so you'd better go pick her up. Trust me, you don't want to be late."

Oz proceeded to give Bishop instructions. After getting Lucy, he was to immediately drive to the George Washington Bridge, then head south on the New Jersey Turnpike. While he took down the instructions, Bishop decided to try something. Reaching into his pocket, he pulled out the prepaid, disposable cell phone he'd recently purchased. He dialed Fitzgerald's cell number and pressed Send.

His suspicion was confirmed almost immediately. When the call connected, he heard the number ring somewhere in the background where Oz was. *Gotcha*, Bishop thought. Without missing a beat, he continued taking down the directions from Oz.

"You'll be contacted with further instructions once you're on the road. And don't forget, we'll be watching you." Oz hung up. Bishop put the phone down. Pennetta stared at him, waiting for an explanation. He went over all of it, emphasizing that Oz had instructed him to bring Lucy and that they'd be tracked as they traveled. Given the schedule Oz had put forward, he needed to get started soon, which didn't leave them much time to figure something out. "You know what he wants, right?" Pennetta asked.

"Absolutely," Bishop said. "He wants to kill us."

"That's right. His plan is to get all of you in the same place and make sure it's the last place any of you will ever see. And just like that, all of the trouble goes away and the commissioner goes to Washington."

They needed to come up with their own plan, quickly, and Bishop had an idea. He told Pennetta about his little trick—that while he was on the phone with Oz, he'd called Fitzgerald using his prepaid cell. Sure enough, he heard the chief's phone ringing in the background while he talked to Oz. Bishop thought they could turn the tables on Oz and Fitzgerald. If he and Lucy were going to be tracked by their cell phones, why couldn't he do the same thing? They had to find out where Oz and Fitzgerald were, and he was hoping that his call to the chief would be the key. He reached out to a contact he had at Verizon and gave her the information. She said she'd get back to him as soon as she came up with something.

Then Bishop was multitasking. Watching him work the phones on a normal day was a sight: he'd have two landlines and two cells going at once. One would be for PI business, two would be for personal business and making connections, and the fourth would be all monkey business. But now the activity was more frenzied than usual and much more focused. All the phone lines and all of his energy and attention were zeroed in on the task at hand. He called Eddie, who still had his car, and told him he needed to shoot up to Greenwich—at the speed of light—and get Lucy's cell phone. "Don't worry about why," Bishop said, "just get it done."

Bishop's plan was pretty simple. He had no intention of driving south with Lucy. If Oz was going to track them by their cell phones, then only the phones actually needed to be in Bishop's car. He would give Eddie and Paul his phone and Lucy's phone and they would drive the car according to the directions from Oz. The calls from Oz to Bishop's phone could be forwarded, without detection, to Bishop's prepaid cell. And in the event the car was actually being tracked by spotters, which Bishop thought was highly unlikely, detection of Eddie and Paul would be difficult with the top up and the windows blacked out.

But in order for the plan to work, Bishop had to find out where A. J. was being held. Bishop was explaining the plan to Pennetta as they got in the car to drive to Republic Airport. Just as he was finishing up, the phone rang. It was his contact at Verizon special services. After several minutes of listening, Bishop's face broke into a wide smile. "Sweetheart," he said excitedly, "you're the best. Next week, dinner anywhere you want and whatever else your little heart desires. I'll call you."

Bishop turned to Pennetta, still smiling. "We got the motherfuckers." His friend at Verizon said the call to Fitzgerald's phone had gone to a cell tower in Morganton, North Carolina. That was the critical piece of information required to set Bishop's plan in motion. When the second call came from Oz, Eddie and Paul were on the road in Bishop's Porsche, driving south on the turnpike. Oz had no idea that his calls were being forwarded to Bishop, nor was there any way for him to know that Bishop had pinpointed the town where he and Fitzgerald were holding A. J.

26

SATISFIED THAT HE had the situation completely in hand, Oz was now in the basement facing A. J. Flanking him were the chief and a Middle Eastern–looking man A. J. had never seen before. A naked lightbulb hung close to A. J.'s head and the harsh light caused him to squint. Oz was the first to speak. "Mr. Ross," he said stiffly, "I'm sure by now you know what I'm capable of, so I'm not going to try and scare you. The fact is, you should be scared. Nevertheless, I'm told you're an honorable, courageous man, and I'm sure you're determined to hold out. So rather than waste time asking you questions you're not going to answer, we'll start with a little pain. Hopefully, once you fully understand how serious I am, that'll speed things up."

A fourth man, also apparently Middle Eastern, came down the stairs holding a bag of ice in one hand, and a large carving knife and a sharpener in the other. A. J. was pulled into the center of the room, where there was a table with a square of butcher block on it.

Oz took out his weapon. He was carrying an HK nine-millimeter. "This is how it's going to work," he said. "The chief is going to unbind you, and you're going to stand up and place your left hand flat on the butcher block. If you flinch or move, I'll put a bullet in one of your knees."

One of the men who'd gone upstairs was coming down again. This time he was carrying an IV pole and what looked like bags of plasma. A. J. looked at this and then back at Oz with real concern in his eyes. Oz smiled and with an almost reassuring nod said, "Yes, my friend, we've done this before. If need be, we can keep you alive for days."

A belt was placed around A. J.'s neck like a dog collar and then tightened. His restraints were taken off; he stood up as instructed and put his left hand on the butcher block. One of the Arab men sharpened the knife for several seconds and then walked over to the table. Oz nodded to the man holding the knife, who placed it over the first joint of A. J.'s left pinky. Then, like a chef chopping a carrot, he leaned on both ends of the knife and pressed down with his weight.

The pain was searing and caused A. J.'s knees to buckle, his eyes to tear, and his vision to get blurry. For a moment he thought he might puke. But he didn't scream and he didn't move his hand. The man holding the belt around A. J.'s neck laughed. "Shut up," Oz harshly snapped at him, and he stopped immediately. "You think this is a joke?" Fitzgerald turned away in disgust. A. J. was reseated in the chair and the man who did the cutting tied off his pinky at the second joint. Although the basement was cool, A. J. was soaked in sweat. All four men were staring at him.

"Quite painful, isn't it, Mr. Ross?" Oz asked. "You'd think with modern technology there'd be better ways to extract information. But my experience has been that this is the most efficient. So, before I extract another piece of your finger, I'll ask you once, what do you know and who else knows it?"

A. J. realized he was playing some kind of bizarre mental chess, and every time he made the wrong move, every time he lost a piece, it would actually be a piece of *him*. His reply to Oz was vague but had just enough information in it to hold his attention. "I know the connection between the three of you," A. J. said, looking in Fitzgerald's direction. A. J. saw that Oz betrayed the hint of a smile at that statement. Before he could follow up, A. J. added, "And I know the connection between you and Brock." A. J. was now looking at Oz, who blushed with anger.

"When you say 'connection,'" Oz looked at A. J. and asked, "what do you mean?"

A. J. was searching for an answer. His finger was throbbing, and he was trying to work through the pain and use his skills as an investigative reporter, his ability to understand what people were thinking, to save his own life. "There are two things going on here," A. J. said, trying to hold it together, "what went down with the chief all those years ago and what's going on with you now."

Oz nodded and the two men picked him up, placed his hand on the butcher block, and took the second joint of his finger.

Pennetta was unloading the equipment from his car onto his plane, two big military duffel bags and a long rifle case. He was resigned to what they were about to do. Once he had flipped that switch, he became a machine. While he packed the plane, Bishop was still working the phones. Now that he knew the town where A. J. was being held, he needed to get the exact location. When his Verizon contact gave him Morganton, he'd remembered the chief loved to hunt and that his wife had a farm somewhere that had been in her family for a long time.

One of Bishop's go-to guys, someone he depended on more than just about anyone else, was a computer geek he called Gigabyte. Gigabyte was his intel wizard, the guy who would get him phone dumps, credit card bills, bank statements, and practically any other critical personal information that was stored somewhere on a computer. Bishop asked Gigabyte to do a property-and-land-deeds search in Morganton as well as the surrounding areas. He gave him all of Fitzgerald's pedigree information and asked him to check the chief's wife as well, since the property could be in her family name.

Pennetta meanwhile was getting his plane ready to fly. It was a 1975 Cessna Skylane 182. He went through his preflight safety check—wings, flaps, tires, fuel, and gauges. His plan was to head to the closest municipal airport, which was in Hickory, about a twenty-minute drive from Morganton. This left him almost no room for error. The drive to Hickory was about 670 miles. His Cessna's range on a full tank was a hair over 600 miles, which, given that his route would be more direct than driving, meant he'd just make it. The plane would be running on fumes as he got to Hickory.

As Pennetta was having the gas tank topped off, Bishop came out from the flight office looking very pleased with himself. He had not only the address where he believed A. J. was being held, but the satellite pictures as well, thanks to Google Earth. The cruising speed on the Cessna was 139 knots, but Pennetta could push that to about 175. If all went according to plan, they'd get to A. J. several hours ahead of Eddie and Paul in Bishop's Porsche.

A. J.'s left pinky was completely gone and his hand was a bloody mess. It had taken three cuts to lose one finger. When they cut off the last piece, A. J. passed out. When he regained consciousness after a few minutes, Oz told him he had nine more to go. A. J. now thought that his best shot was to try to work Fitzgerald. He clearly seemed to be the weak link, the one man of the four whose heart didn't seem to be in it. "Why are you protecting these scumbags?" he asked him. "Don't you realize who these people are? I've covered the department a long time and your rep has always been as good as anyone's. Whatever you did with Brock all those years ago has nothing to do with this."

Fitzgerald was listening carefully, but A. J. was really struggling. He felt like he was about to pass out again. He was fighting with everything he had to stay conscious while at the same time trying to find some strategy, some way, to connect with Fitzgerald. His mind was all over the place; images and strands of information came and went like he was in a fever dream. He saw Bishop and Brock at the Sheraton in New York. He pictured his walk with Bishop at the softball field. He remembered him talking about the hookah bar's owner. "*I held that fat guy's head to the fire,*" he could hear Bishop say, thinking he'd mangled the expression. "*He said the cops told him to keep his mouth shut.*"

A. J. decided it was worth a shot. "Don't you see the bigger picture?"

he said to Fitzgerald. "Don't you realize that all of this is about the raid and Brock going to Washington, not the old drug deal? Who tipped off the terrorists before ESU hit the door? I know it wasn't you, Chief. It was this scumbag," A. J. said, looking at Oz. With that, Oz went over to A. J. and struck him across the face with a left hook, knocking him and the chair over. The chief looked at Oz for a long moment. "I need a cigarette," he said.

Oz told his men to take A. J. upstairs to the shower. "Clean him up and bring him to, then we'll start all over again."

Fitzgerald went outside. It was early afternoon. He looked out at the property and wondered why he hadn't spent more time here over the years. It was so beautiful. They owned several hundred acres that stretched up into the mountains. The land was held in a trust so it could never be sold. If his wife's family hadn't done that, he thought, he surely would have sold this farm and used the money for his daughter. Who knows, but maybe he wouldn't have been forced to enter into a deal with Brock, Anderson, and Church Jackson for money to try to save his daughter's life. "What's the difference at this point?" he said out loud. "What's done is done." He felt his eyes fill with tears. Things were getting worse and worse. First the drug deal, then torture and maybe murder, and now what? Terrorism? Was the raid some kind of fucking setup?

He turned around and saw Oz staring at him with an odd look on his face. The moment was broken by A. J.'s screams. The two Arabs were literally rubbing salt into A. J.'s open wound. Oz turned and went back inside. Fitzgerald followed him a few minutes later and saw Oz at the laptops tracking what he thought was Bishop and Lucy in the Boxster. The Porsche still had plenty of miles to cover. It was on Interstate 78 West and approaching 81 South in Maryland. They still had plenty of miles to cover before reaching North Carolina.

Fitzgerald looked toward the bathroom, where he could hear the Arabs scuffling with A. J. "Enough now," Oz yelled to his men. "Ice him up and bring him downstairs." Oz looked back at Fitzgerald. "We all make choices," he said as if he'd read the chief's mind, "and then we have to live with the consequences. Sometimes those can be difficult. Whatever happens, it's always best not to look back. I know this is a dirty business, but you'll have your house back soon. This'll all be over and these characters will be fertilizer for your farm."

27

MAYOR NICHOLAS DOMENICO bit into a strawberry and immediately bent forward at the waist so the juice wouldn't drip on his tie or his crisp white shirt. "This is really good," he said to no one in particular. The mayor finished the strawberry and decided to stand by the fruit bowl and have several more pieces. It was almost six o'clock and he was hungry. The day had been a blur of meetings and appearances that all seemed to run together—a sit-down with the schools chancellor on class size, an appearance before the city council to discuss better radios for the fire department, face time at a nursing home in Sheepshead Bay, a short press conference, and a spot on an afternoon drive-time radio show. Lunch had never happened and he was happy to munch on some fresh fruit.

Domenico was in the green room at Fox, waiting to be interviewed by Bill O'Reilly. The taped segment would air that night and likely include the usual set of questions about leadership, the state of America's national security, and his presidential ambitions. The mayor was eating melon two pieces at a time when he heard a minor commotion outside in the hallway. There was even a little light applause for the arrival of Commissioner Brock. When he walked in, the two men embraced and then Domenico excused everyone else—the various members of his entourage and those of Brock's.

"Congratulations," Brock said with a big smile.

"What the hell for?" the mayor asked, now eating pineapple.

"All the speculation about you running for the White House."

"At this point it's all bullshit. But it does keep my name in the head-lines. Listen, I had you come here because I needed to talk to you face-to-face," Domenico said, moving away from the fruit bowl toward Brock. "I'm gonna get asked about you when I go on here in about ten minutes. And everywhere I go for at least the next several weeks people are gonna continue to ask about you. How's the vetting process going?"

"Fine, sir. My attorneys are responding promptly to inquiries from the White House; my tax returns are in order. There've been a few hic-cups, but the attorney general is okay with everything."

"I'm not gonna bullshit you, Larry. I've been hearing rumors."

"What kind of rumors, Mayor?"

"The kind of shit I don't wanna hear, that's what kind. Stuff about large gifts, questionable deals, and even speculation that something wasn't right about the Brooklyn raid. You have to understand we're joined at the fucking hip at this point. So any shit that comes down on you is gonna get on me as well."

Brock waited a moment before responding. "Sir, I believe every-thing is all right. There are things in my past you know about, and now the White House knows about them too. They've told me they're fine with it."

"I'm not feeling reassured. So I'm gonna ask again," Domenico said, looking hard into Brock's eyes. "Is there anything I need to know about? Actually, let me rephrase. Is there anything that needs to be taken care of that won't be taken care of?"

"Absolutely not, sir. I'm all over this."

"Okay, as long as we're clear on this. You're only good to me as long as you're good *for* me. Understand? I love you like a brother, Larry, but this is business. Don't ever forget that. Embarrass me and I'll cut you off in a fucking heartbeat."

"I understand," Brock said.

One of the producers knocked on the door. "Mayor Domenico, we need you in makeup, sir."

"I'll be right there," he said. Then, turning back to Brock as he was putting his suit jacket on, the mayor said, "Don't fuck me, Larry. We've been together a long time. It'd be a shame to lose you now."

Pennetta was driving a rented SUV to Chief Fitzgerald's farmhouse. The equipment he'd brought for the operation was in the back. Google Maps had provided an incredibly detailed layout of the area, which Bishop was sitting in the passenger seat and studying. While he was doing that, Pennetta was prepping him on the mission and going over critical details. Bishop willingly relinquished all control of the operation. As an ESU commander, this was what Zito trained for, planned for, and lived for, every day of his life.

While they talked about their plan for snatching A. J., Pennetta hoped that Bishop was up to the task. Being a cop in the South Bronx and then a Manhattan private detective probably wasn't the best training to take part in a dangerous covert operation, but neither one of them had a choice. This was their only shot at freeing A. J. If they failed, he'd likely be dead within twenty-four hours—if he wasn't dead already.

About a mile from the farmhouse, they turned onto an access road to the high power lines running along the base of the mountains. This was their staging area, the place where they'd gear up. Pennetta had decided that Bishop would go in and extract A. J. while he covered him with his sniper rifle. They parked in a covered spot where the car was visible from the main road and pulled out the gear. Pennetta had camouflage clothes and face paint for Bishop. He'd wanted Bishop to take an MP5 as his weapon, but Bishop refused, convinced he should stick to what he was good at—and he believed he was very good at close-quarters combat with his .45. He did, however, allow Pennetta to give him a Colt Commander in a shoulder rig as a backup.

Pennetta was reluctant to use any NYPD weapons or equipment, so he'd brought his latest showpiece, an M40A3 sniper rifle he was testing for a friend who worked for the manufacturer. It was one of a handful of handmade weapons of its kind in use outside of the Marine Corps.

While he was getting suited up in his camo gear, Bishop tried to stave off a case of nerves by keeping things light. "You gotta be fucking kidding me," he said at one point. "How big are these pants? If I'm gonna get killed today, how's it gonna look when the news cameras roll and I'm wearing my grandpa's pants?"

Pennetta almost smiled.

"I saw that," Bishop teased him.

Pennetta tossed him a belt. "Shut up and tuck the long pants into your boots," he told Bishop.

"Next mission," Bishop said, "I'll do the shopping."

It was getting late in the day and the sun was starting to set. A. J. was back in the basement being watched by one of the men, which seemed unnecessary given how battered and depleted he was. The other man Oz had brought in was upstairs at the computers monitoring the travel progress of the Boxster.

Oz was watching the dirt road and the entrance to Fitzgerald's farm with binoculars. The chief walked up behind him and asked, "What's the plan?" Without turning around or looking away from the binoculars, Oz replied, "The plan is simple. Once they come over the wooden bridge, one of my men will block the road behind them. They'll have no way out. We have some heavy artillery in the trunk of the Honda fixed with silencers, not that anyone would hear anything out here. We'll take them into the basement first for serious interrogation."

"Why don't we just get it over and done with?" Fitzgerald interrupted. "Let's kill them."

"No," Oz snapped. "If that's what we intended to do, it would've been done already, and it would've been staged to look like an accident. We need to talk to them, we need to find out what they know. The commissioner's future depends on it."

• • •

Like all strong, effective military and law enforcement leaders, Pennetta was a control freak, totally anal about his work. So he and Bishop were well prepared. They knew the terrain, they had prearranged positions, and they had point-to-point throat radios for communication. Pennetta set up on the high ground in the woods opposite the Fitzgerald farmhouse. He cleared a flat area for his M40A3 sniper rifle, which weighed nearly twenty pounds, and got it solidly positioned on a bipod. Then he lay down flat on his stomach, made sure there were no small rocks or tree branches beneath him, and checked the farmhouse through his scope. From where he was positioned, he'd be shooting at a distance of eight hundred yards—not terribly long for a Marine Corps sniper but not exactly the average distance of an NYPD shoot-out. Given the fact that the overwhelming number of gun battles for the NYPD occurred in an area of less than twelve feet, Pennetta, who was a world-class shot, was cursing under his breath, wishing he'd put in more time on the sniper range.

Bishop had a longer hike to get in position, looping around through the woods to come up directly behind the farmhouse without being spotted. Once they were both in position, they'd share reconnaissance: exactly how many men were in the farmhouse, A. J.'s location, possible strategies for getting him out with the least amount of contact. Pennetta compiled most of this information using his scope, which had both standard night-vision capabilities and thermo-imaging. With a laser range finder for both black heat and white heat, he could pick out the bad guys in the dark, through the trees, and around corners, by the body heat they gave off.

From Pennetta's vantage point, he counted three bodies, and all were moving around freely. That told him that either A. J. was dead and buried at another location, or he was in the basement, which would explain why Pennetta was not picking up his image.

As he relayed this information over the point-to-point, Bishop had just finished mother-fucker-ing his way through the woods (albeit very quietly, under his breath) and was coming up to the rear of the house.

He removed his backpack and pulled out his own set of infrared glasses. From behind the house he saw the old barn, the building supply shed, and the outhouse, positioned precisely as he'd seen them on the satellite photos. He also saw Fitzgerald's truck and an old Honda. He suspected Oz and his assembled cretins were heavily armed, and he was seriously starting to wonder how the hell he'd ever get to A. J. Then he saw the old-fashioned double storm-shelter doors on the side of the house leading down to the basement and smiled.

When Oz returned to the basement, followed by Fitzgerald, it was A. J. who initiated the interrogation. "Who set up the Jafaari kid?" he asked. Fitzgerald just stood there and looked at him.

"I can understand the rest of them," A. J. continued, "you know, thinking they'd be martyrs, that they were gonna die for Allah. Although how fast you think they would've given it up if they knew they were gonna die for Lawrence Brock? But where'd you get the Jafaari kid? He doesn't seem to fit."

A. J. was totally winging it, but at the same time he was starting to put everything together in his head. "Come on, Chief, don't play stupid. Don't tell me you had no idea what Brock was up to. It's like when a volunteer fireman starts a fire so he can go put it out and be the hero. The whole thing was a fucking setup, although I'm sure nobody told the guys in the apartment."

Oz looked at A. J. He wasn't happy, but he was impressed at how sharp A. J. was even after the torture and the loss of blood. He let him continue so he could find out what else he knew.

"And all this old shit," A. J. continued, looking directly into Fitzgerald's eyes, "it was never about Supreme, it was never about Anderson. It was all about lousy timing. Anderson got a little greedy, and when Internal Affairs finally decided to make waves, it just didn't work well with Brock's agenda. Remember Son of Sam? That's what Brock and this motherfucker Oz are like. David Berkowitz didn't get caught actually killing anybody, he got caught because he got a parking ticket. *A lousy fucking parking ticket.* First Anderson, then Supreme, and now *you*, Chief, are like that parking ticket."

Even Oz had to smile. "Okay, Mr. Ross, who else knows about your conspiracy theory? Think before you answer, because the next thing you lose will be your hand."

With that Oz nodded, but as his men were getting ready to put A. J.'s bloodied hand back on the butcher block, the telephone rang. Oz went upstairs to take the call.

Fitzgerald looked at the ground. He didn't want to make eye contact with A. J.

"Is this where your career ends, Chief? This the way you want to go out, being a member of a terrorist cell?"

Fitzgerald turned around and walked up the stairs.

Pennetta counted two people coming up out of the basement by the heat signatures he saw on his scope. He knew in his gut, and from years of experience, that they had A. J. down there. He told Bishop over the radio that this was the moment to move in. As the sun was setting, Bishop ran along the tree line as far as he could until he could make the break. Then, in a low crouch, he ran the twenty yards from the woods to the door, unsurprised to find it unlocked. Treading lightly, he went down eight steps to the second door. Through the shadows he could see one guy, who was about five feet seven, one hundred sixty pounds, standing over A. J. Bishop's heart started to race. If this were a movie and he were Stallone or the Rock, he'd have pulled out a knife and thrown it perfectly so it pierced the bad guy's throat, killing him instantly. But Bishop knew he could barely cut a steak. He also knew he wasn't fast enough to shoot the guard and get A. J. out before they all came running downstairs.

Bishop really wanted to get Zito on the radio, but he had no transmission in the basement. He knew he had to move. But how? He withdrew the Kimber from his holster and was steeling himself to blow the motherfucker away when he got lucky. The man watching A. J. suddenly smacked him across the face and then went upstairs. Bishop could hear him calling one of the other guys for prayer time. "Praise be to Allah," Bishop said to himself, and smiled.

He holstered his .45, pulled out the commando knife Pennetta had given him, and walked over to A. J. He cut the flex cuffs and whispered into his ear, "Can you move?" A. J. nodded and his face broke into a smile. Bishop saw his bloodied left hand where the missing pinky used to be. He pulled A. J. up on unsteady legs and walked him to the door at the back of the basement, grabbing a rag and wrapping it around his hand. He pulled out the Colt Commander from his shoulder holster and gave it to A. J., then told him to run to the edge of the woods and wait. "Now," he said, pushing A. J. forward as he heard the sound of footsteps on the stairs.

He slipped back into the shadows, hugging the wall, and waited. He watched the guy look at the empty chair and the trail of blood to the door. As he ran to the rear door, Bishop grabbed him around the throat from behind with his left forearm, pulled his neck back, and stabbed him in the side of his throat. Blood sprayed everywhere. It reminded Bishop of when he'd wash a car as a kid and he'd put his thumb over the open hose, shooting the water all over.

Oz was about to go back downstairs and cut off A. J.'s hand. Fitzgerald stopped him. "Let me do this," he said. "Let me go down there and talk to him and see if I can get it done."

Now Bishop could hear Fitzgerald coming slowly down the stairs. He moved into the center of the room, in full view, so the chief could see him, covered in blood, knife in hand, standing over the body of one of Oz's men. The shock on Fitzgerald's face practically lit up the dim cellar.

Finally, Fitzgerald spoke. "You don't have to die," he said. It made Bishop angry. He dropped the knife and both men simultaneously went to their holsters. Like the thousands of times they had faced off in friendly competition at the range, they came up in their point-and-shoot stance. Only this time when they fired, they shot directly at each other.

Bishop was knocked down and felt like he'd been hit in the chest three times with a baseball bat. He was waiting for the chief to stand over him and finish him off. But nothing happened. When Bishop got to his feet he realized that while both of them were wearing vests, only Bishop had successfully executed the Mozambique—two to the body and one to the head. Fitzgerald was dead. Bishop briefly stood over him, but there was no time to linger. At the sound of the shots everyone had gone into overdrive.

Oz's second guy picked up the M16 that was leaning on the table and ran to the entrance of the basement. When he looked down, he saw Bishop and started firing. That was all Pennetta, who'd never taken his eyes off his scope, needed. Exhaling calmly, he took aim, held his breath, and slowly squeezed the trigger. The lone shot through the window exploded the man's heart onto the inside wall of the basement staircase.

Oz pulled out a nine-millimeter and crawled to the basement. He'd barely registered the dead bodies on the floor when he heard a movement, emptied his mag, and made his way to the back door. He needed to get to the Honda. Oz was moving to the car with the keys in his hand when he heard footsteps from behind.

"Turn around," A. J. said. He wanted to look Oz in the eye when he blew his brains out. He wasted no time pulling the trigger as Oz turned to face him. But nothing happened. Oz laughed. A. J. hadn't depressed the thumb safety before trying to shoot. He reached in the back of his pants and pulled out his stiletto. He started toward A. J., who tried one last time to shoot. A. J. was circling but Oz was closing the distance quickly.

A. J. grabbed a branch off the ground and swung it around just in time to block Oz's thrust and avoid being stabbed.

Oz was now a man possessed. He charged at A. J. again. A. J. lifted the big branch over his head like a lumberjack and came down hard, forcing Oz to block the branch with his knife hand. A. J., sweating, dizzy, and breathing hard, lunged for the knife. Both men went down. They rolled down the hill into the dirt driveway about twenty-five yards from the house.

• • •

Bishop didn't realize he'd been hit until he tried to get up and it felt like his right leg was dead. He crawled up the steps and saw that there was no one left in the house to kill. Making his way out onto the deck, he saw A. J. locked in a life-and-death struggle with Oz. As they stopped rolling about thirty yards away from where he stood, Oz ended up on top and leaned all of his weight on the knife to try to plunge it directly into A. J.'s chest.

A. J. was resisting with what little strength and energy he had left, but Bishop could see he was slowly losing the battle. The knife point was just about to break his skin and the drool from Oz's open mouth was hitting him in the face. A. J. knew he had nothing left, and he started to close his eyes and think of Nikki and the kids. He didn't want Oz's face to be the last thing he saw before he died.

Bishop got down on one knee. His body was shaking, and he knew he was going into shock. But he also knew he had to try to save A. J. He sighted in on the head of Oz, and letting out a breath, he slowly started to squeeze the trigger.

He never heard the shot from Pennetta's rifle, only saw the wide pink spray as the top of Oz's head exploded.

28

A. J. PUT HIS head back and closed his eyes. He could feel the sun and a slight breeze on his face. He was thinking about the words; he had to find exactly the right words. But he was having trouble concentrating. It'd been almost two weeks since the shooting in North Carolina, and his emotions were still a little frayed. He'd cried twice, both times because he was happy, happy to be alive, happy to be with his family, and happy to return to work. He laughed every time he thought about the image of him, Bishop, and Zito walking away from the farmhouse. What a sight they must've been, though there was no one there to see it. A dirt-covered Zito with smeared camo face paint running down his cheeks, half-carrying Bishop, who'd been shot in the leg, walking next to an exhausted, unsteady, battered, and bruised A. J. with a bloodsoaked rag wrapped around his now four-fingered hand.

"Hey, motherfucker, are you gonna move your car or not?"

A. J. opened his eyes. It was just after eleven in the morning, and he and Bishop were in the car in midtown. A cabdriver behind them screamed again in a slight Middle Eastern accent.

"The light's green, motherfucker, MOVE!"

Bishop and A. J. looked at each other and smiled. Then they both looked at the cabbie. "Absolutely," Bishop said. "Have a great day."

262

Bishop hit the gas and they sped downtown on Fifth Avenue. They were on their way to police headquarters. In a very compressed period of time, their relationship had matured the way all good ones do—there was no longer a need for constant forced chatter. They were comfortable enough to sit together in silence. Bishop's XM radio was playing—what else?—the sounds of the seventies, specifically "Easy," by the Commodores. A. J. was happy to be lost in his thoughts.

Since they'd been back, the papers were filled almost every day with coverage of Fitzgerald, Anderson, Supreme, and Oz. And, of course, Brock. What started in the headlines ended in headlines: CORRUPT CHIEF COOKS BOOKS, read the *Daily News*. AIDE TO COMMISSIONER IN DRUG SCAM WITH CHIEF, the *Times* wrote. And the *Post*, more playfully, ran with NYPD'S CHIEF WAMPUM. The stories were all interesting, but they were woefully incomplete. More often, however, they were just wrong. Fitzgerald and Oz took the rap. Terrorism, the Middle East, and the raid were never mentioned. And no one blamed Brock for anything except being a lousy, distracted manager. The op-ed columnists carped that he should've known what those close to him were doing.

After about fifteen minutes, Bishop pulled up in front of One Police Plaza. They sat in the car for a moment and neither one of them said anything. "Let me come up with you," Bishop protested halfheartedly. "We should do this together."

"I don't think so," A. J. said. "I think we've done more than enough together lately. People are starting to talk."

"Seriously, I don't wanna be accused, yet again, of not stepping in to help," he said as A. J. opened the car door. "You're always telling me I need to care about things, to actually give a shit. Well, most people wouldn't have lifted a pinky to help you." Bishop purposely didn't look at A. J.'s bandaged hand.

"I'm glad to see you haven't gotten any funnier," A. J. said without smiling. "This is something *I* need to finish. I'll catch up with you later."

"You sure you don't want me to wait for you?" Bishop asked, making one last attempt to change A. J.'s mind. "The last time somebody dropped you off here alone things didn't turn out so well."

This time A. J. smiled. "Now that's amusing. See you later."

A. J. cleared security and stepped off the elevator on the fourteenth floor. Against the advice of his doctor and his wife, A. J. had stopped taking painkillers. They made him feel light-headed and foggy, like his brain was working in a lower gear. But his hand was throbbing now as he held up his visitor's pass and was buzzed in through the security doors to the area outside the commissioner's office. "Good morning," Brock's secretary said. "He's expecting you."

She led A. J. into Brock's office and said the commissioner was on his way. *He's still playing games*, A. J. thought as he sat down on the couch. *Fine. This time I'm ready.* The pain kept him focused as he looked around the office at the trappings of power: enormous mahogany desk, huge thronelike leather chair, large windows overlooking lower Manhattan and the East River. And, of course, the mementos. Dozens of vanity photographs with politicians and celebrities: the president, two popes, stars and starlets, athletes, and at least half a dozen foreign heads of state.

A. J. started thinking about North Carolina again. When the shooting had stopped, Zito wanted to contact the local authorities. A. J. agreed. But Bishop convinced them that dealing with the local cops would create too many complications, raise too many questions, and get them entangled in a never-ending web of legal issues. Instead, they called Victoria Cannel and had her get in touch with the Feds. When they returned to New York, they were fully debriefed by the FBI, the CIA, and Homeland Security over several days of fairly intense interrogations. Once the interviews were completed, they assumed Brock was finished. Not only would he lose everything, he'd be facing very serious criminal charges. They waited with great anticipation for him to be dragged out of his office in handcuffs—and the subsequent explosion of headlines. When that didn't happen, Zito, Bishop, and A. J. used their contacts to find out what was going on.

The answer didn't satisfy anyone. It was beyond anything any of them could've anticipated. Homeland Security had thrown a blanket over the entire affair. Beyond murder, corruption, and drug-dealing charges for Oz, Chief Fitzgerald, and Kevin Anderson—all of whom were dead anyway—everything else was now classified until further notice. Using the Intelligence Identities Protection Act, which makes it a federal crime to release classified information that could harm the government's foreign intelligence activities, the Feds had completely shut them and everyone else down. A. J., Bishop, and Zito were forbidden, under threat of federal prosecution, from talking about any aspect of what had happened—other than the claims and charges that had already been made public. And there was no definitive evidence tying Brock to any of these activities. It was an incredibly bitter pill for them to swallow.

And while there might have been a time earlier in A. J.'s life when he would've considered writing the story and defying the Feds, his days of being a renegade—of believing in telling the story no matter the costs—were behind him. He had a family, and a lifetime of experience as a journalist had taught him that telling the truth was not always the best thing. Sometimes the consequences could be devastating.

Suddenly the private door behind Brock's desk flew open and the commissioner walked in wearing warm-up pants and a sleeveless T-shirt. He had a towel draped over his head and was soaked in sweat. He'd just worked out, and his hands were taped like he'd been boxing or maybe working the heavy bag. Brock was just about finished unwrapping his right hand as A. J. stood up.

Without a word, Brock stepped around the desk toward A. J. and, in one uninterrupted movement, threw his towel in A. J.'s face, pushed him back down on the couch, and removed a Walther PKK/S from the back of his waistband. Racking a round in the chamber, he pointed the gun in A. J.'s face.

"I could just splatter you all over the couch right now and be done with it," Brock said with little real malice.

A. J. smiled. After all he'd been through, it was going to take more than this bullshit bravado to rattle him. "Go ahead, tough guy," he said, staring directly into Brock's eyes. "Who're you gonna blame it on? All your patsies are gone. No more Oz, no more Fitzgerald. You're all alone now."

Stepping back and putting the gun on the desk so he could unwrap his other hand, Brock shook his head slowly in disgust. "This has been a fucking spectacular pain in the ass. But make no mistake, shithead, that's all it's been. The Feds don't have anything on me and neither do you. It's all circumstantial. The president's sent word that he thinks my services would be better utilized outside the confines of a federal post. I really did want Homeland Security. But I'll survive. There'll be other opportunities. I let the president know that I'd rather stay in New York as police commissioner. After all, A. J., if I left, who'd be here to keep an eye on your beautiful little family, right?" Brock said with a wink.

The commissioner went to his chair and sat down heavily. He took a cigar out of an ornate wooden box near the phone. As he leaned forward, A. J. smoothly grabbed the gun off the desk and pointed it at Brock's face. Brock was a little surprised and he almost smiled. A. J. was angry but in control.

"You deluded son of a bitch," he said. "Are you nuts? You really think there's any way you're going to remain PC after everything you've done? You think I'd let that happen? Make no mistake, motherfucker, you're going to resign immediately."

"And why's that?"

A. J. was squeezing the gun so tight that his bandaged hand had started to bleed. He was in a shooter's stance, feet shoulder-width apart, both hands on the weapon. Drops of blood were dripping on the commissioner's carpet.

"You're gonna resign as police commissioner because I say so." A. J. took one hand off the gun, reached into the inside pocket of his blazer, and pulled out a book covered in ornately engraved black leather with a zipper around the outside. Brock recognized it almost immediately. It was the pocket-sized Koran that Oz always carried.

"It's funny, you know," A. J. said. "With everything going on and all the excitement, I forgot to give this to the Feds. I took it out of Oz's pocket, right after Zito blew his brains all over me and the North Carolina dirt. Did you ever get a chance to look at it? Really interesting reading. Especially all the handwritten entries detailing his various activities. Oz was very organized. I had it translated by an imam I'm friends with uptown."

A. J. slipped the book back into his pocket and walked around the desk so he was standing over the commissioner.

"Get up, asshole," A. J. said to him. Seething, Brock complied. He wanted to put his hands around A. J.'s throat and choke the life out of him, but A. J. had the gun stuck in his chest and pointed directly at his heart.

"You don't have the balls to pull the trigger," Brock said finally.

A. J. took a small breath and adjusted his position slightly as if he were about to shoot. Instead, he delivered a hard, swift, perfectly aimed knee to Brock's balls, giving it everything he had. The commissioner crumpled instantly, curling up in a ball on the rug. A. J. decocked the gun, dropped the magazine on the floor, and racked out the round in the chamber.

"Fuck you, Brock," A. J. said as he turned to leave. The commissioner, still curled up on the floor, teeth clenched, reached out and grabbed A. J.'s pants leg. Swiftly, and stunningly, A. J. swiveled, reached down, grabbed Brock's hand, and bent the pinky completely back, breaking it instantly.

"That doesn't exactly even the score, but it's a start."

A. J. strode past Brock's assistant and into the elevator, where he could still hear the commissioner howling.

29

THE POLICE COMMISSIONER'S secretary was nothing if not loyal—especially to Mayor Domenico. While the mayor had a long history with Brock and basically trusted him, he also knew the commissioner could be difficult to control. So he had taken a few precautions—trust but verify. This meant skillfully placing someone at the center of Brock's activities—a highly recommended, experienced secretary the commissioner was happy to hire, who would dependably and quietly report to Domenico on the commissioner's activities.

A. J. had barely walked out of Brock's office when the commissioner's secretary phoned the mayor, as requested, to let him know the meeting was over. Brock had no idea Domenico had given the encounter his blessing less than twenty-four hours earlier in a clandestine, late-night meeting with A. J. and Bishop underneath the one-hundred-year-old Hell Gate Bridge in the South Bronx. With his sense of the dramatic, Bishop had chosen the desolate, almost ghostly spot, a place he was familiar with from his days in the Fortieth Precinct. Cops sometimes went there to disappear for a while or engage in off-the-books activity while on duty.

It didn't take much convincing to get the mayor to agree to a meeting. The Feds had filled him in, so when A. J. called, he immediately said yes. A. J. barely had to mention he had information that could affect Domenico's presidential ambitions.

It was a short meeting. Domenico came with only a small security detail in his official black Chevy SUV. Though the mayor had no idea who Bishop was, he'd met A. J. on many occasions and detested him for dogging his administration in the magazine.

"Nice fuckin' location," the mayor said as he climbed out of the car. "A little creepy for my taste, but whatever. Okay, you got me here, now you've got ten minutes. Start talking. And this better be worth my time."

"Are you kidding me with that—" Bishop snapped before A. J. cut him off.

"Understand," A. J. said, "we're beyond angry. But that's not why we're here. Nevertheless, I suggest you show us a little more respect."

Now it was Domenico's turn to snap. "You arrogant little cocksuckers. Who the fuck do you think you are? Get to the point, A. J. I don't have all night. I don't like you, you don't like me, and a little courtesy's not gonna change that. What do you have for me?"

"If I were you I'd throttle it back," Bishop said. "We're holding all the fuckin' cards here."

"If that were true we wouldn't be having this meeting, tough guy," Domenico said. "I know you can't nail Brock, so let's get on with it."

"Look," A. J. said, losing his patience. "It's true our hands are tied here by every goddamned agency in Washington. That is, up to a point. We can't kill your guy, but we can kill your national political ambitions. So I suggest you listen to me carefully. You already know I've agreed not to write about this for the sake of the national interest. Officially. But hey, I can't be held responsible if rumors start to pop up on the Internet. Regularly. People will begin to ask questions, maybe do a little digging. You understand where I'm going with this? I want that sick motherfucker out of public life."

To make sure Domenico understood the stakes, A. J. took out Oz's pocket Koran. The mayor quickly saw the light and they made a deal.

• • •

The next evening, a few hours after A. J.'s meeting with Brock at One Police Plaza, the local news shows and the national network and cable broadcasts all carried the story that New York's police commissioner had scheduled a prime-time press conference for eight fifteen that evening to make a major announcement. Bishop and Lucy met at Bell's at about eight, and the place was buzzing over the Brock story. "Did you talk to A. J.?" Lucy asked Bishop.

"No," he said, "I left him a message to meet us here."

"There's no way he's coming," Lucy said.

"How do you know?"

"Trust me," she said, "I know him."

John, the headwaiter, turned the television on just as the networks were breaking into their regular programming to cover the press conference. "This is so exciting," Lucy said to Bishop. "You know A. J. totally engineered this. How do you think he got Brock to cave?"

Bishop looked at Lucy like he was considering her question. "You promised you were going to go to V with me. I hope you're gonna keep your promise."

Lucy shook her head. "Are you nuts?" she said. "You bring that up *now*, with what's about to happen? Besides, I didn't promise. And if we do go, it's gotta be our secret," she said, playfully smacking him in the back of his head.

Bishop's cell phone rang. "Hey, if that's A. J.," she said before he answered, "and you mention V, you'll never see me step foot in that place— at least not with you."

"Hey, partner," Bishop said to A. J. on the phone. "When are you getting here?"

"What's this 'partner' shit?"

"Come on," Bishop said, "it's just an expression."

Lucy was pulling on Bishop's shirt. "Lemme talk to him, lemme have the phone." Bishop relented.

"Hey, boss," she said. "Are you in front of the television? Brock is just walking up to the microphones. Wait, let's hear what he has to say."

"Call me back when you're ready," A. J. said to her.

Brock was standing at the lectern in an impeccably tailored suit, and he kept his right hand under his left to hide the splint on his pinky. Behind Brock were the usual suspects—what Bishop referred to as the "battling bobbleheads": the deputy PC, the fire commissioner, the head of Emergency Management, and various other city agency bosses jockeying to get some TV face time.

"Good evening," Brock said, looking directly into the cameras. "I come before you tonight to announce that I am withdrawing my name from consideration as secretary of Homeland Security, and I am resigning as New York City's police commissioner, effective immediately. I have discussed these decisions with the president and with Mayor Domenico. Given the dire recent events around the world, I firmly believe I can better serve this great nation by leaving government service and taking up the fight against ISIS . . ."

The press corps erupted. Cameras flashed, reporters leapt out of their seats shouting questions, and arms waved furiously. Brock simply turned and walked out. Ever the survivor, he had managed to find a way out.

Bishop looked depressed, almost sullen. He stood up, paused for a moment, and then leaned in and gently kissed Lucy on her cheek before walking out of Bell's into the cool Manhattan night.

Lucy was puzzled for a moment. Then she called A. J.

"So, what'd you think?" she asked, a hint of excitement still in her voice.

"About Brock?" A. J. asked.

"C'mon, A. J."

"Okay, okay. I think it's a good but difficult lesson. In the real world, the good guys don't always win."

"At least he's resigning as PC," Lucy said in a somber tone. "He's going to fight ISIS as a private citizen? What's that mean?"

"I'm not really sure," A. J. said after a long pause. "I guess it means he's still in the game. He lives to fight another day. At least we're not walking away empty-handed. "

A. J. hung up and walked slowly into his office. He sat down at his laptop and stared at the screen. After a few minutes he closed the computer. His hand was throbbing and he was totally spent, but the Motrin was starting to work.

"Annie," he yelled, "are you ready?"

"Coming, Dad. I just need to grab my bat bag."

"Okay, I reserved the batting cage for nine thirty, so let's make tracks."

ACKNOWLEDGMENTS

This book could not have been done without the collective love, knowledge, patience, and support of the following people. You have our most sincere gratitude:

Judith Regan

Ron Hogan

Colby & Taylor Horowitz

Terry (Mom) & Matthew (Bro) Stanton

Brad and Lamia Jacobs and Family

Jim Conroy

Jay Novik

John, KK, Sinclair and Schiller Ranch

Big Al Sessa

Sly and Jennifer Stallone

Bill Bratton

Rikki Klieman

Megyn Kelly, Esq.

Marilyn Chinitz, Esq.

John Herzfeld and Rebekah Chaney

Phil Houston and the QVerity Team

Shirene Coburn and Coburn Communications

The Fitzgerald Family

David Zinczenko

Dan Abrams

Stephen Lang

Lara Spencer

Kimberly Guilfoyle, Esq.

Dr. Raja Flores

Dr. Emilio Biagiotti

Mark Speranza

Jon and Brandis Dietelbaum

Al and Donna Parlato and Family

Robert Strent, Esq.

Rich Gaspari

Frank Daconti

Robert Sharenow

Frank Shea

Marc Victor

Kevin Reilly

Pat Rogers

Bill Lappe

Chief Steve Silks

Chief Tom Fahey

Insp. Russell Green

Noah Oppenheim

Joe Tacopina, Esq.

Dr. Jeff Dorfman

The Musano Family

Frank and Barbara Hoffman

Stephanie Levinson

Steve and Rafael

Tara Lane

Victoria Gotti

Dan Magnan

John Miller

Ira Rosen

Paul Pietropaulo

Brian Kilmeade

Neal P. Cavuto

Andrew Wilkow

Larry Shire

Matt Zimmerman

Chris Coumo

Santina Lucci

Chris Viasto